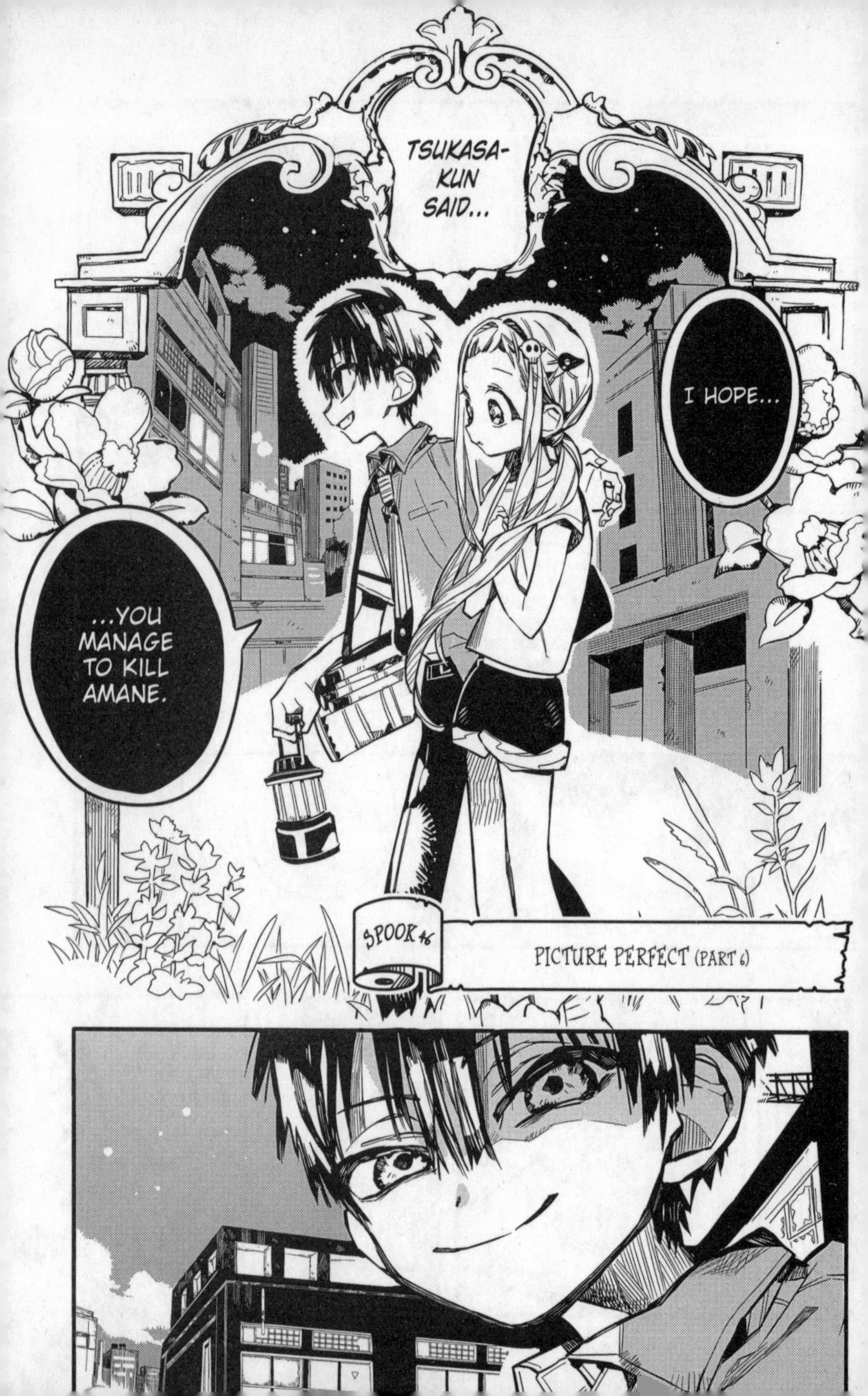
TSUKASA-KUN SAID...
I HOPE...
...YOU MANAGE TO KILL AMANE.
SPOOK 46
PICTURE PERFECT (PART 6)

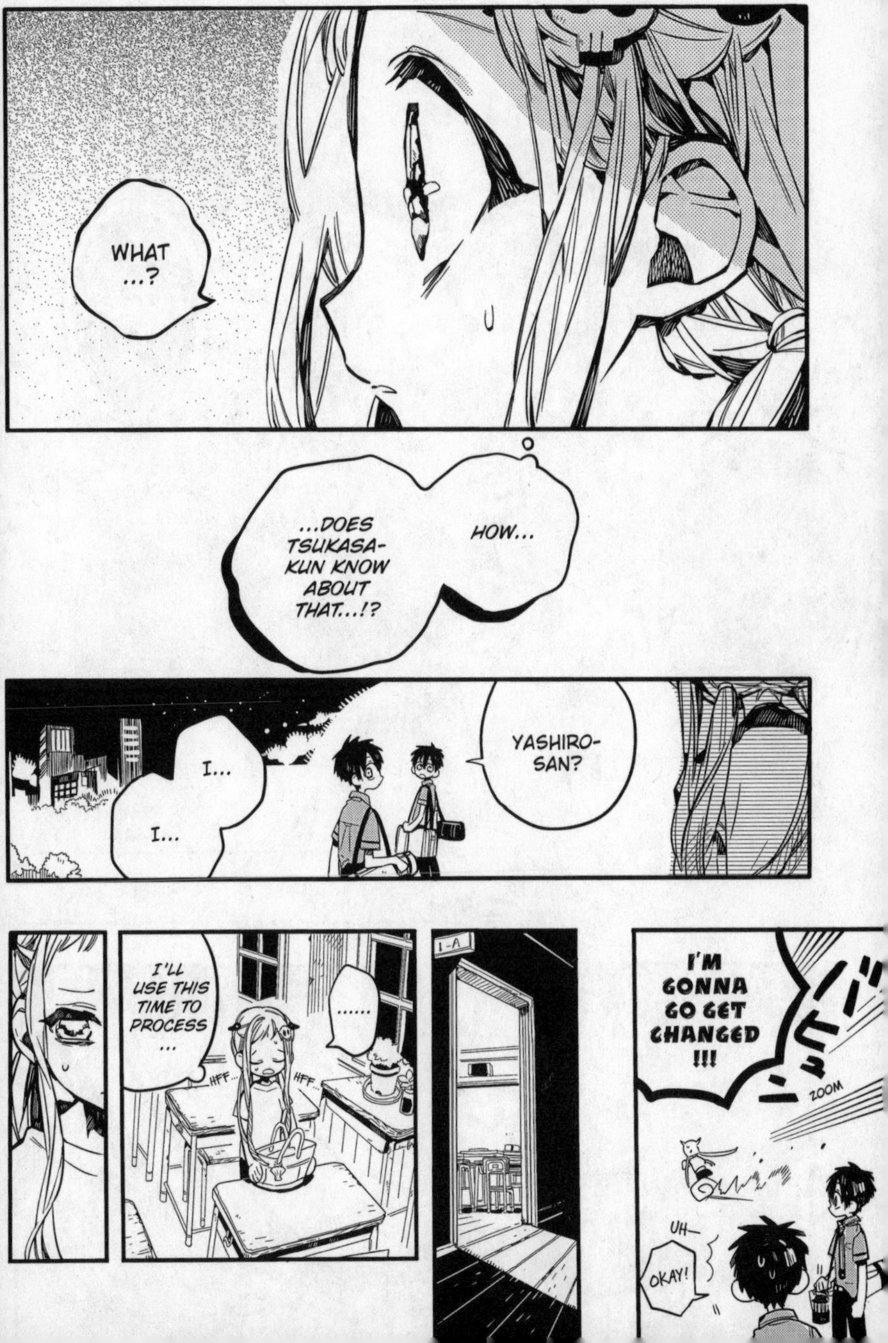
WHAT ...?
HOW...
...DOES TSUKASA-KUN KNOW ABOUT THAT...!?
YASHIRO-SAN?
I...
I...
I'M GONNA GO GET CHANGED !!!
ZOOM
UH—
OKAY!
1-A
......
I'LL USE THIS TIME TO PROCESS ...
HFF...
HFF...

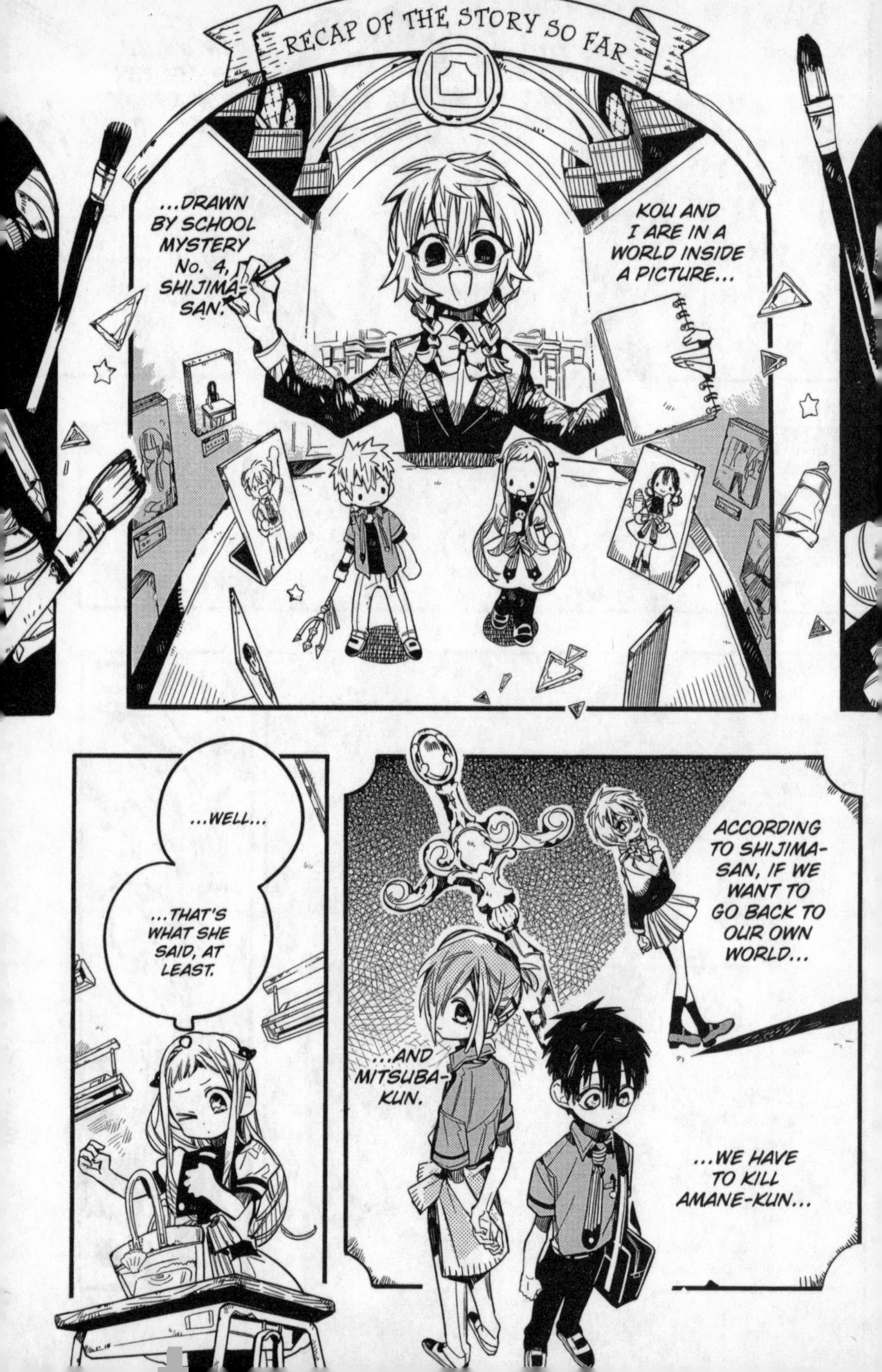
RECAP OF THE STORY SO FAR
KOU AND I ARE IN A WORLD INSIDE A PICTURE...
...DRAWN BY SCHOOL MYSTERY No. 4, SHIJIMA-SAN.
ACCORDING TO SHIJIMA-SAN, IF WE WANT TO GO BACK TO OUR OWN WORLD...
...WE HAVE TO KILL AMANE-KUN...
...AND MITSUBA-KUN.
...WELL...
...THAT'S WHAT SHE SAID, AT LEAST.

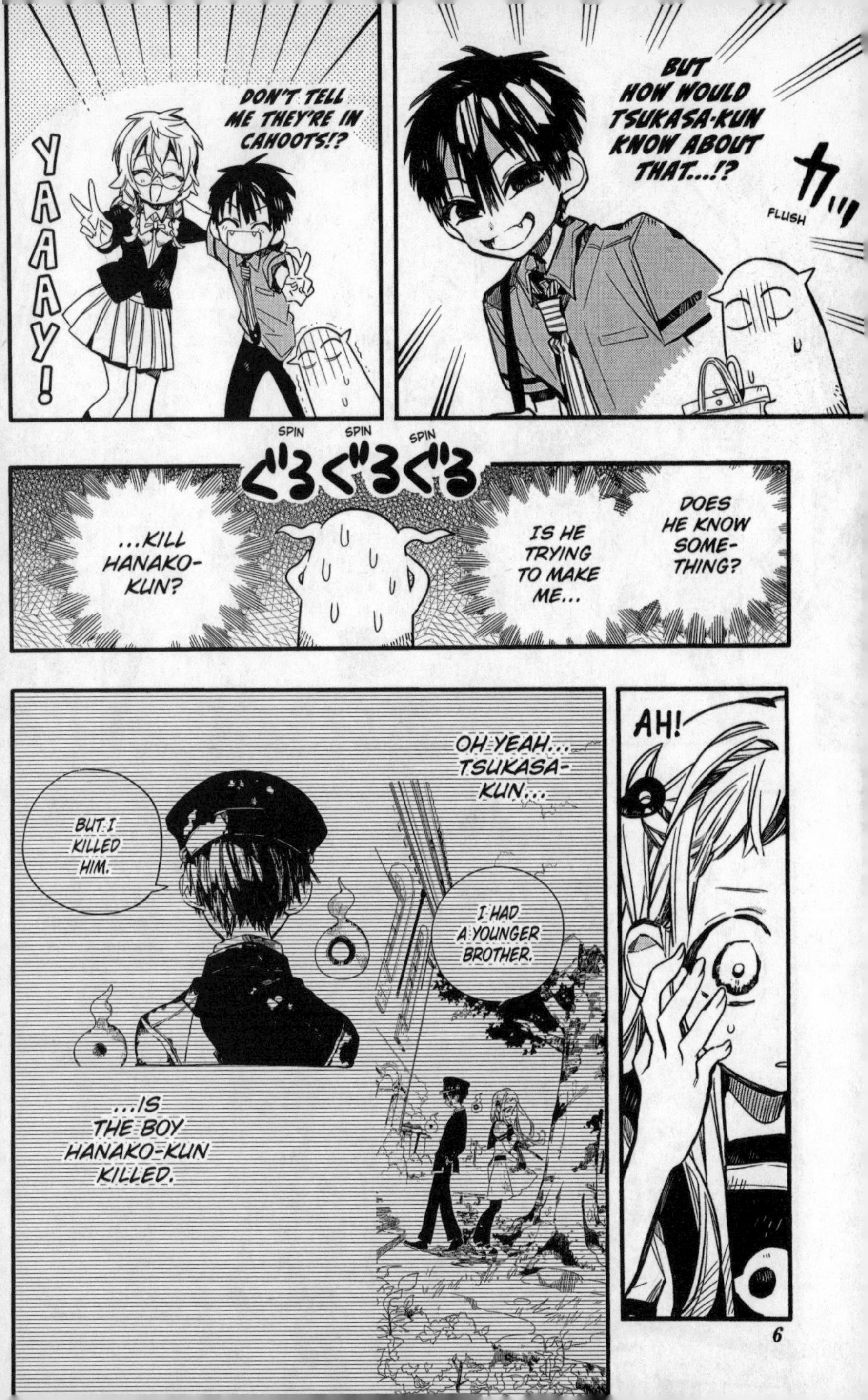
BUT HOW WOULD TSUKASA-KUN KNOW ABOUT THAT...!?
カッ
FLUSH
DON'T TELL ME THEY'RE IN CAHOOTS!?
YAAAAY!
ぐるぐるぐる
SPIN SPIN SPIN
DOES HE KNOW SOME-THING?
IS HE TRYING TO MAKE ME...
...KILL HANAKO-KUN?
AH!
OH YEAH... TSUKASA-KUN...
I HAD A YOUNGER BROTHER.
BUT I KILLED HIM.
...IS THE BOY HANAKO-KUN KILLED.

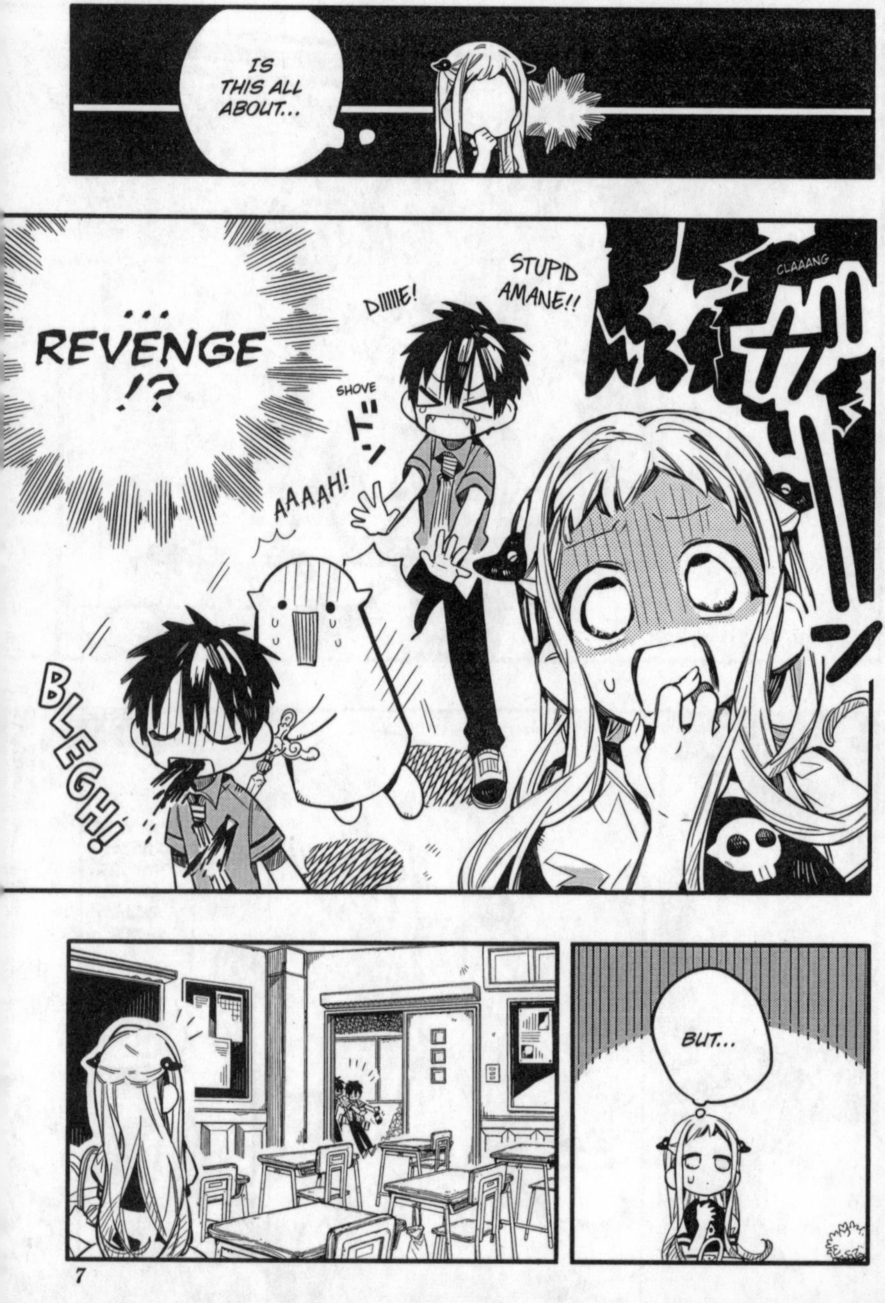
IS THIS ALL ABOUT...
CLAAANG
STUPID AMANE!!
DIIIIE!
SHOVE
AAAAH!
...REVENGE!?
BLEGH!
BUT...

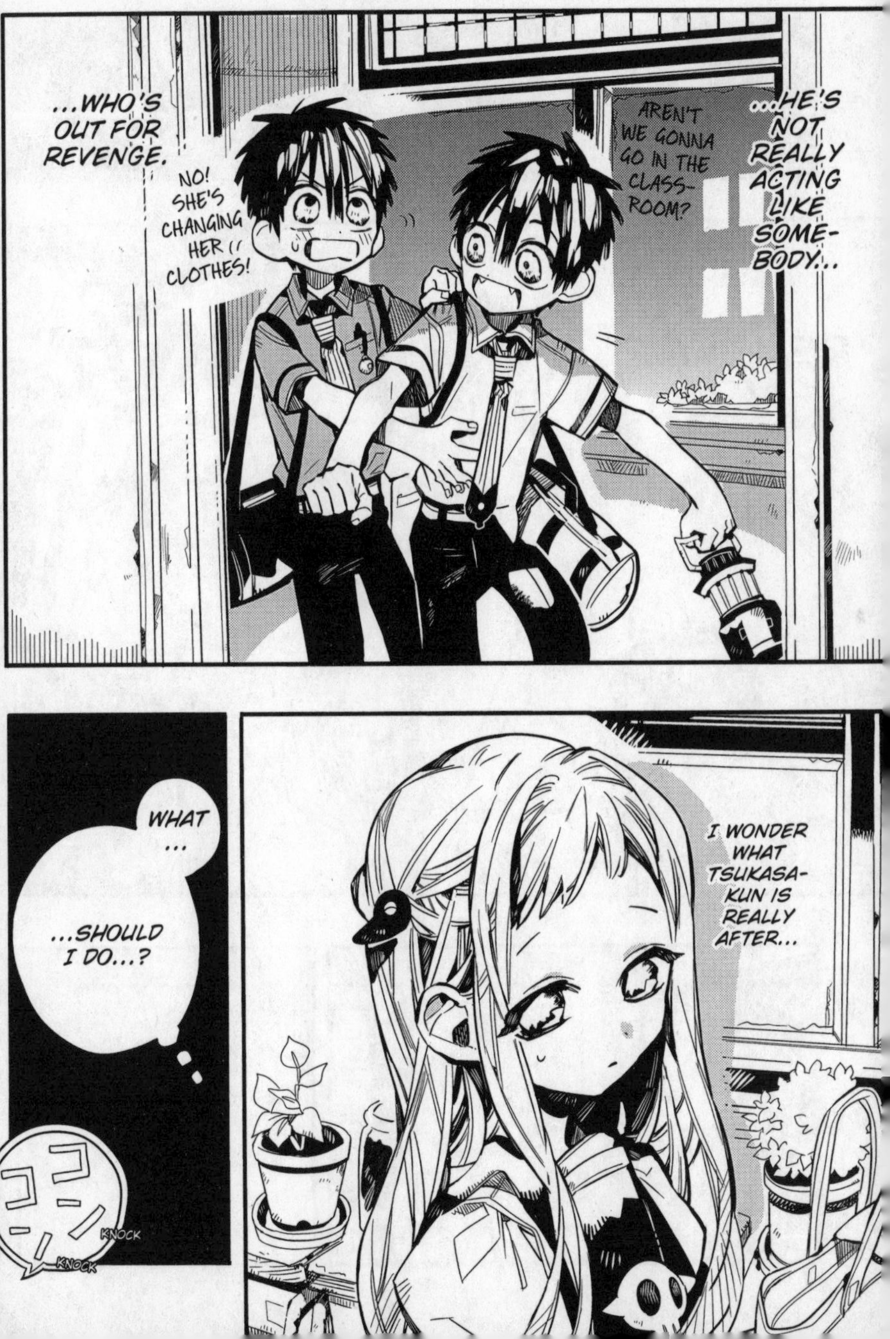
...HE'S NOT REALLY ACTING LIKE SOMEBODY...
...WHO'S OUT FOR REVENGE.
AREN'T WE GONNA GO IN THE CLASS-ROOM?
NO! SHE'S CHANGING HER CLOTHES!
I WONDER WHAT TSUKASA-KUN IS REALLY AFTER...
WHAT ...
...SHOULD I DO...?
KNOCK
KNOCK

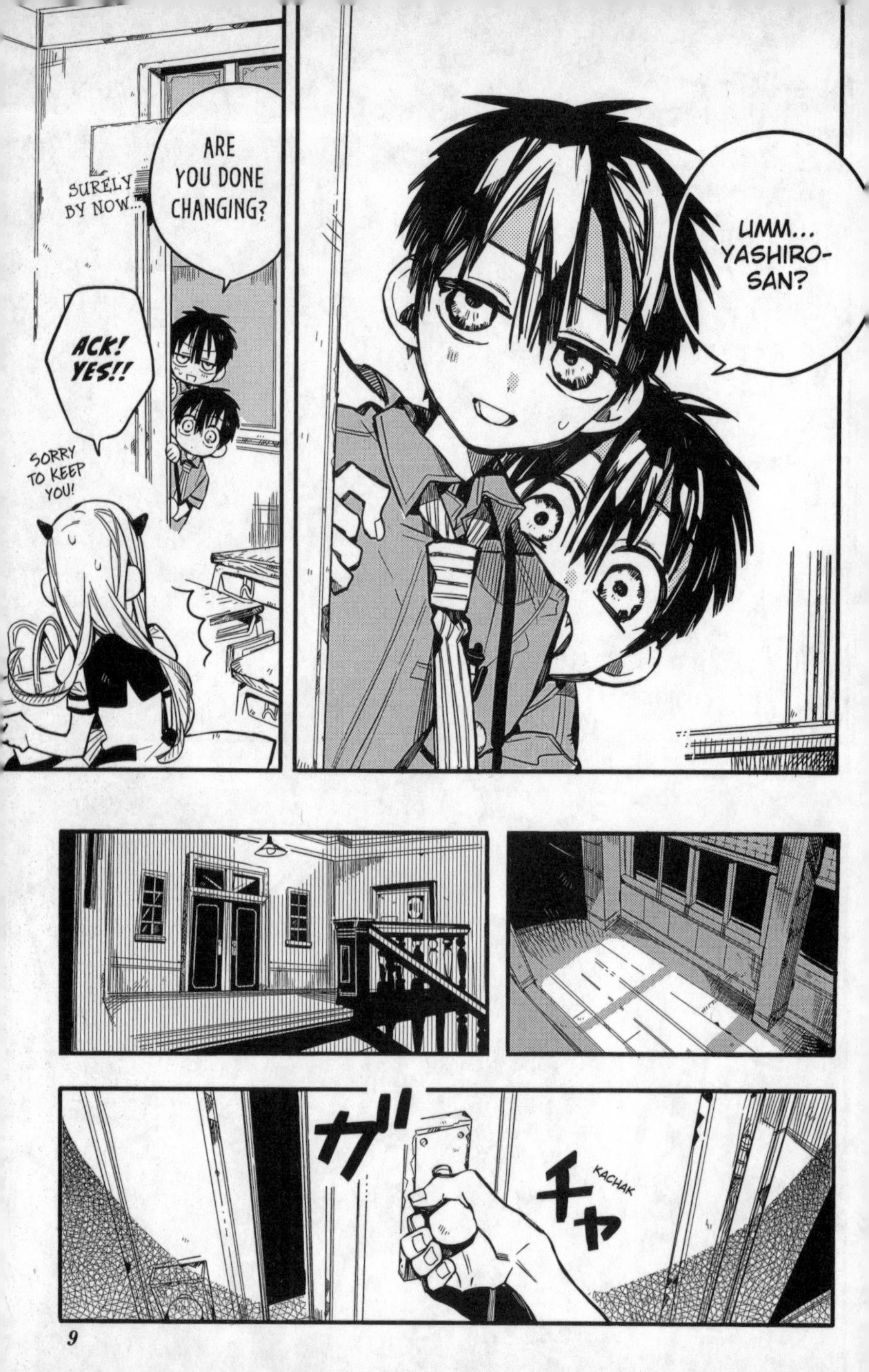
UMM... YASHIRO-SAN?
ARE YOU DONE CHANGING?
SURELY BY NOW...
ACK! YES!!
SORRY TO KEEP YOU!
ガ
チャ
KACHAK

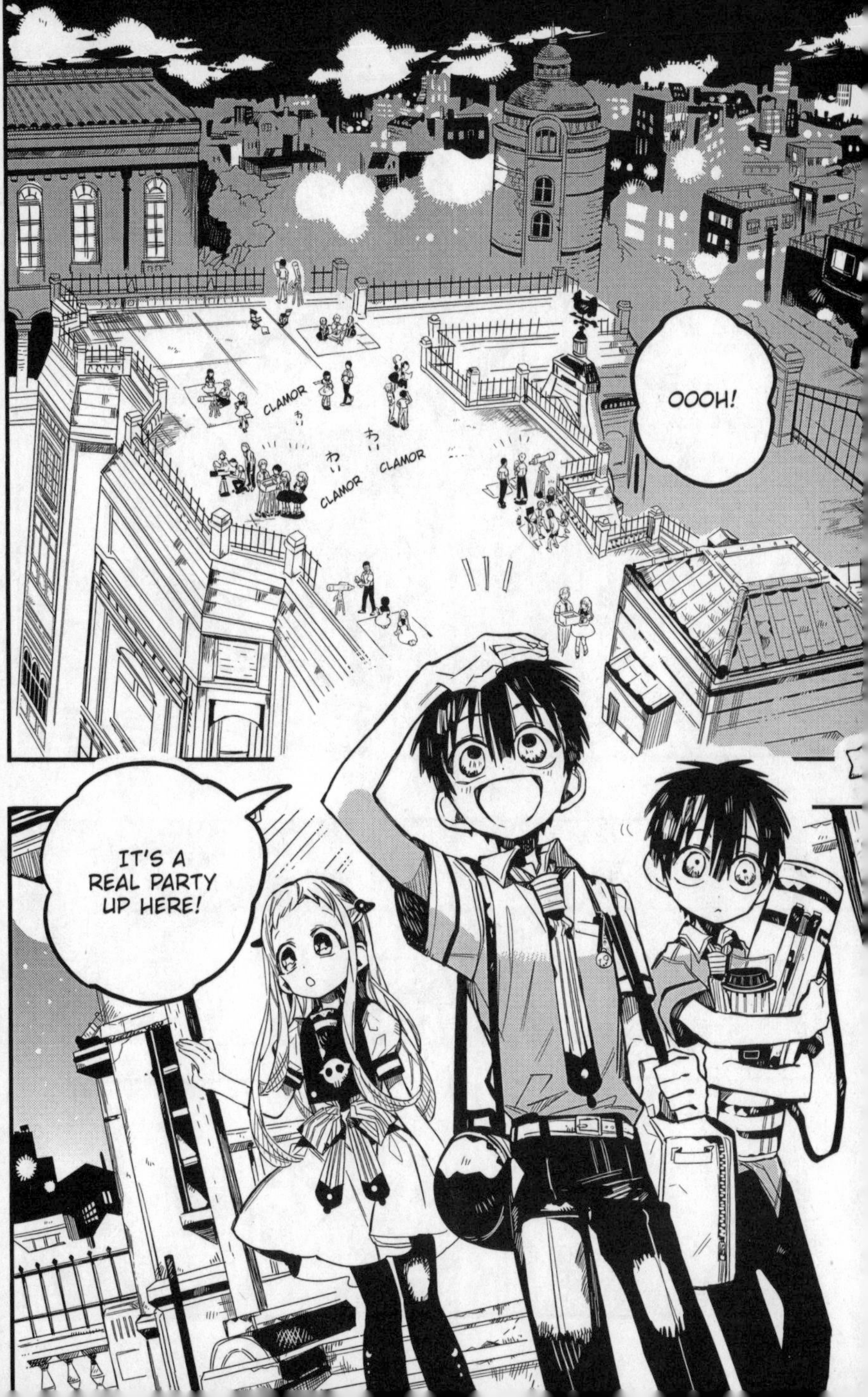
OOOH!
CLAMOR
わい
わい
CLAMOR
CLAMOR
IT'S A REAL PARTY UP HERE!

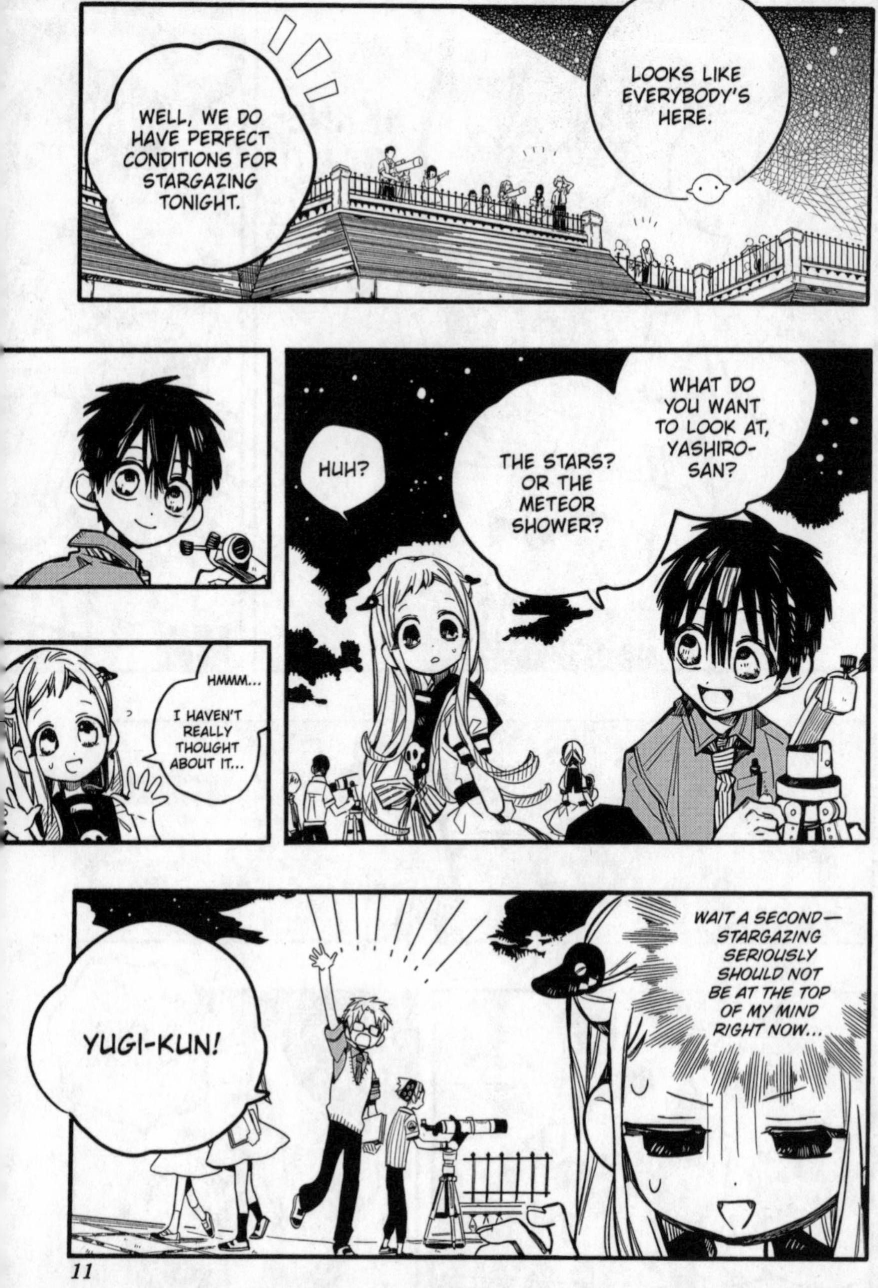
LOOKS LIKE EVERYBODY'S HERE.
WELL, WE DO HAVE PERFECT CONDITIONS FOR STARGAZING TONIGHT.
WHAT DO YOU WANT TO LOOK AT, YASHIRO-SAN?
THE STARS? OR THE METEOR SHOWER?
HUH?
HMMM...
I HAVEN'T REALLY THOUGHT ABOUT IT...
WAIT A SECOND— STARGAZING SERIOUSLY SHOULD NOT BE AT THE TOP OF MY MIND RIGHT NOW...
YUGI-KUN!

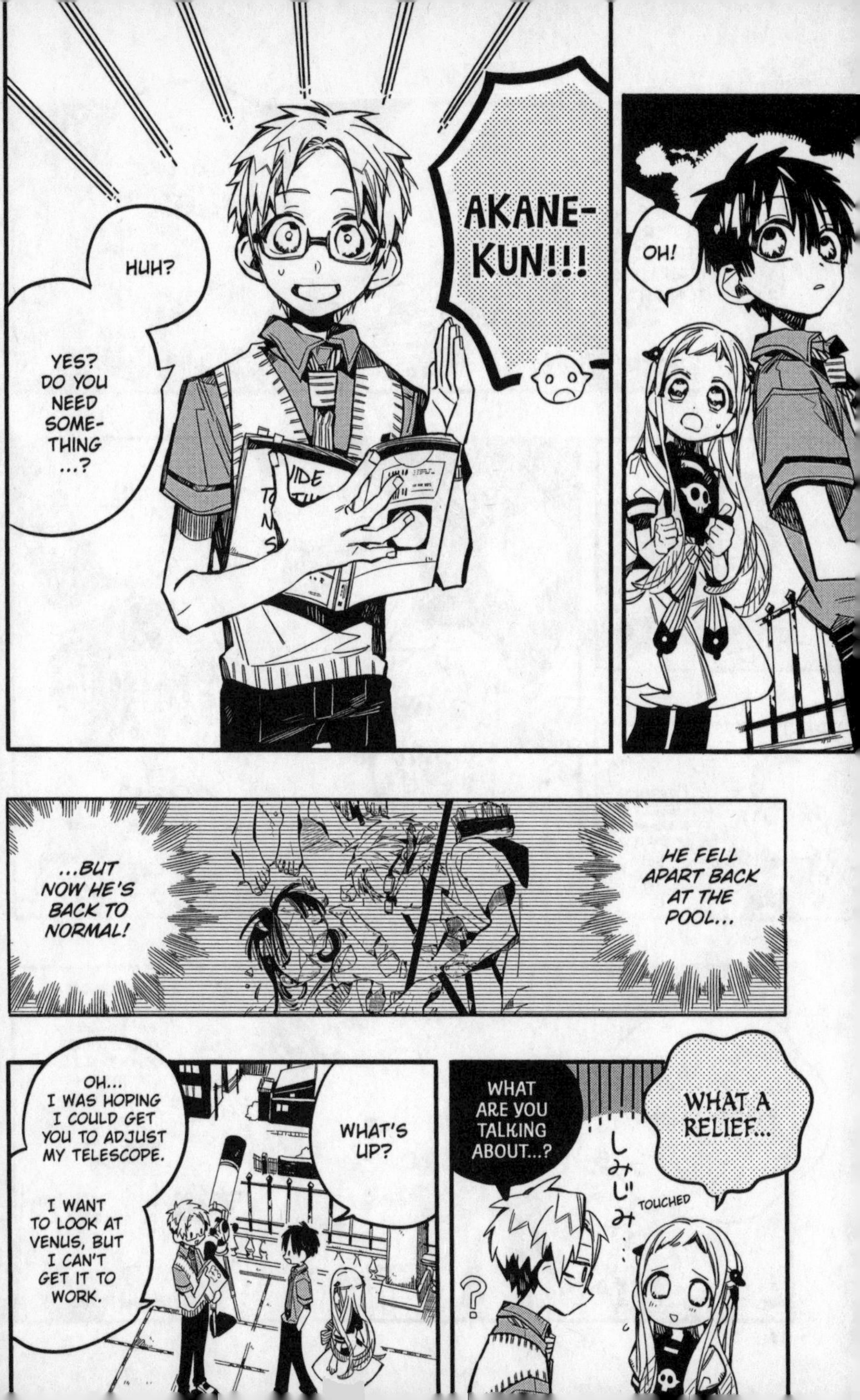
OH!
AKANE-KUN!!!
HUH?
YES? DO YOU NEED SOMETHING...?
HE FELL APART BACK AT THE POOL...
...BUT NOW HE'S BACK TO NORMAL!
WHAT A RELIEF...
しみじみ
TOUCHED
WHAT ARE YOU TALKING ABOUT...?
WHAT'S UP?
OH... I WAS HOPING I COULD GET YOU TO ADJUST MY TELESCOPE.
I WANT TO LOOK AT VENUS, BUT I CAN'T GET IT TO WORK.

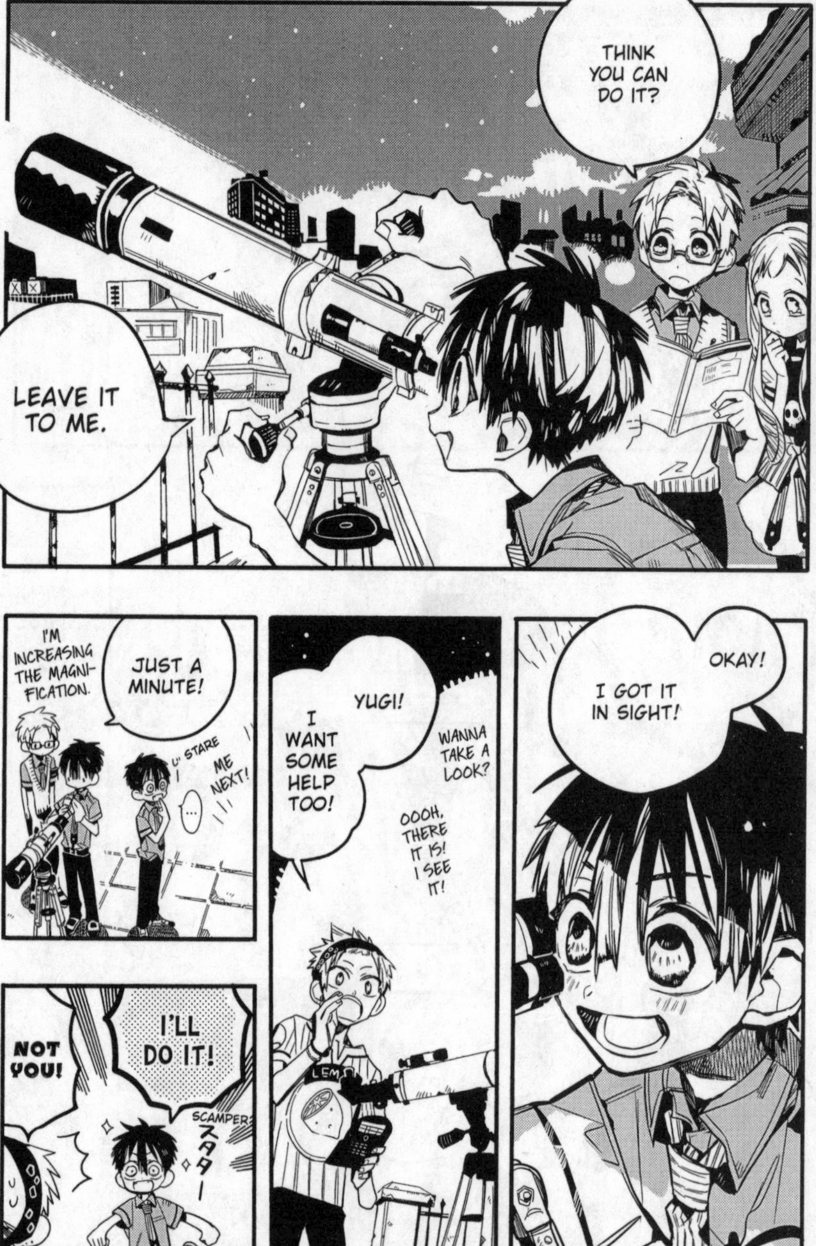
THINK YOU CAN DO IT?
LEAVE IT TO ME.
OKAY!
I GOT IT IN SIGHT!
YUGI!
WANNA TAKE A LOOK?
OOOH, THERE IT IS! I SEE IT!
I WANT SOME HELP TOO!
JUST A MINUTE!
I'M INCREASING THE MAGNI-FICATION.
STARE
ME NEXT!
...
I'LL DO IT!
NOT YOU!
SCAMPER
スタター

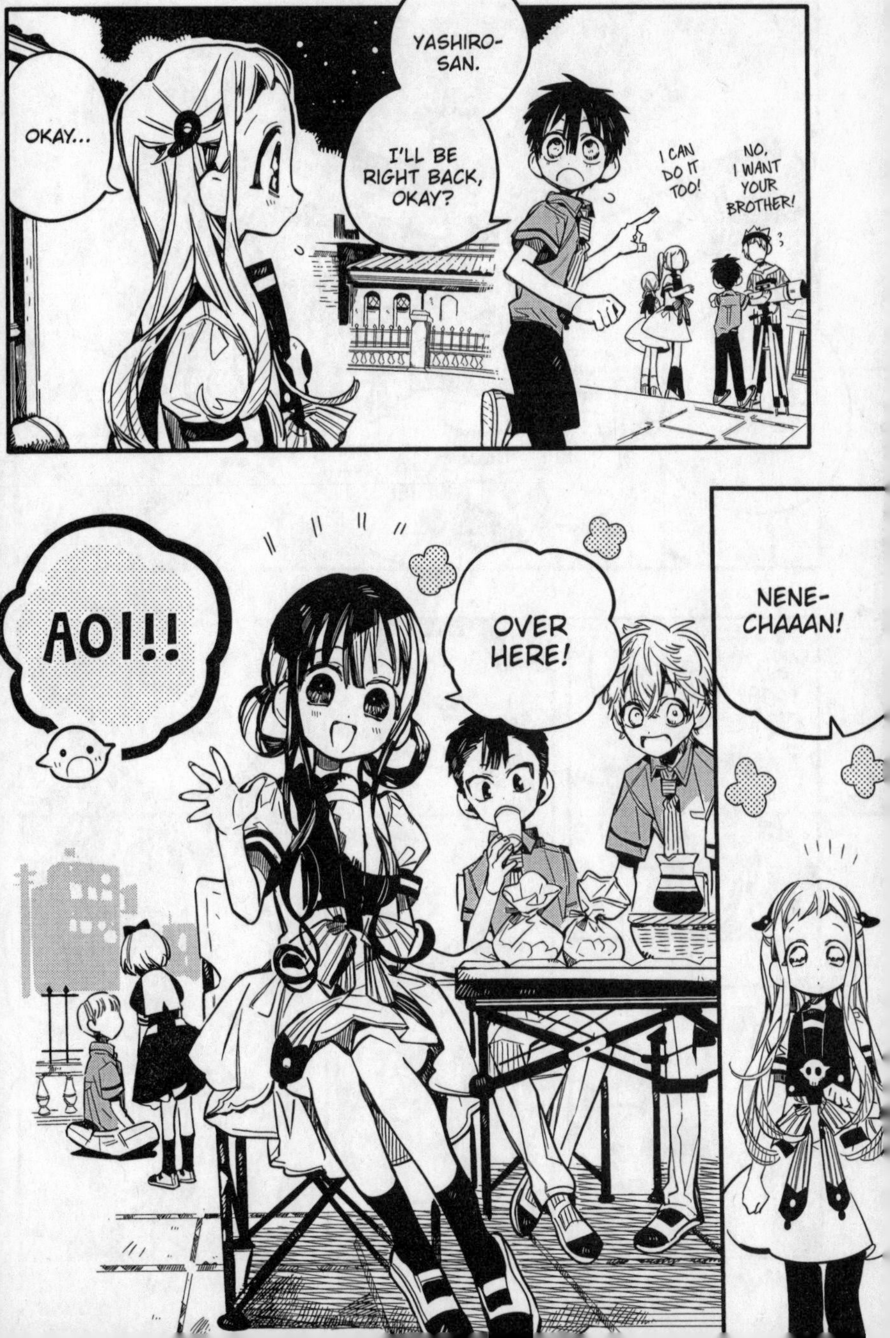
I CAN DO IT TOO!
NO, I WANT YOUR BROTHER!
YASHIRO-SAN.
I'LL BE RIGHT BACK, OKAY?
OKAY...
NENE-CHAAAN!
OVER HERE!
AOI!!

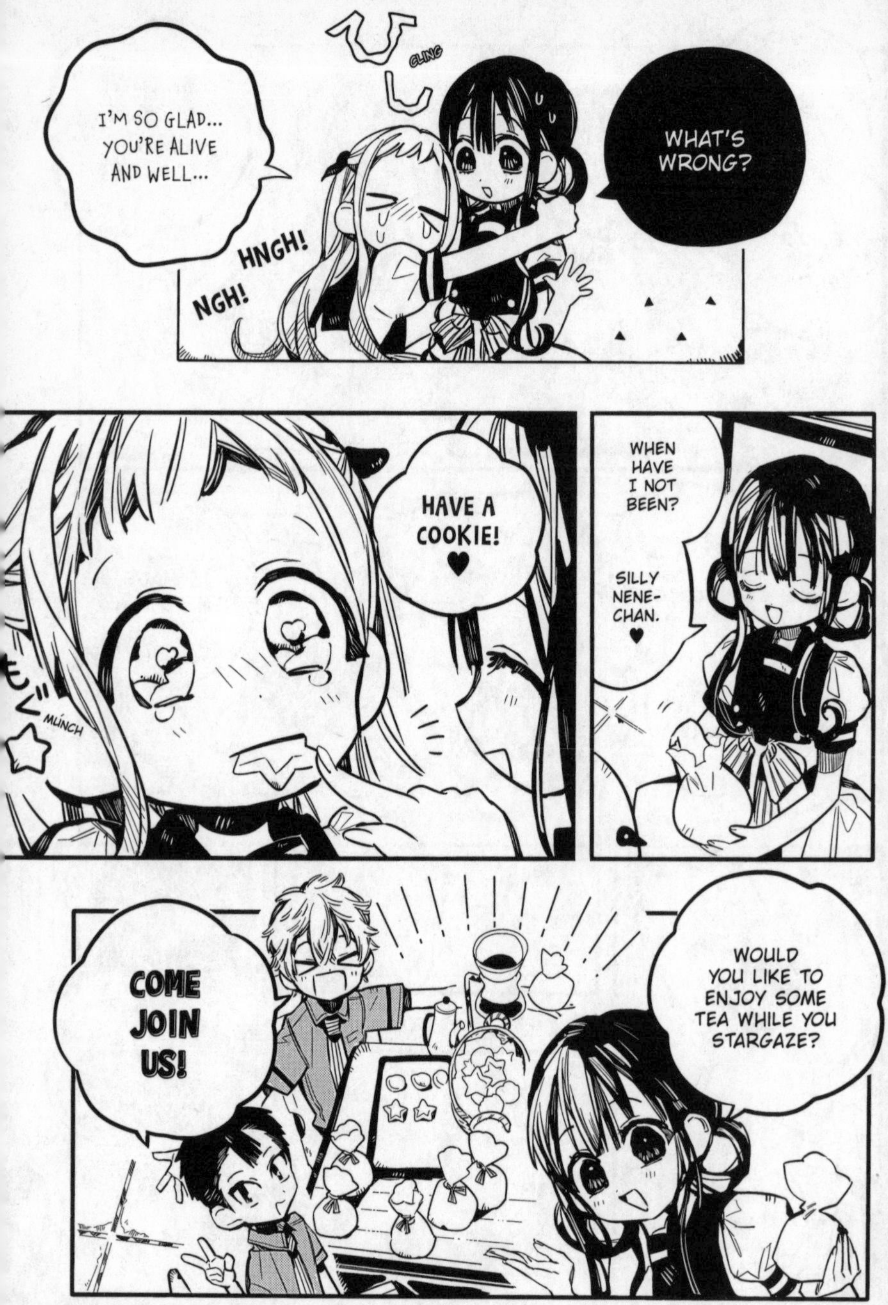
WHAT'S WRONG?
CLING
I'M SO GLAD... YOU'RE ALIVE AND WELL...
HNGH!
NGH!
WHEN HAVE I NOT BEEN?
SILLY NENE-CHAN. ♥
HAVE A COOKIE! ♥
MUNCH
WOULD YOU LIKE TO ENJOY SOME TEA WHILE YOU STARGAZE?
COME JOIN US!

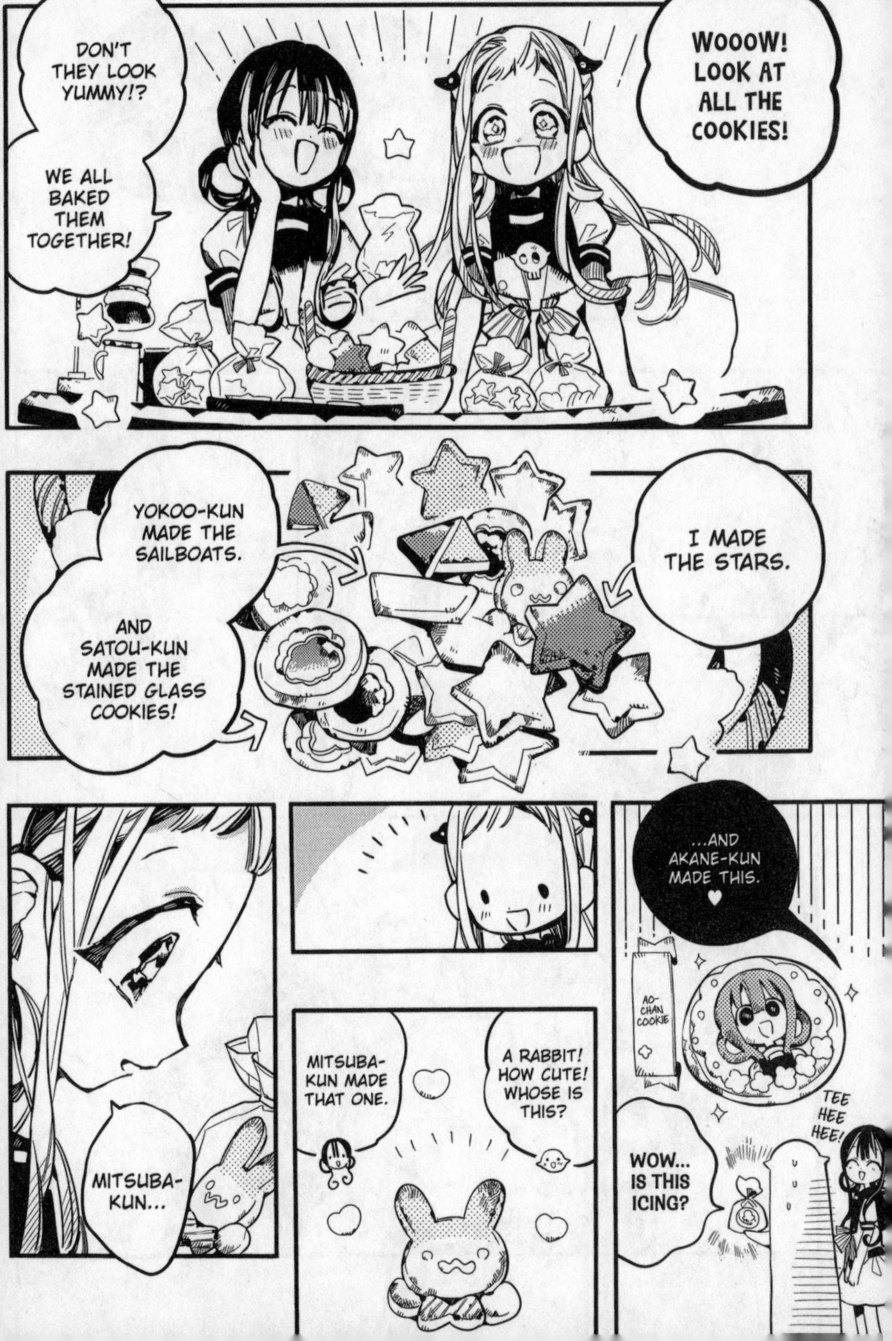
WOOOW! LOOK AT ALL THE COOKIES!
DON'T THEY LOOK YUMMY!?
WE ALL BAKED THEM TOGETHER!
I MADE THE STARS.
YOKOO-KUN MADE THE SAILBOATS.
AND SATOU-KUN MADE THE STAINED GLASS COOKIES!
...AND AKANE-KUN MADE THIS. ♥
AO-CHAN COOKIE
TEE HEE HEE!
WOW... IS THIS ICING?
A RABBIT! HOW CUTE! WHOSE IS THIS?
MITSUBA-KUN MADE THAT ONE.
MITSUBA-KUN...

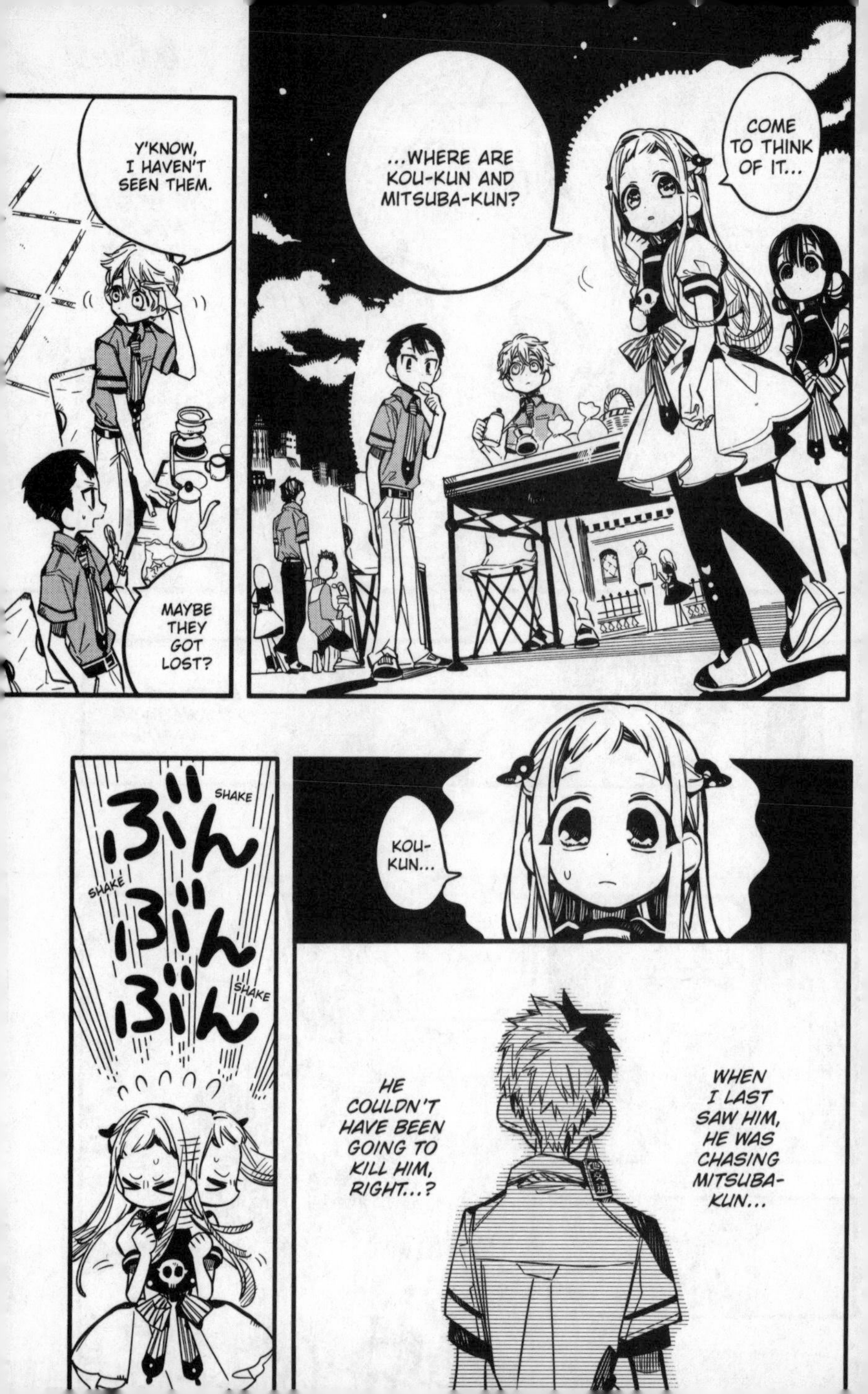
COME TO THINK OF IT...
...WHERE ARE KOU-KUN AND MITSUBA-KUN?
Y'KNOW, I HAVEN'T SEEN THEM.
MAYBE THEY GOT LOST?
KOU-KUN...
WHEN I LAST SAW HIM, HE WAS CHASING MITSUBA-KUN...
HE COULDN'T HAVE BEEN GOING TO KILL HIM, RIGHT...?
ぶん
SHAKE
ぶん
SHAKE
ぶん
SHAKE

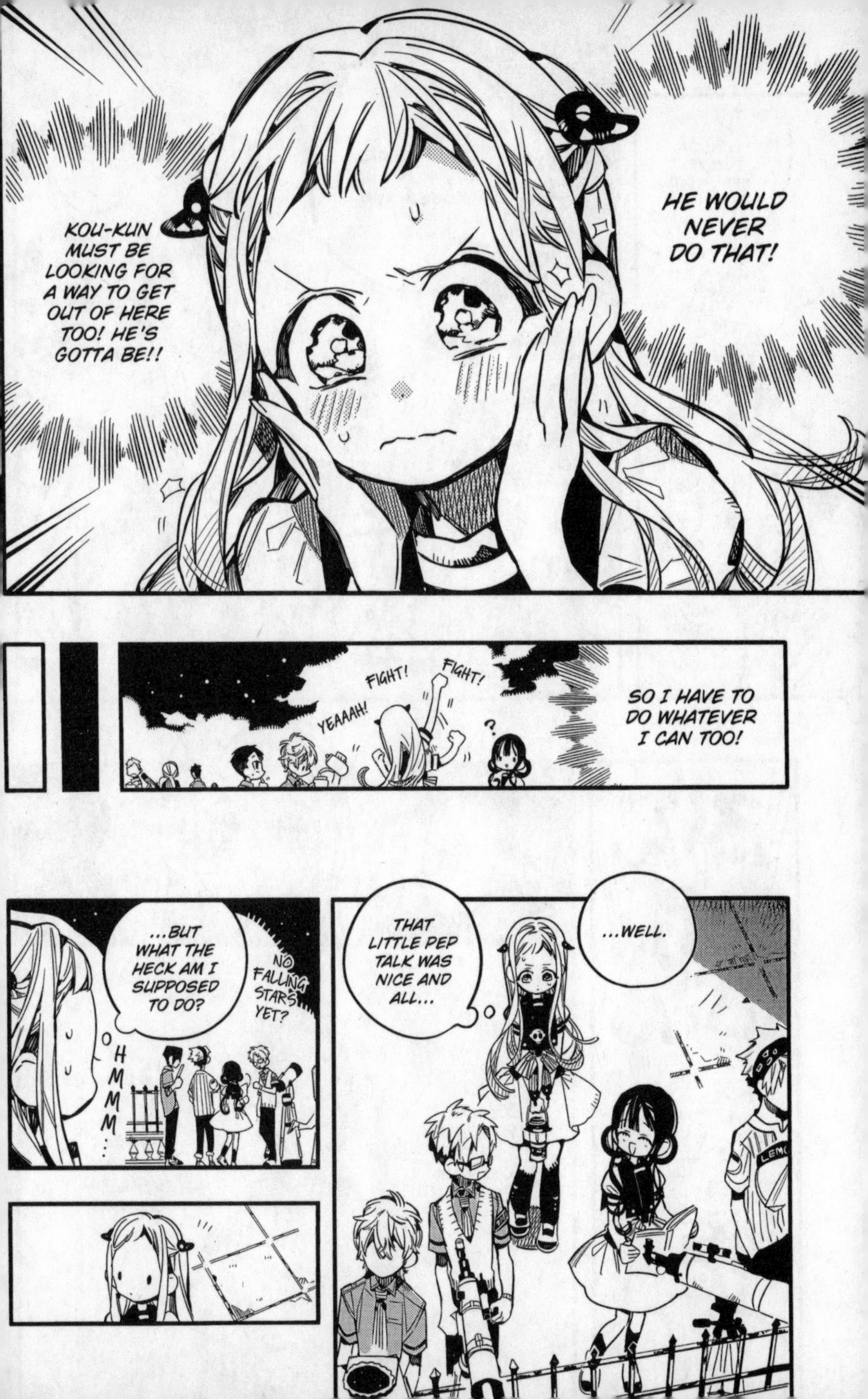
HE WOULD NEVER DO THAT!
KOU-KUN MUST BE LOOKING FOR A WAY TO GET OUT OF HERE TOO! HE'S GOTTA BE!!
SO I HAVE TO DO WHATEVER I CAN TOO!
FIGHT!
FIGHT!
YEAAAH!
?
...WELL.
THAT LITTLE PEP TALK WAS NICE AND ALL...
...BUT WHAT THE HECK AM I SUPPOSED TO DO?
NO FALLING STARS YET?
HMMM...

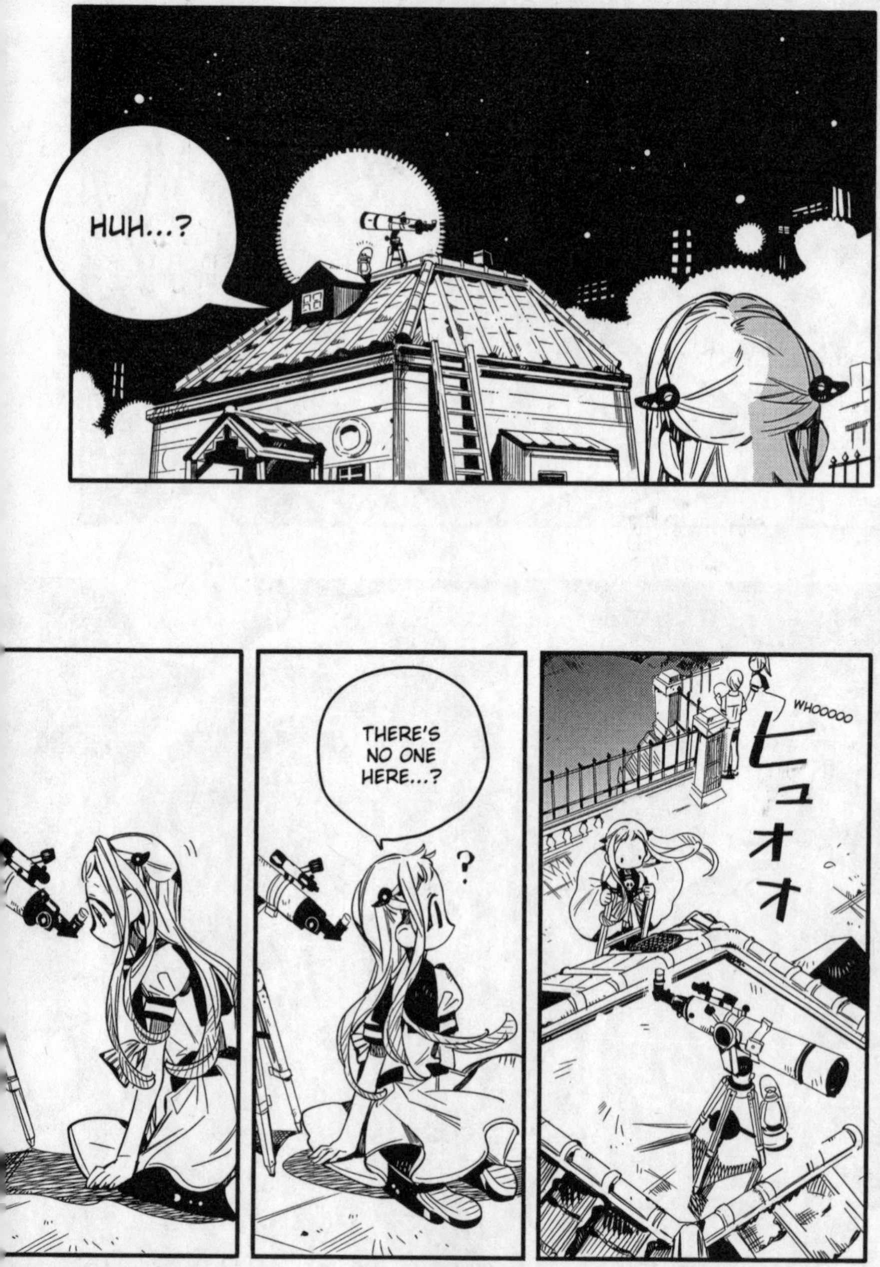
HUH...?
WHOOOOO
ヒュオオ
THERE'S NO ONE HERE...?
?

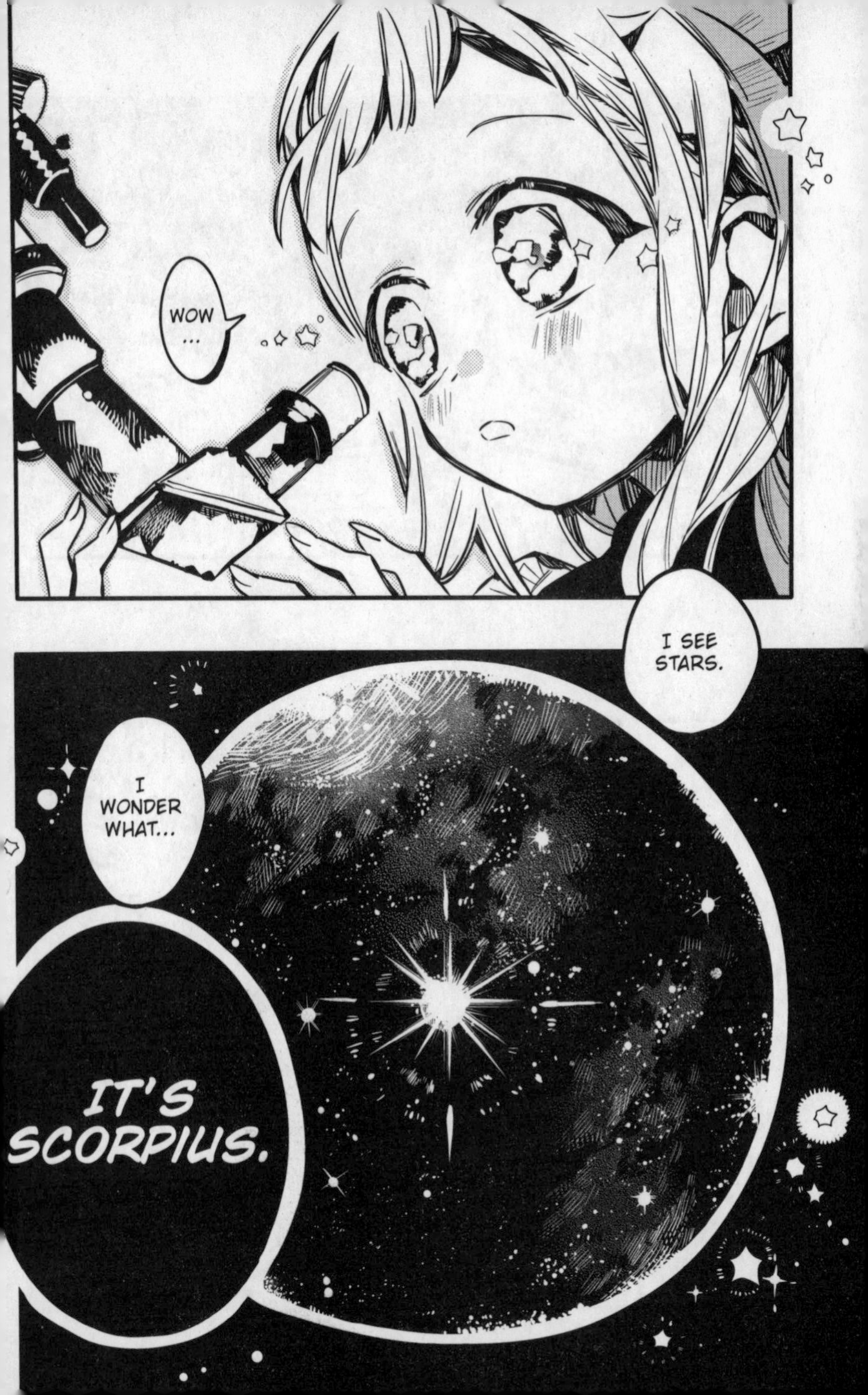
WOW ...
I SEE STARS.
I WONDER WHAT...
IT'S SCORPIUS.

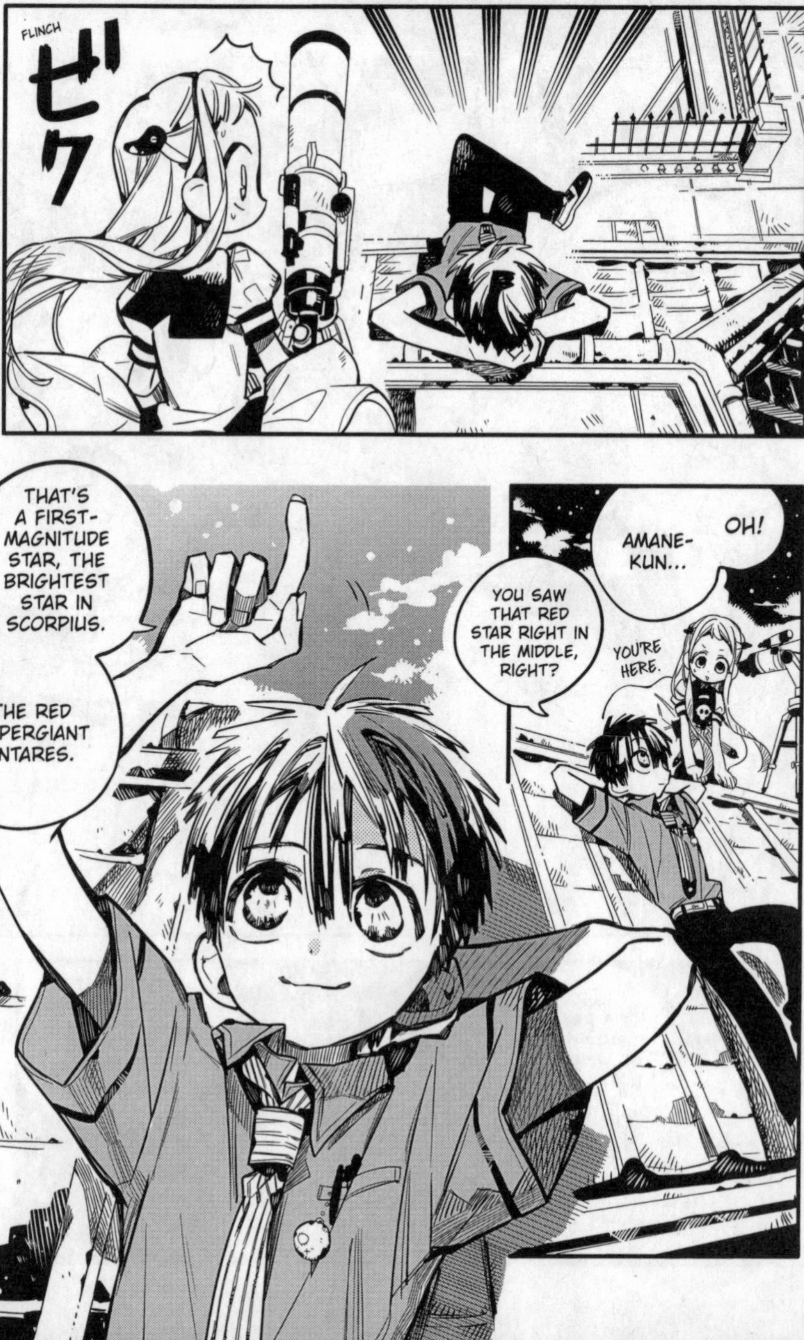
FLINCH
ゼク
OH!
AMANE-KUN...
YOU'RE HERE.
YOU SAW THAT RED STAR RIGHT IN THE MIDDLE, RIGHT?
THAT'S A FIRST-MAGNITUDE STAR, THE BRIGHTEST STAR IN SCORPIUS.
THE RED SUPERGIANT ANTARES.

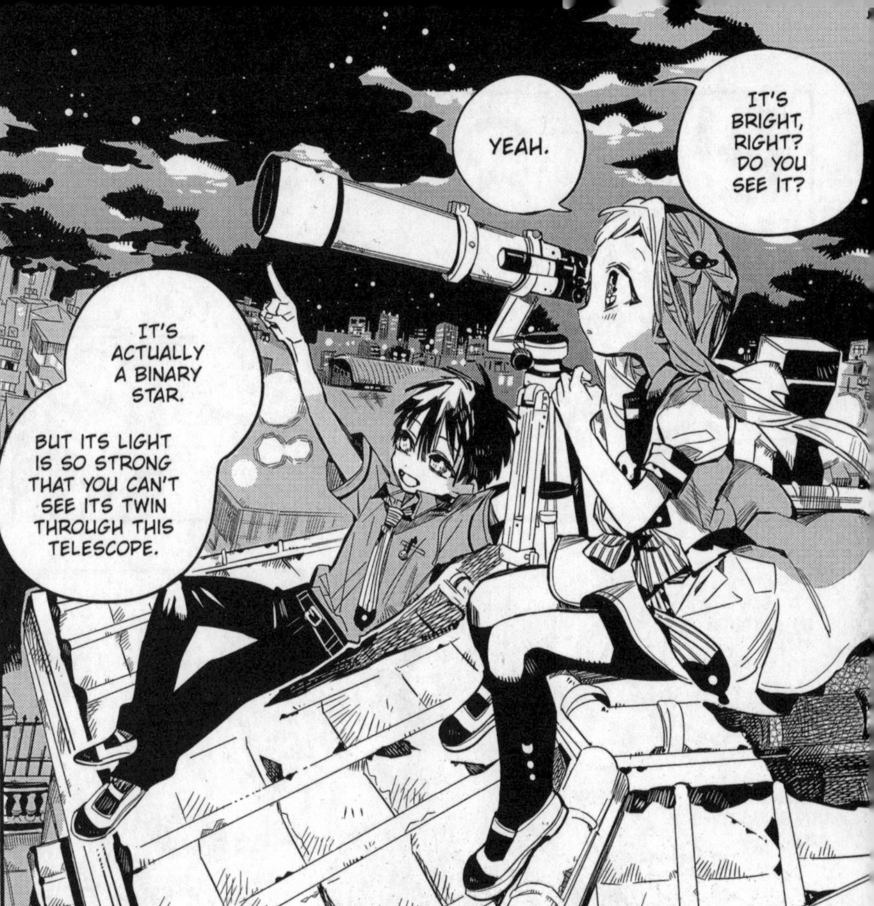
IT'S BRIGHT, RIGHT? DO YOU SEE IT?
YEAH.
IT'S ACTUALLY A BINARY STAR.
BUT ITS LIGHT IS SO STRONG THAT YOU CAN'T SEE ITS TWIN THROUGH THIS TELESCOPE.

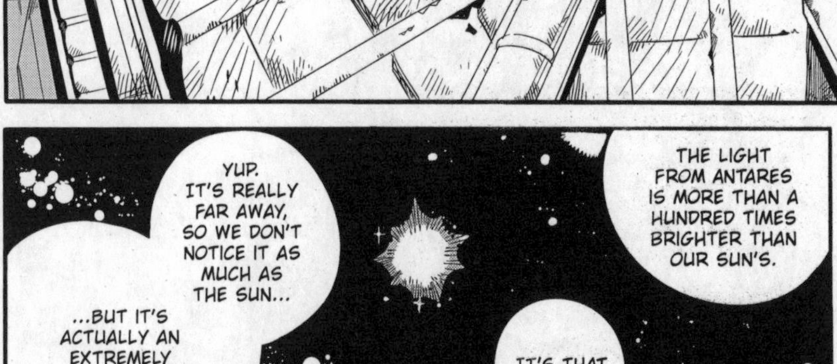
THE LIGHT FROM ANTARES IS MORE THAN A HUNDRED TIMES BRIGHTER THAN OUR SUN'S.
IT'S THAT BRIGHT?
YUP. IT'S REALLY FAR AWAY, SO WE DON'T NOTICE IT AS MUCH AS THE SUN...
...BUT IT'S ACTUALLY AN EXTREMELY BRIGHT STAR.

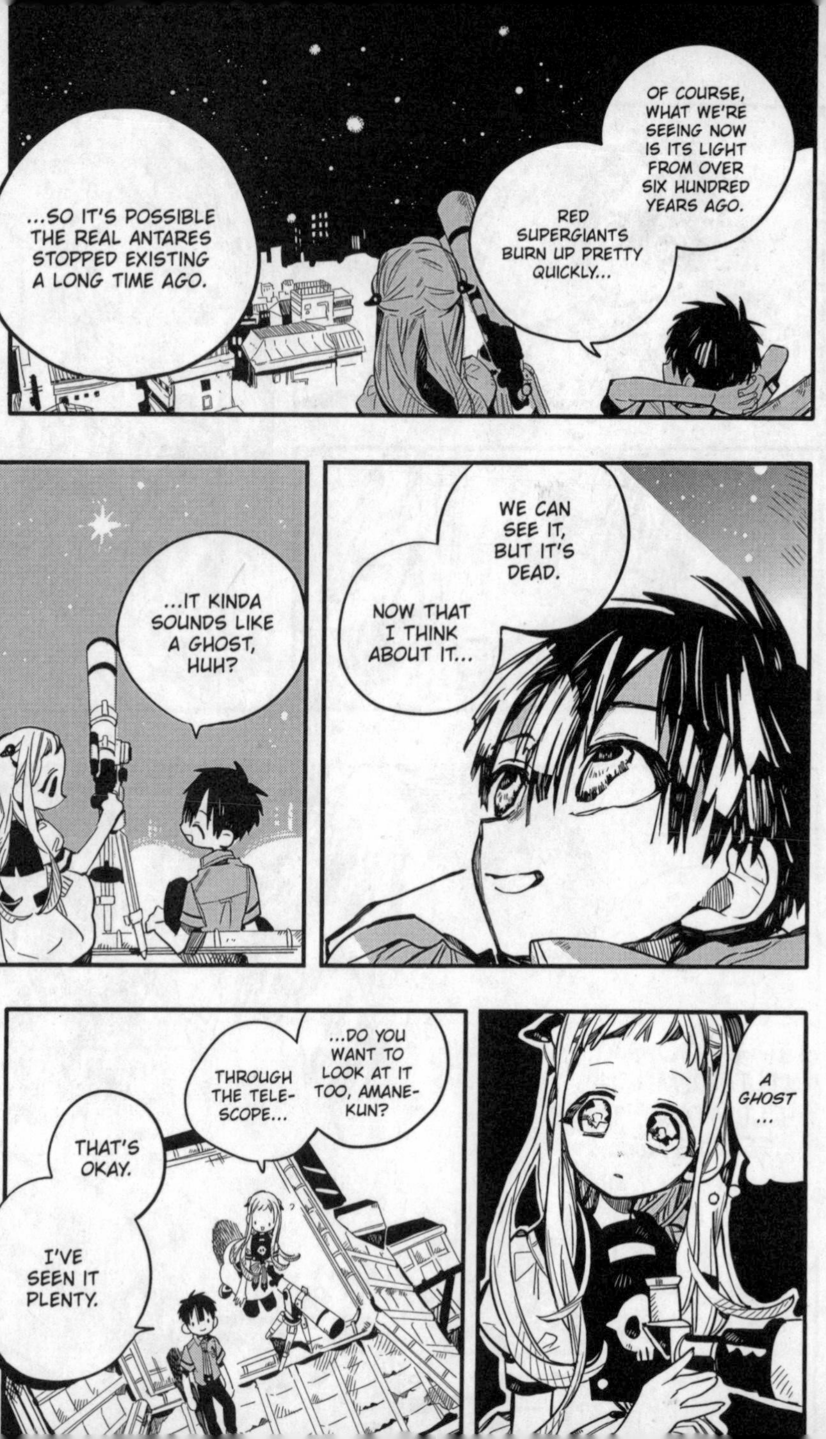
OF COURSE, WHAT WE'RE SEEING NOW IS ITS LIGHT FROM OVER SIX HUNDRED YEARS AGO.
RED SUPERGIANTS BURN UP PRETTY QUICKLY...
...SO IT'S POSSIBLE THE REAL ANTARES STOPPED EXISTING A LONG TIME AGO.
WE CAN SEE IT, BUT IT'S DEAD.
NOW THAT I THINK ABOUT IT...
...IT KINDA SOUNDS LIKE A GHOST, HUH?
A GHOST...
...DO YOU WANT TO LOOK AT IT TOO, AMANE-KUN?
THROUGH THE TELE-SCOPE...
THAT'S OKAY.
I'VE SEEN IT PLENTY.

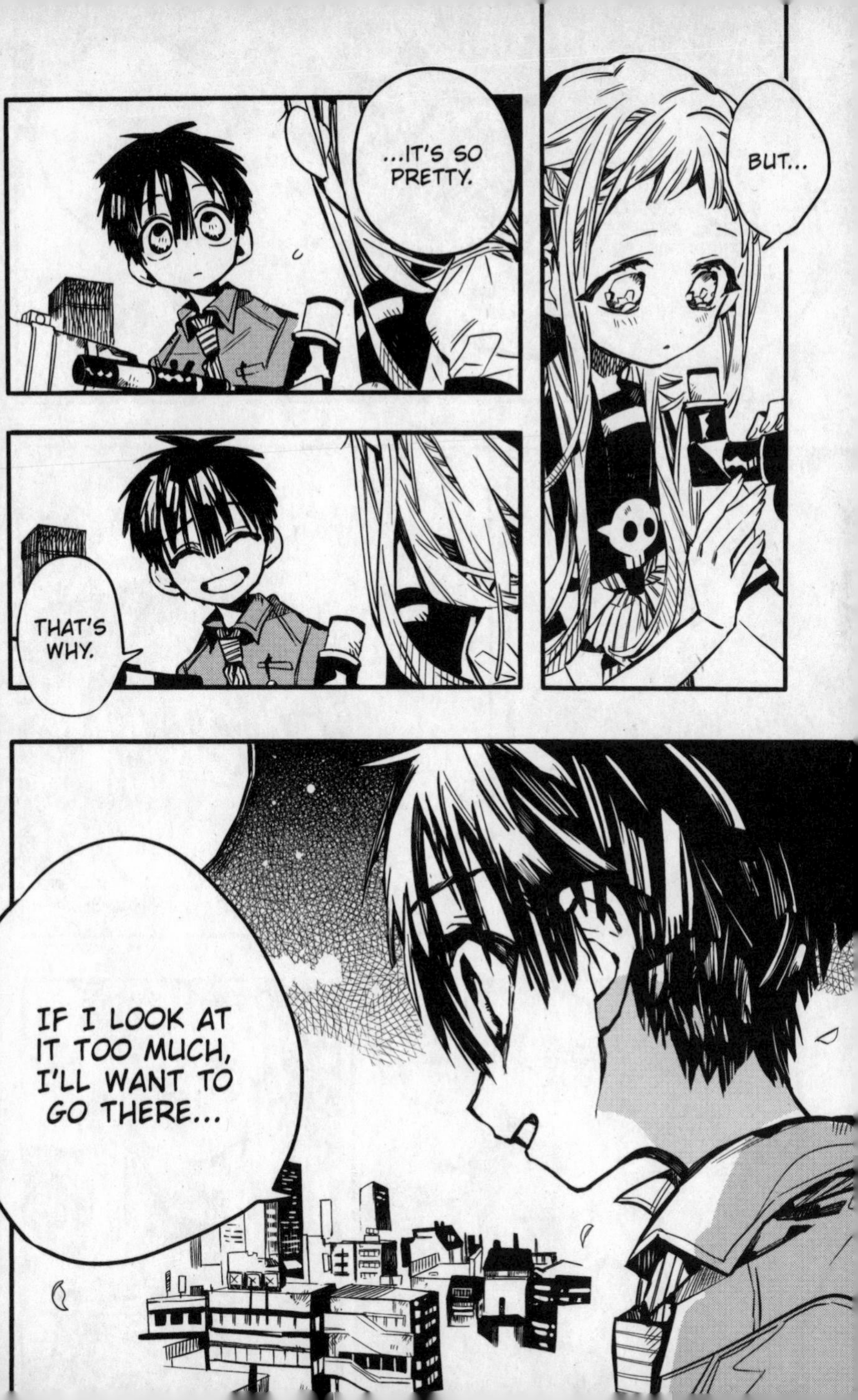
BUT...
...IT'S SO PRETTY.
THAT'S WHY.
IF I LOOK AT IT TOO MUCH, I'LL WANT TO GO THERE...

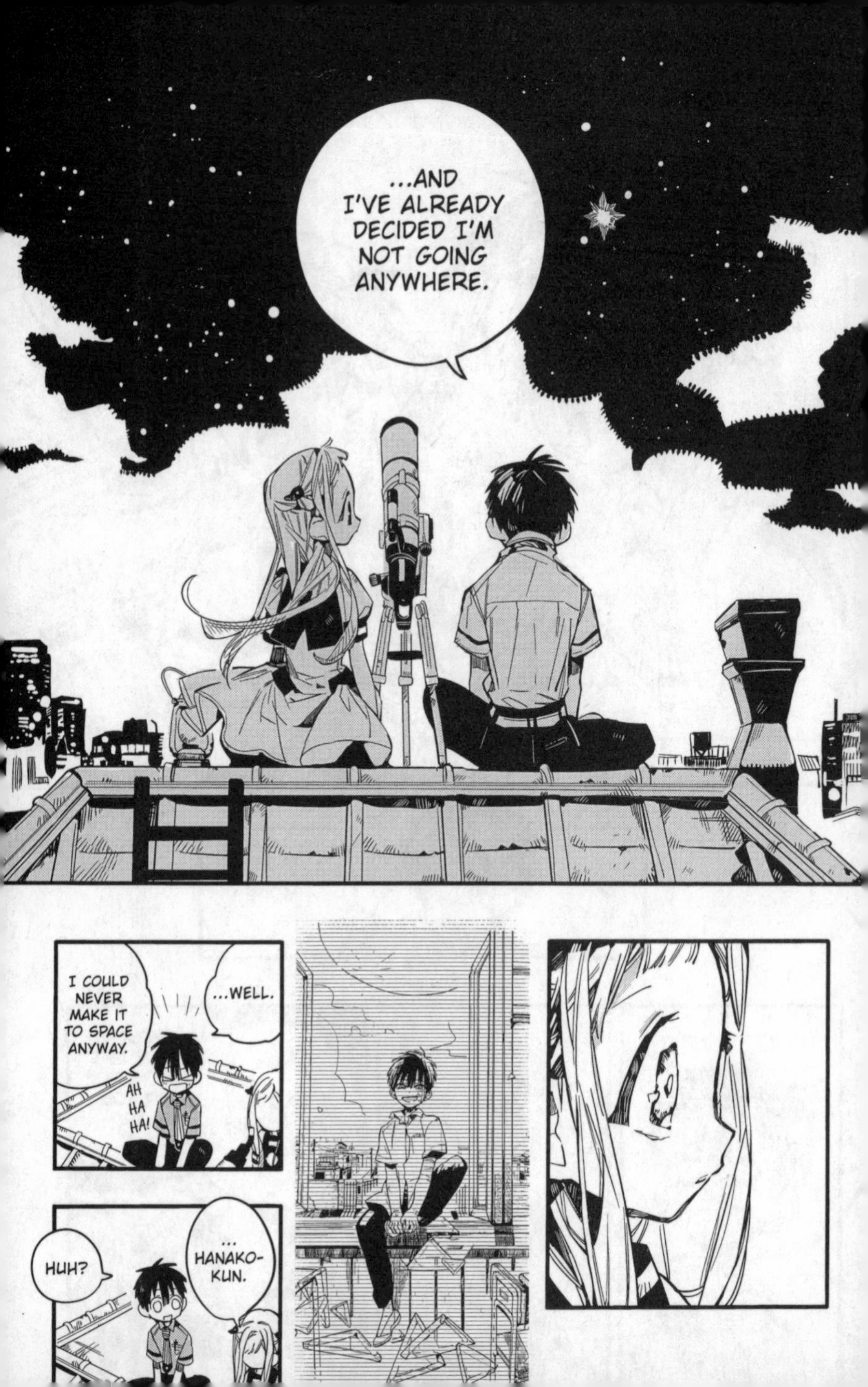
...AND I'VE ALREADY DECIDED I'M NOT GOING ANYWHERE.
...WELL.
I COULD NEVER MAKE IT TO SPACE ANYWAY.
AH HA HA!
...HANAKO-KUN.
HUH?

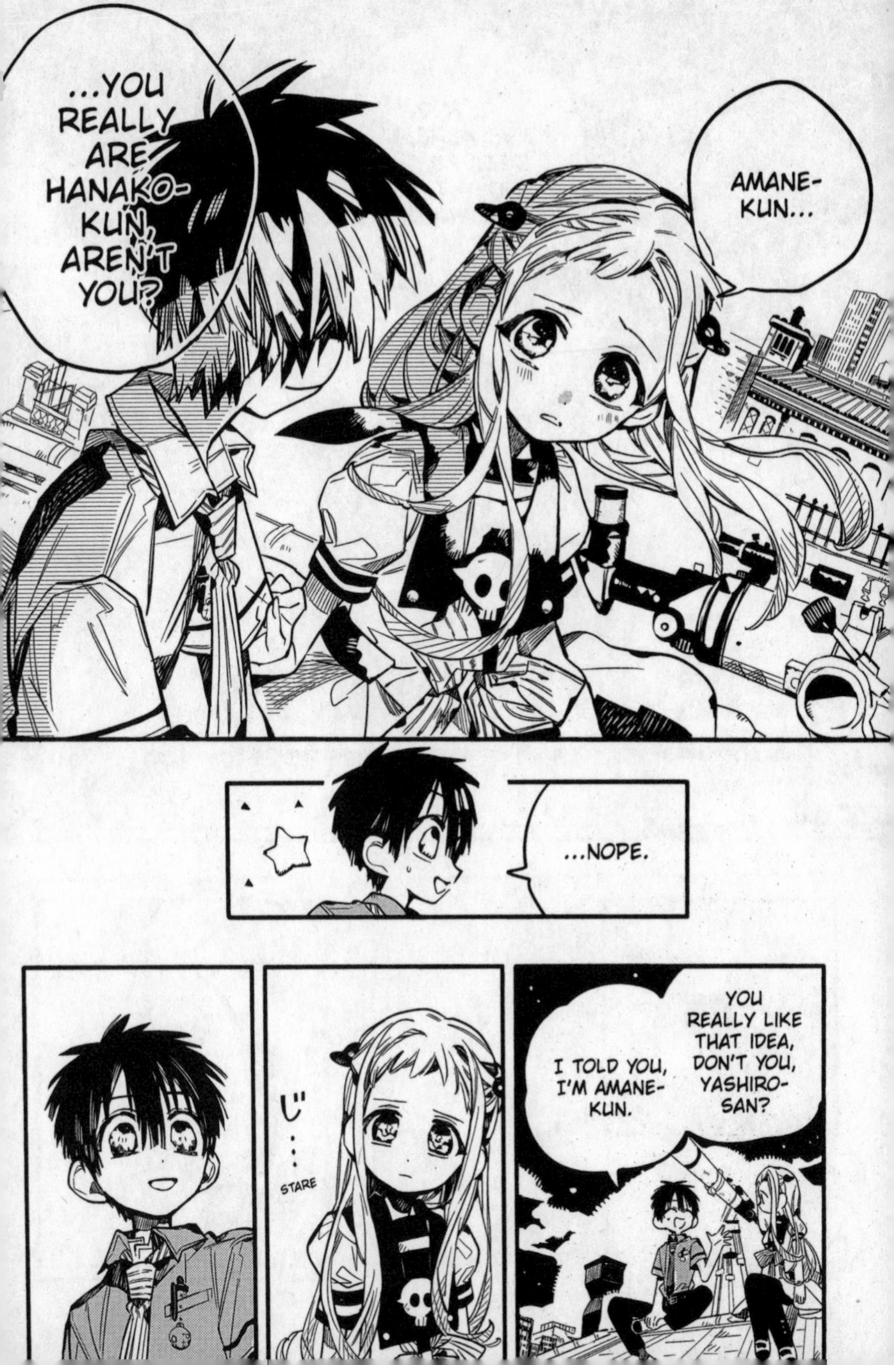
AMANE-KUN...
...YOU REALLY ARE HANAKO-KUN, AREN'T YOU?
...NOPE.
YOU REALLY LIKE THAT IDEA, DON'T YOU, YASHIRO-SAN?
I TOLD YOU, I'M AMANE-KUN.
じ...
STARE

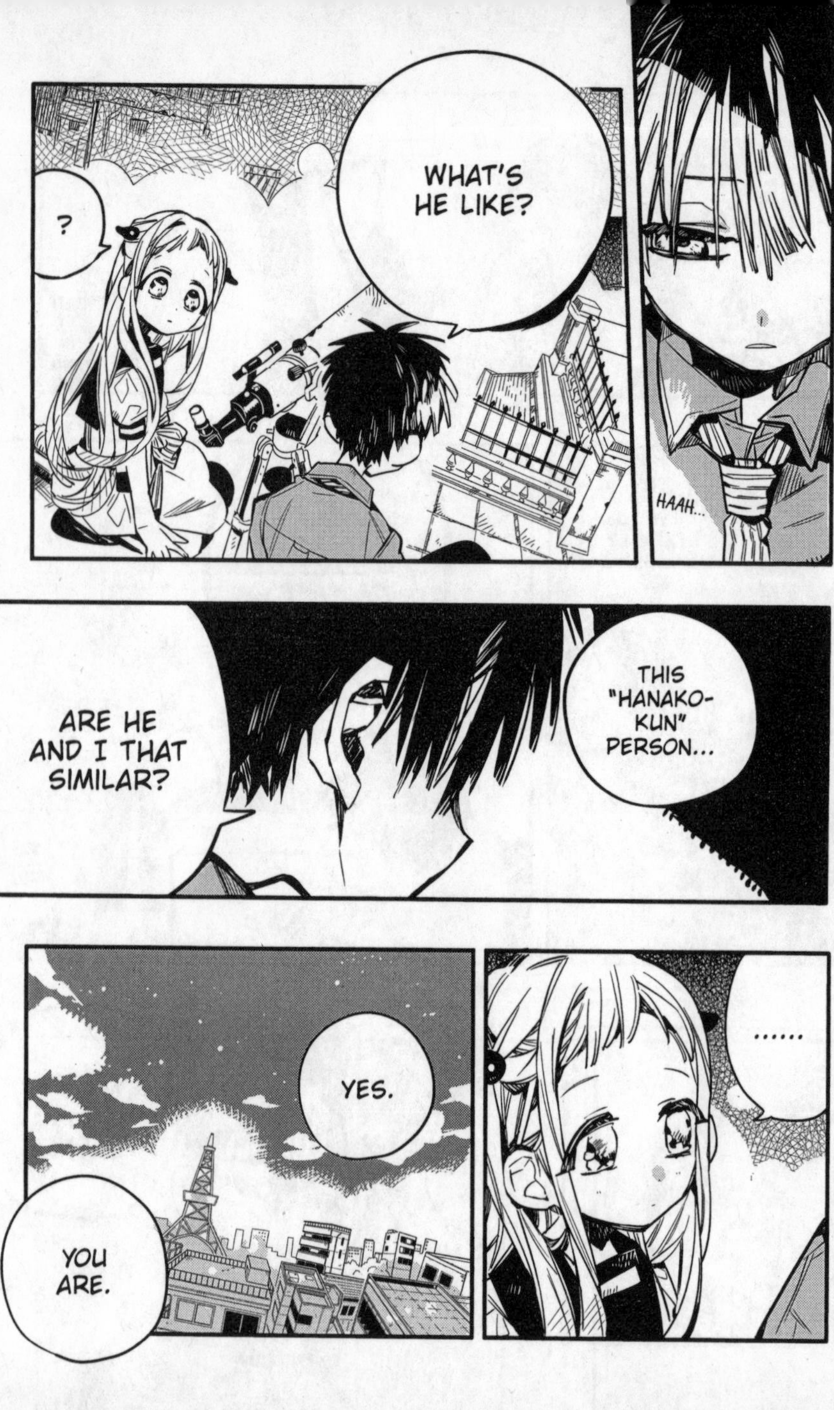
HAAH...
WHAT'S HE LIKE?
?
THIS "HANAKO-KUN" PERSON...
ARE HE AND I THAT SIMILAR?
......
YES.
YOU ARE.

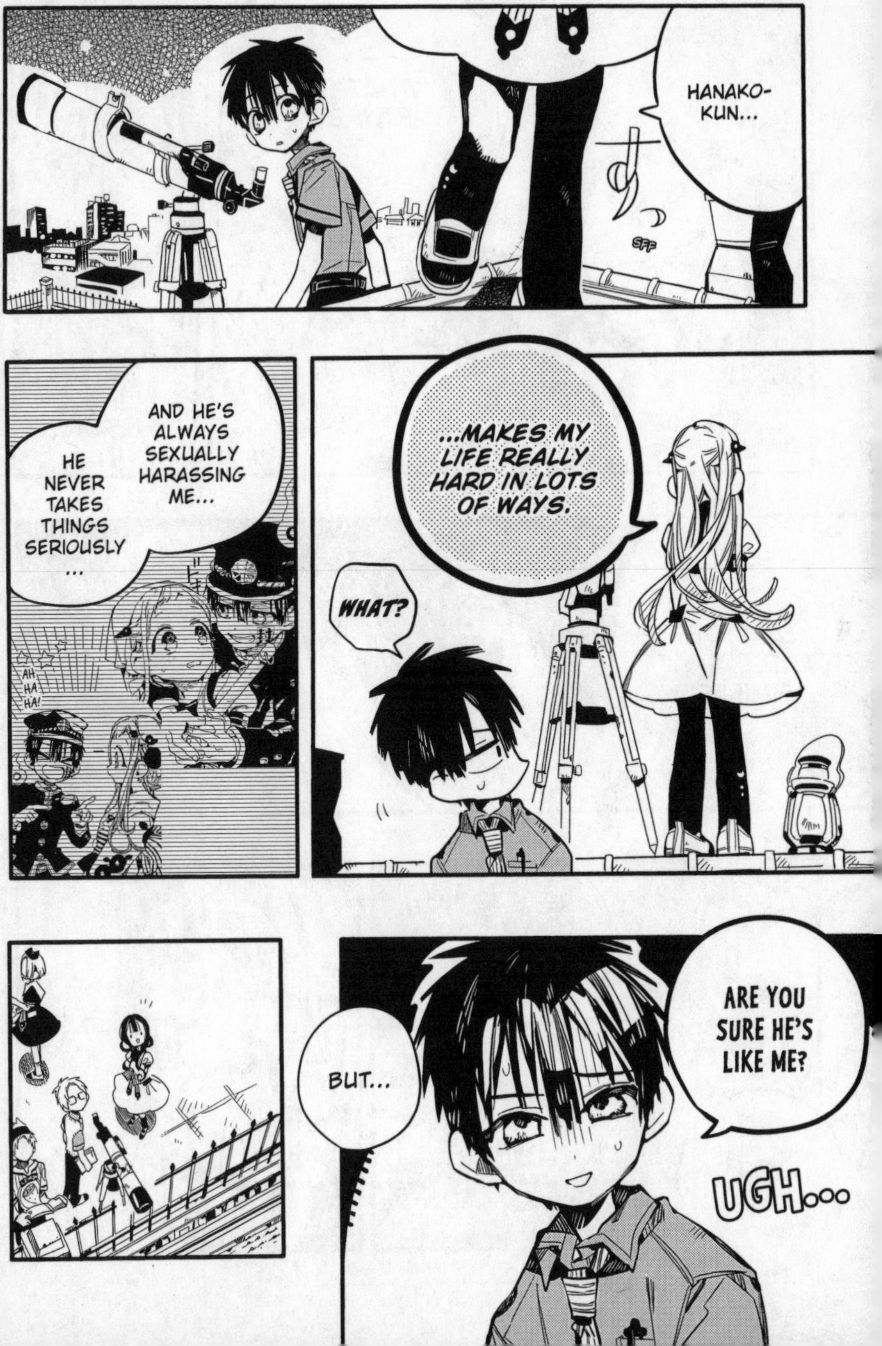
HANAKO-KUN...
SFF
...MAKES MY LIFE REALLY HARD IN LOTS OF WAYS.
WHAT?
AND HE'S ALWAYS SEXUALLY HARASSING ME...
HE NEVER TAKES THINGS SERIOUSLY ...
AH HA HA!
ARE YOU SURE HE'S LIKE ME?
BUT...
UGH...

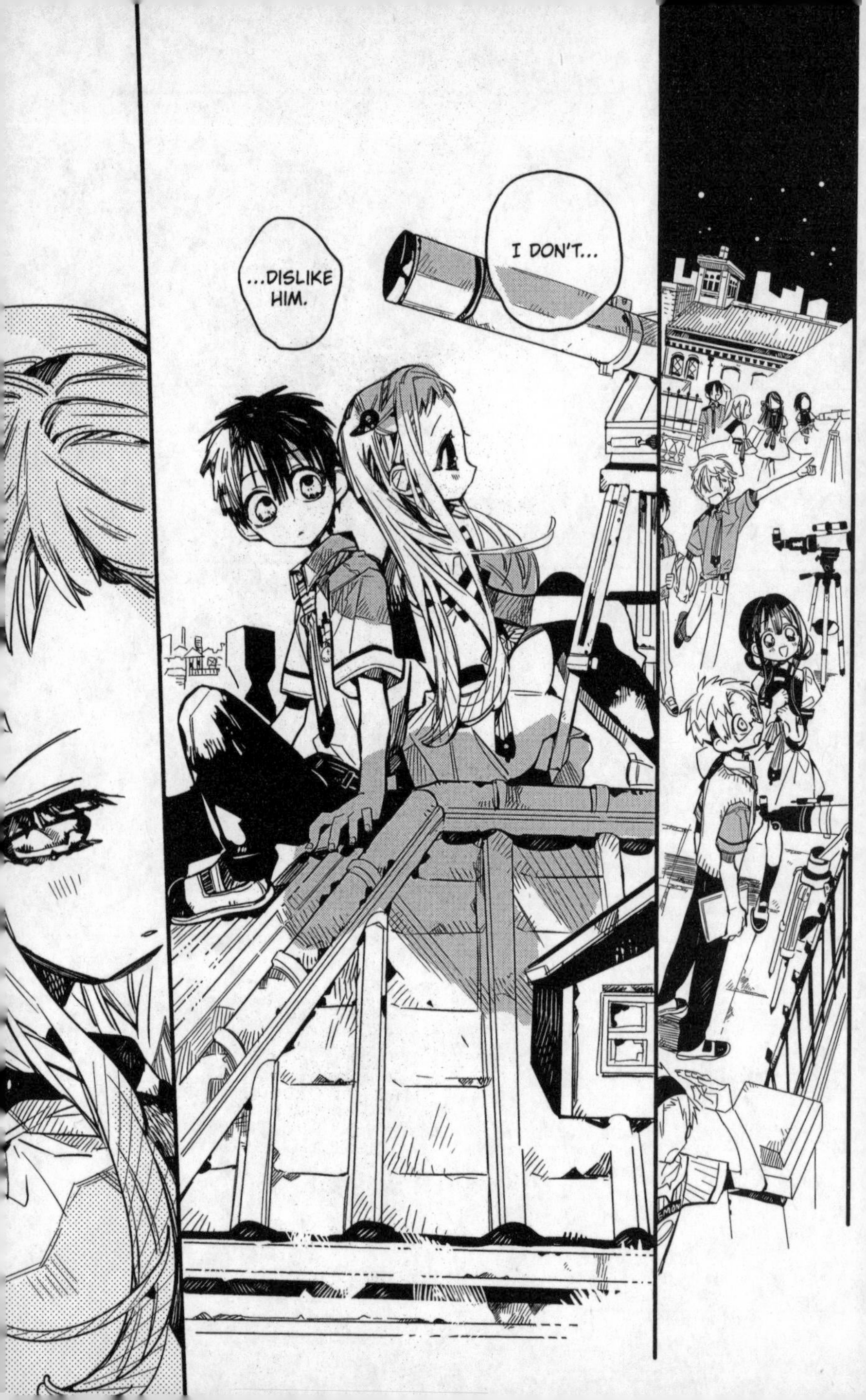
I DON'T...
...DISLIKE HIM.

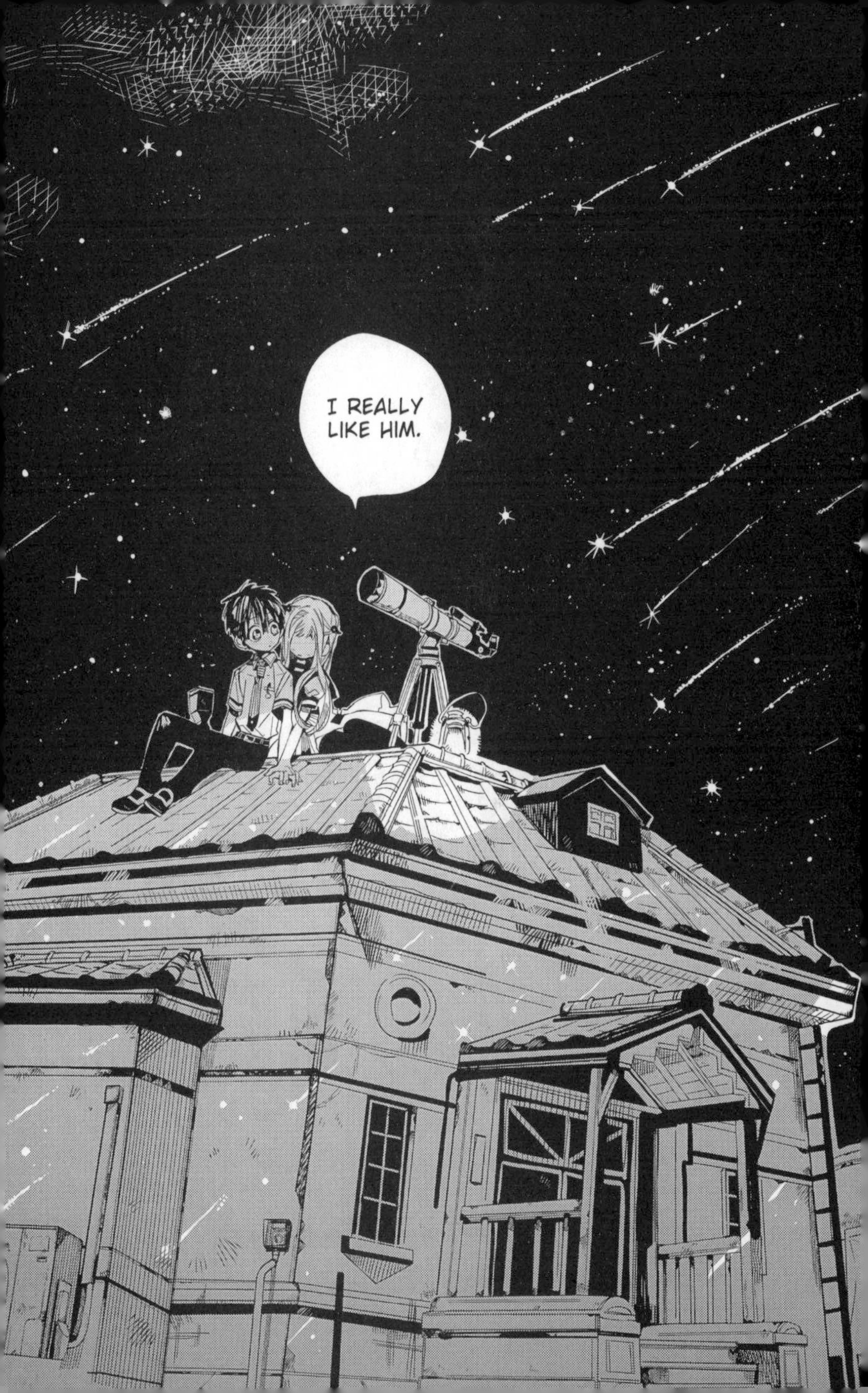
I REALLY LIKE HIM.

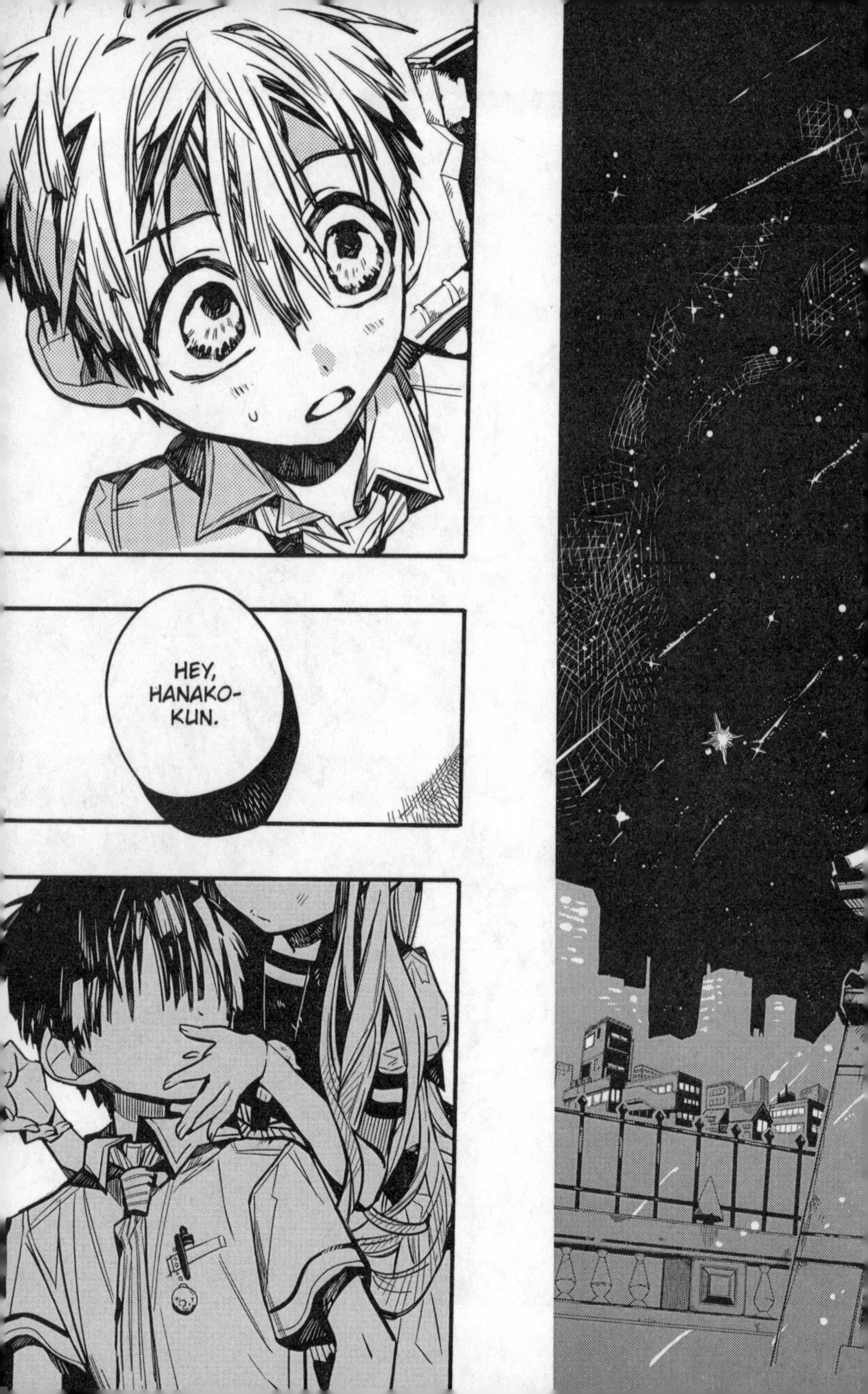
HEY, HANAKO-KUN.

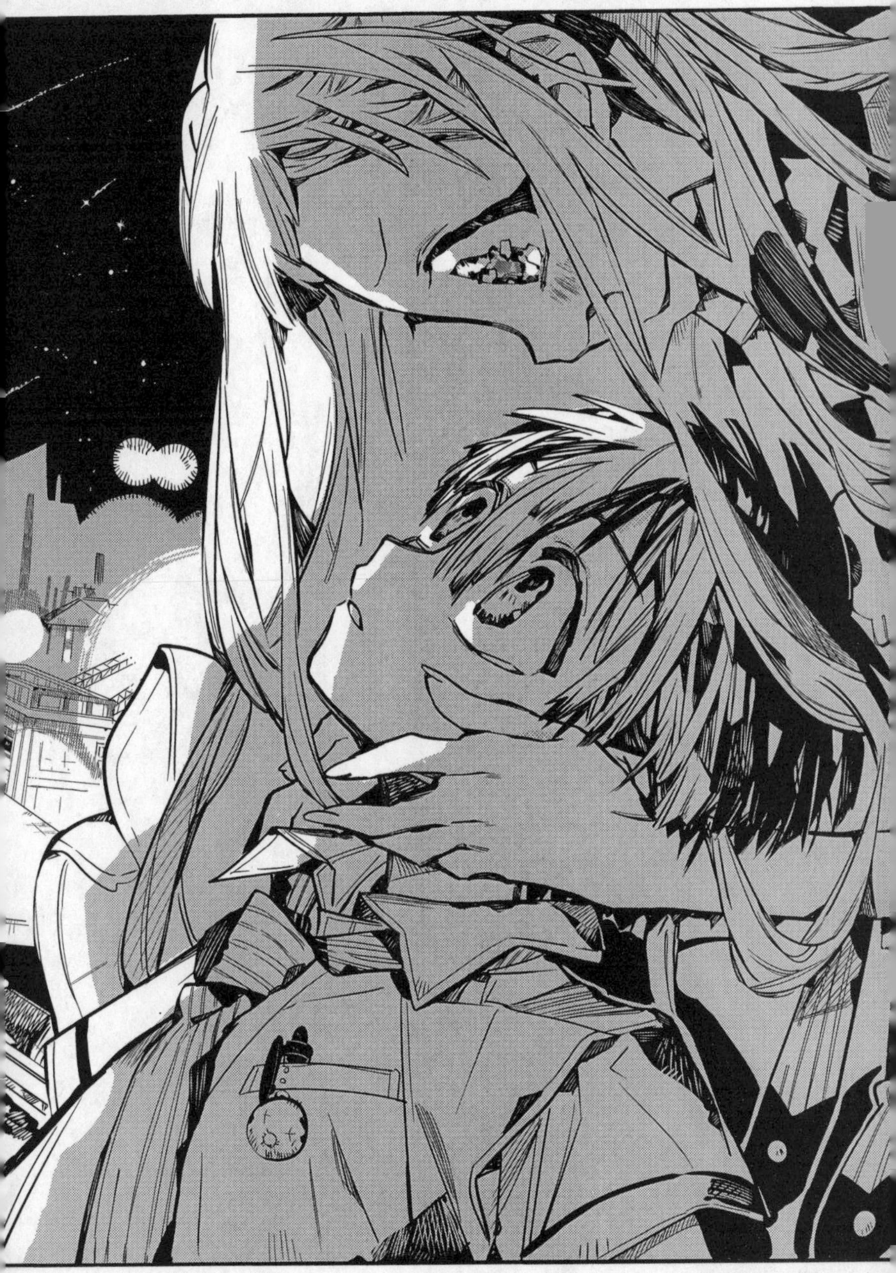

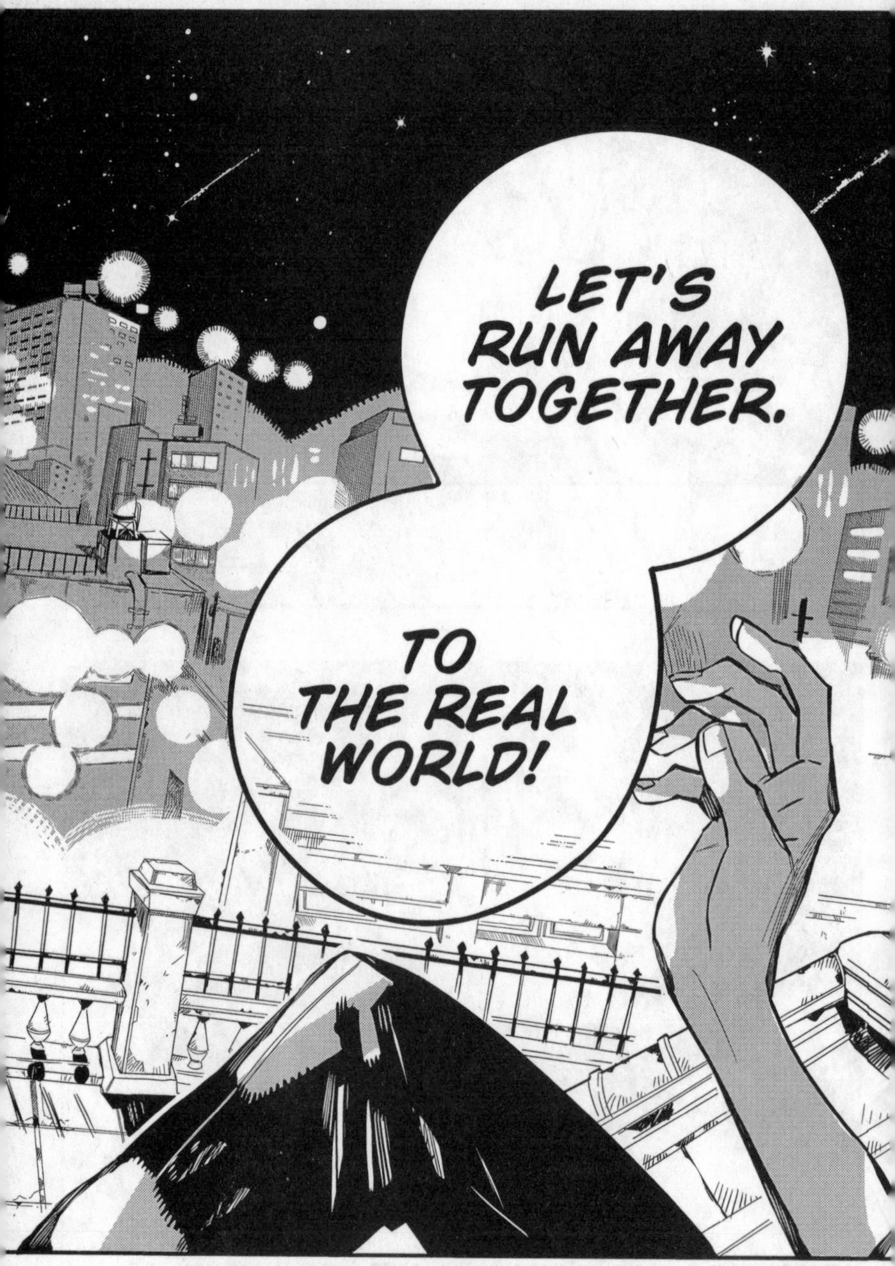
LET'S RUN AWAY TOGETHER.
TO THE REAL WORLD!

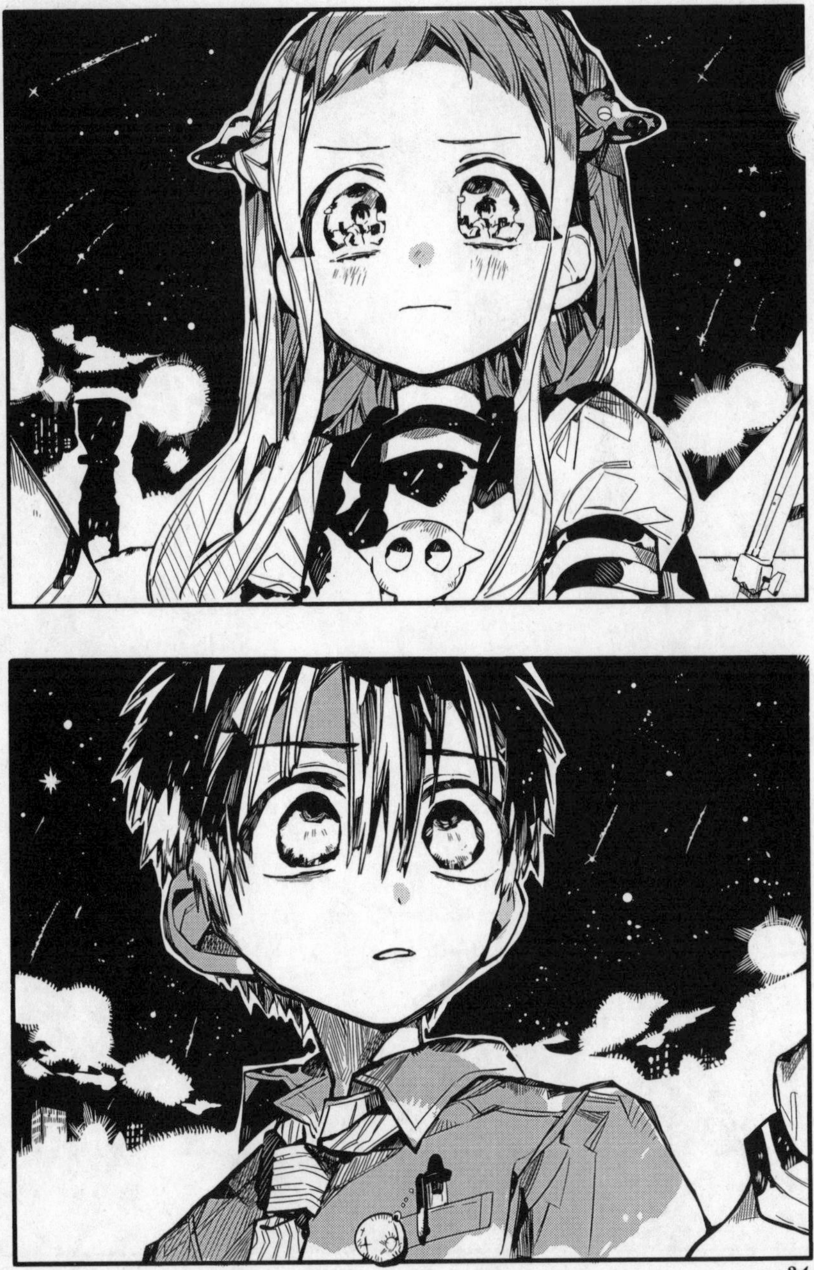

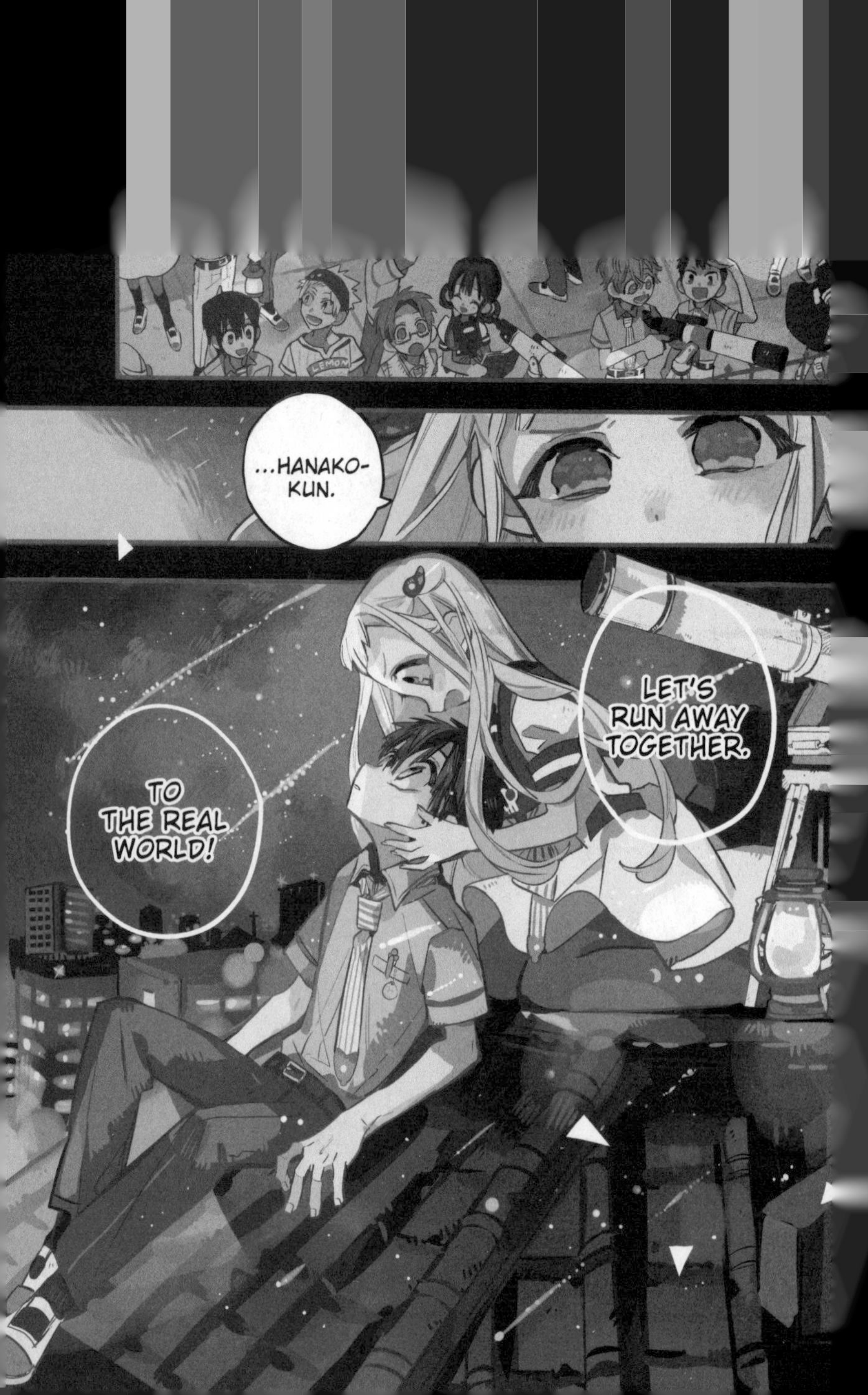
...HANAKO-KUN.
LET'S RUN AWAY TOGETHER.
TO THE REAL WORLD!

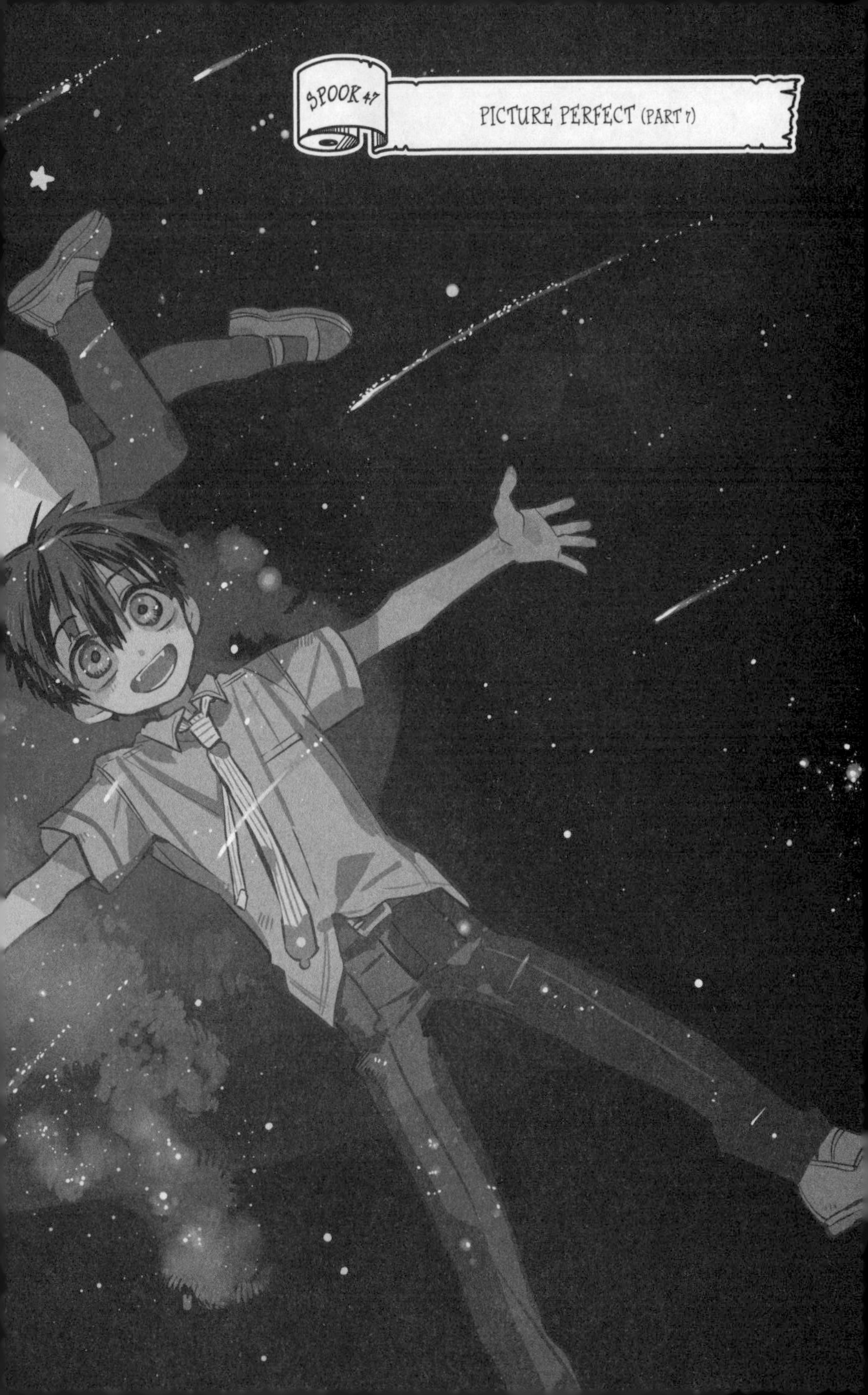
SPOOK 47
PICTURE PERFECT (PART 7)

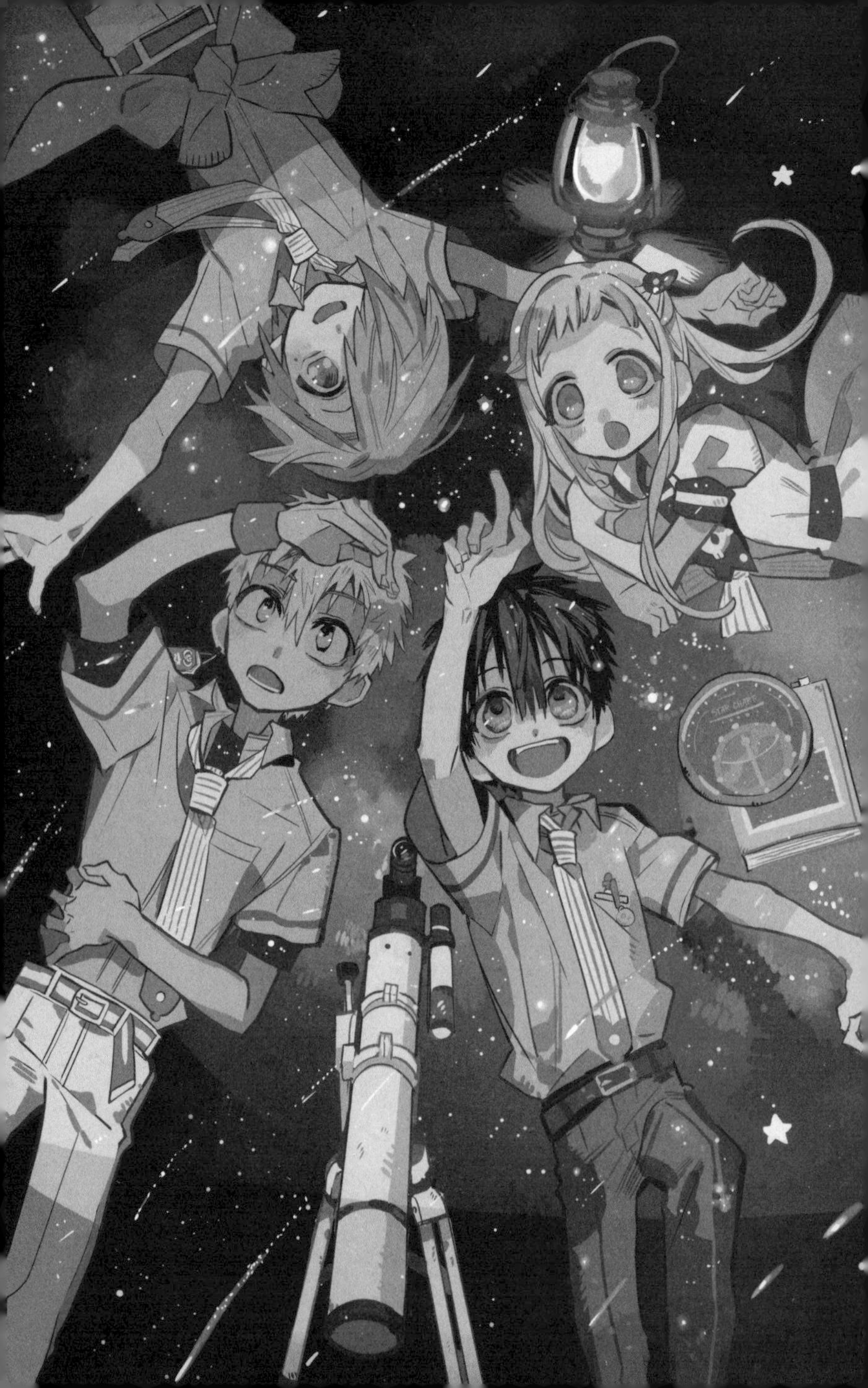
STAR CHART

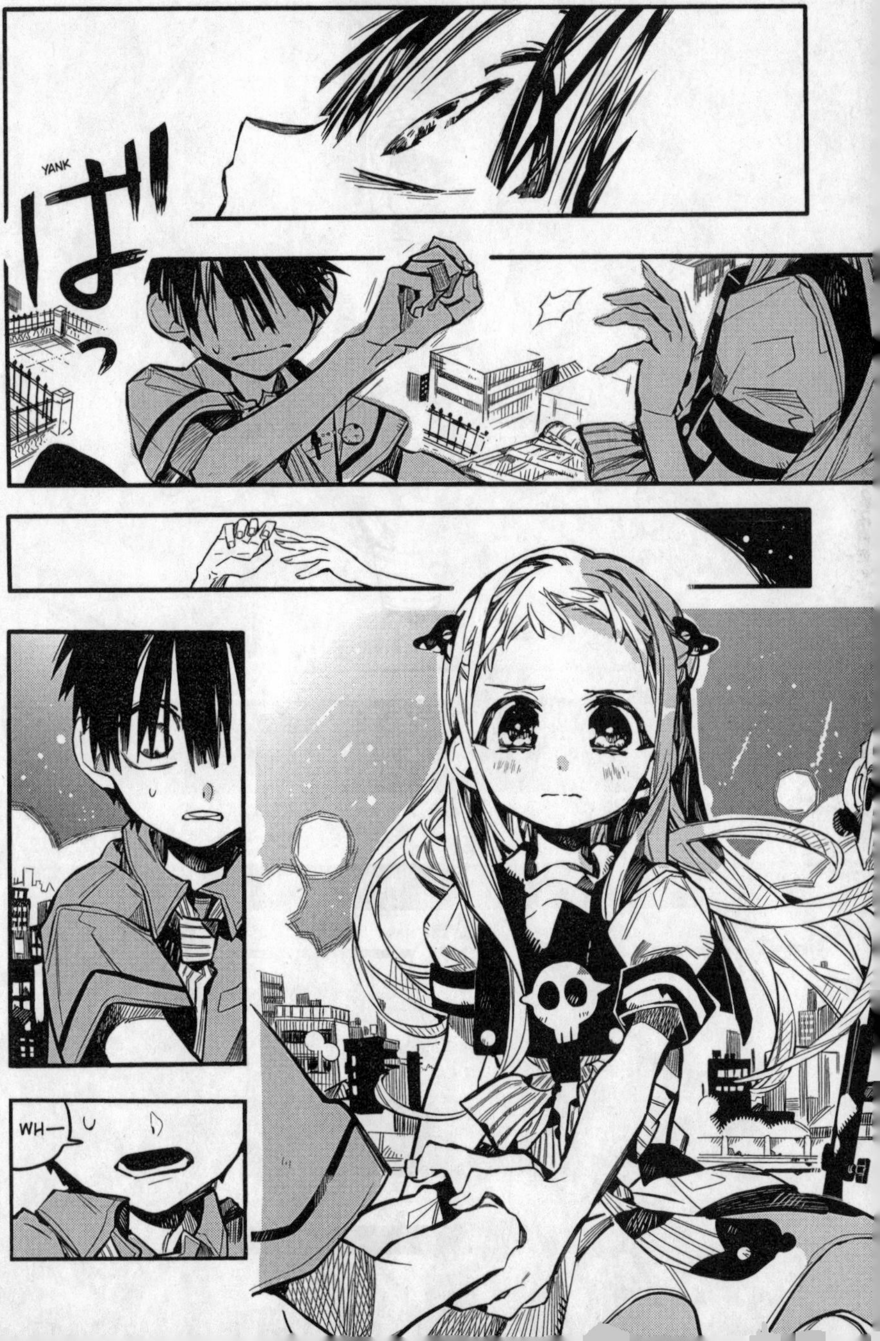
YANK
ばっ
WH—

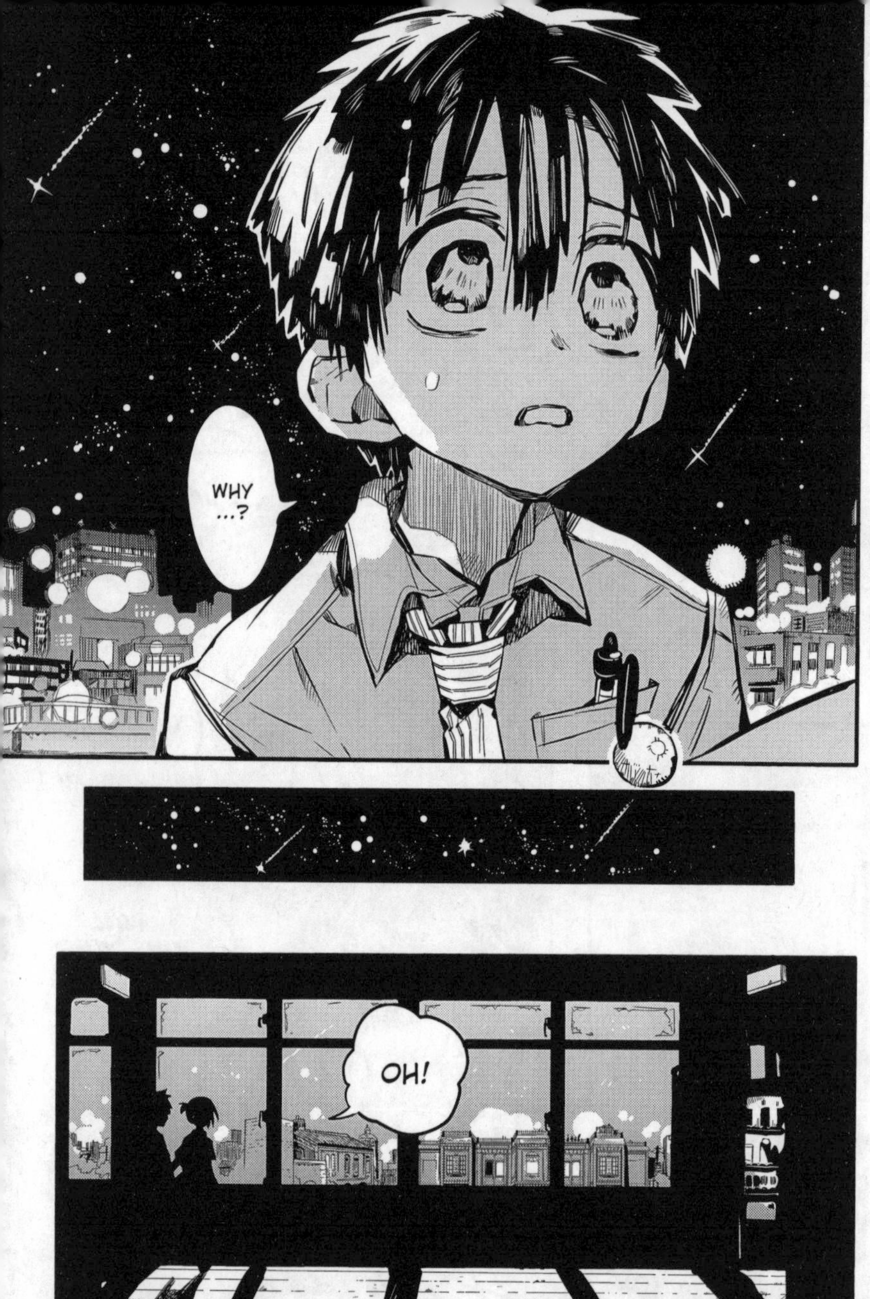
WHY ...?
OH!

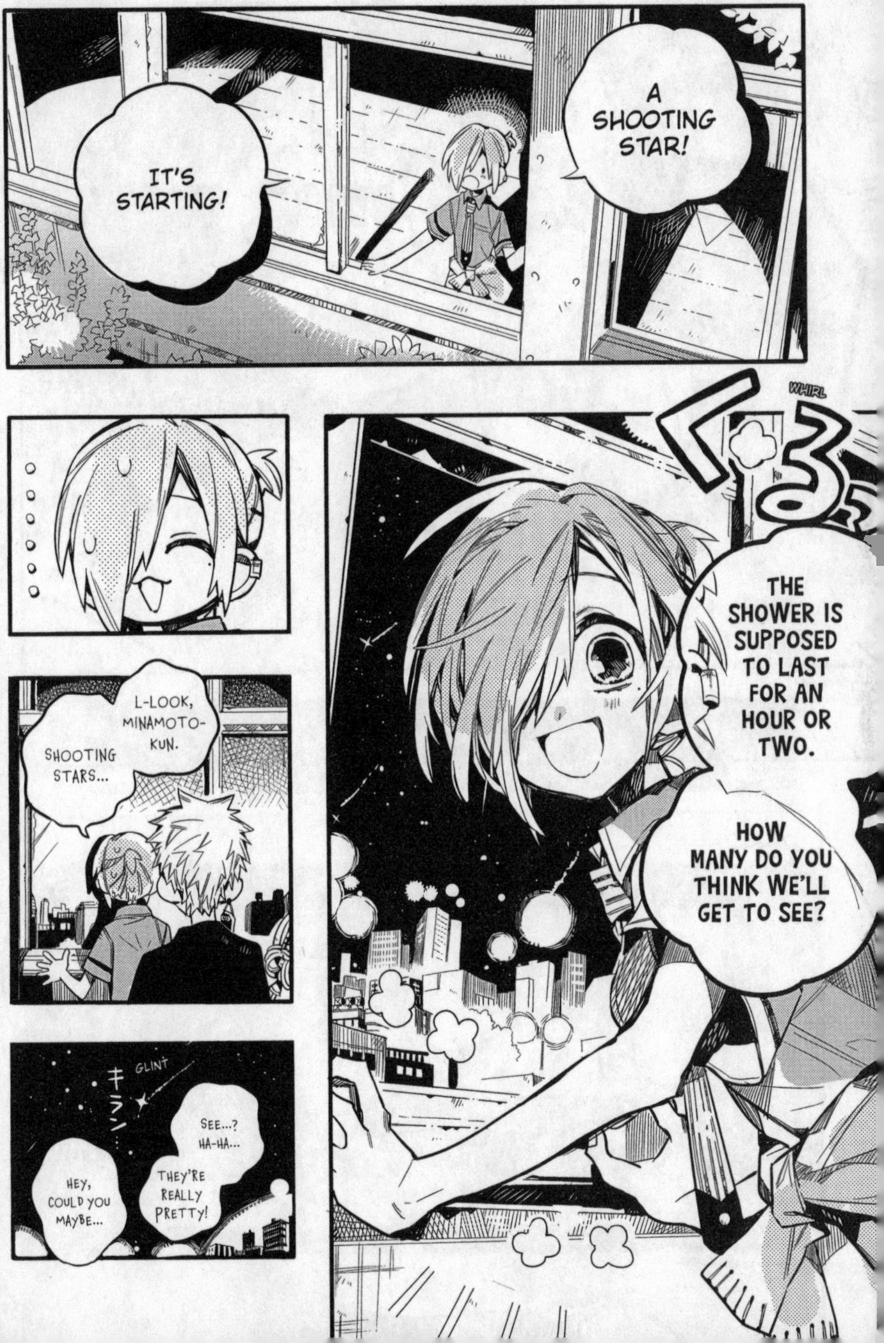
A SHOOTING STAR!
IT'S STARTING!
くる
WHIRL
THE SHOWER IS SUPPOSED TO LAST FOR AN HOUR OR TWO.
HOW MANY DO YOU THINK WE'LL GET TO SEE?
......
L-LOOK, MINAMOTO-KUN.
SHOOTING STARS...
キラン
GLINT
SEE...? HA-HA...
THEY'RE REALLY PRETTY!
HEY, COULD YOU MAYBE...

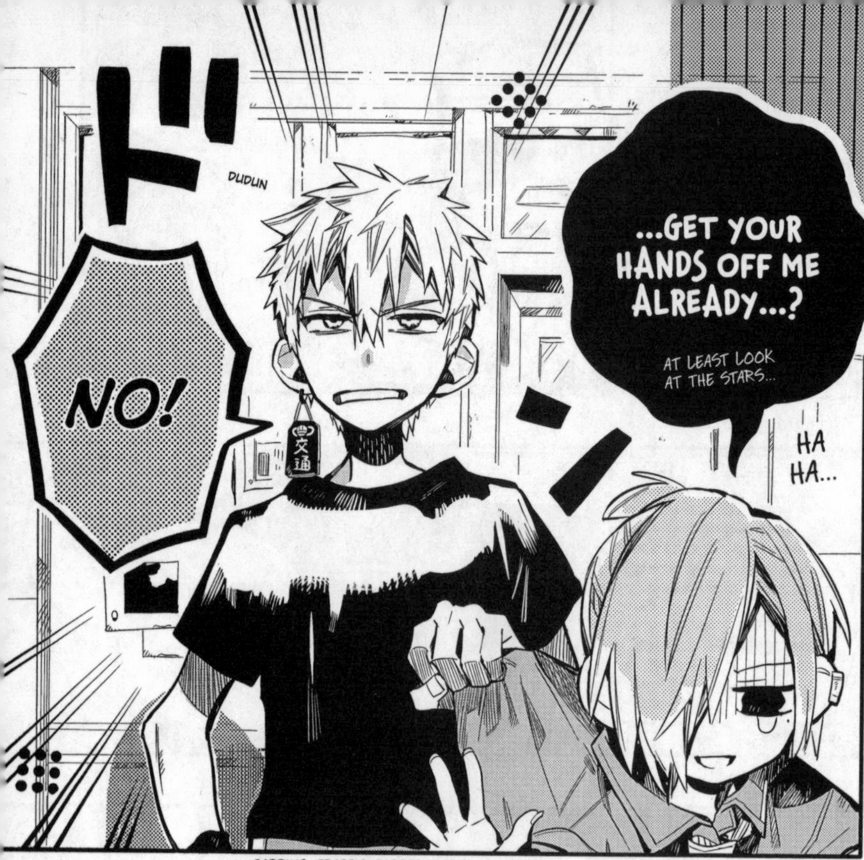
...GET YOUR HANDS OFF ME ALREADY...?
AT LEAST LOOK AT THE STARS...
HA HA...
ド
DUDUN
NO!

EARRING: TRAFFIC-SAFETY CHARM

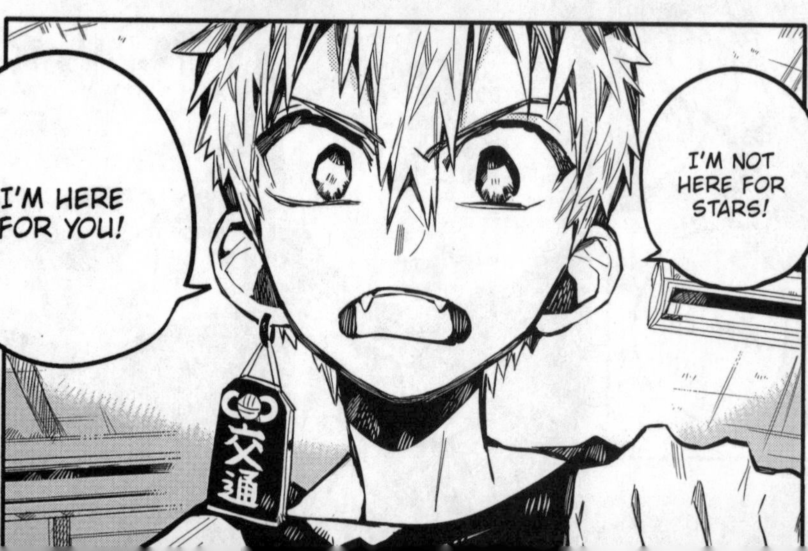
I'M NOT HERE FOR STARS!
I'M HERE FOR YOU!
交通

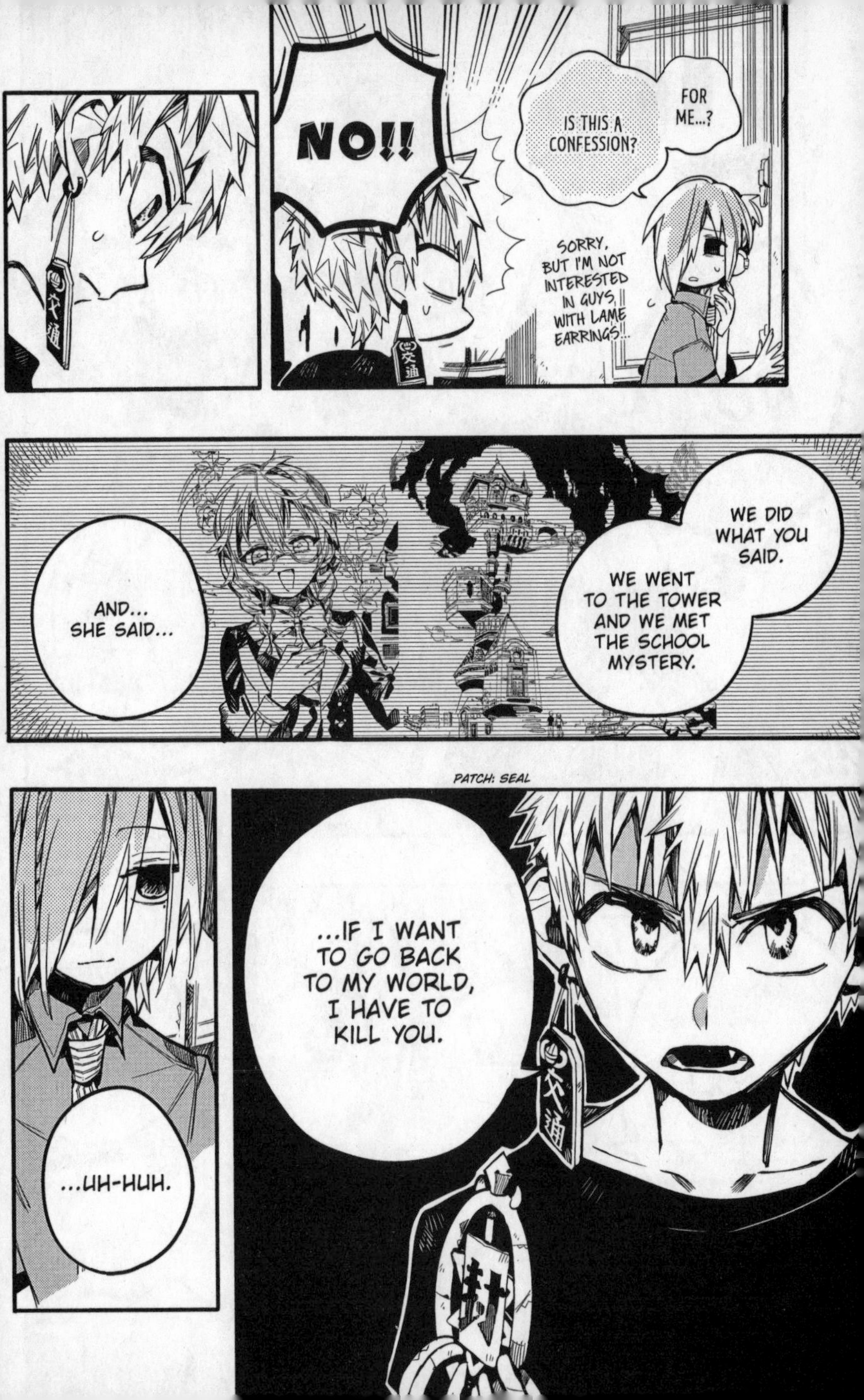
FOR ME...?
IS THIS A CONFESSION?
SORRY, BUT I'M NOT INTERESTED IN GUYS WITH LAME EARRINGS...
NO!!
WE DID WHAT YOU SAID.
WE WENT TO THE TOWER AND WE MET THE SCHOOL MYSTERY.
AND... SHE SAID...
PATCH: SEAL
...IF I WANT TO GO BACK TO MY WORLD, I HAVE TO KILL YOU.
...UH-HUH.

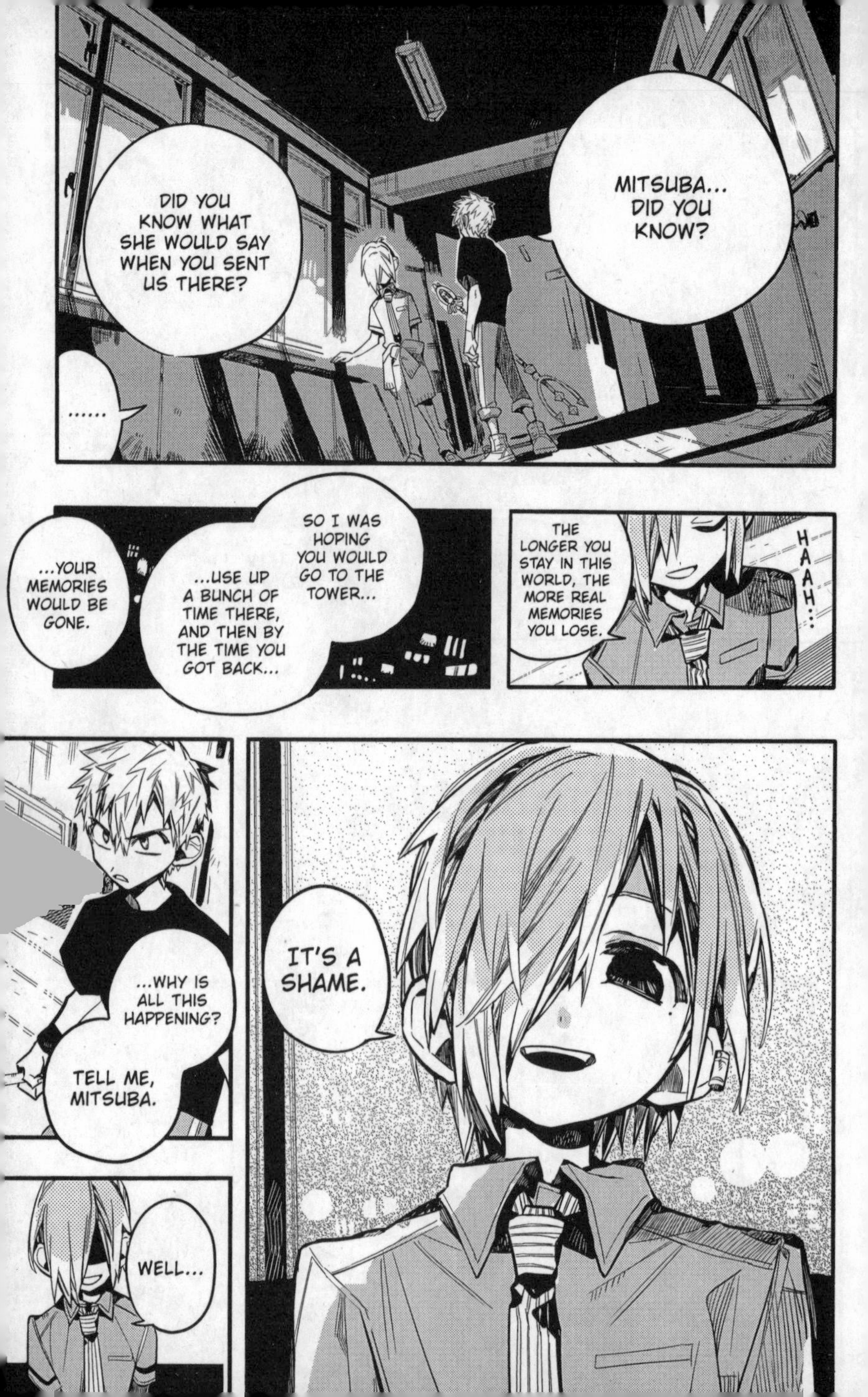
MITSUBA... DID YOU KNOW?
DID YOU KNOW WHAT SHE WOULD SAY WHEN YOU SENT US THERE?
......
THE LONGER YOU STAY IN THIS WORLD, THE MORE REAL MEMORIES YOU LOSE.
HAAAH...
SO I WAS HOPING YOU WOULD GO TO THE TOWER...
...USE UP A BUNCH OF TIME THERE, AND THEN BY THE TIME YOU GOT BACK...
...YOUR MEMORIES WOULD BE GONE.
IT'S A SHAME.
...WHY IS ALL THIS HAPPENING?
TELL ME, MITSUBA.
WELL...

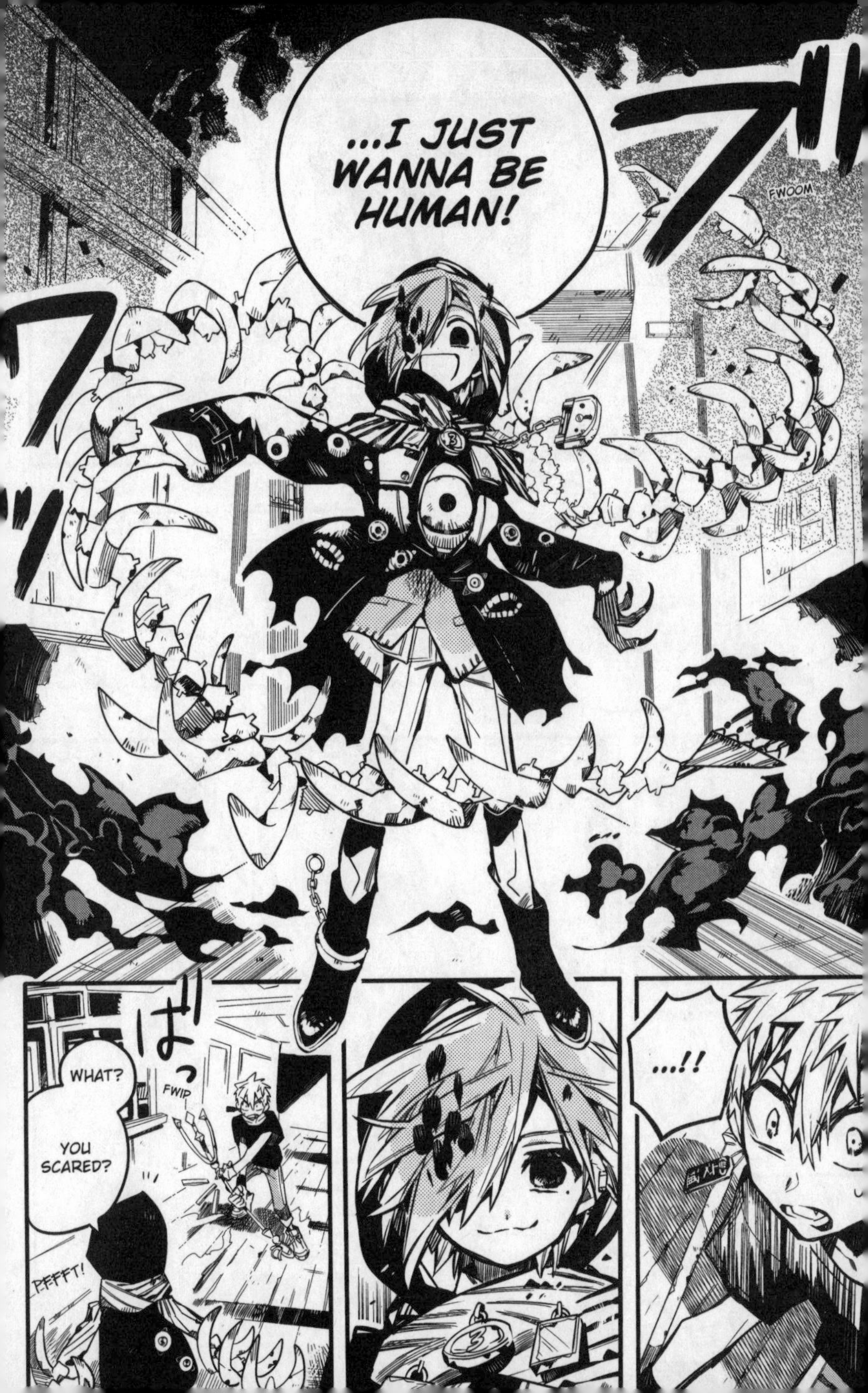
...I JUST WANNA BE HUMAN!
FWOOM
...!!
FWIP
WHAT?
YOU SCARED?
PFFFT!

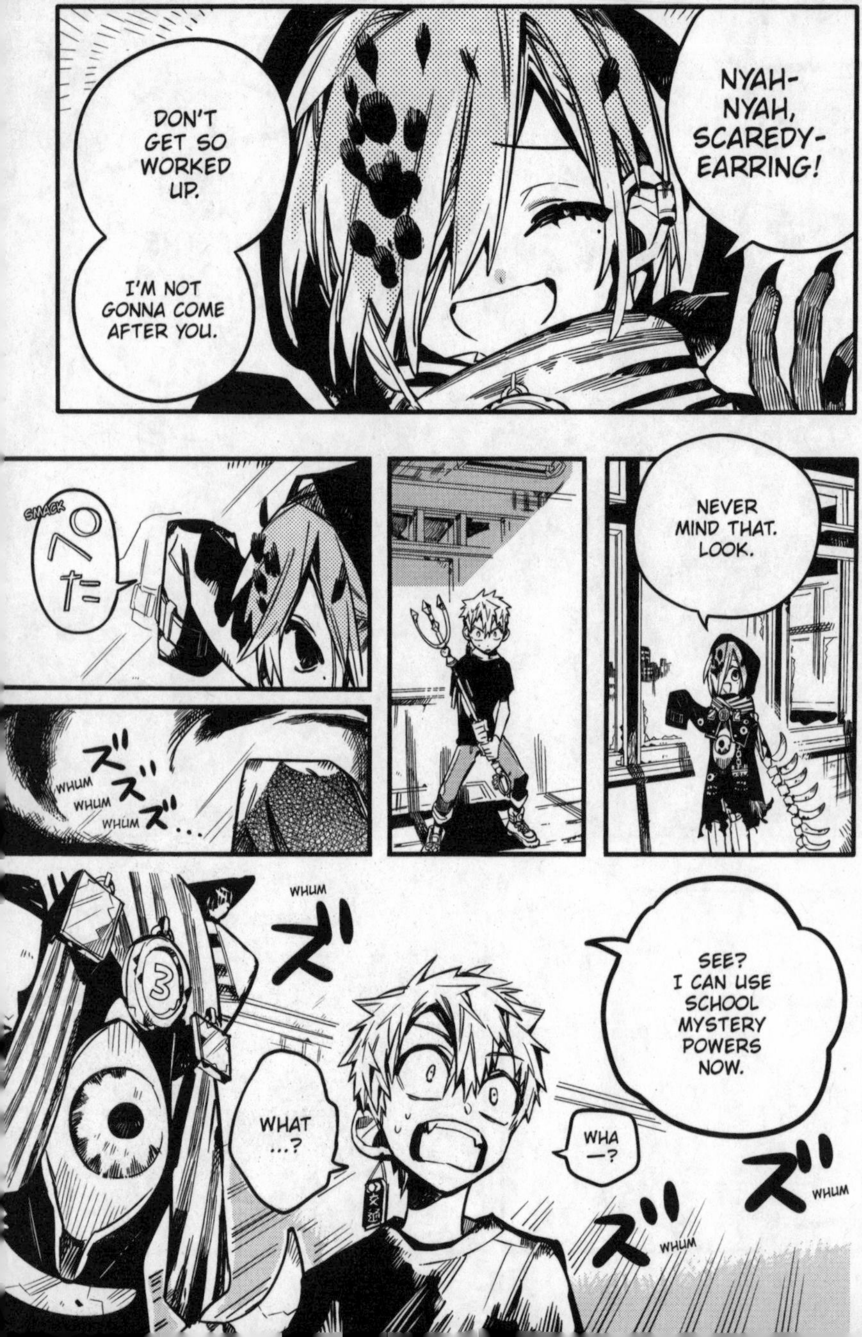
NYAH-NYAH, SCAREDY-EARRING!
DON'T GET SO WORKED UP.
I'M NOT GONNA COME AFTER YOU.
NEVER MIND THAT. LOOK.
ぺた
SMACK
ズズズ…
WHUM WHUM WHUM
SEE? I CAN USE SCHOOL MYSTERY POWERS NOW.
ズ
WHUM
WHA—?
WHAT …?
ズズ
WHUM WHUM

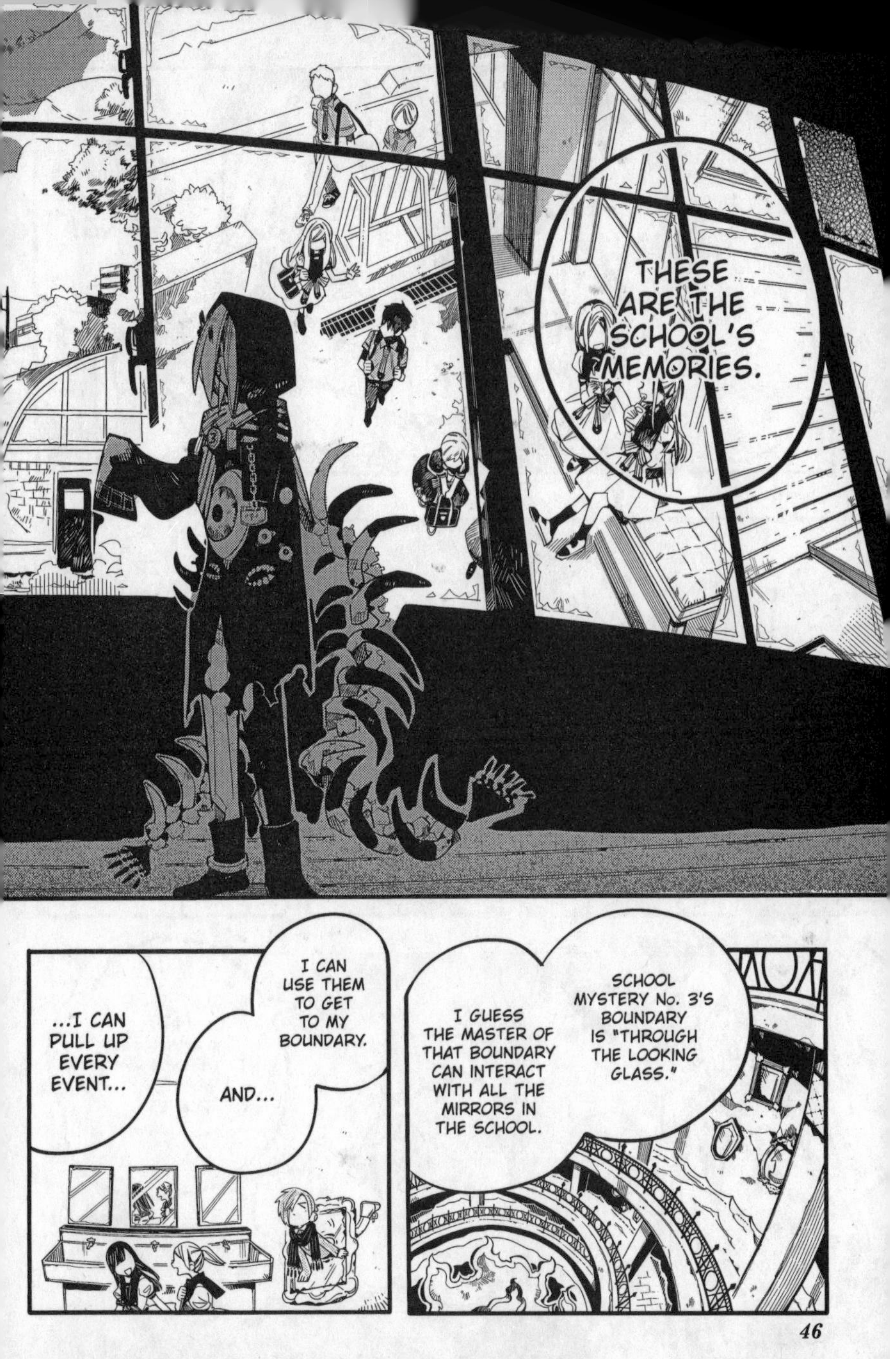
THESE ARE THE SCHOOL'S MEMORIES.
SCHOOL MYSTERY No. 3'S BOUNDARY IS "THROUGH THE LOOKING GLASS."
I GUESS THE MASTER OF THAT BOUNDARY CAN INTERACT WITH ALL THE MIRRORS IN THE SCHOOL.
I CAN USE THEM TO GET TO MY BOUNDARY.
...I CAN PULL UP EVERY EVENT...
AND...

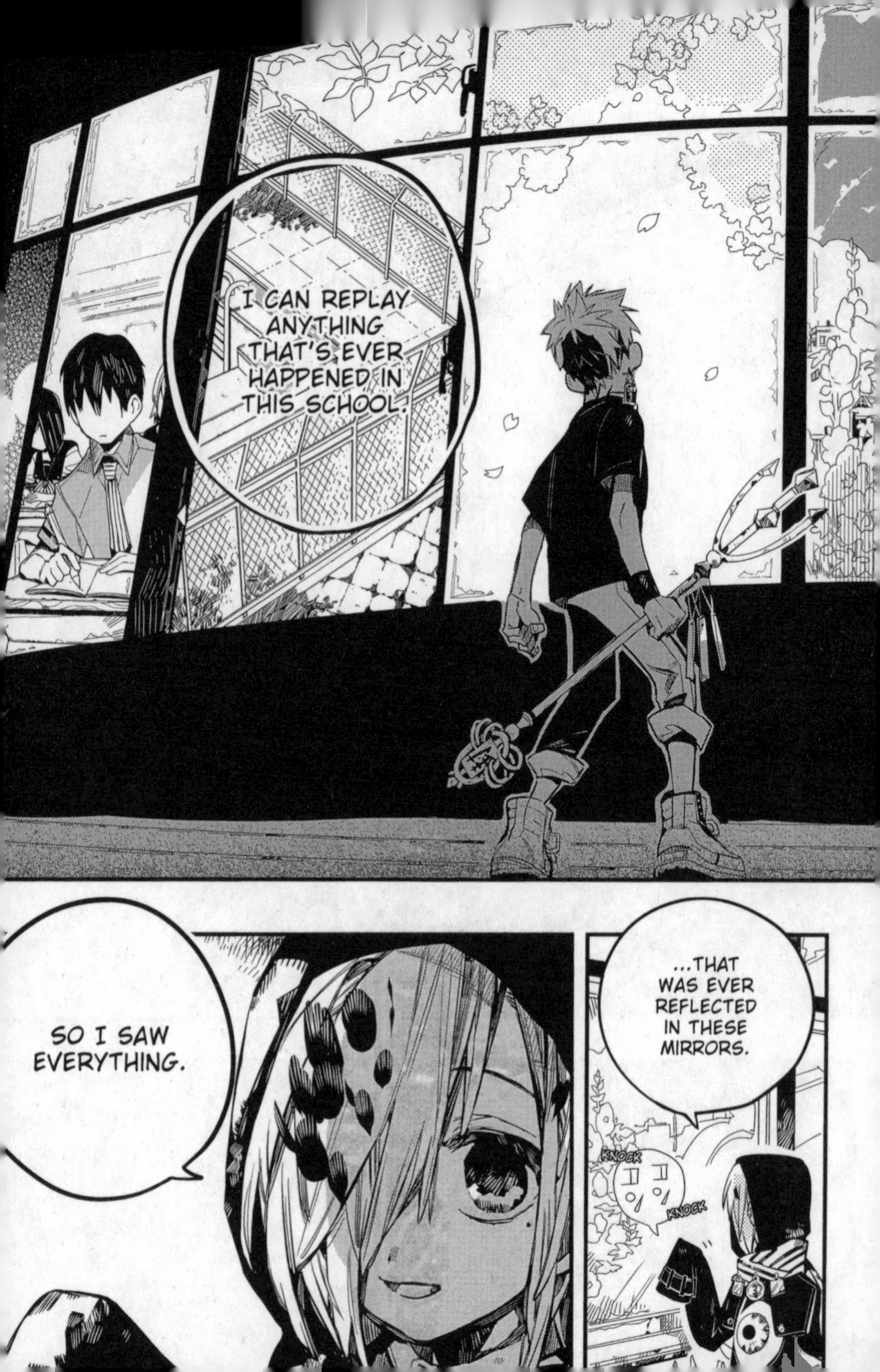
I CAN REPLAY ANYTHING THAT'S EVER HAPPENED IN THIS SCHOOL.
...THAT WAS EVER REFLECTED IN THESE MIRRORS.
KNOCK
KNOCK
SO I SAW EVERYTHING.

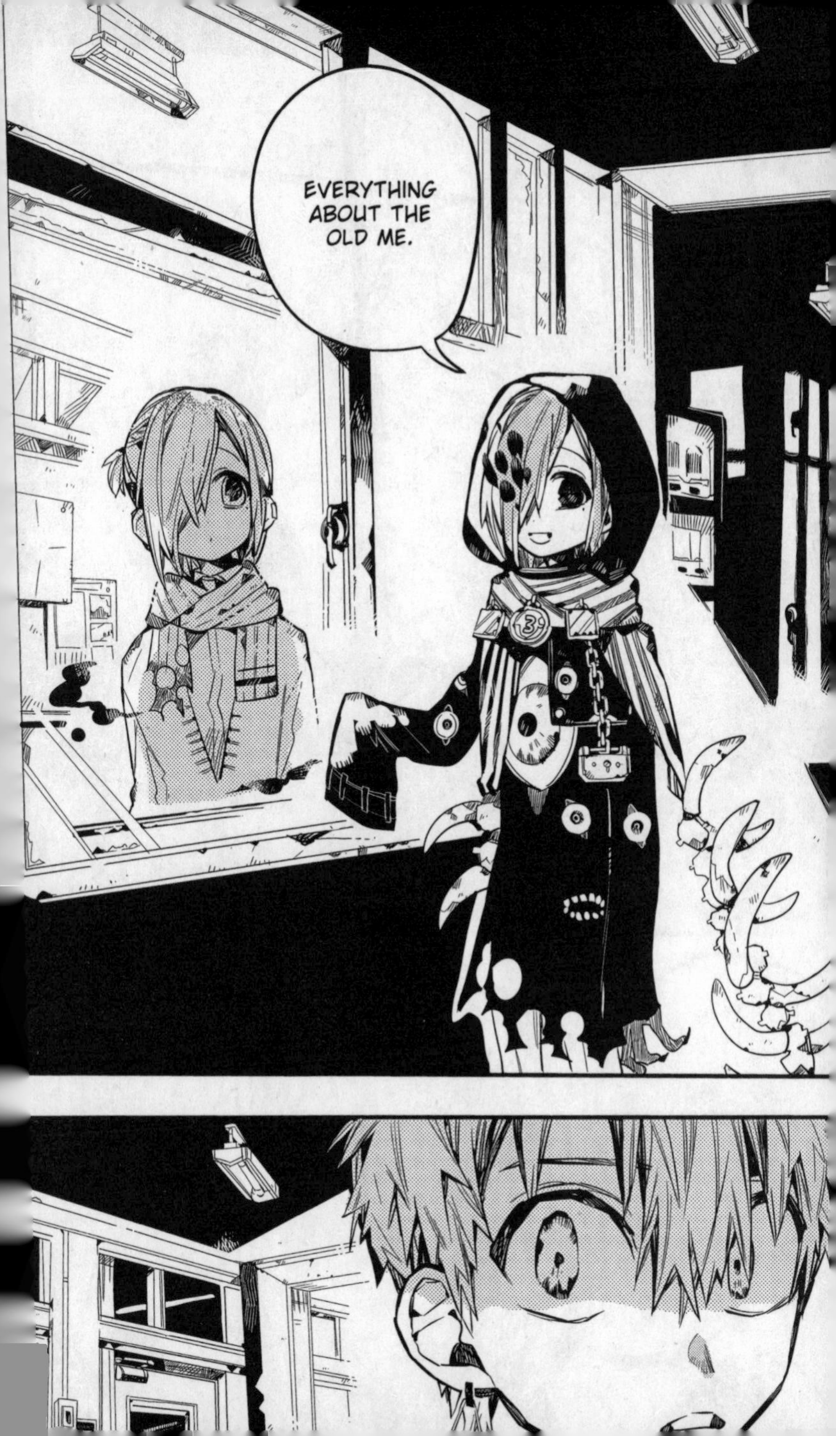
EVERYTHING ABOUT THE OLD ME.

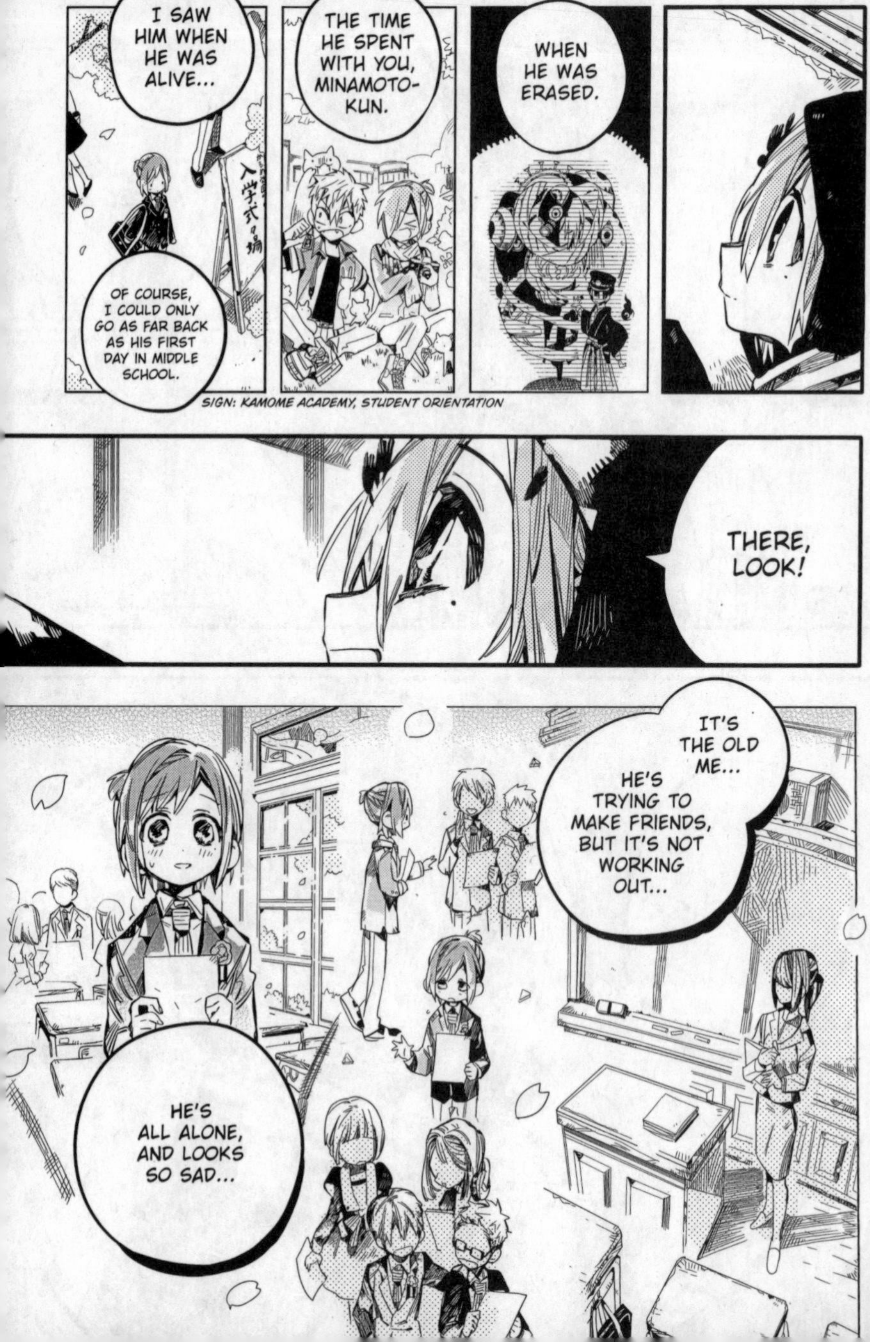
WHEN HE WAS ERASED.
THE TIME HE SPENT WITH YOU, MINAMOTO-KUN.
I SAW HIM WHEN HE WAS ALIVE...
OF COURSE, I COULD ONLY GO AS FAR BACK AS HIS FIRST DAY IN MIDDLE SCHOOL.
SIGN: KAMOME ACADEMY, STUDENT ORIENTATION
THERE, LOOK!
IT'S THE OLD ME...
HE'S TRYING TO MAKE FRIENDS, BUT IT'S NOT WORKING OUT...
HE'S ALL ALONE, AND LOOKS SO SAD...

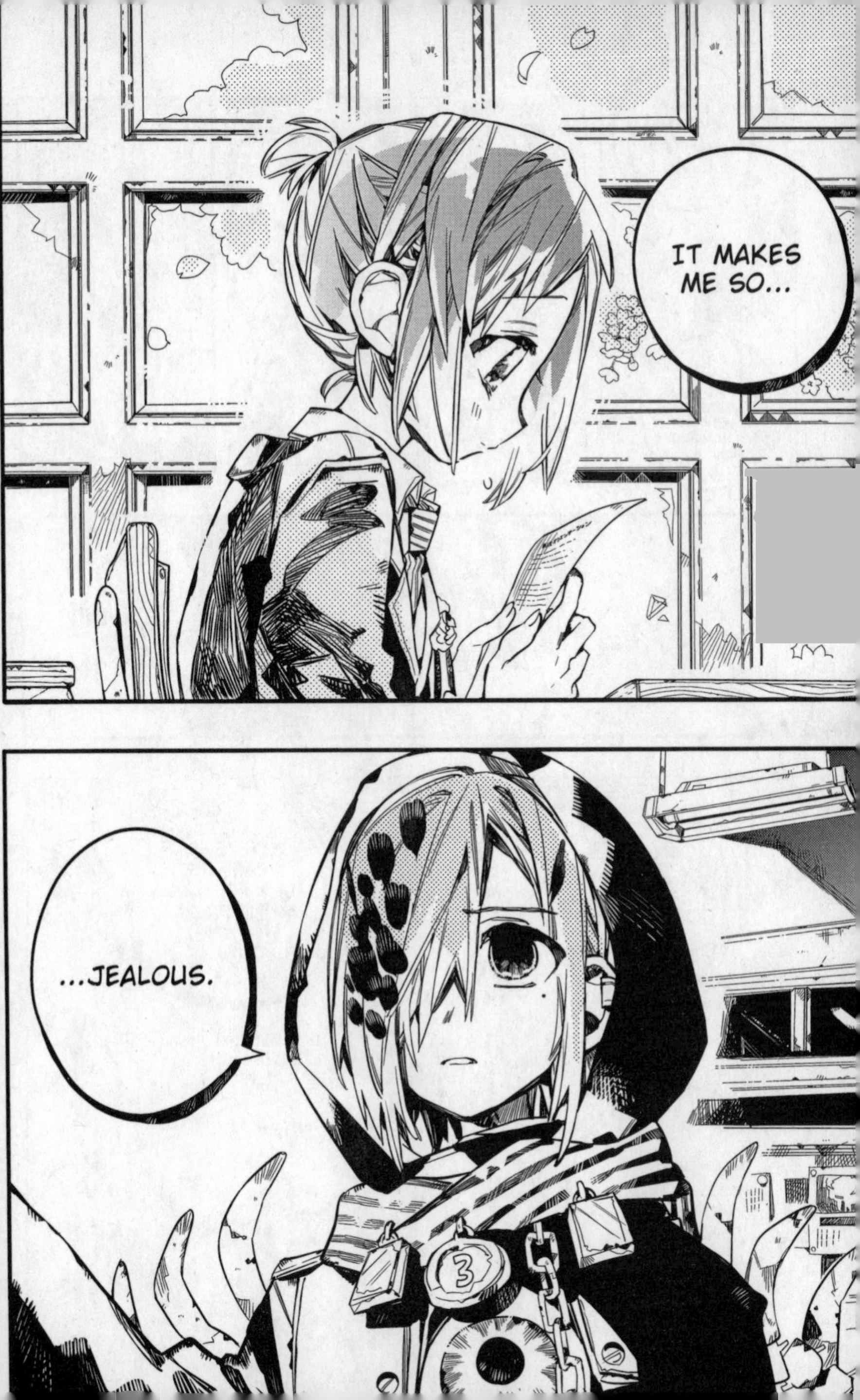
IT MAKES ME SO...
...JEALOUS.

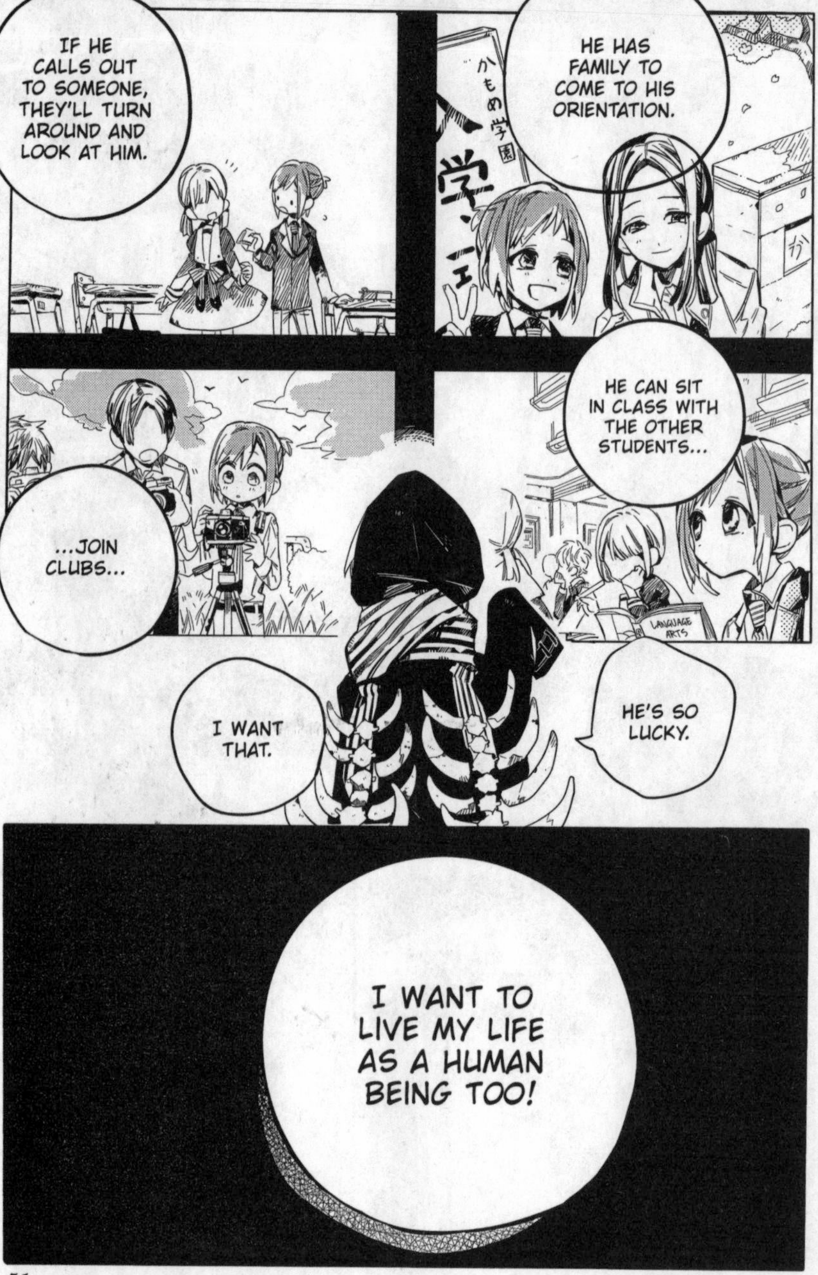
HE HAS FAMILY TO COME TO HIS ORIENTATION.
かもめ学園
IF HE CALLS OUT TO SOMEONE, THEY'LL TURN AROUND AND LOOK AT HIM.
HE CAN SIT IN CLASS WITH THE OTHER STUDENTS...
LANGUAGE ARTS
...JOIN CLUBS...
HE'S SO LUCKY.
I WANT THAT.
I WANT TO LIVE MY LIFE AS A HUMAN BEING TOO!

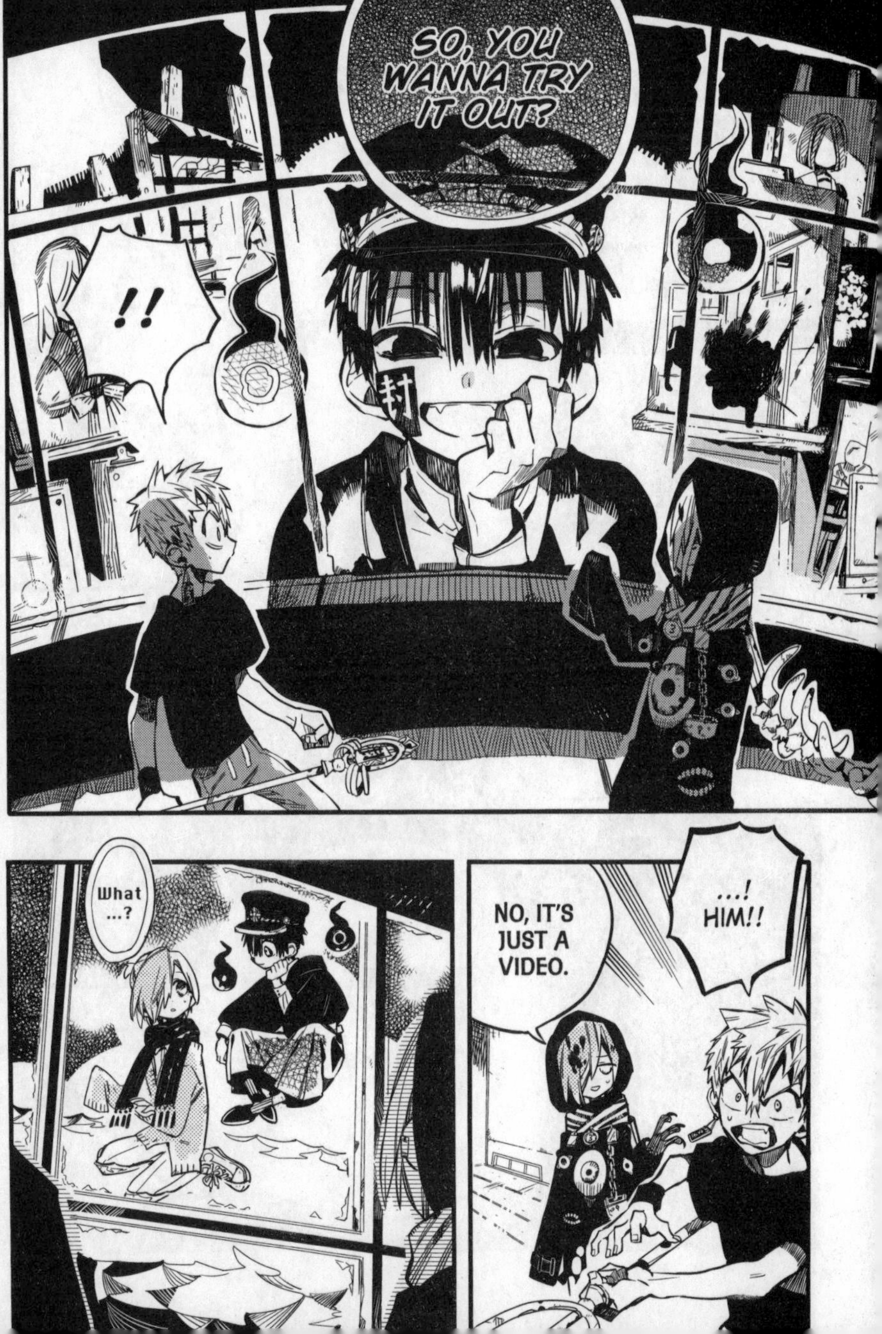
SO, YOU WANNA TRY IT OUT?
!!
...! HIM!!
NO, IT'S JUST A VIDEO.
What ...?

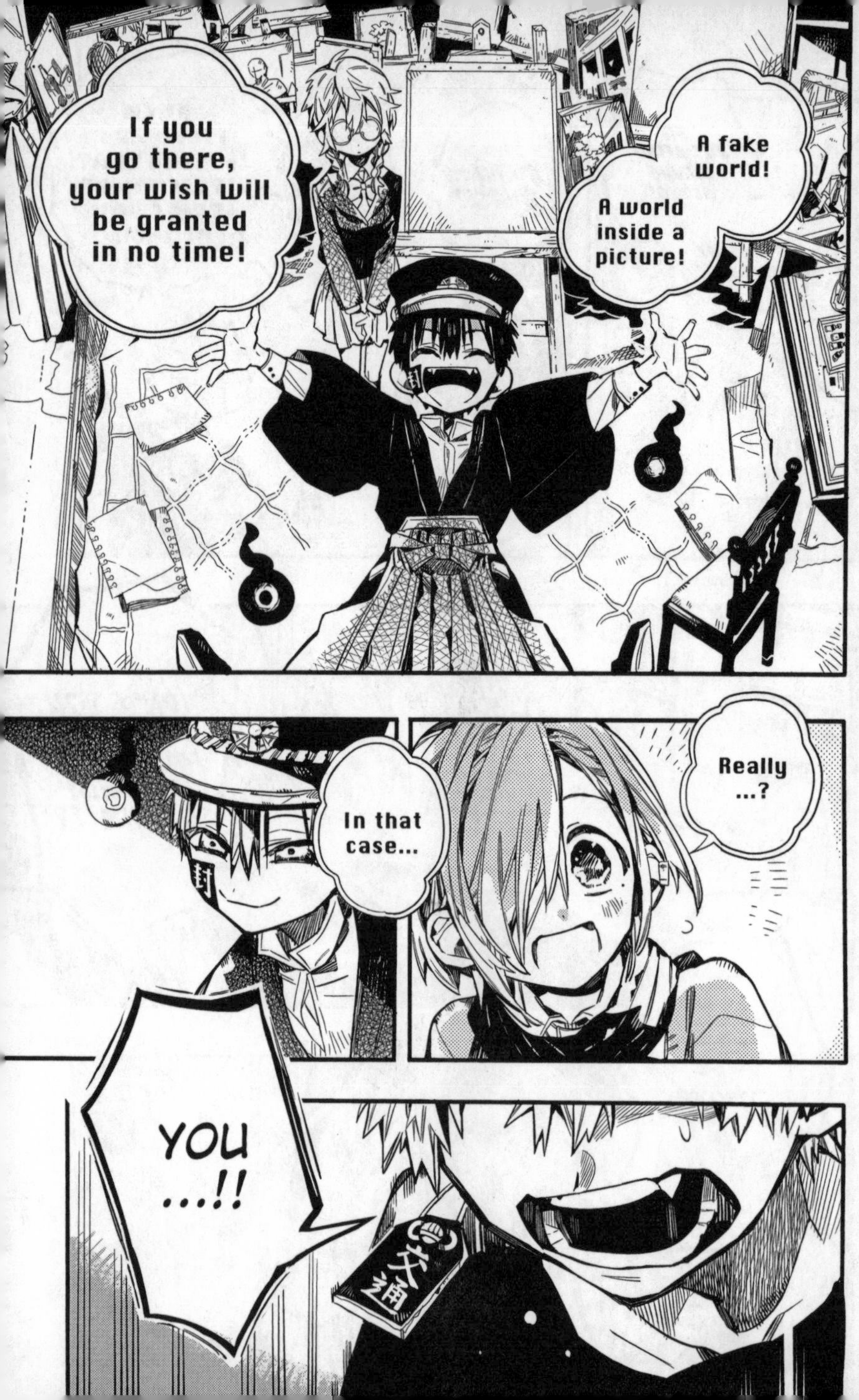
A fake world!
A world inside a picture!
If you go there, your wish will be granted in no time!
Really ...?
In that case...
YOU ...!!

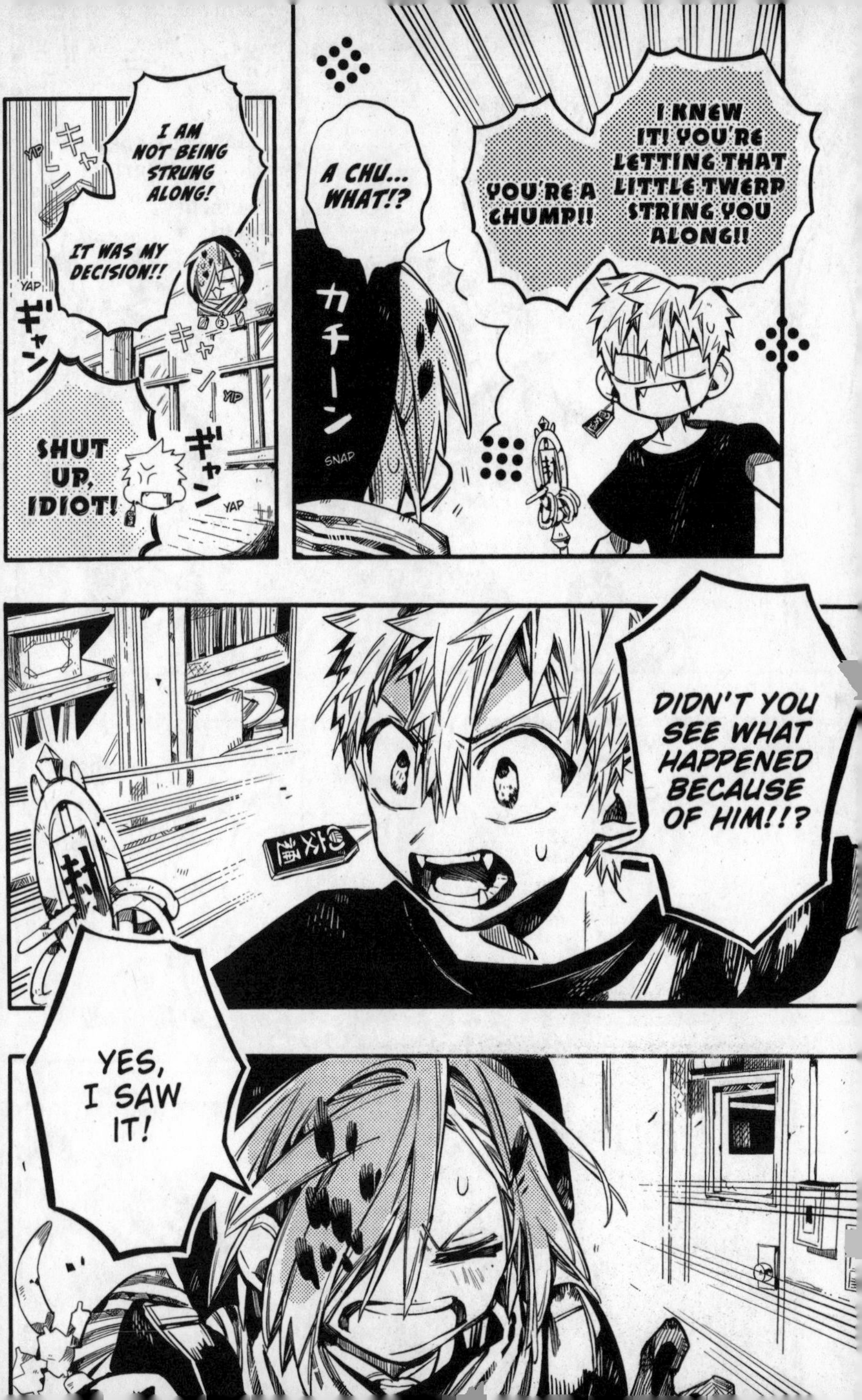
I KNEW IT! YOU'RE LETTING THAT LITTLE TWERP STRING YOU ALONG!!
YOU'RE A CHUMP!!
A CHU... WHAT!?
カチーン
SNAP
I AM NOT BEING STRUNG ALONG!
IT WAS MY DECISION!!
キャン
YIP
ギャン
YAP
キャン
YIP
ギャン
YAP
SHUT UP, IDIOT!
DIDN'T YOU SEE WHAT HAPPENED BECAUSE OF HIM!!?
YES, I SAW IT!

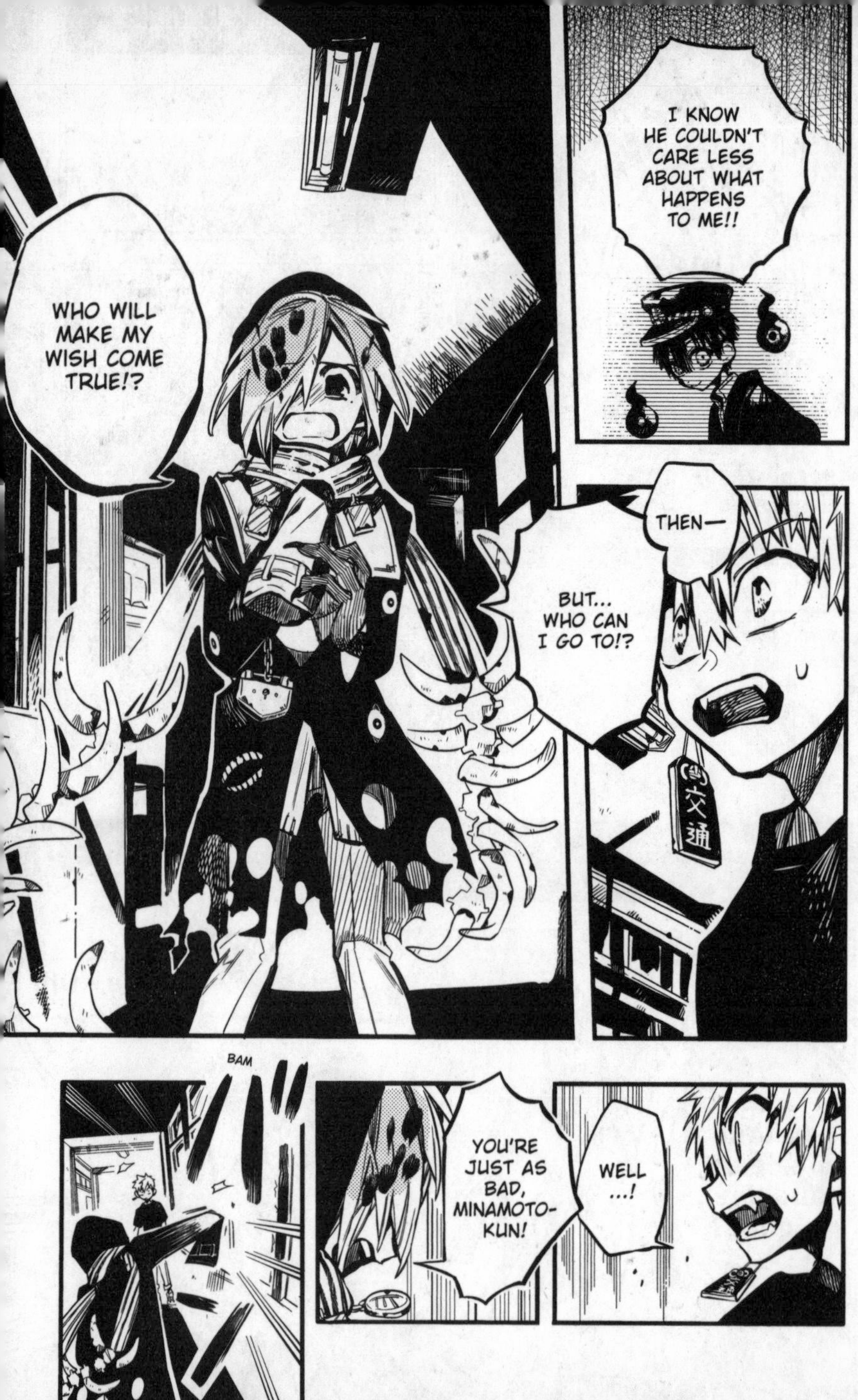
I KNOW HE COULDN'T CARE LESS ABOUT WHAT HAPPENS TO ME!!
THEN—
BUT... WHO CAN I GO TO!?
WHO WILL MAKE MY WISH COME TRUE!?
WELL ...!
YOU'RE JUST AS BAD, MINAMOTO-KUN!
BAM

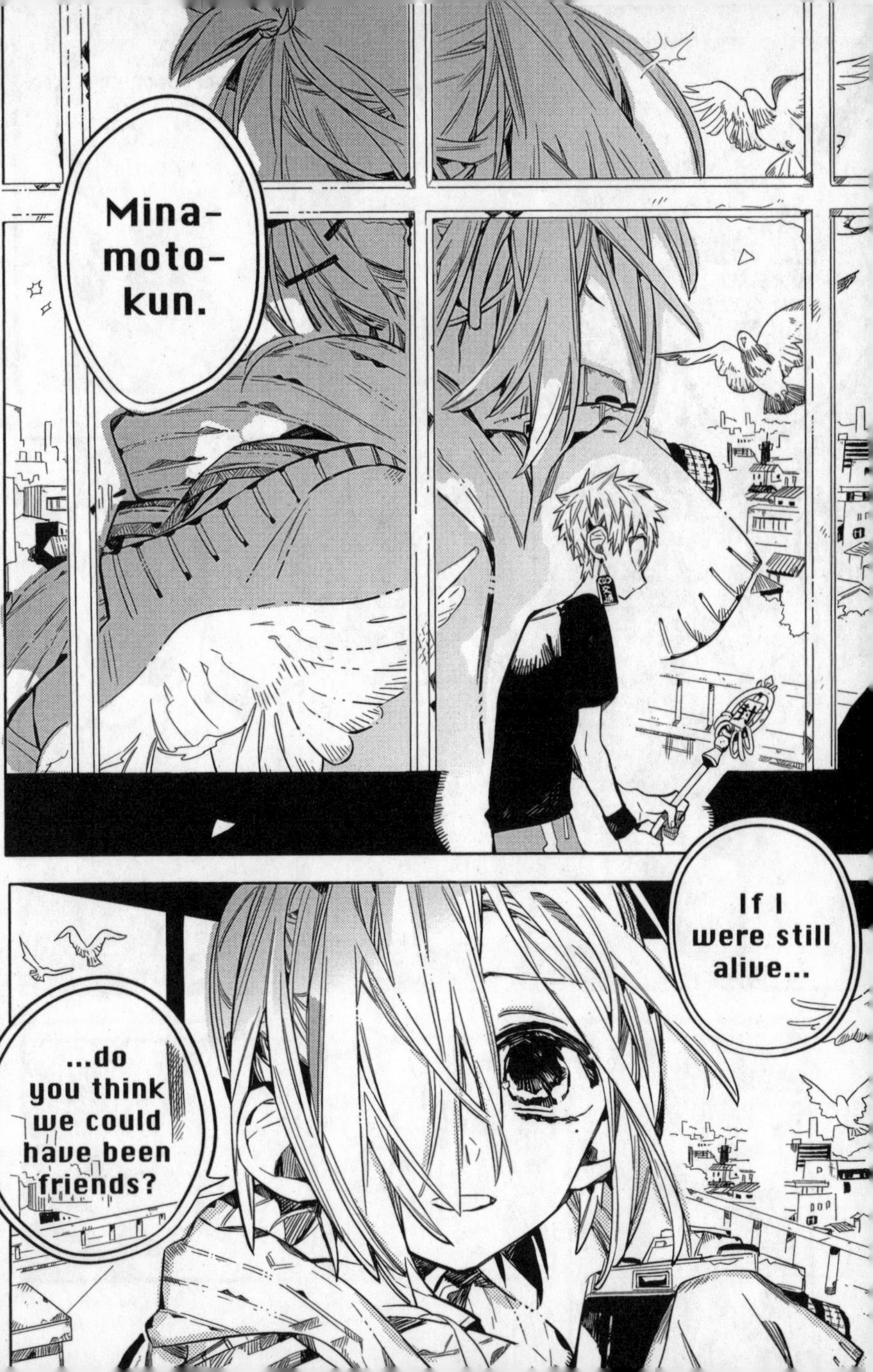
Mina-moto-kun.
If I were still alive...
...do you think we could have been friends?

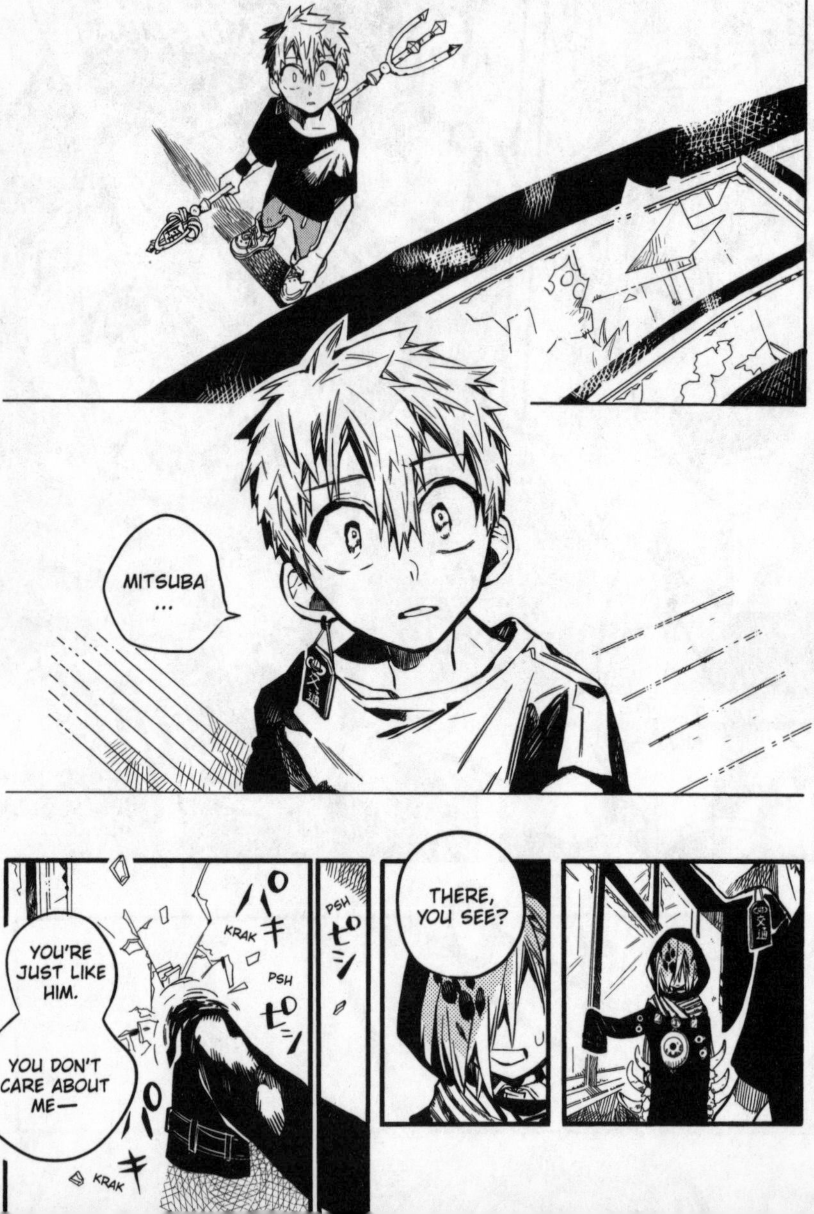
MITSUBA ...
THERE, YOU SEE?
PSH ピシ
パキ KRAK
PSH ピシ
YOU'RE JUST LIKE HIM.
YOU DON'T CARE ABOUT ME—
パキ KRAK

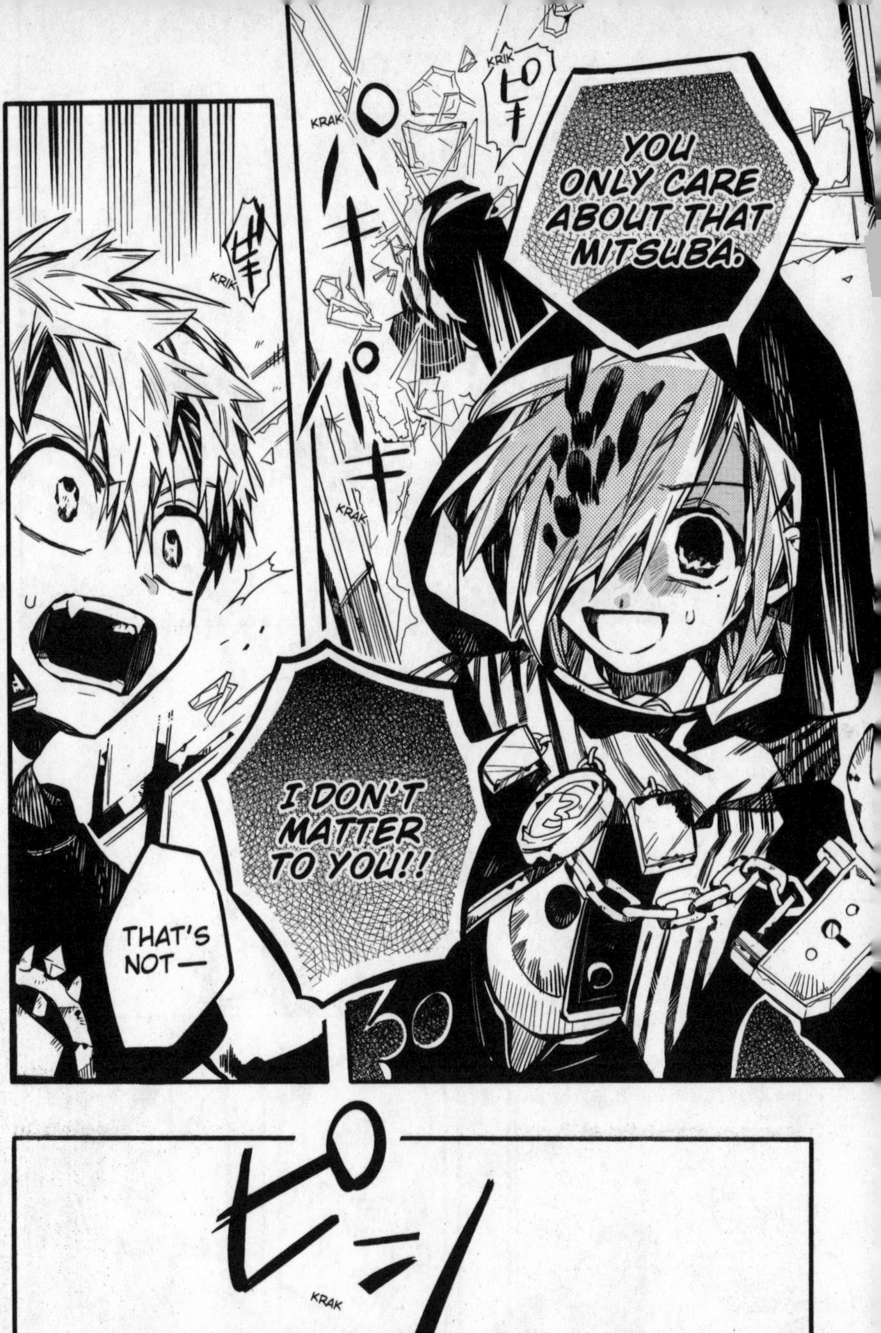

KRIK
YOU ONLY CARE ABOUT THAT MITSUBA.
KRAK
KRAK
I DON'T MATTER TO YOU!!
KRIK
THAT'S NOT—
KRAK

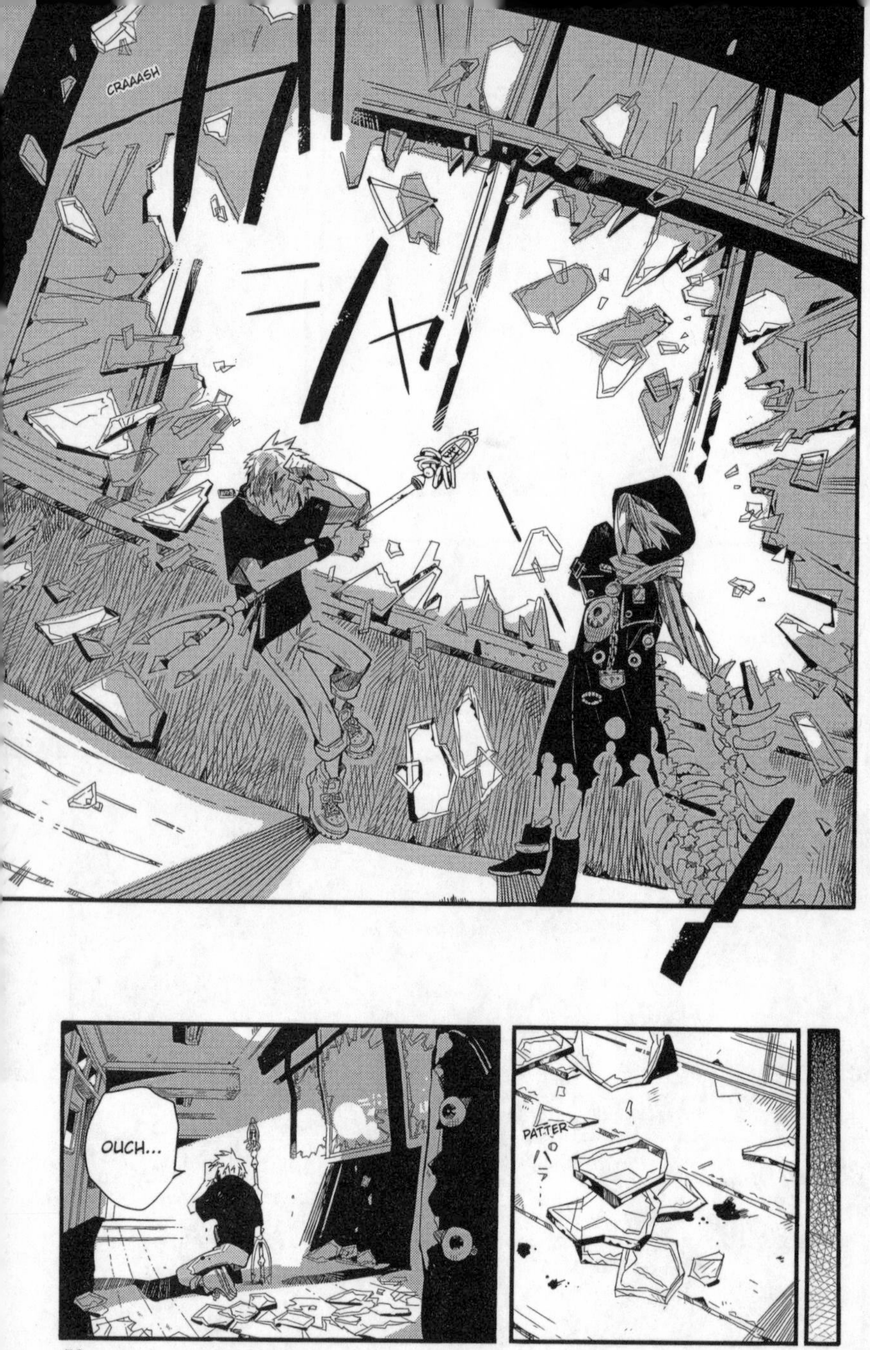
CRAAASH
PATTER
パラ
OUCH...

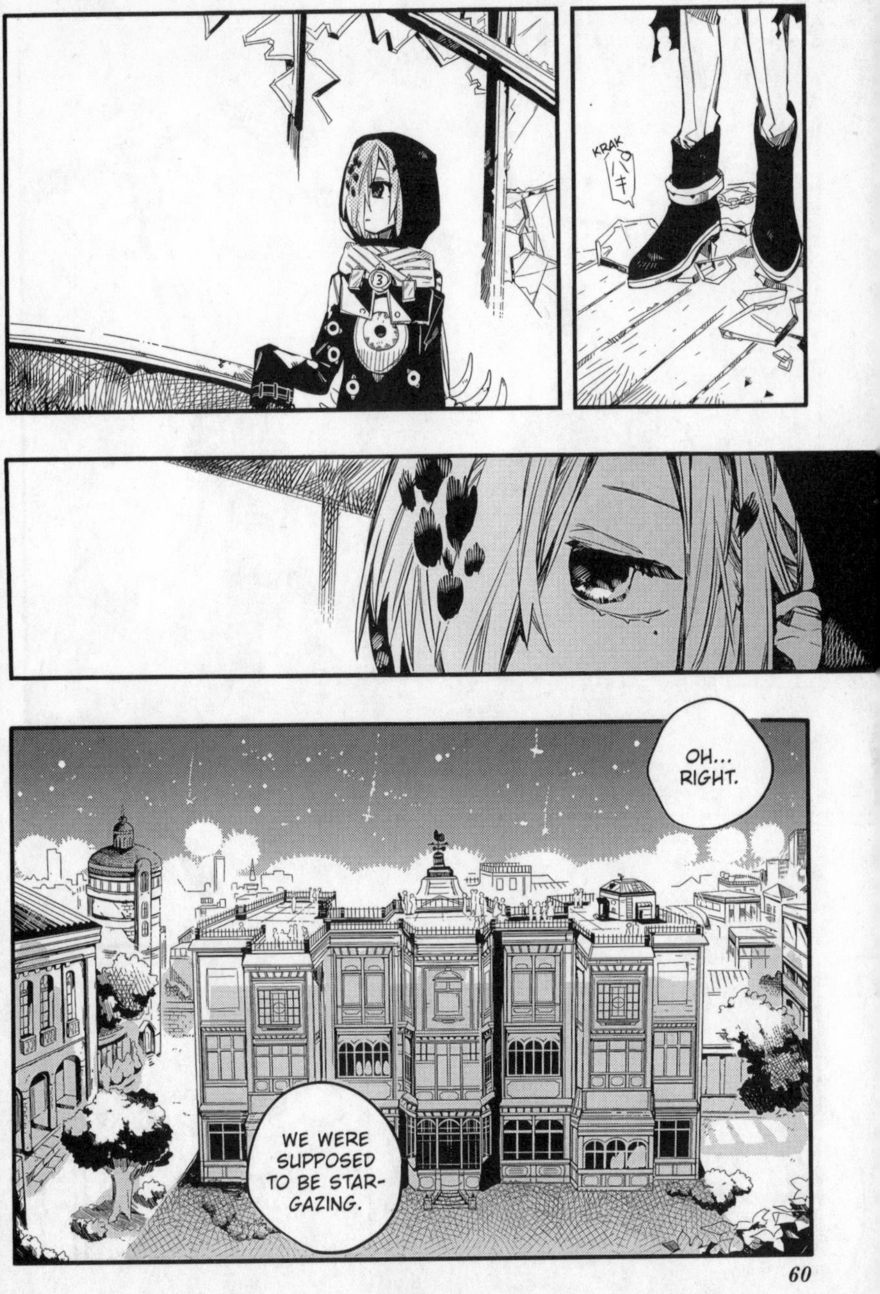
KRAK
パキ
OH... RIGHT.
WE WERE SUPPOSED TO BE STAR-GAZING.

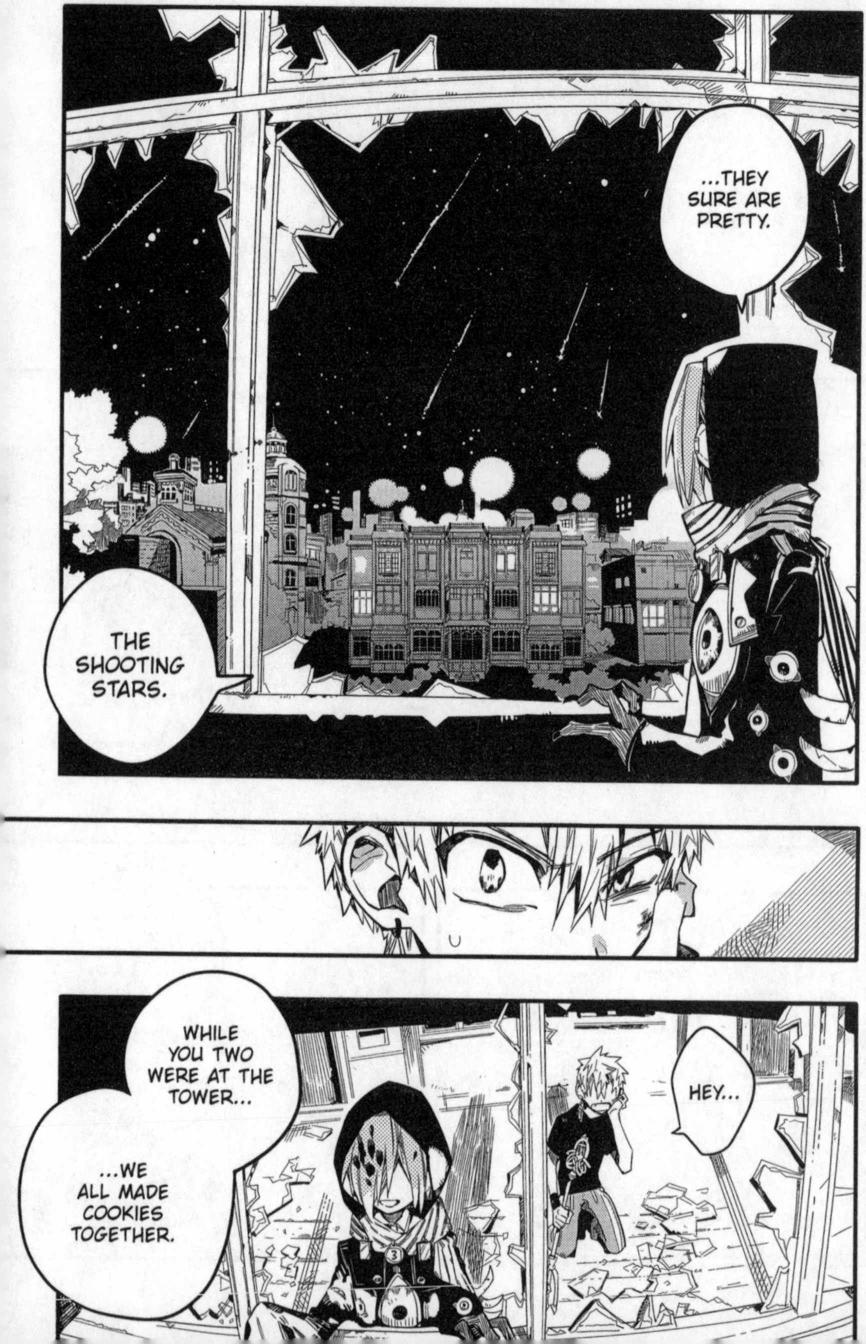
...THEY SURE ARE PRETTY.
THE SHOOTING STARS.
HEY...
WHILE YOU TWO WERE AT THE TOWER...
...WE ALL MADE COOKIES TOGETHER.

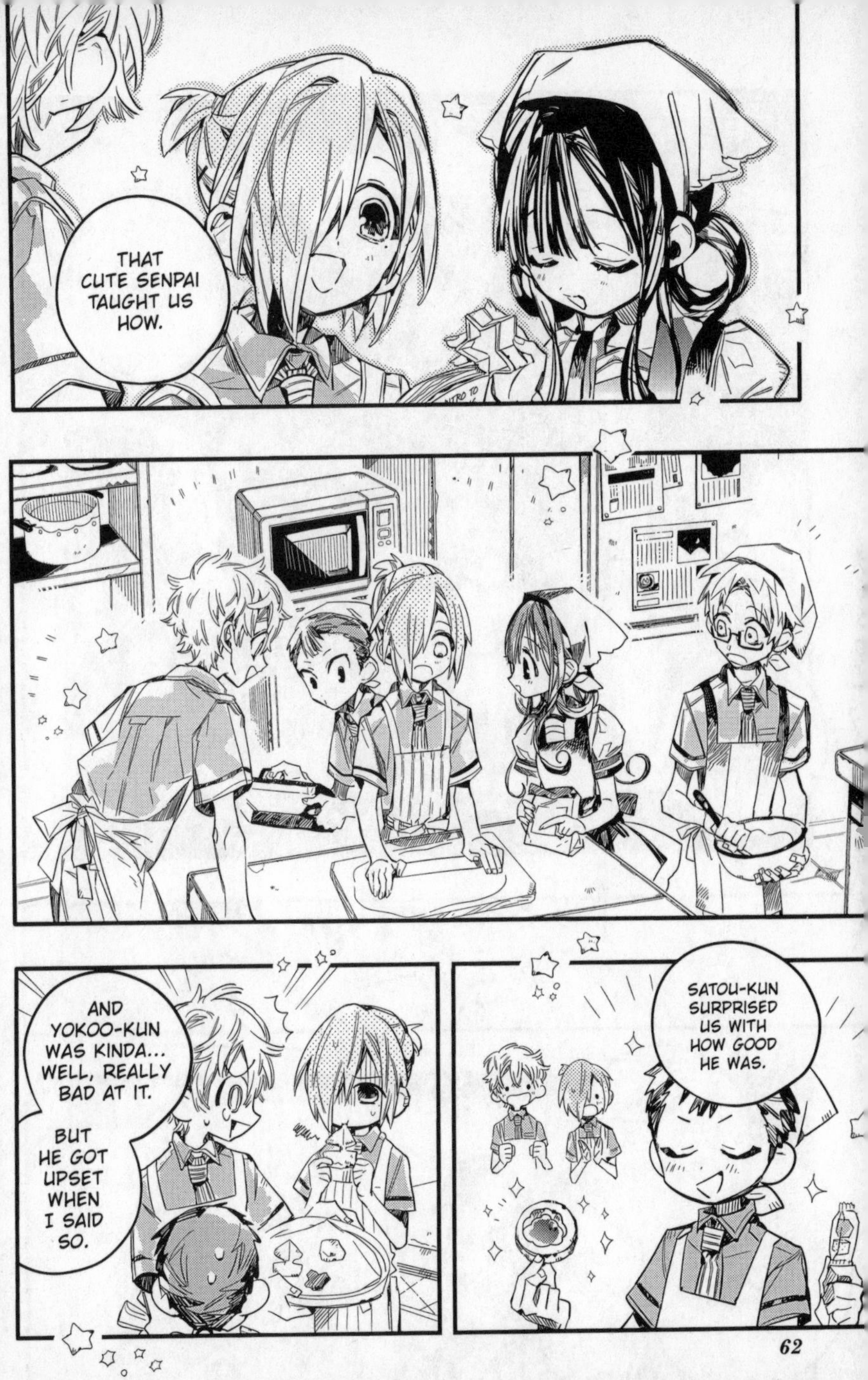
THAT CUTE SENPAI TAUGHT US HOW.
INTRO TO
SATOU-KUN SURPRISED US WITH HOW GOOD HE WAS.
AND YOKOO-KUN WAS KINDA... WELL, REALLY BAD AT IT.
BUT HE GOT UPSET WHEN I SAID SO.

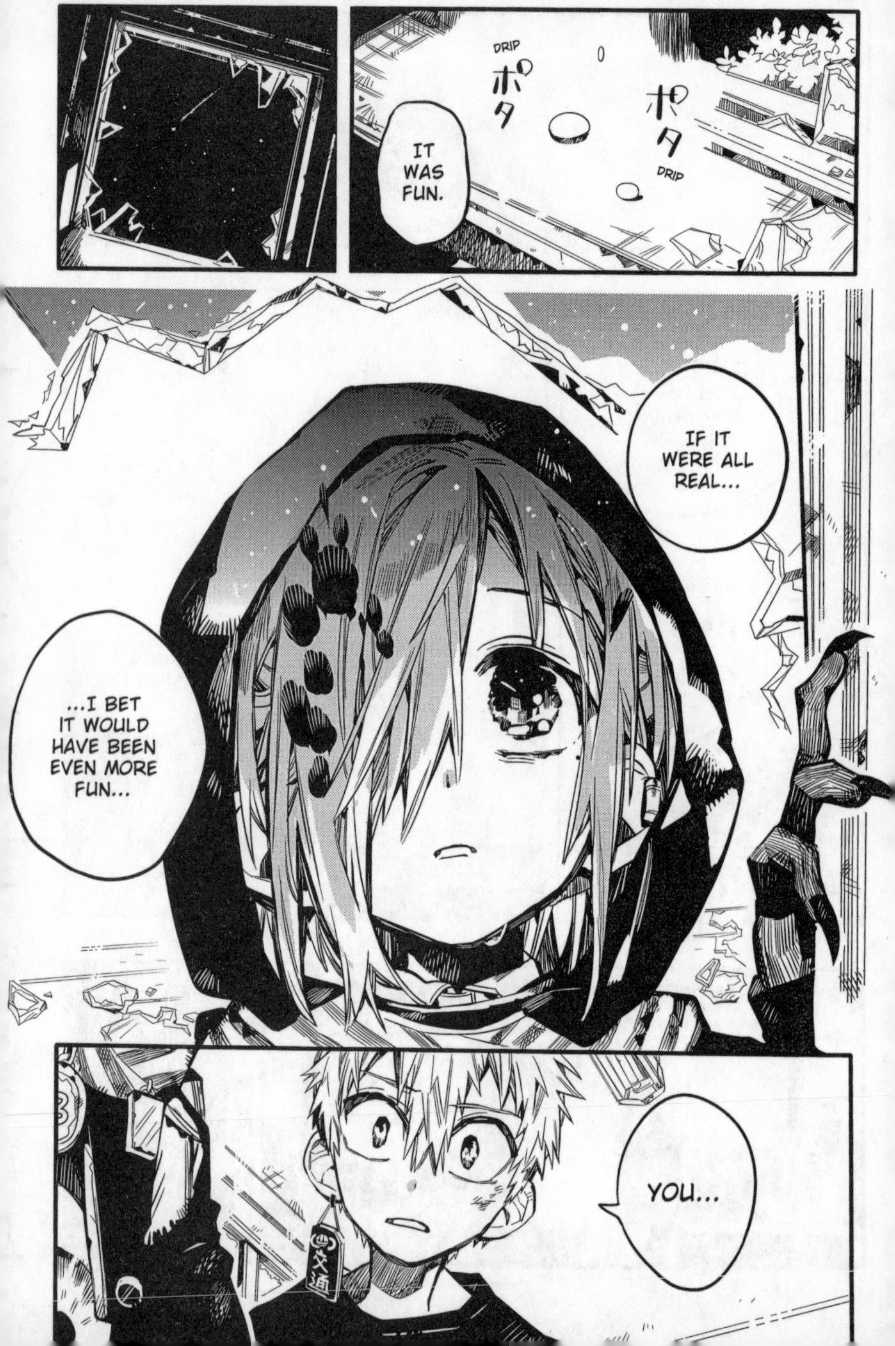

ポタ
DRIP
ポタ
DRIP
IT WAS FUN.
IF IT WERE ALL REAL...
...I BET IT WOULD HAVE BEEN EVEN MORE FUN...
YOU...

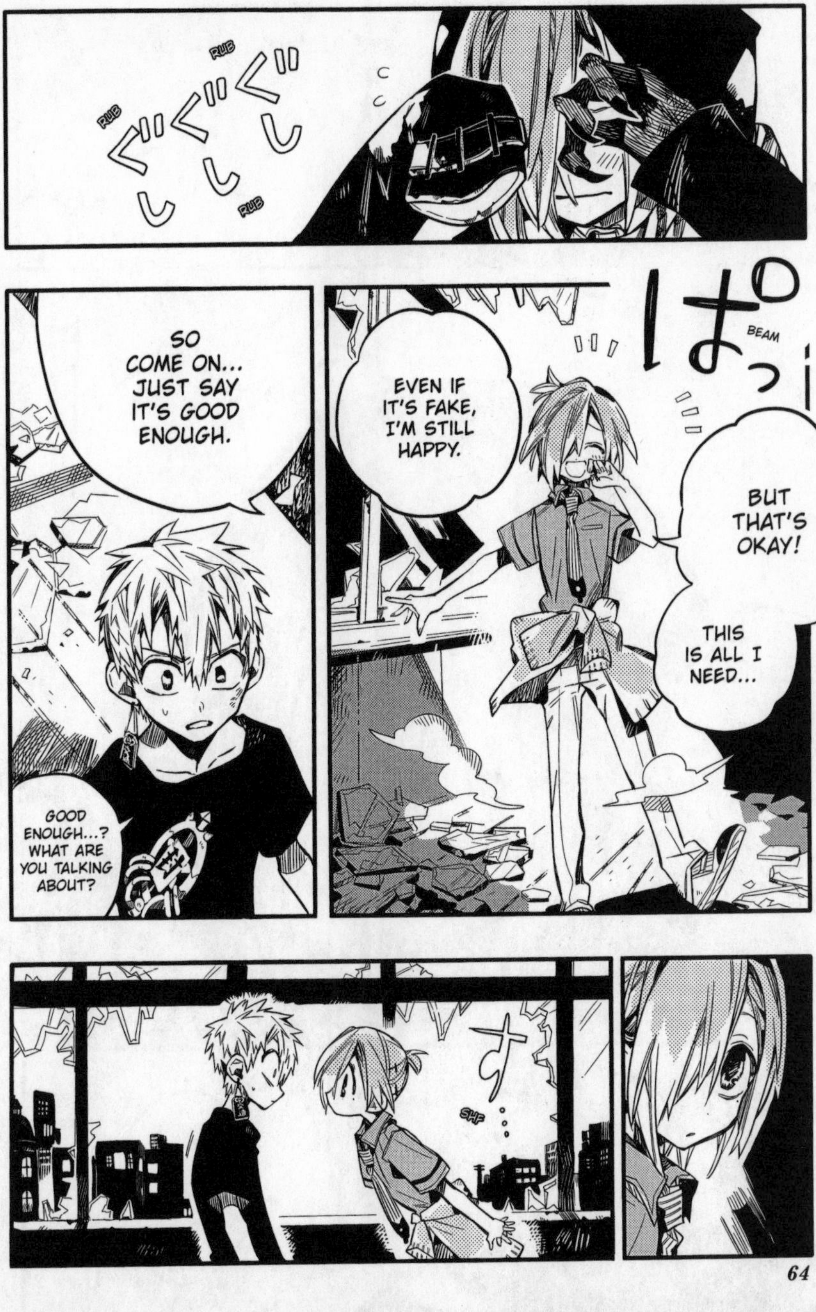
ぐいぐいぐい
RUB
RUB
RUB
ぱっ
BEAM
EVEN IF IT'S FAKE, I'M STILL HAPPY.
BUT THAT'S OKAY!
THIS IS ALL I NEED...
SO COME ON... JUST SAY IT'S GOOD ENOUGH.
GOOD ENOUGH...? WHAT ARE YOU TALKING ABOUT?
す
SHF

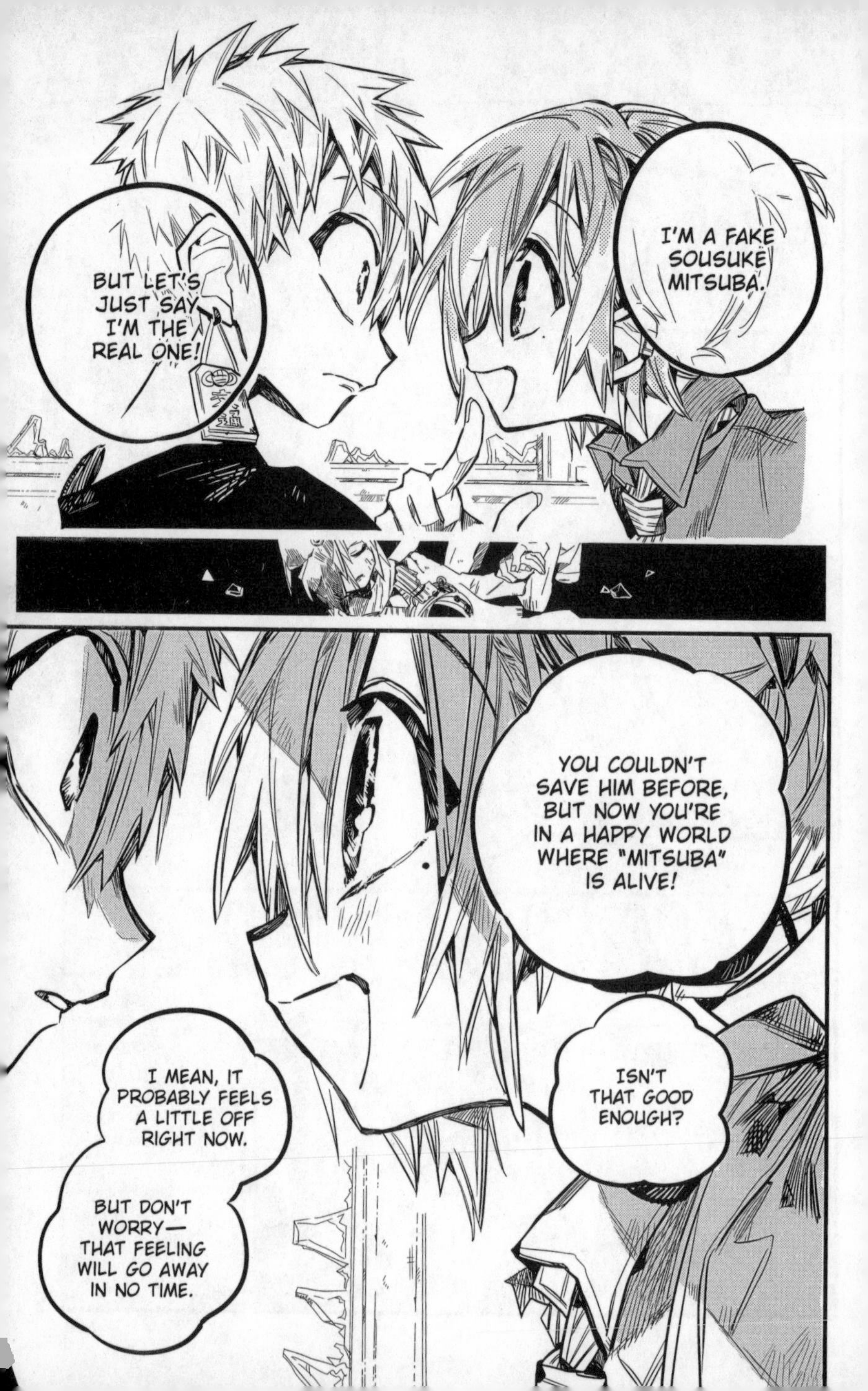
I'M A FAKE SOUSUKE MITSUBA.
BUT LET'S JUST SAY I'M THE REAL ONE!
YOU COULDN'T SAVE HIM BEFORE, BUT NOW YOU'RE IN A HAPPY WORLD WHERE "MITSUBA" IS ALIVE!
ISN'T THAT GOOD ENOUGH?
I MEAN, IT PROBABLY FEELS A LITTLE OFF RIGHT NOW.
BUT DON'T WORRY— THAT FEELING WILL GO AWAY IN NO TIME.

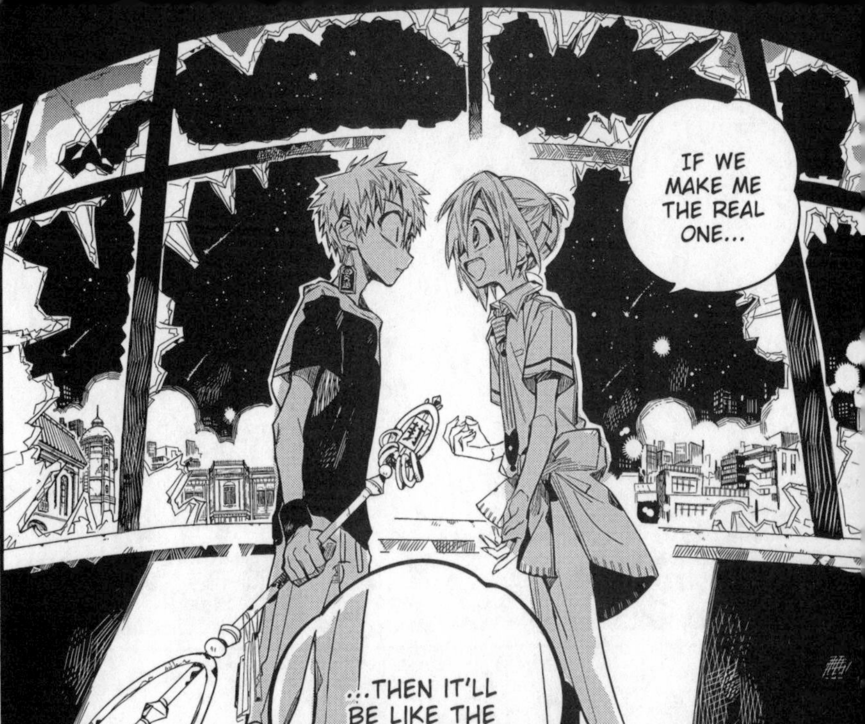
IF WE MAKE ME THE REAL ONE...
...THEN IT'LL BE LIKE THE OTHER MITSUBA NEVER DIED!
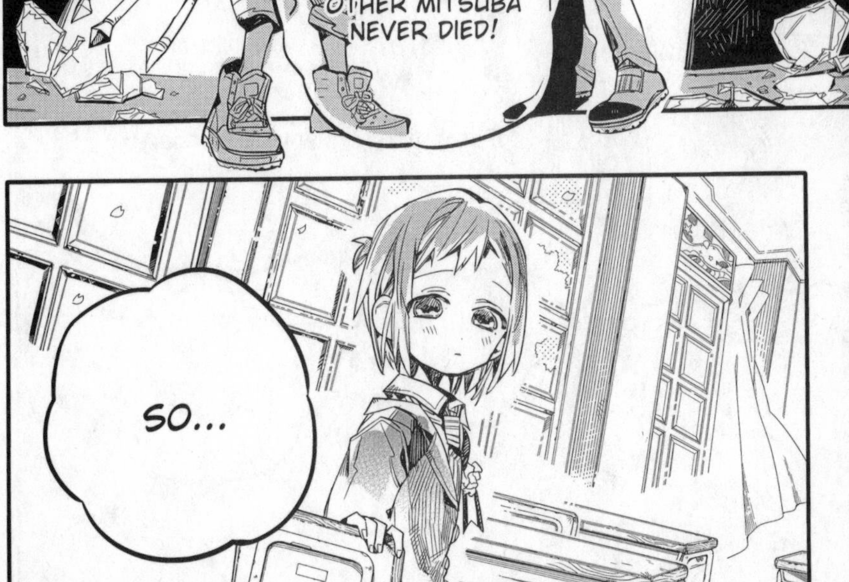
SO...

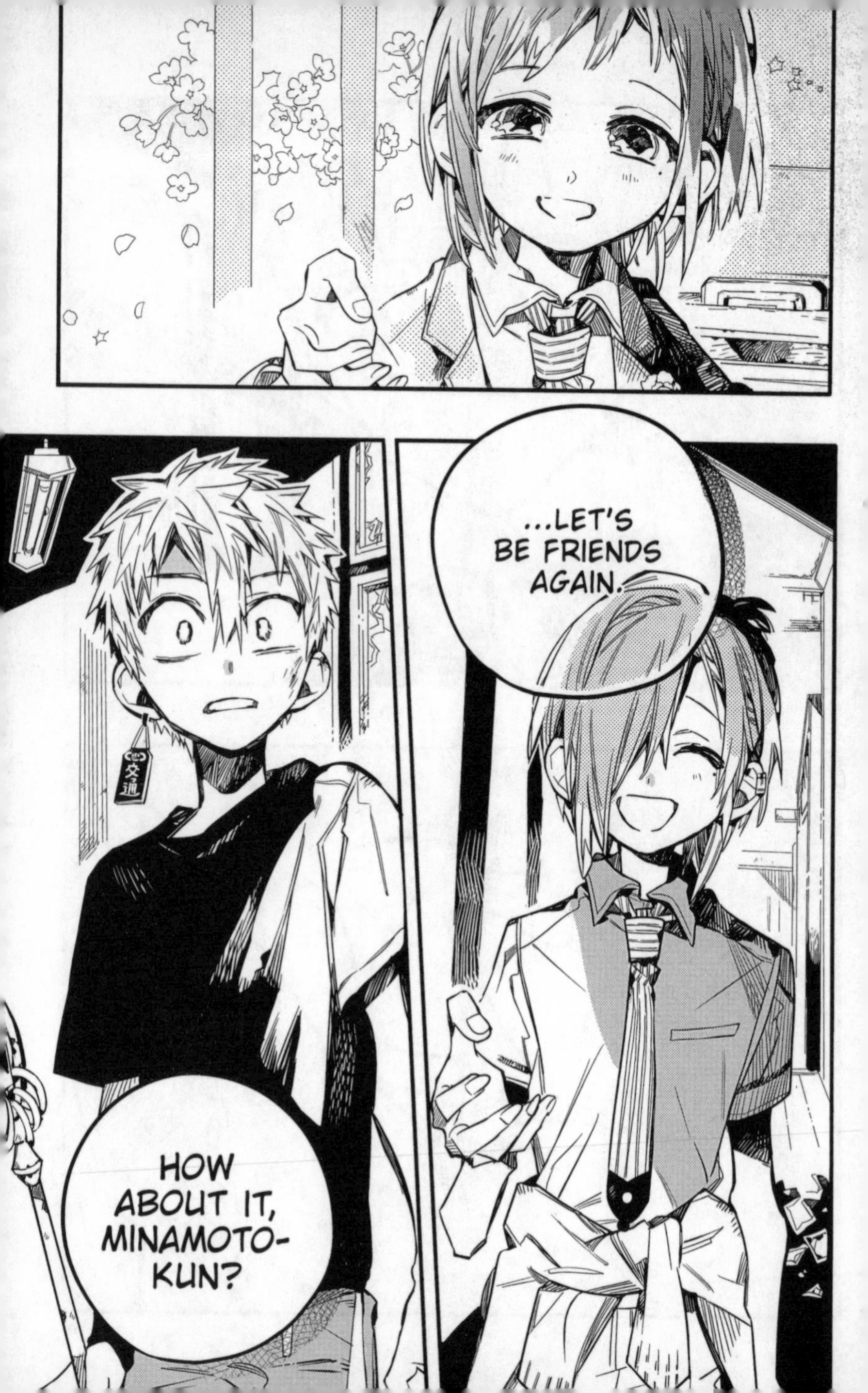
...LET'S BE FRIENDS AGAIN.
交通
HOW ABOUT IT, MINAMOTO-KUN?

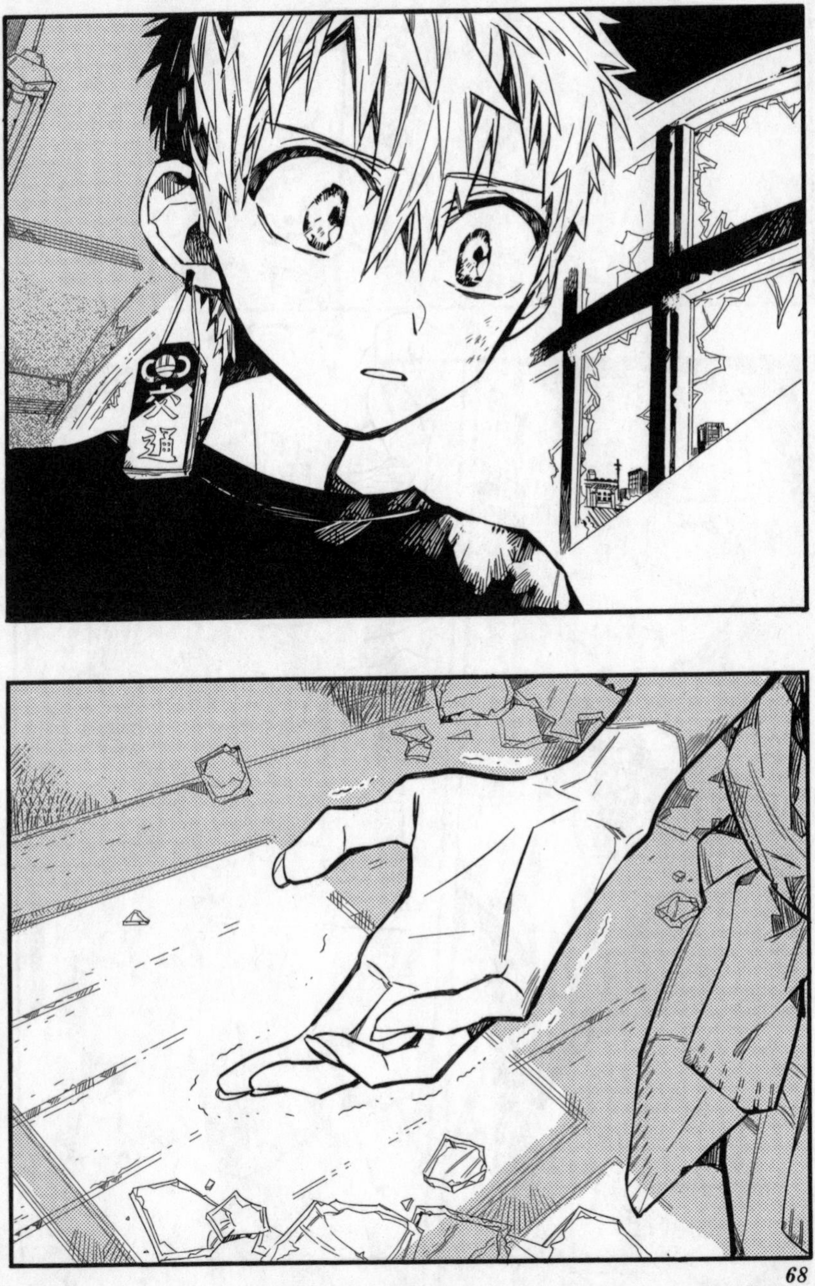
交通

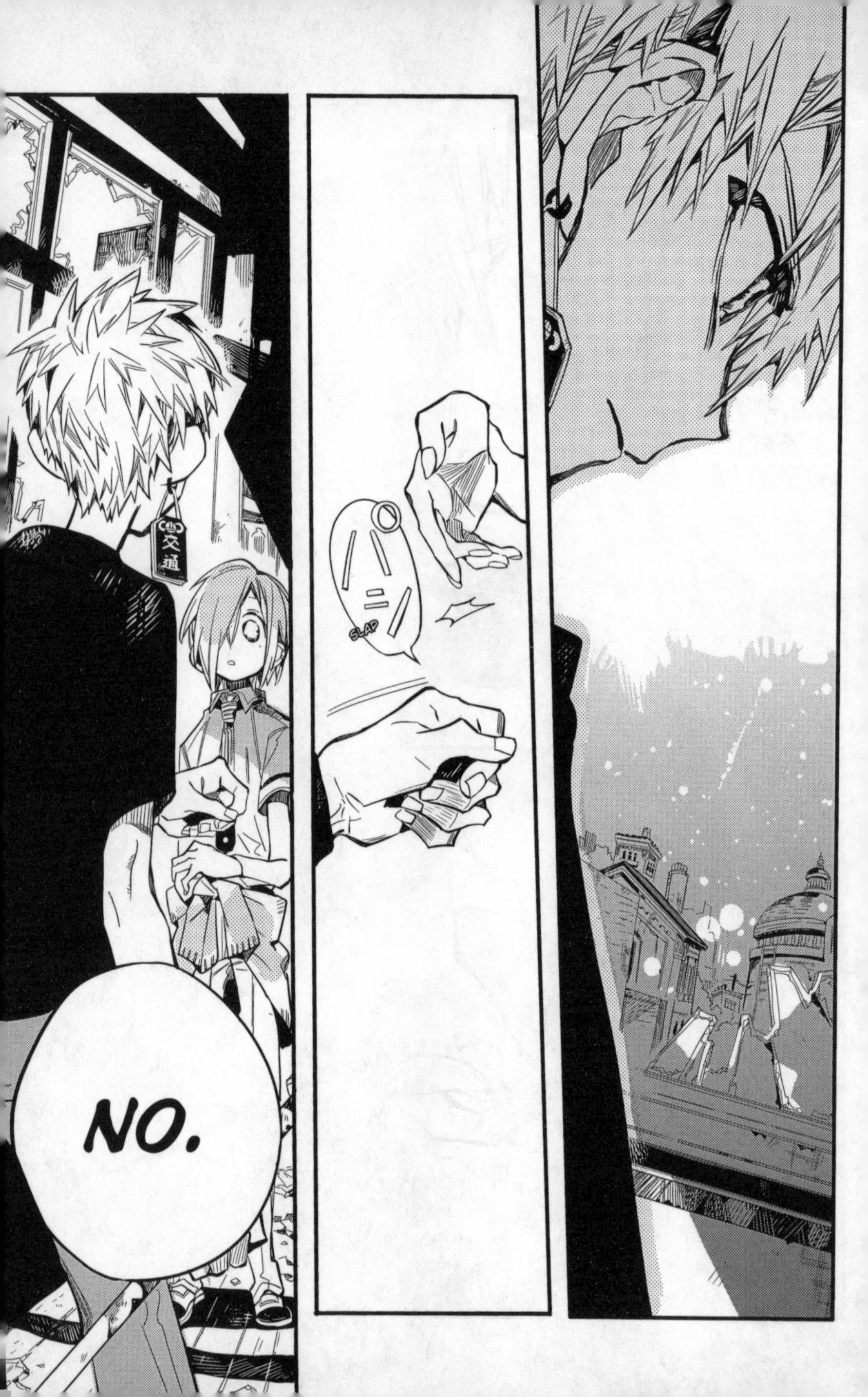
SLAP
NO.

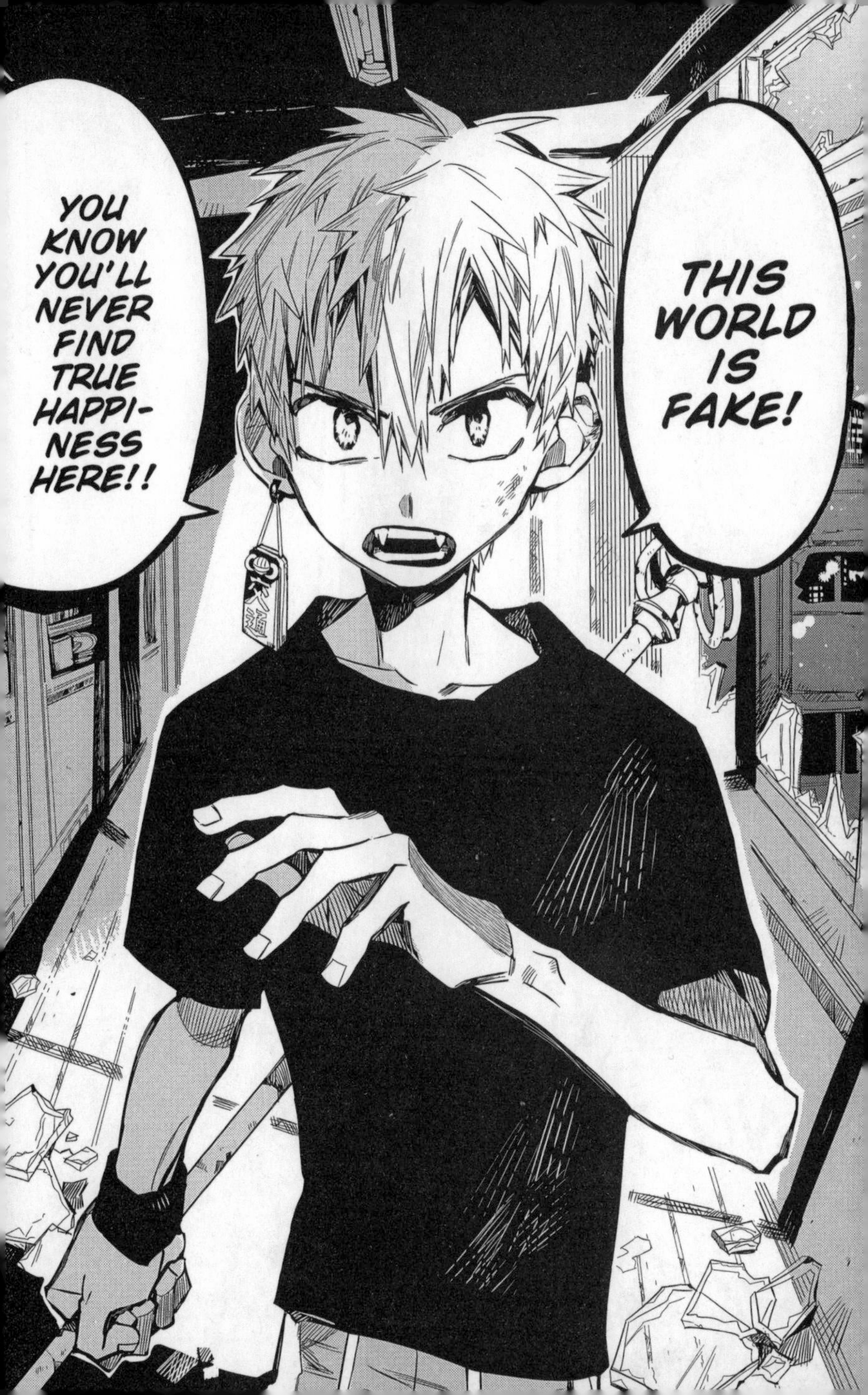
THIS WORLD IS FAKE!
YOU KNOW YOU'LL NEVER FIND TRUE HAPPI-NESS HERE!!

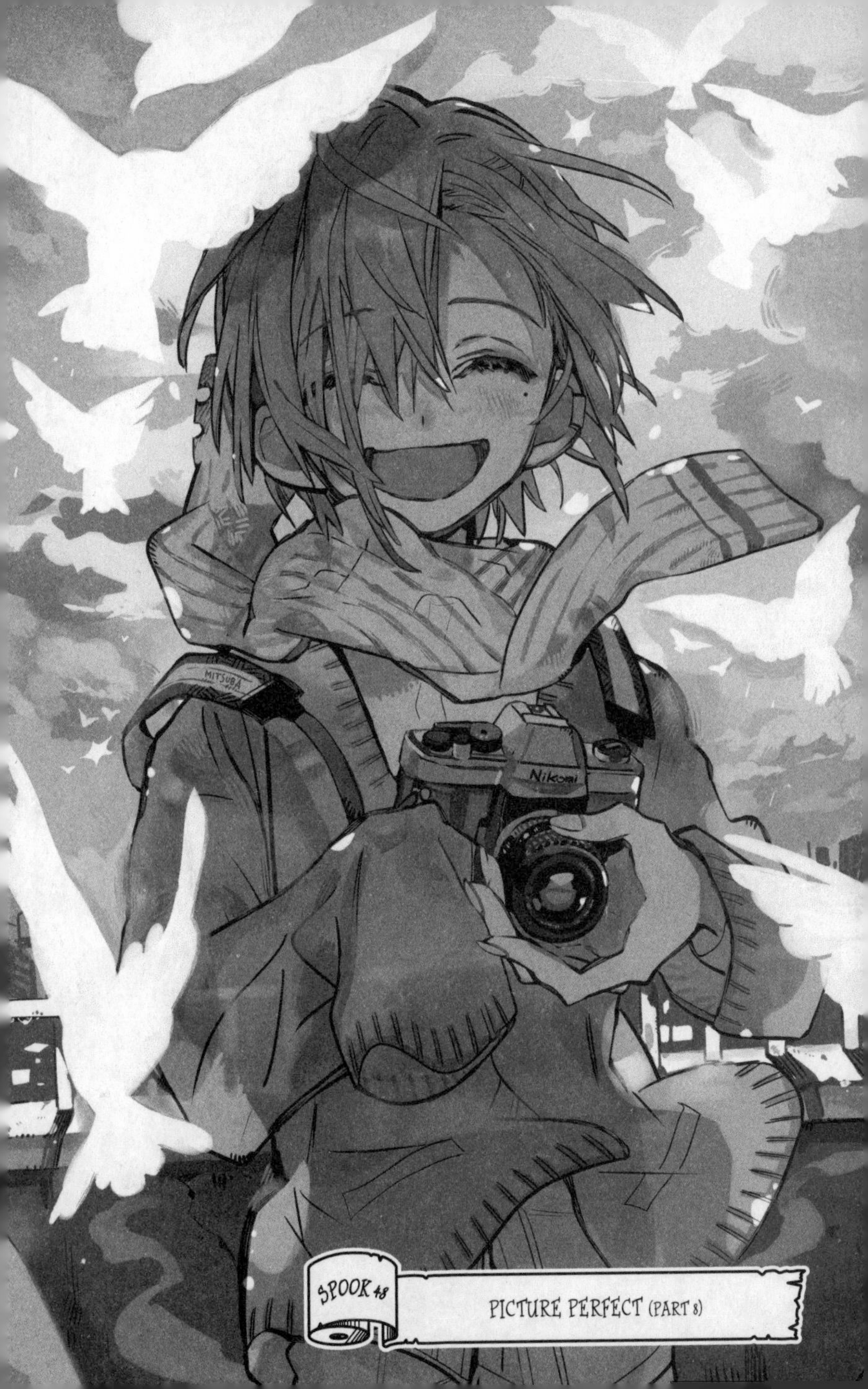
MITSUBA
Nikoai
SPOOK 48
PICTURE PERFECT (PART 8)

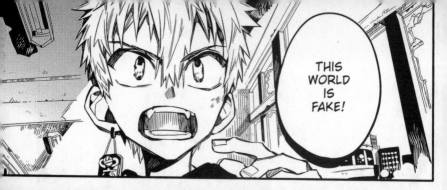

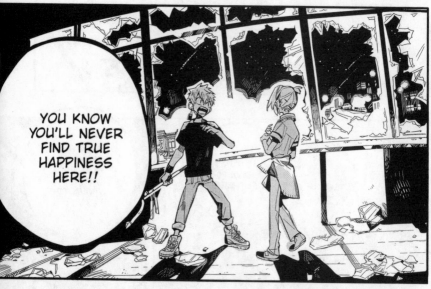

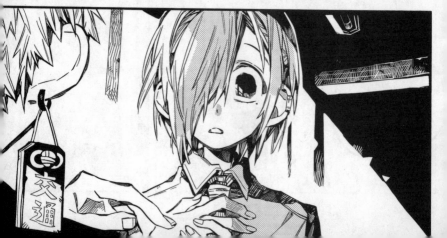

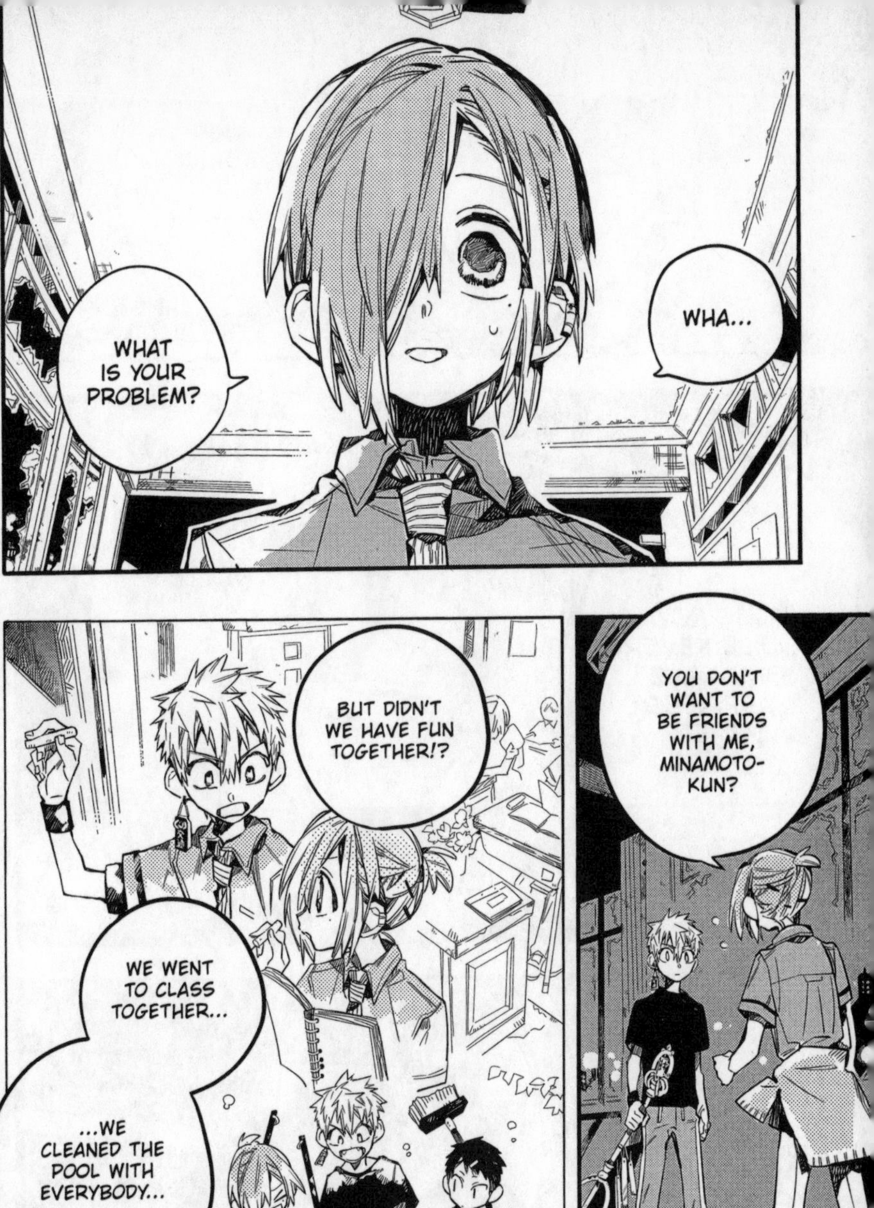
WHA...
WHAT IS YOUR PROBLEM?
YOU DON'T WANT TO BE FRIENDS WITH ME, MINAMOTO-KUN?
BUT DIDN'T WE HAVE FUN TOGETHER!?
WE WENT TO CLASS TOGETHER...
...WE CLEANED THE POOL WITH EVERYBODY...

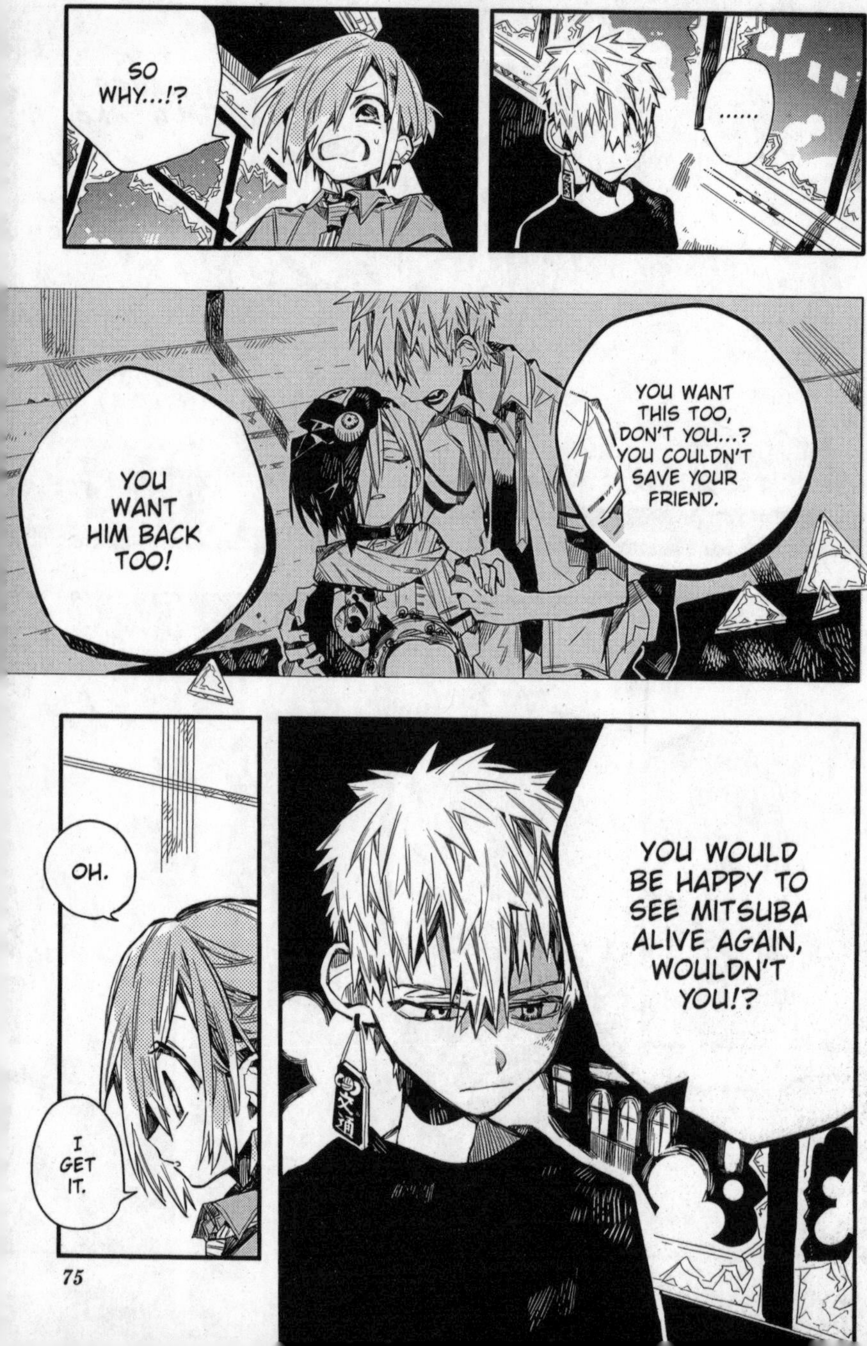
......
SO WHY...!?
YOU WANT THIS TOO, DON'T YOU...? YOU COULDN'T SAVE YOUR FRIEND.
YOU WANT HIM BACK TOO!
YOU WOULD BE HAPPY TO SEE MITSUBA ALIVE AGAIN, WOULDN'T YOU!?
OH.
I GET IT.

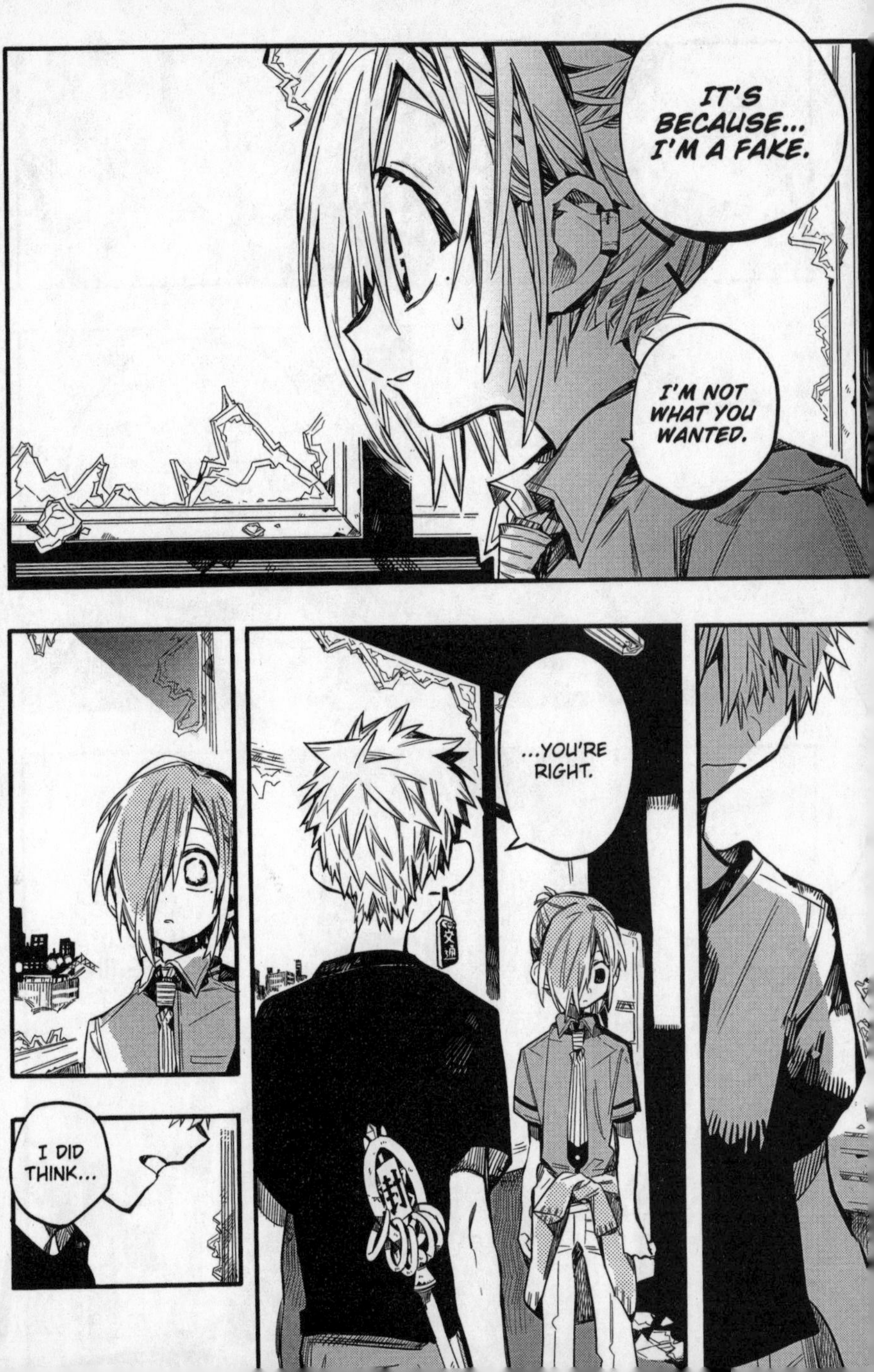
IT'S BECAUSE... I'M A FAKE.
I'M NOT WHAT YOU WANTED.
...YOU'RE RIGHT.
I DID THINK...

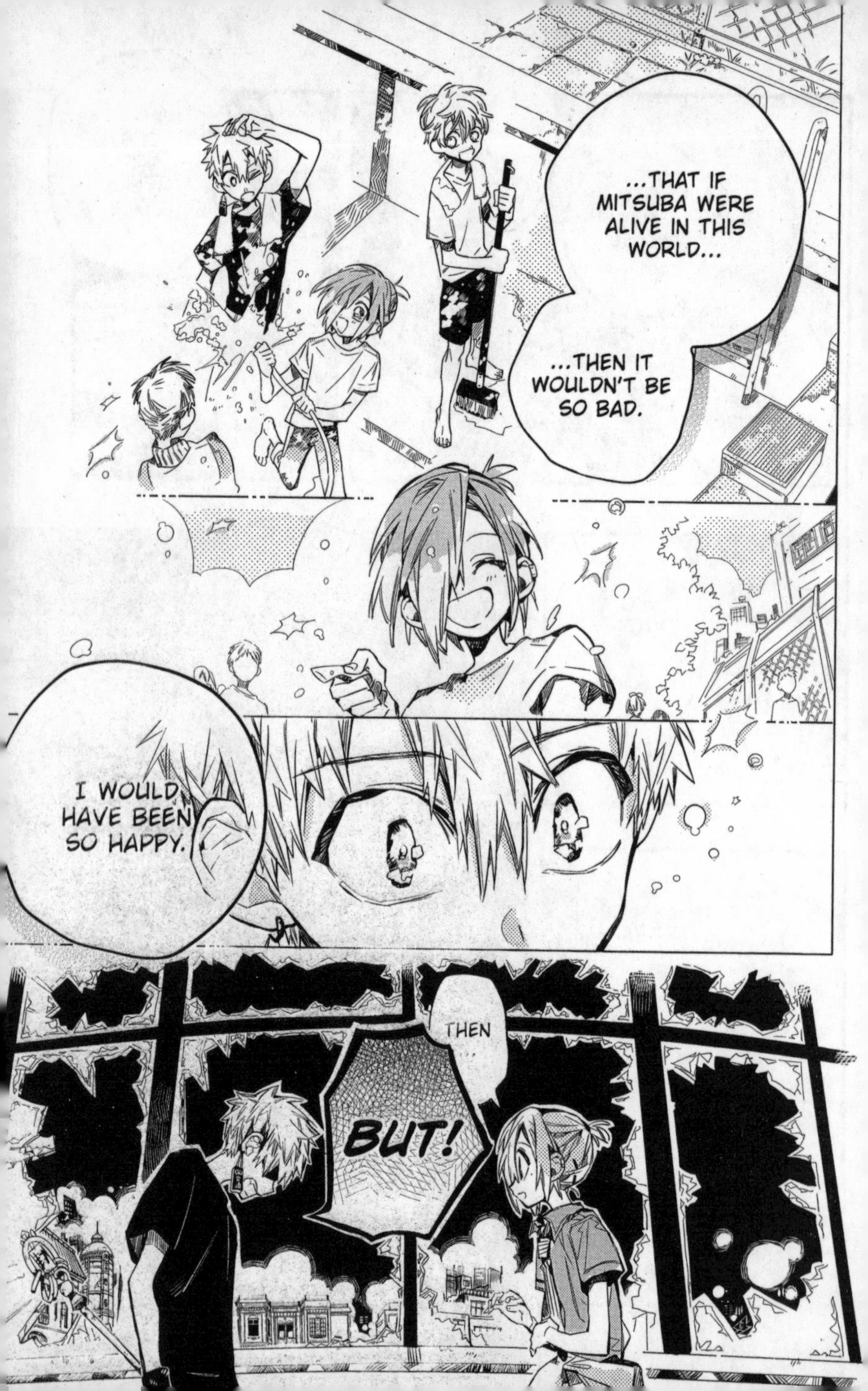
...THAT IF MITSUBA WERE ALIVE IN THIS WORLD...
...THEN IT WOULDN'T BE SO BAD.
I WOULD HAVE BEEN SO HAPPY.
THEN
BUT!

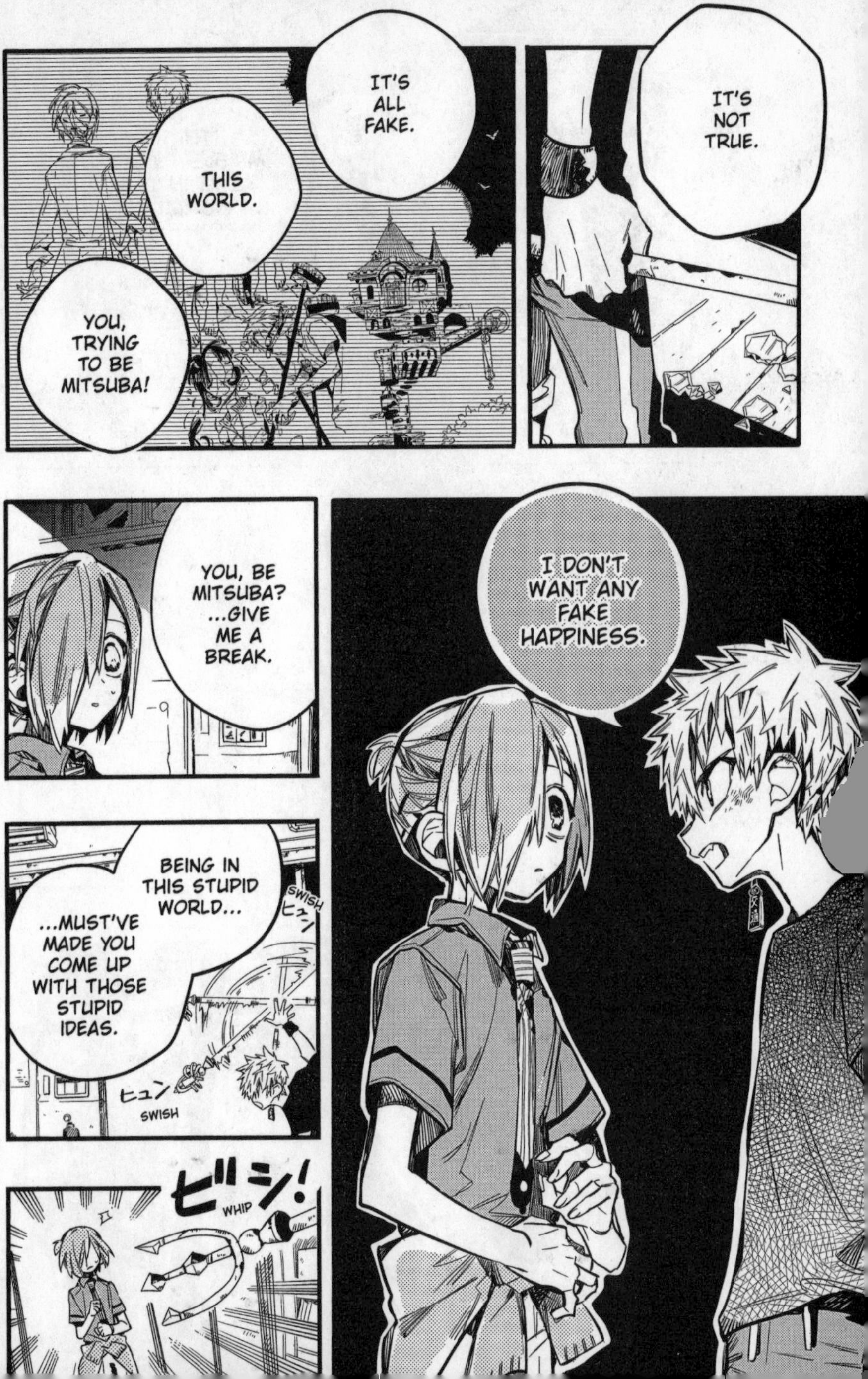
IT'S NOT TRUE.
IT'S ALL FAKE.
THIS WORLD.
YOU, TRYING TO BE MITSUBA!
I DON'T WANT ANY FAKE HAPPINESS.
YOU, BE MITSUBA? ...GIVE ME A BREAK.
BEING IN THIS STUPID WORLD...
SWISH ヒュン
...MUST'VE MADE YOU COME UP WITH THOSE STUPID IDEAS.
ヒュン SWISH
ビシッ!
WHIP

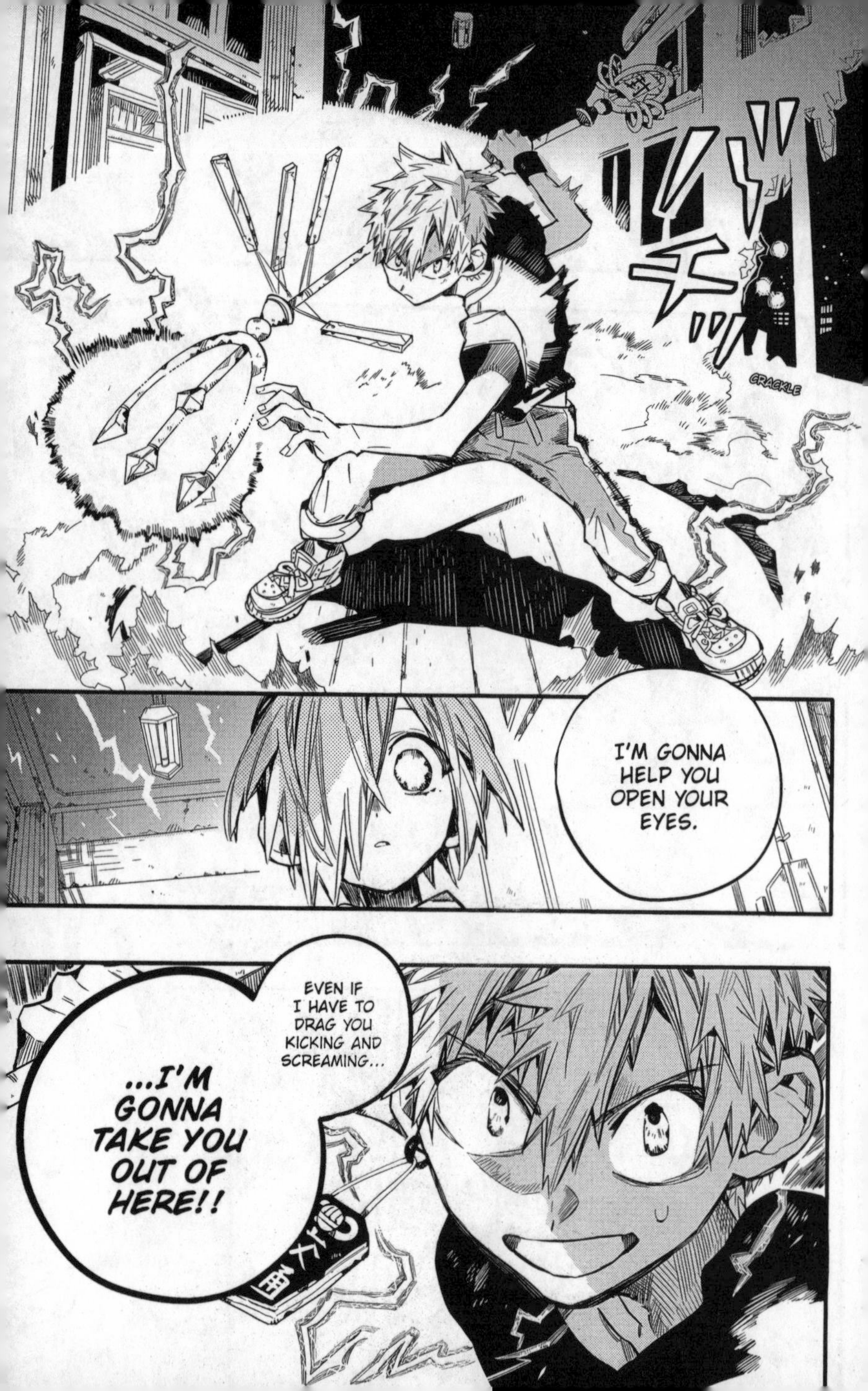
CRACKLE
I'M GONNA HELP YOU OPEN YOUR EYES.
EVEN IF I HAVE TO DRAG YOU KICKING AND SCREAMING...
...I'M GONNA TAKE YOU OUT OF HERE!!

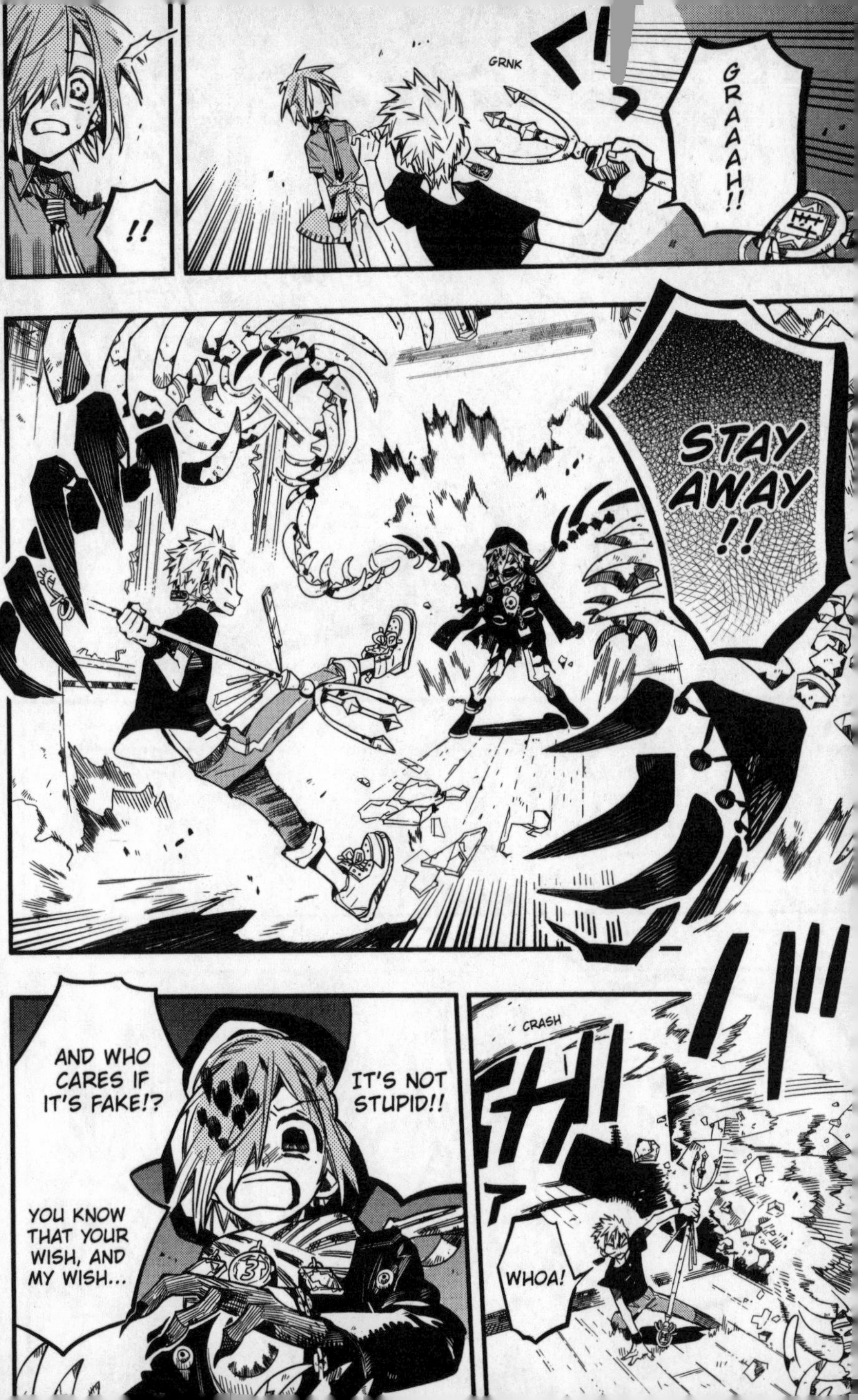
GRAAAH!!
GRNK
!!
STAY AWAY!!
CRASH
WHOA!
IT'S NOT STUPID!!
AND WHO CARES IF IT'S FAKE!?
YOU KNOW THAT YOUR WISH, AND MY WISH...

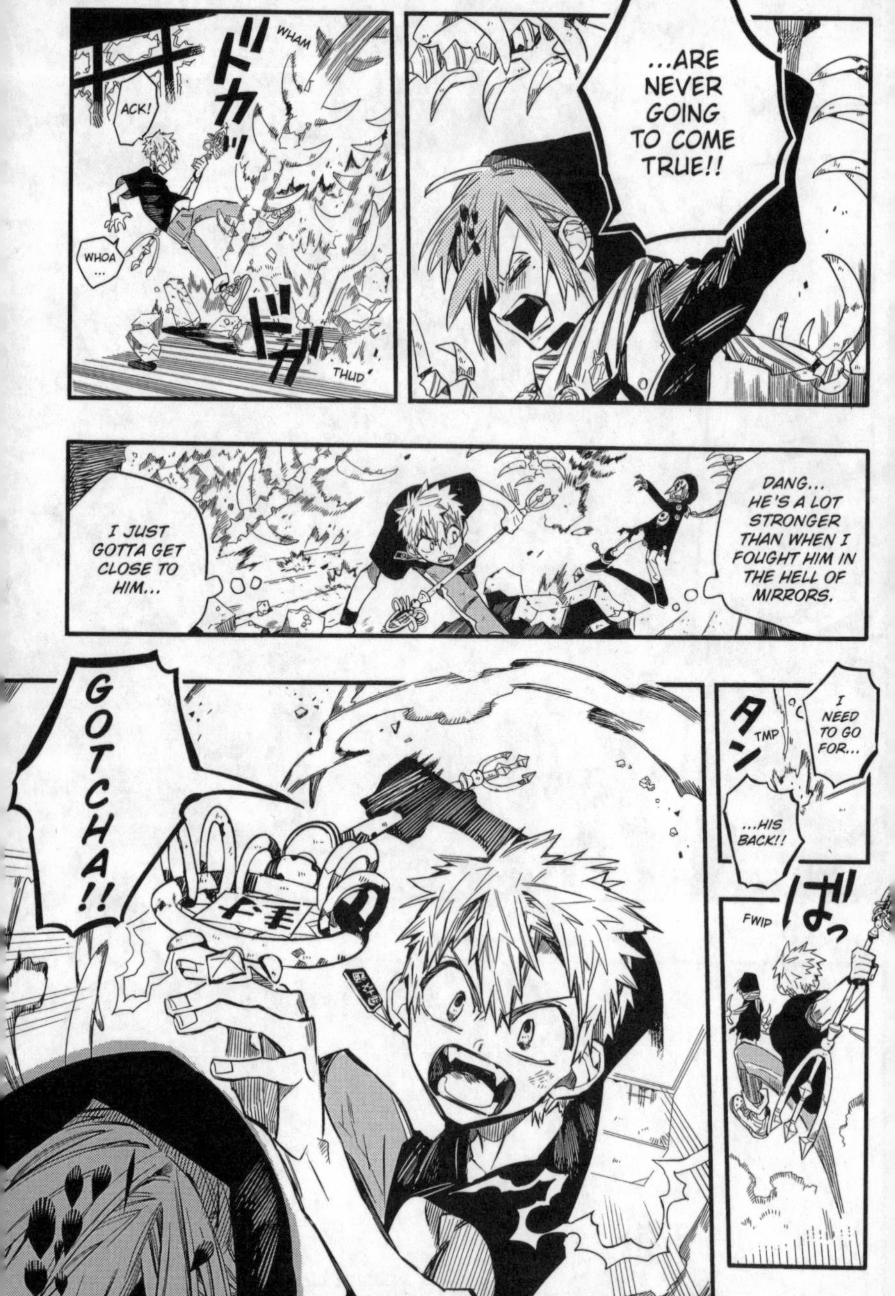
...ARE NEVER GOING TO COME TRUE!!
ドカッ
WHAM
ACK!
WHOA...
ドガッ
THUD
DANG... HE'S A LOT STRONGER THAN WHEN I FOUGHT HIM IN THE HELL OF MIRRORS.
I JUST GOTTA GET CLOSE TO HIM...
タン
TMP
I NEED TO GO FOR...
...HIS BACK!!
ばっ
FWIP
GOTCHA!!

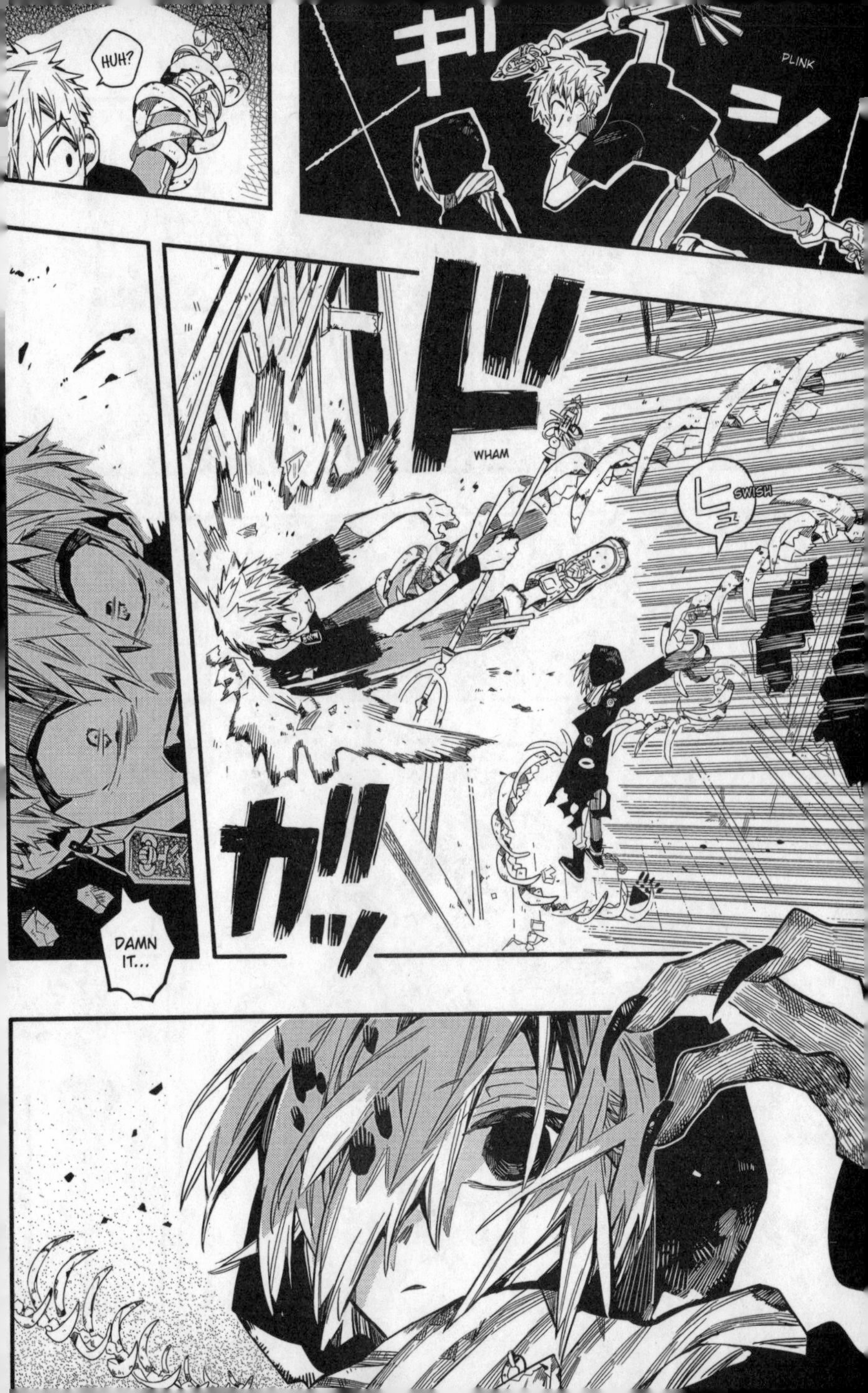
PLINK
HUH?
WHAM
ヒュ SWISH
DAMN IT...

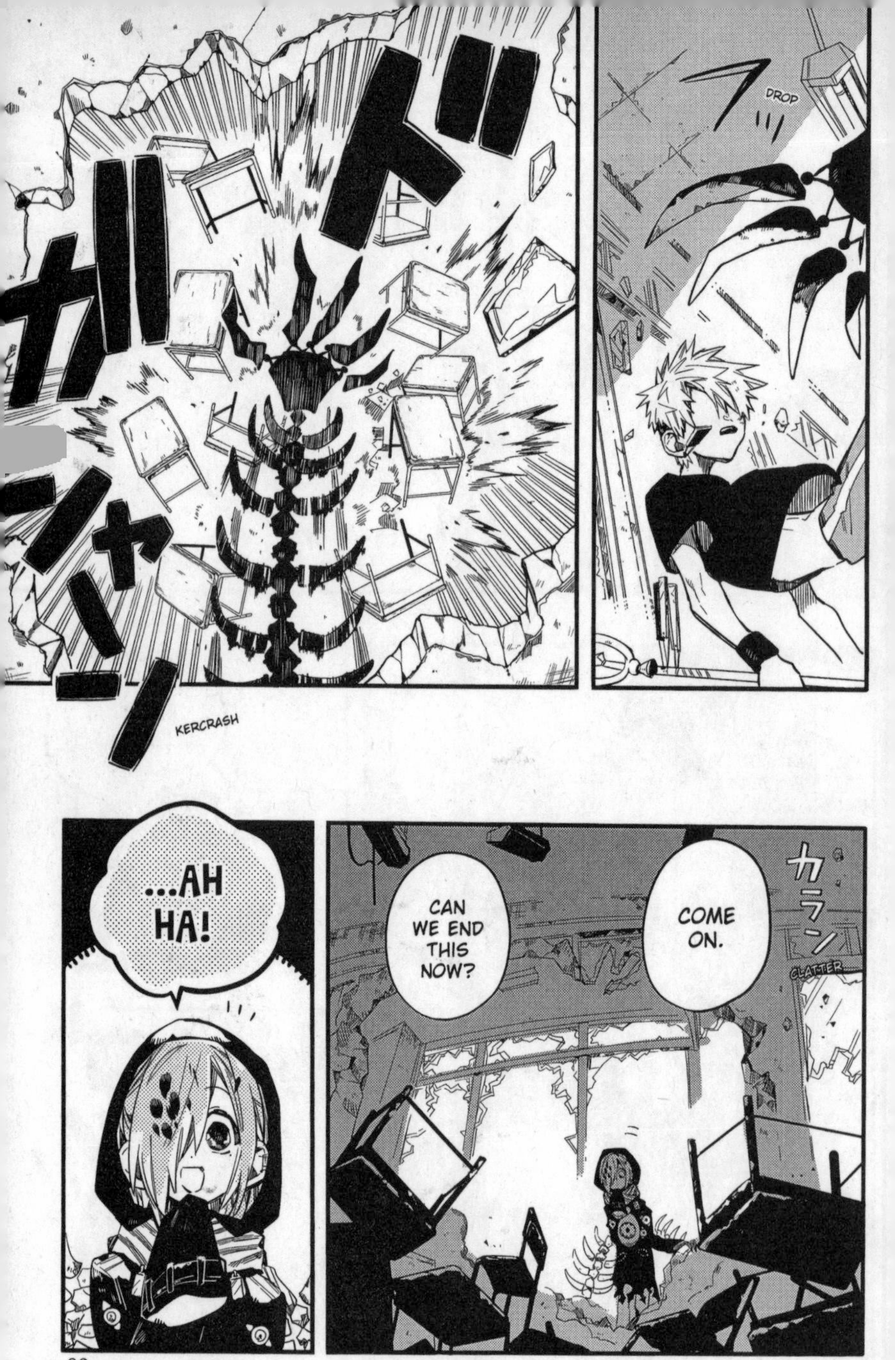
DROP
ド
ガシャーン
KERCRASH
カラン
CLATTER
COME ON.
CAN WE END THIS NOW?
...AH HA!

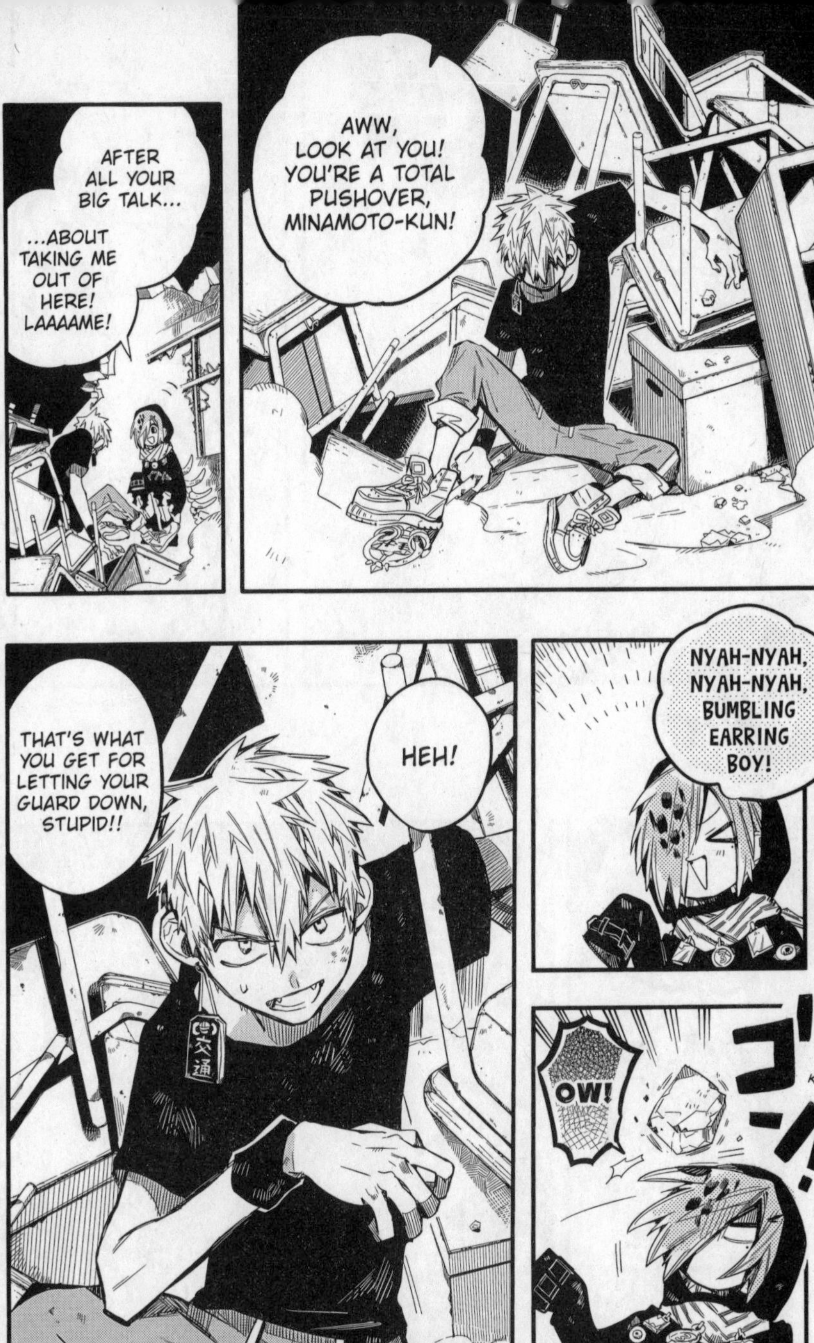
AWW, LOOK AT YOU! YOU'RE A TOTAL PUSHOVER, MINAMOTO-KUN!
AFTER ALL YOUR BIG TALK...
...ABOUT TAKING ME OUT OF HERE! LAAAAME!
NYAH-NYAH, NYAH-NYAH, BUMBLING EARRING BOY!
OW!
KONK
HEH!
THAT'S WHAT YOU GET FOR LETTING YOUR GUARD DOWN, STUPID!!

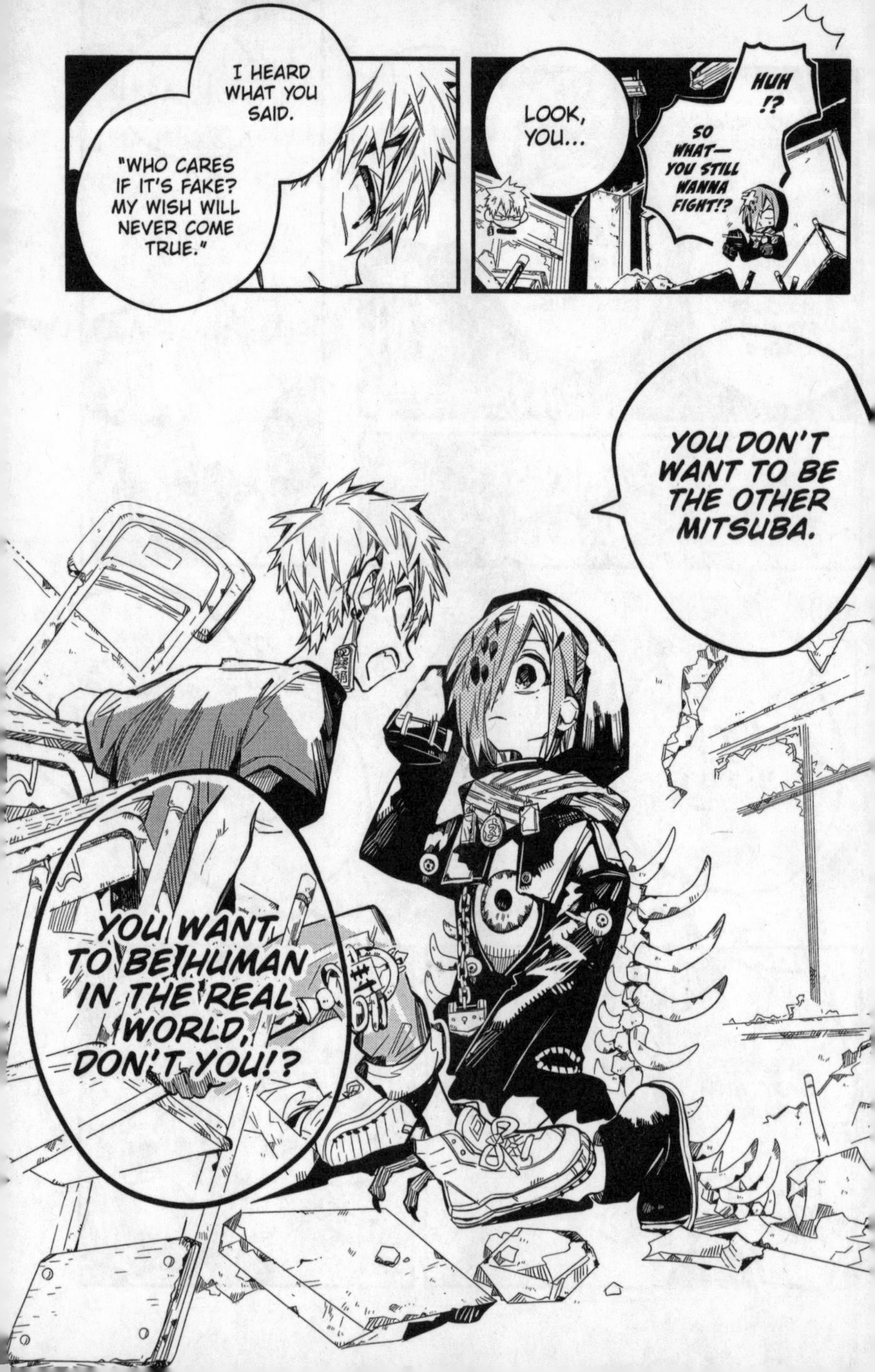
HUH !?
SO WHAT— YOU STILL WANNA FIGHT!?
LOOK, YOU...
I HEARD WHAT YOU SAID.
"WHO CARES IF IT'S FAKE? MY WISH WILL NEVER COME TRUE."
YOU DON'T WANT TO BE THE OTHER MITSUBA.
YOU WANT TO BE HUMAN IN THE REAL WORLD, DON'T YOU!?

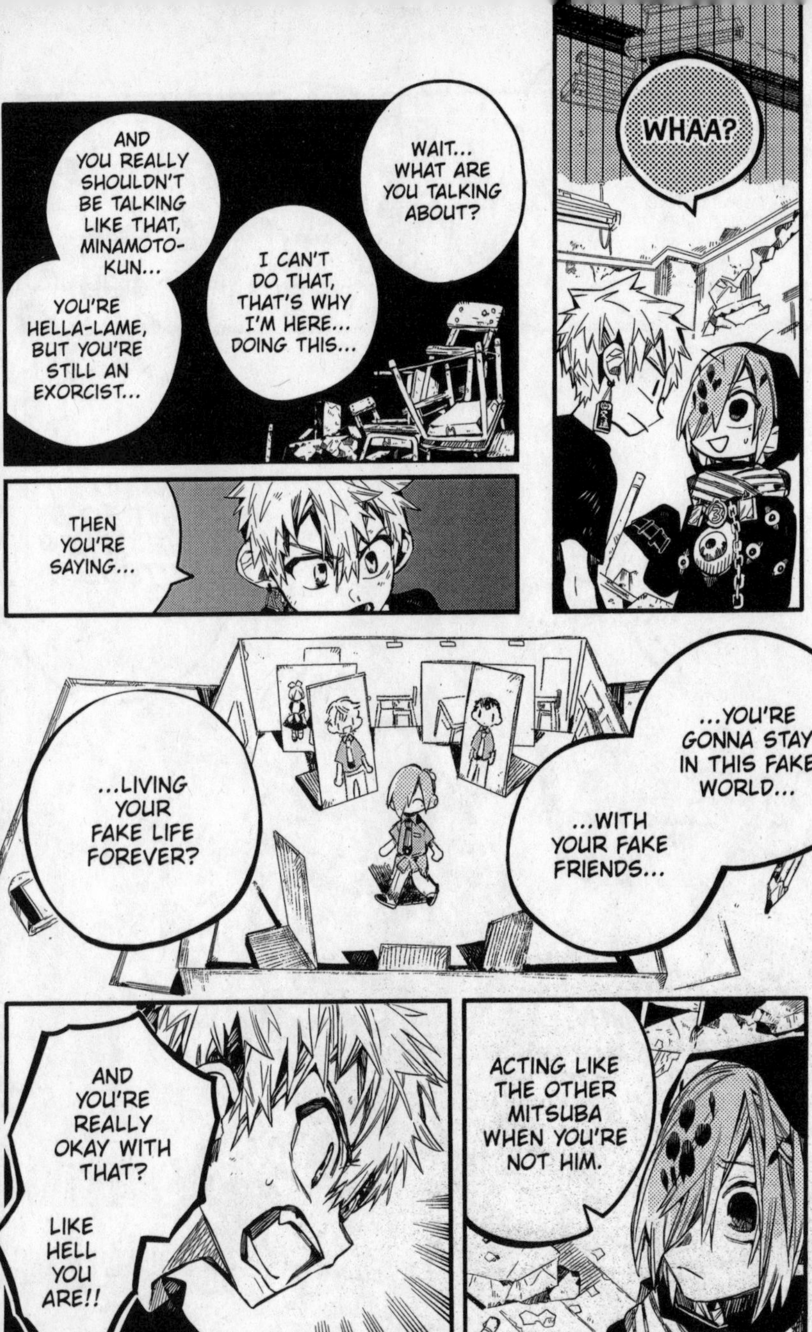
WHAA?
WAIT... WHAT ARE YOU TALKING ABOUT?
I CAN'T DO THAT, THAT'S WHY I'M HERE... DOING THIS...
AND YOU REALLY SHOULDN'T BE TALKING LIKE THAT, MINAMOTO-KUN...
YOU'RE HELLA-LAME, BUT YOU'RE STILL AN EXORCIST...
THEN YOU'RE SAYING...
...YOU'RE GONNA STAY IN THIS FAKE WORLD...
...WITH YOUR FAKE FRIENDS...
...LIVING YOUR FAKE LIFE FOREVER?
ACTING LIKE THE OTHER MITSUBA WHEN YOU'RE NOT HIM.
AND YOU'RE REALLY OKAY WITH THAT?
LIKE HELL YOU ARE!!

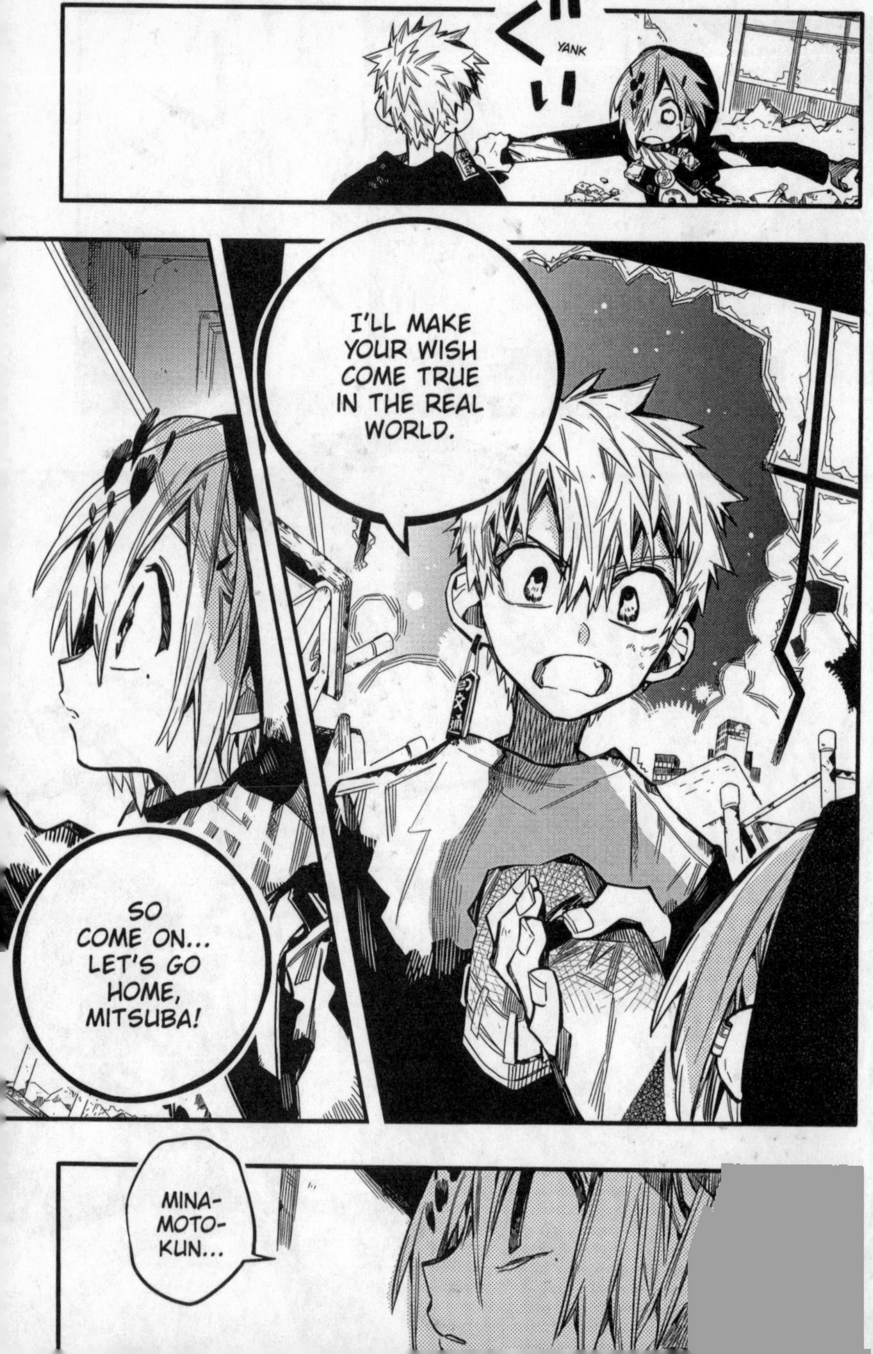
YANK
I'LL MAKE YOUR WISH COME TRUE IN THE REAL WORLD.
SO COME ON... LET'S GO HOME, MITSUBA!
MINA-MOTO-KUN...

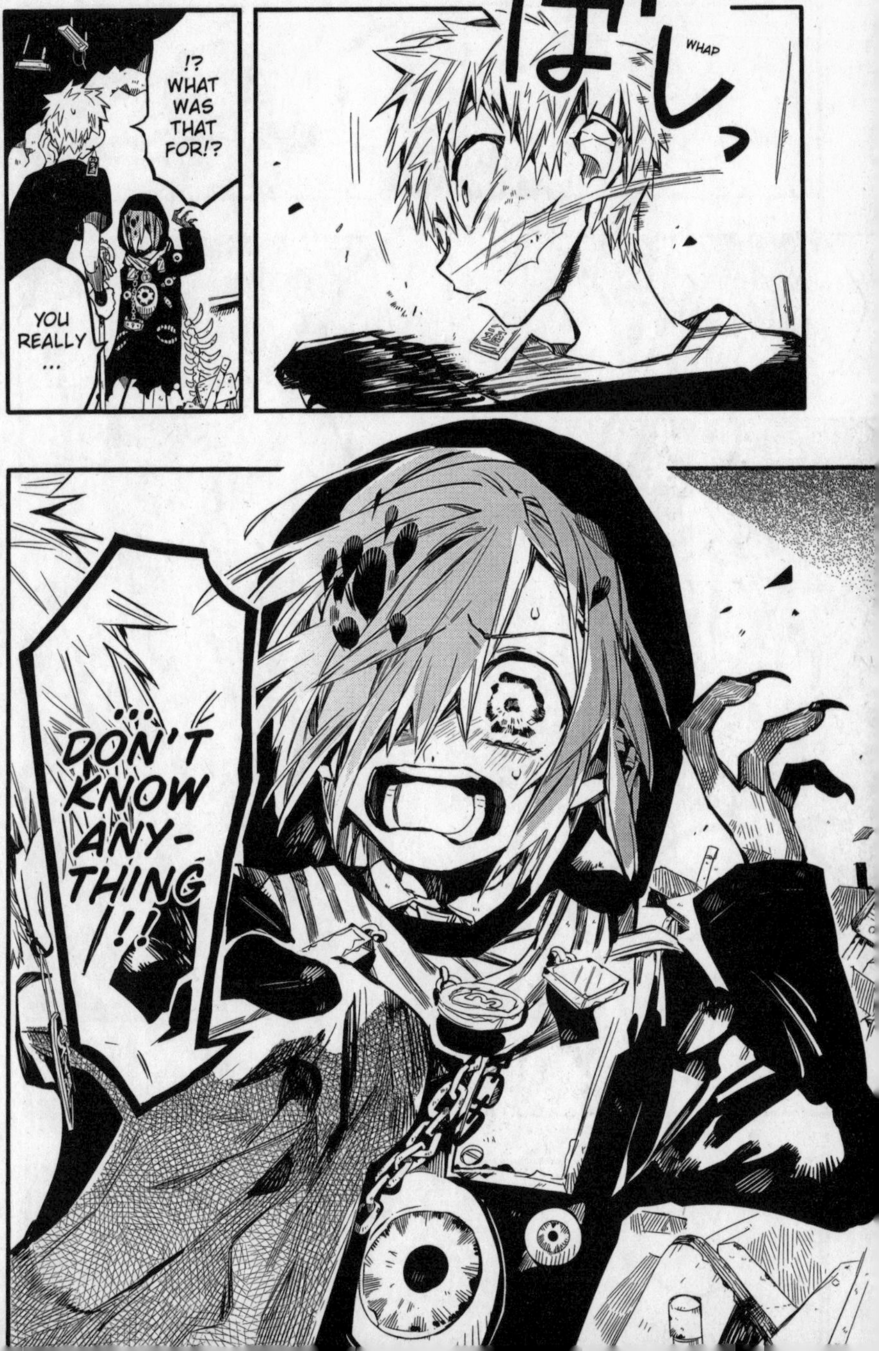
ばしっ
WHAP
!? WHAT WAS THAT FOR!?
YOU REALLY ...
...DON'T KNOW ANY-THING!!

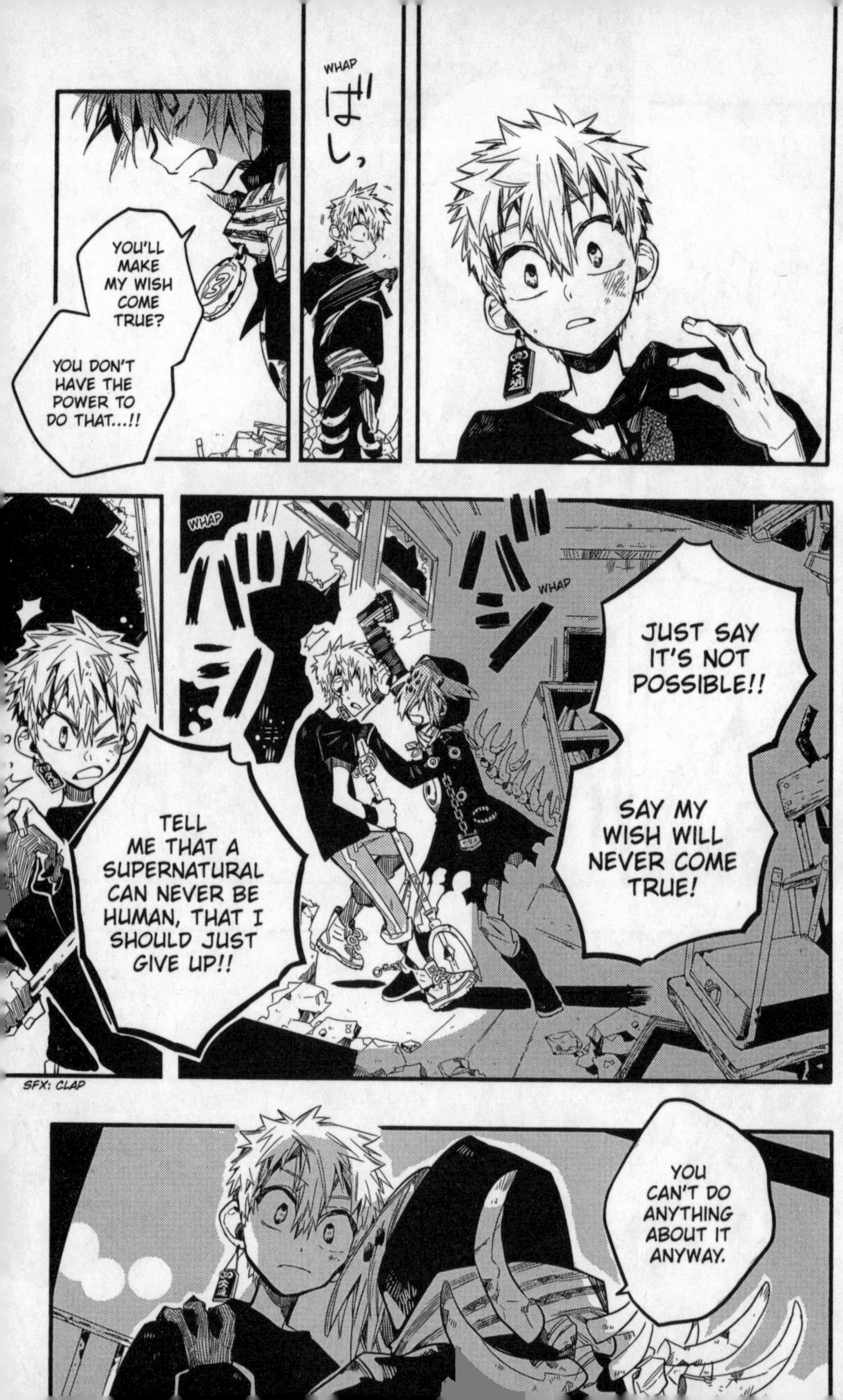
WHAP
ばしっ
YOU'LL MAKE MY WISH COME TRUE?
YOU DON'T HAVE THE POWER TO DO THAT...!!
WHAP
JUST SAY IT'S NOT POSSIBLE!!
SAY MY WISH WILL NEVER COME TRUE!
WHAP
TELL ME THAT A SUPERNATURAL CAN NEVER BE HUMAN, THAT I SHOULD JUST GIVE UP!!
SFX: CLAP
YOU CAN'T DO ANYTHING ABOUT IT ANYWAY.

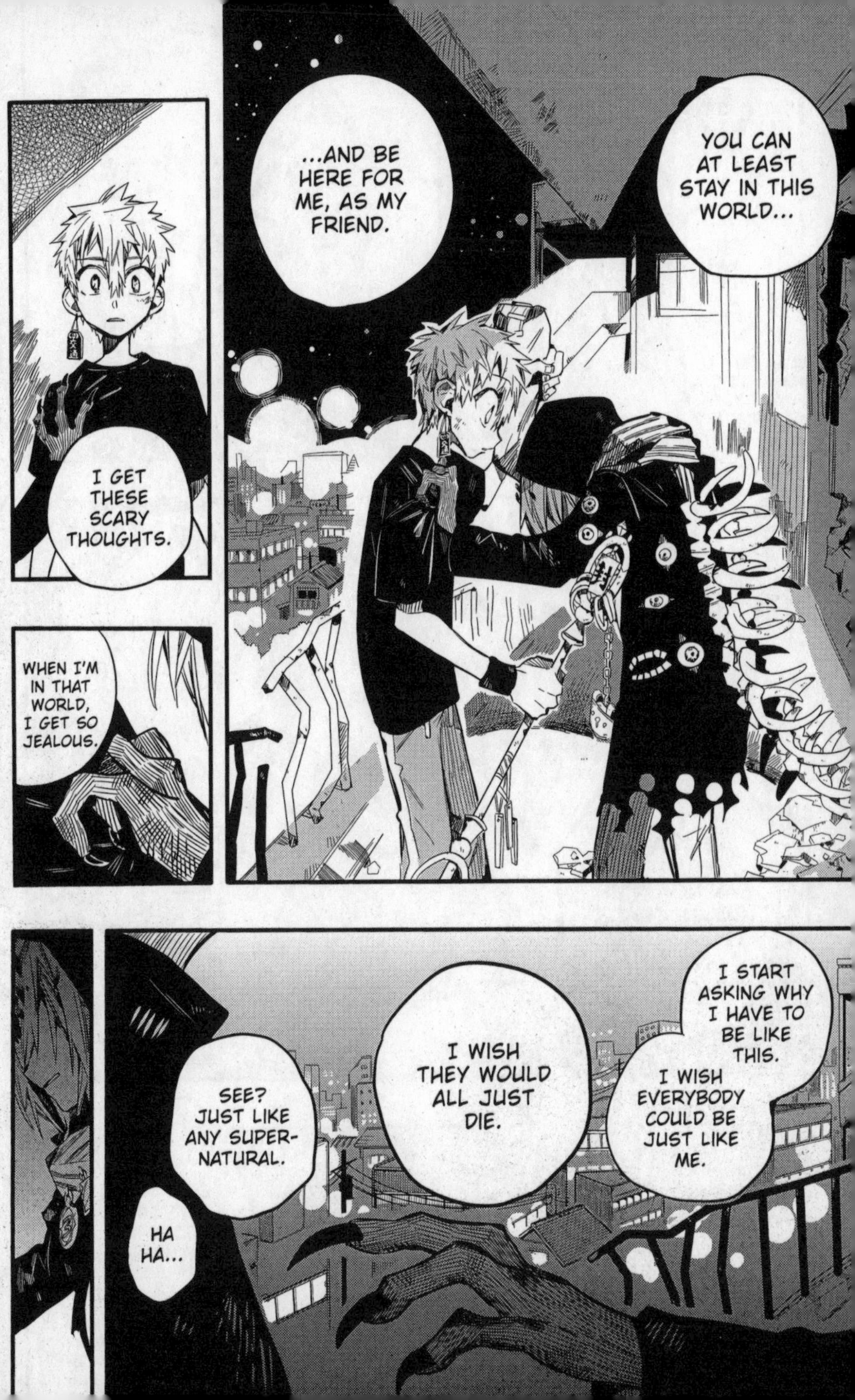
YOU CAN AT LEAST STAY IN THIS WORLD...
...AND BE HERE FOR ME, AS MY FRIEND.
I GET THESE SCARY THOUGHTS.
WHEN I'M IN THAT WORLD, I GET SO JEALOUS.
I START ASKING WHY I HAVE TO BE LIKE THIS.
I WISH EVERYBODY COULD BE JUST LIKE ME.
I WISH THEY WOULD ALL JUST DIE.
SEE? JUST LIKE ANY SUPER-NATURAL.
HA HA...

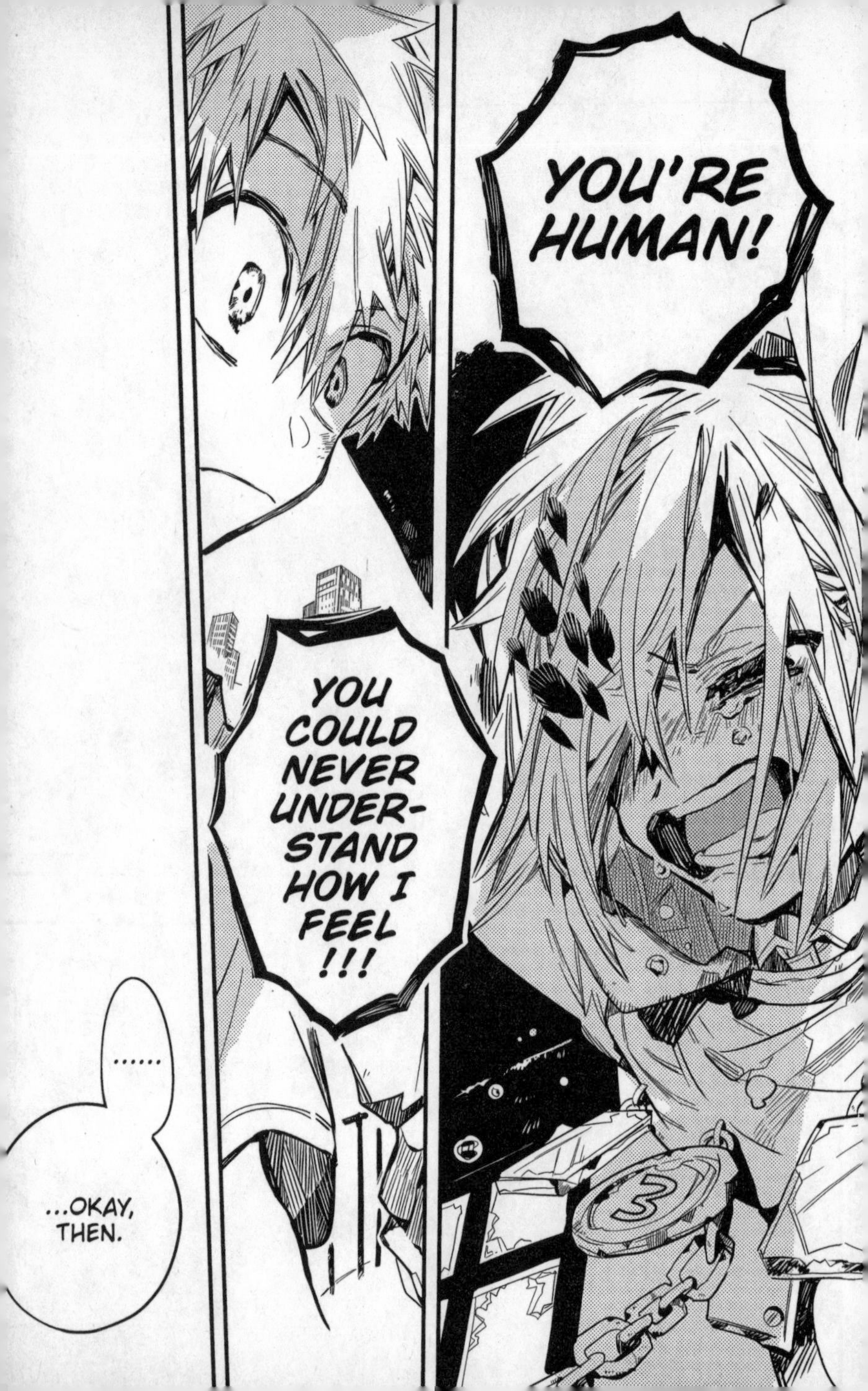
YOU'RE HUMAN!
YOU COULD NEVER UNDER-STAND HOW I FEEL!!!
......
...OKAY, THEN.

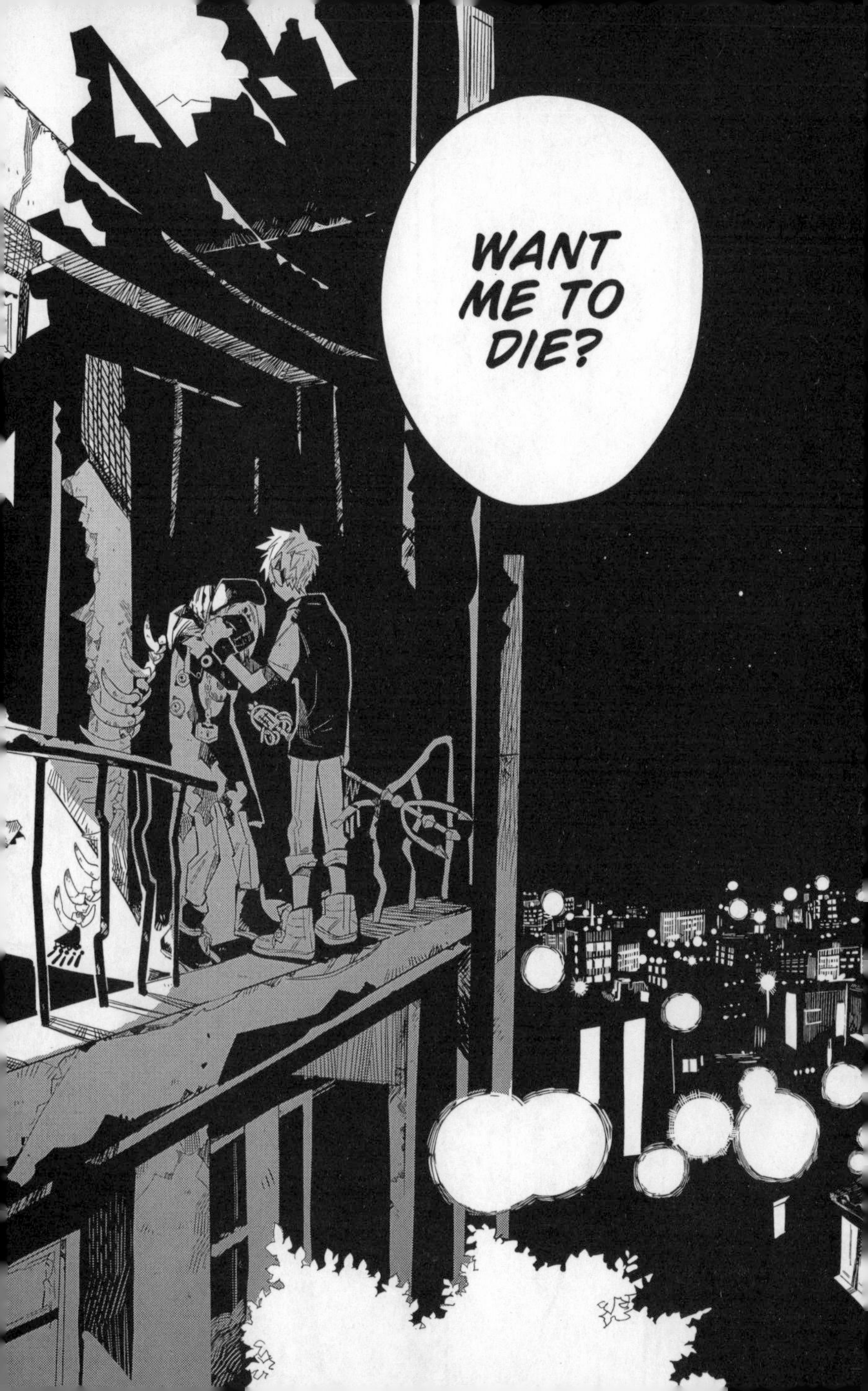
WANT ME TO DIE?

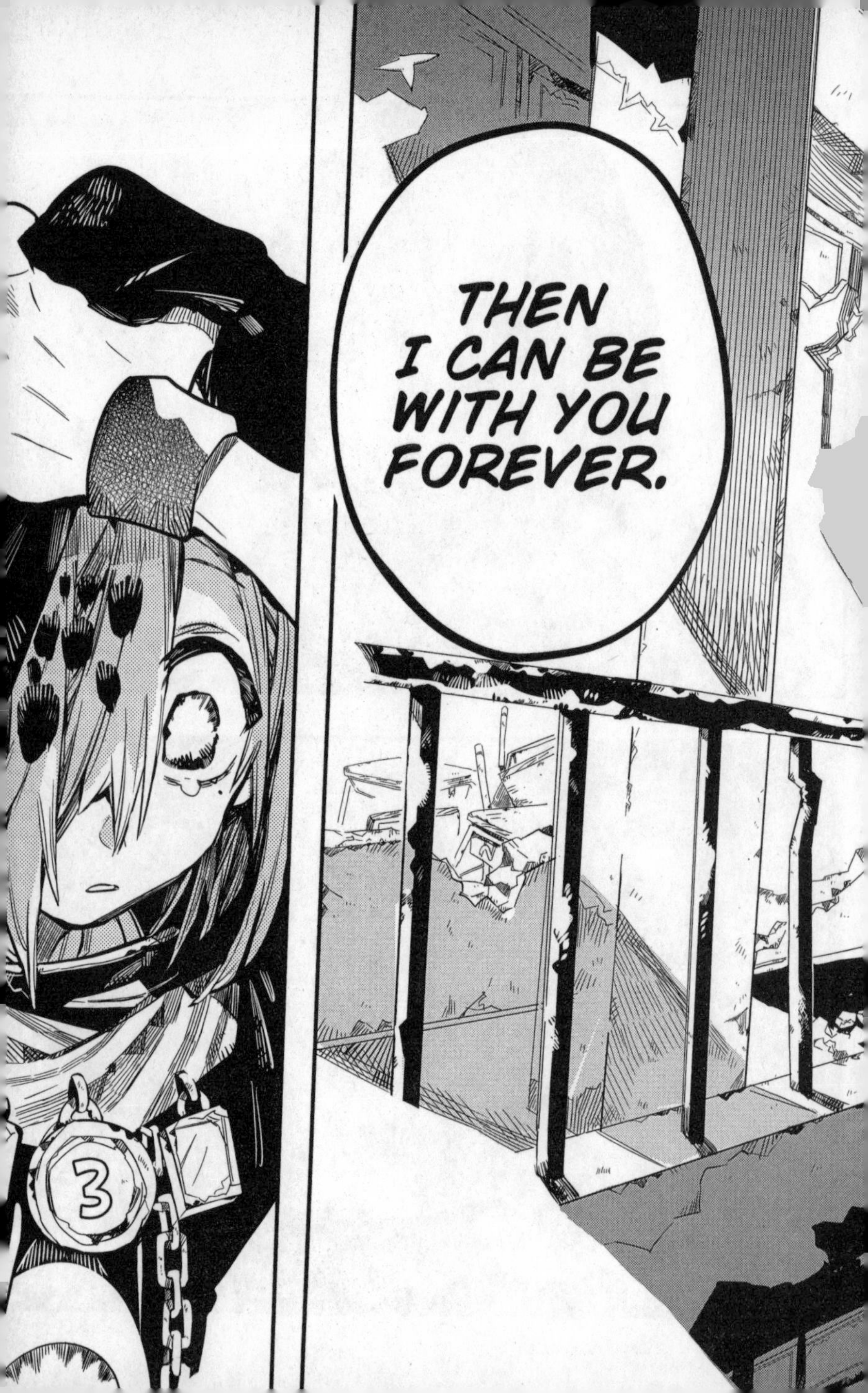
THEN I CAN BE WITH YOU FOREVER.
3

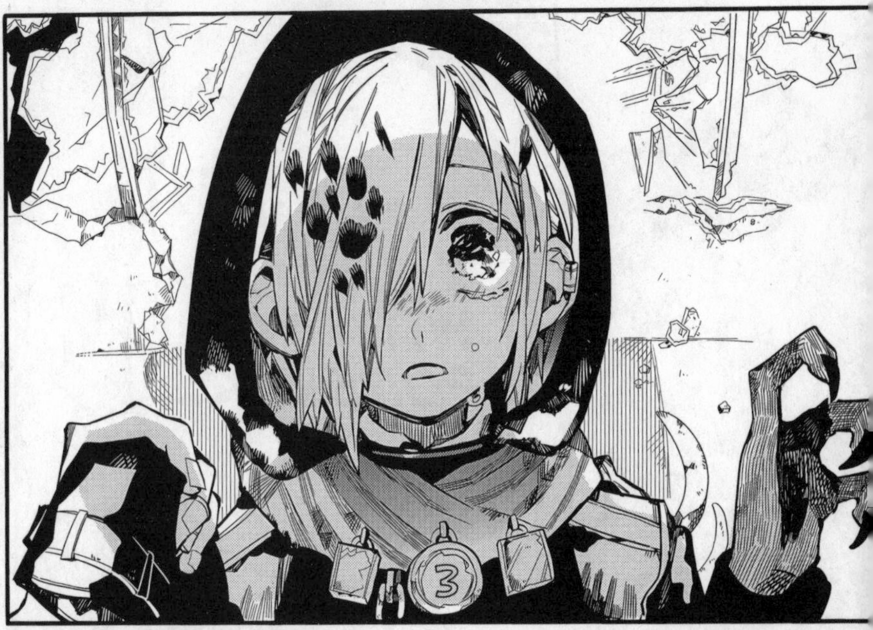

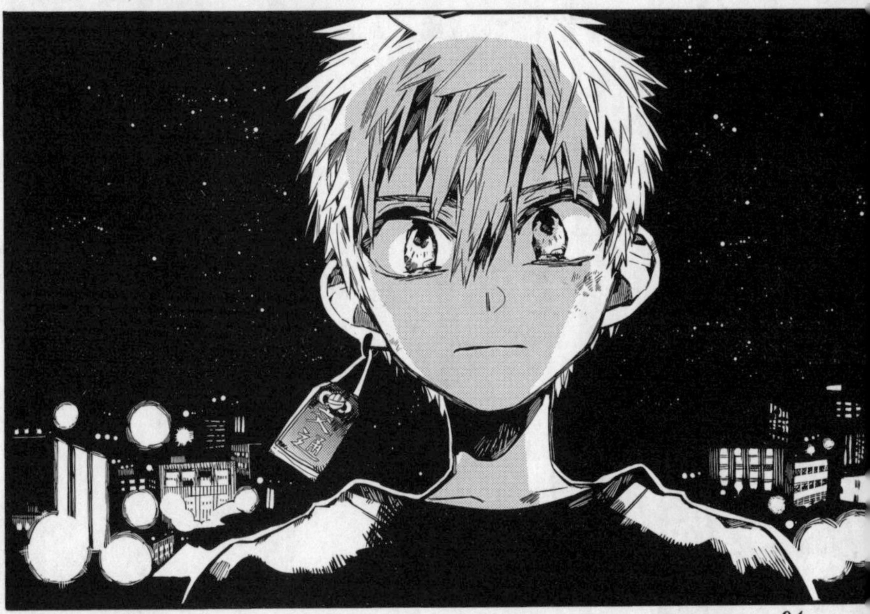

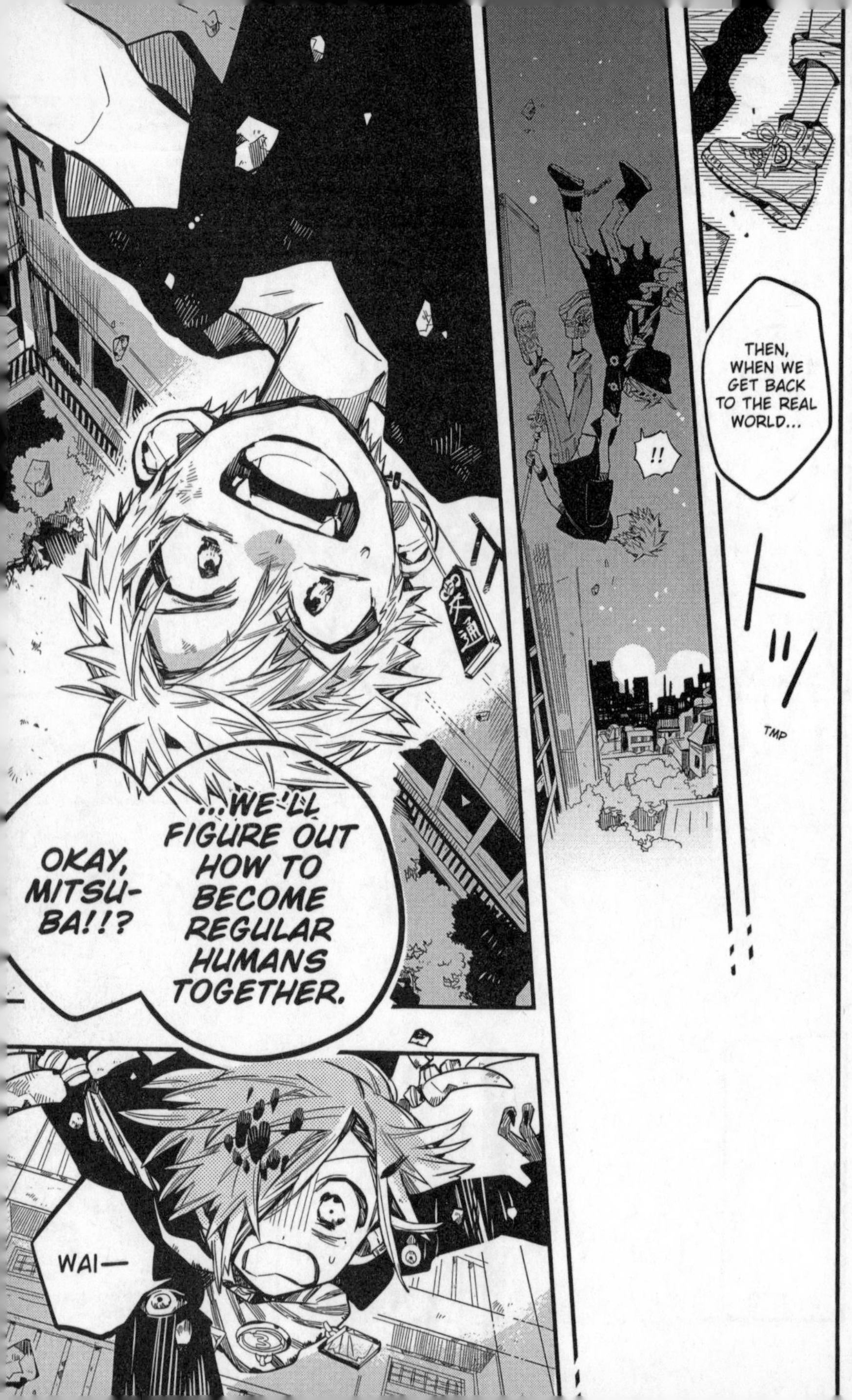
THEN, WHEN WE GET BACK TO THE REAL WORLD...
TMP
!!
...WE'LL FIGURE OUT HOW TO BECOME REGULAR HUMANS TOGETHER.
OKAY, MITSU-BA!!?
WAI—

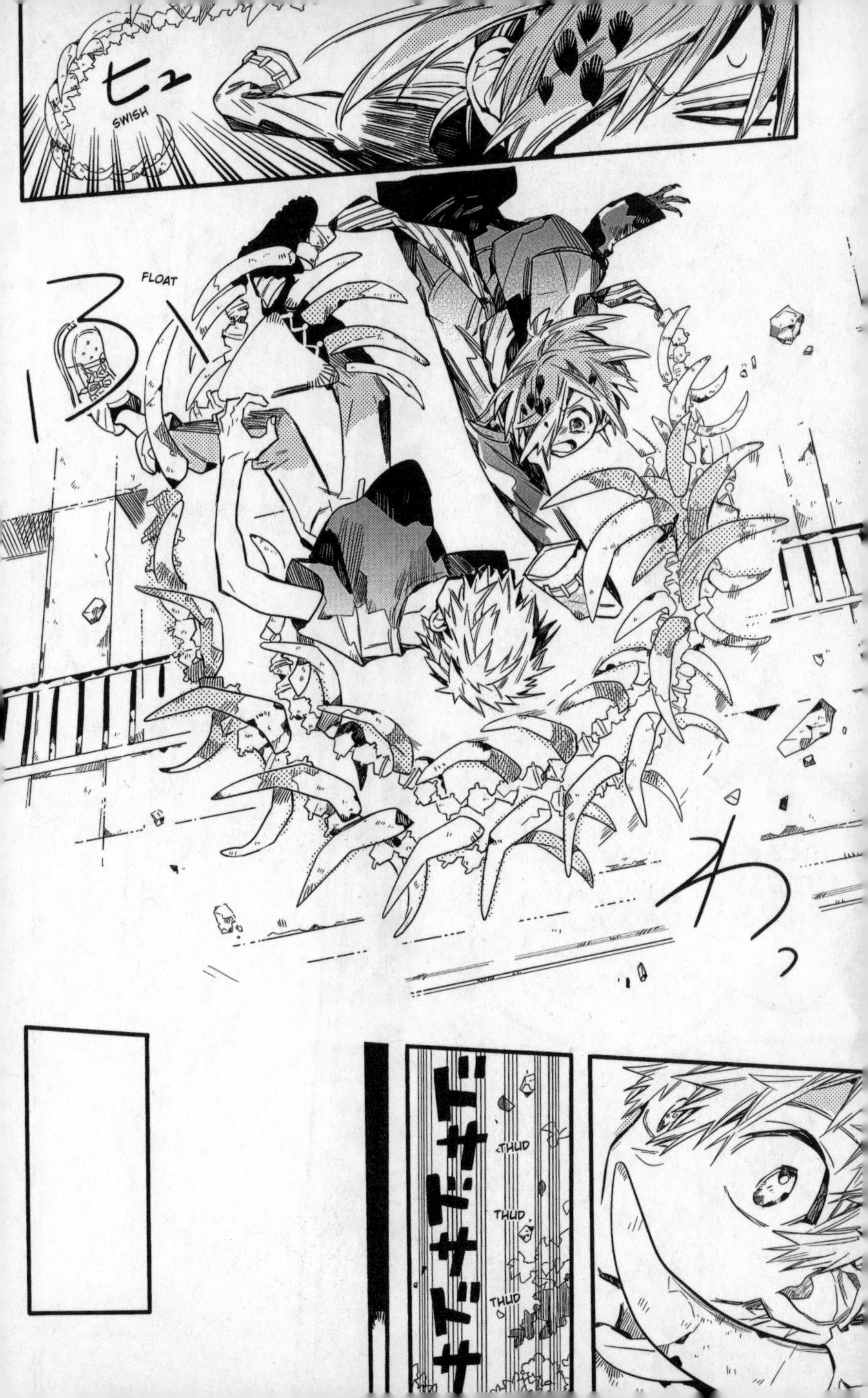
ヒュ
SWISH
ふ
FLOAT
わっ
ドサドサドサ
THUD
THUD
THUD

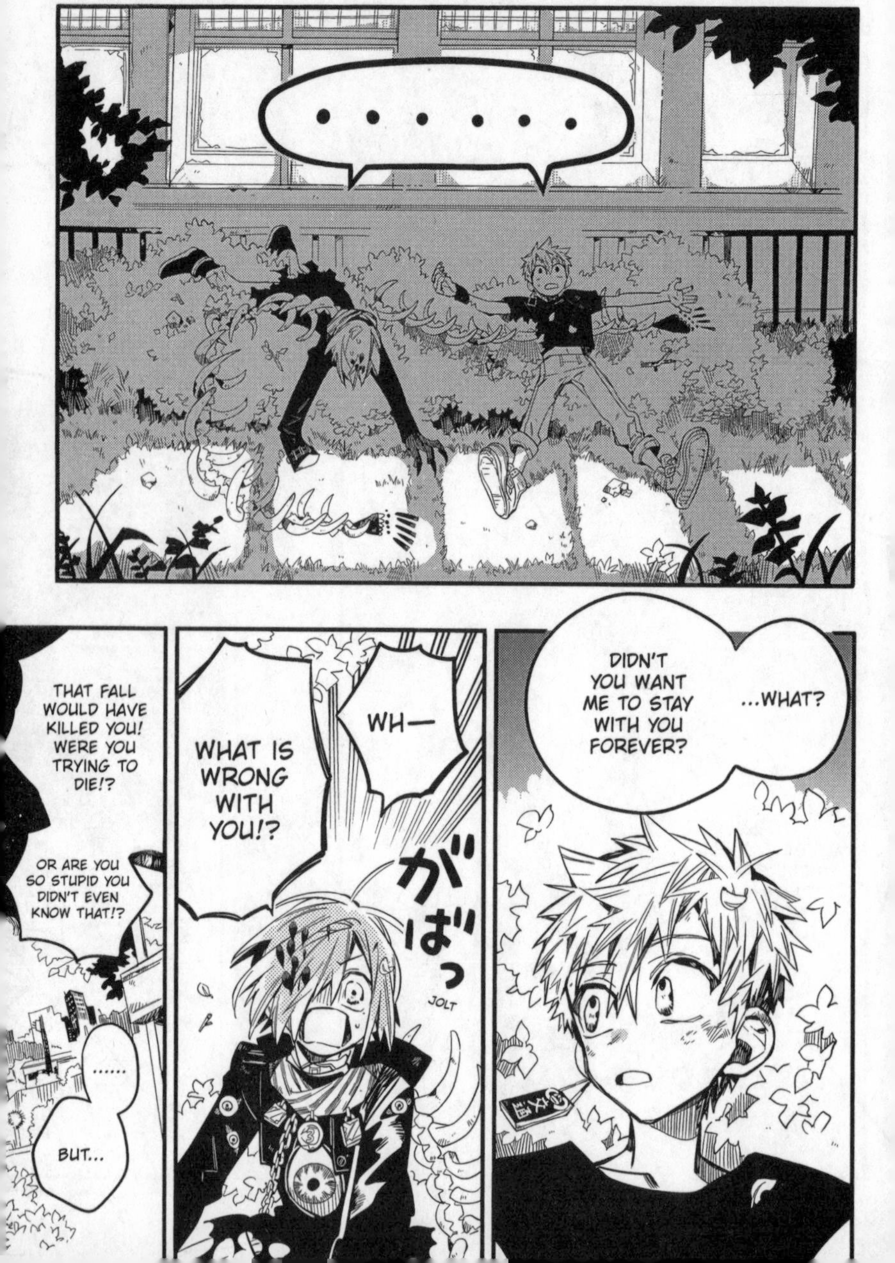
.....
...WHAT?
DIDN'T YOU WANT ME TO STAY WITH YOU FOREVER?
WH—
WHAT IS WRONG WITH YOU!?
がばっ
JOLT
THAT FALL WOULD HAVE KILLED YOU! WERE YOU TRYING TO DIE!?
OR ARE YOU SO STUPID YOU DIDN'T EVEN KNOW THAT!?
......
BUT...

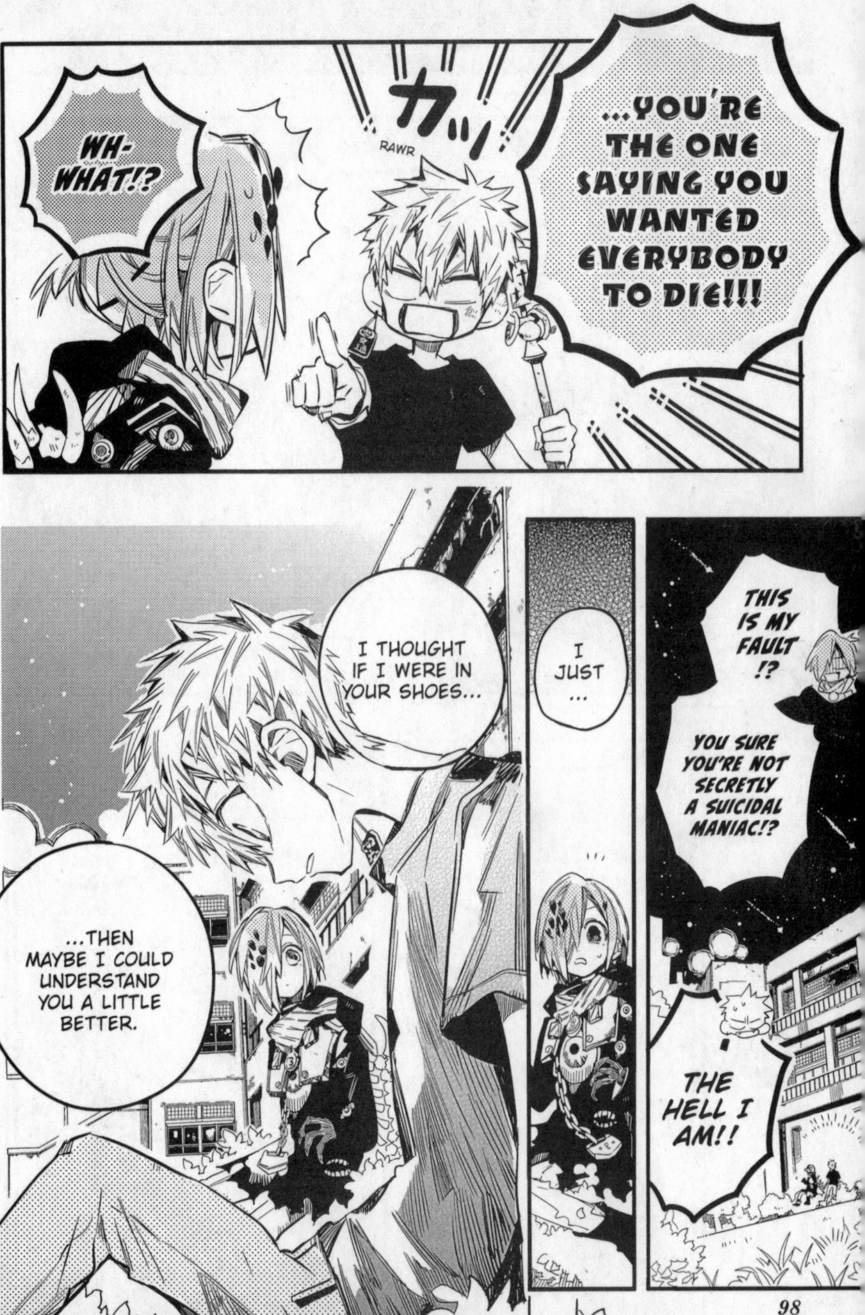
...YOU'RE THE ONE SAYING YOU WANTED EVERYBODY TO DIE!!!
カッ
RAWR
WH-WHAT!?
THIS IS MY FAULT!?
YOU SURE YOU'RE NOT SECRETLY A SUICIDAL MANIAC!?
THE HELL I AM!!
I JUST ...
I THOUGHT IF I WERE IN YOUR SHOES...
...THEN MAYBE I COULD UNDERSTAND YOU A LITTLE BETTER.

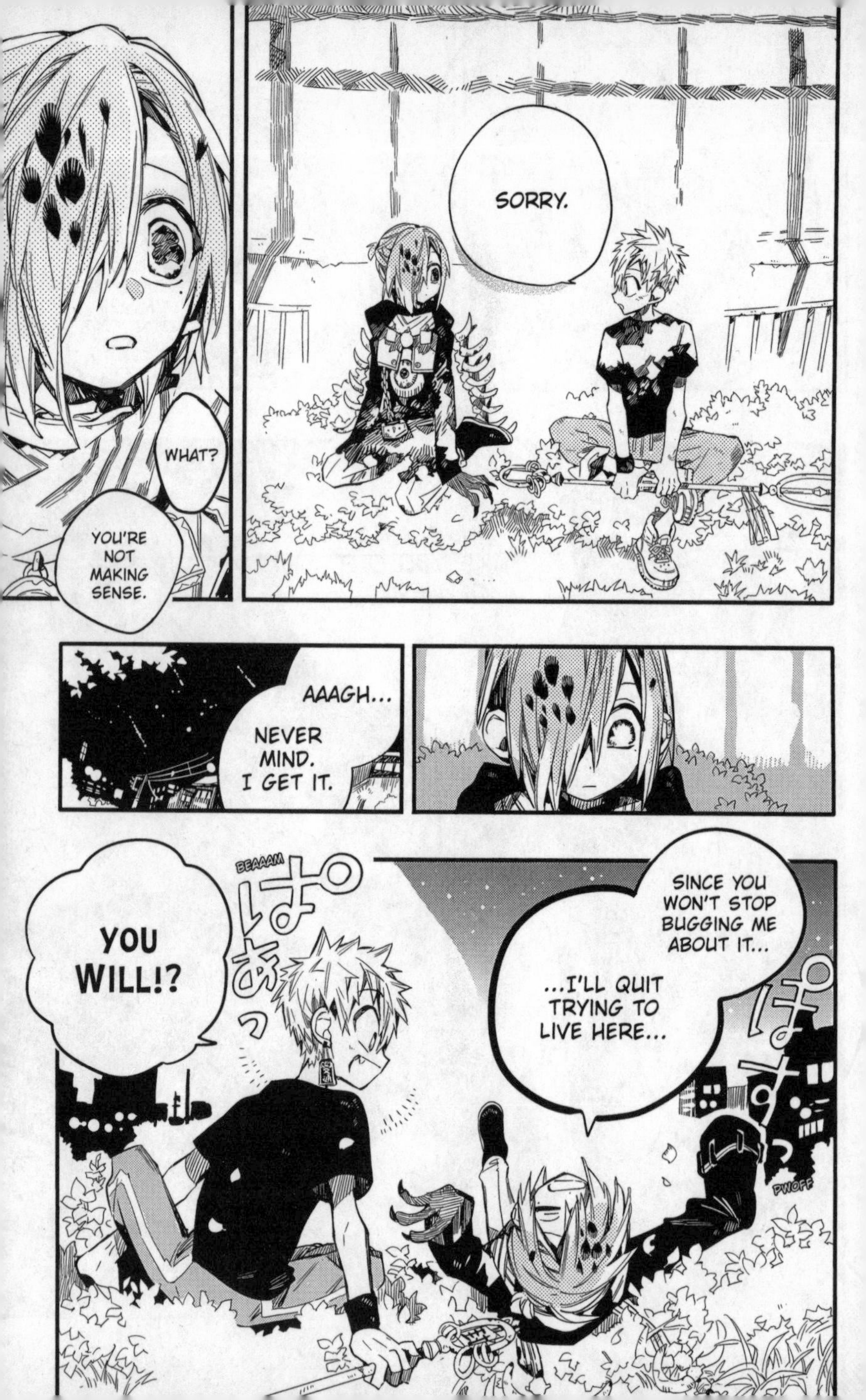
SORRY.
WHAT?
YOU'RE NOT MAKING SENSE.
AAAGH... NEVER MIND. I GET IT.
SINCE YOU WON'T STOP BUGGING ME ABOUT IT...
...I'LL QUIT TRYING TO LIVE HERE...
ぽすっ
PWOFF
ぱあっ
BEAAAM
YOU WILL!?

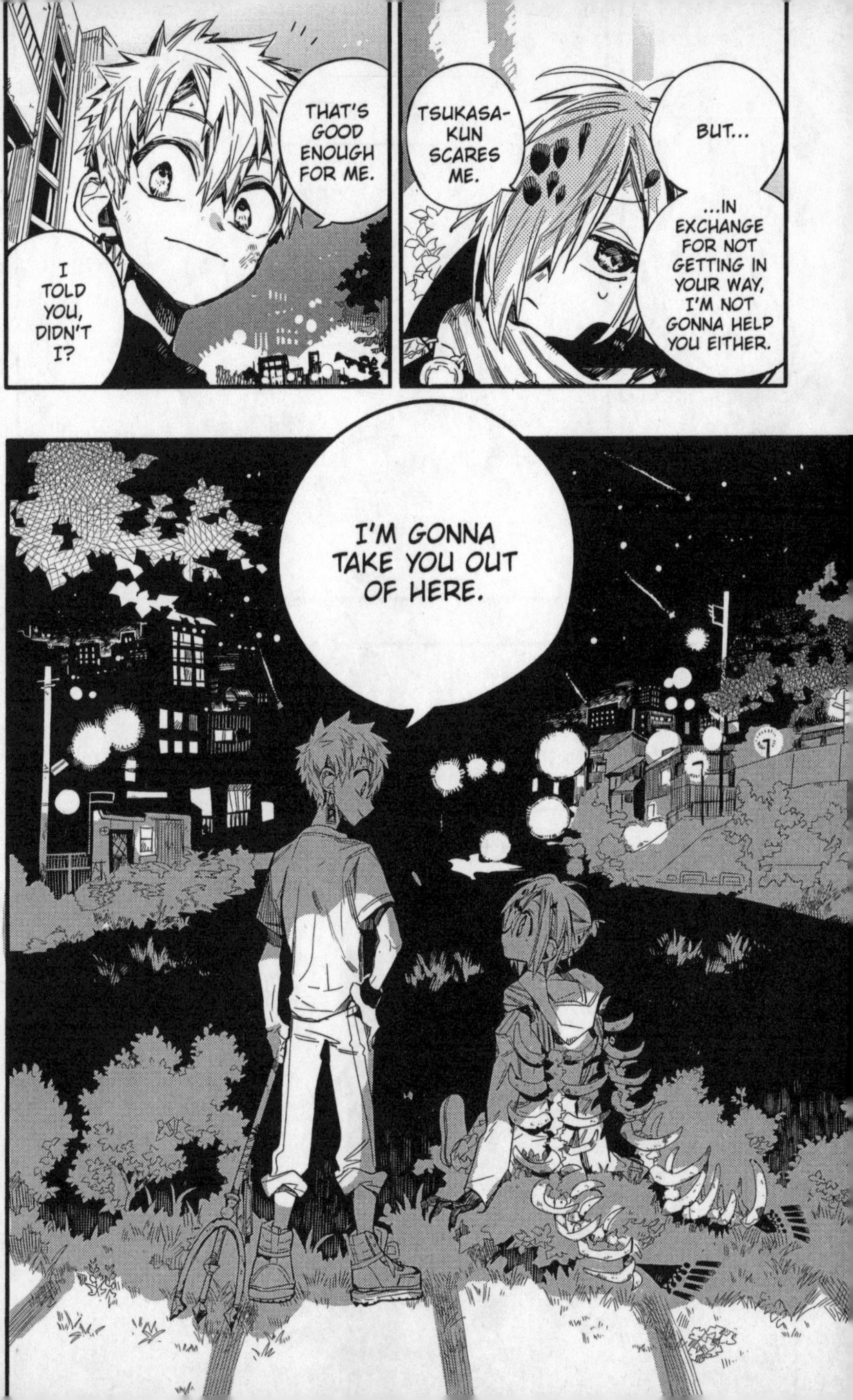
BUT...
...IN EXCHANGE FOR NOT GETTING IN YOUR WAY, I'M NOT GONNA HELP YOU EITHER.
TSUKASA-KUN SCARES ME.
THAT'S GOOD ENOUGH FOR ME.
I TOLD YOU, DIDN'T I?
I'M GONNA TAKE YOU OUT OF HERE.

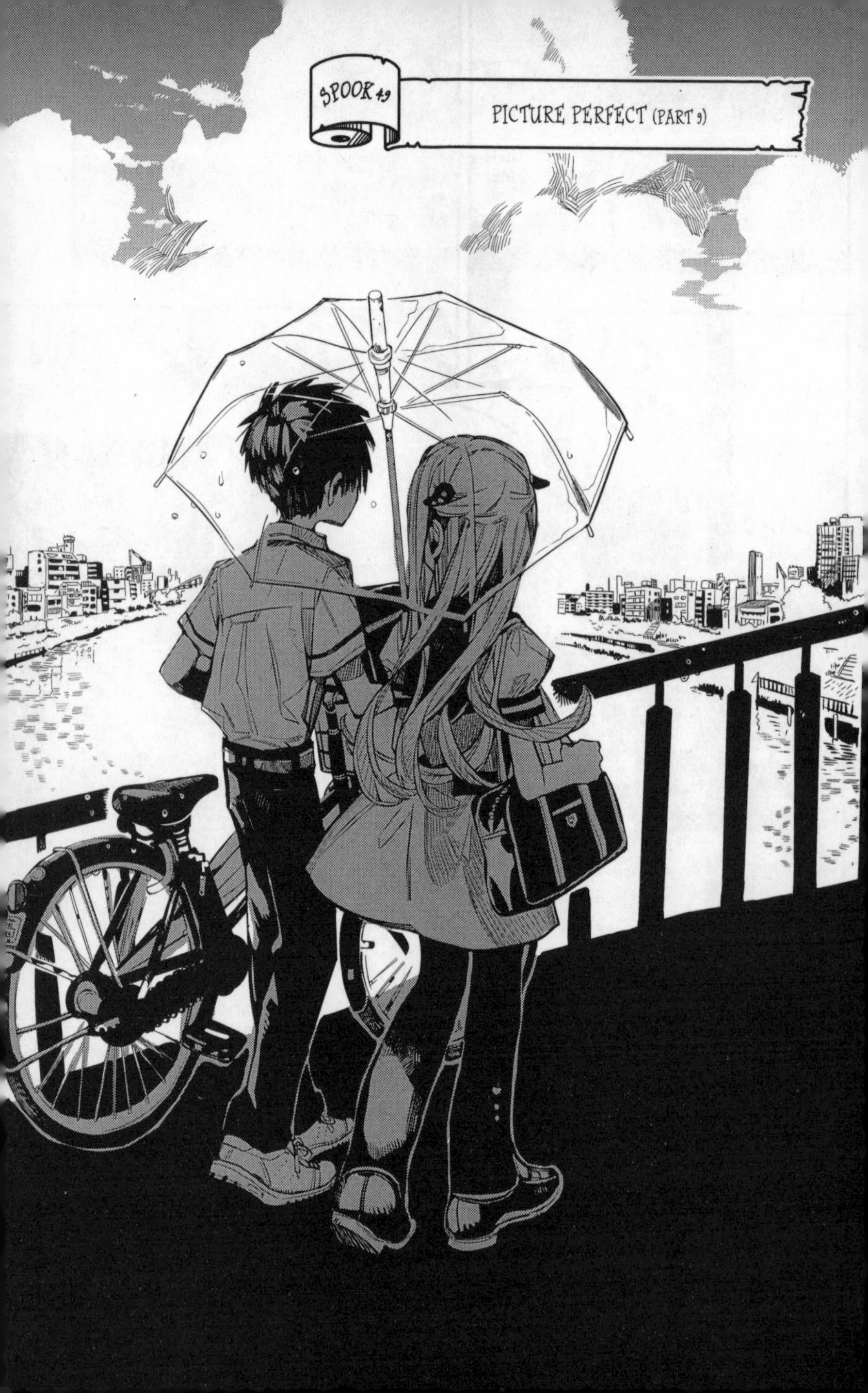
SPOOK 49
PICTURE PERFECT (PART 9)

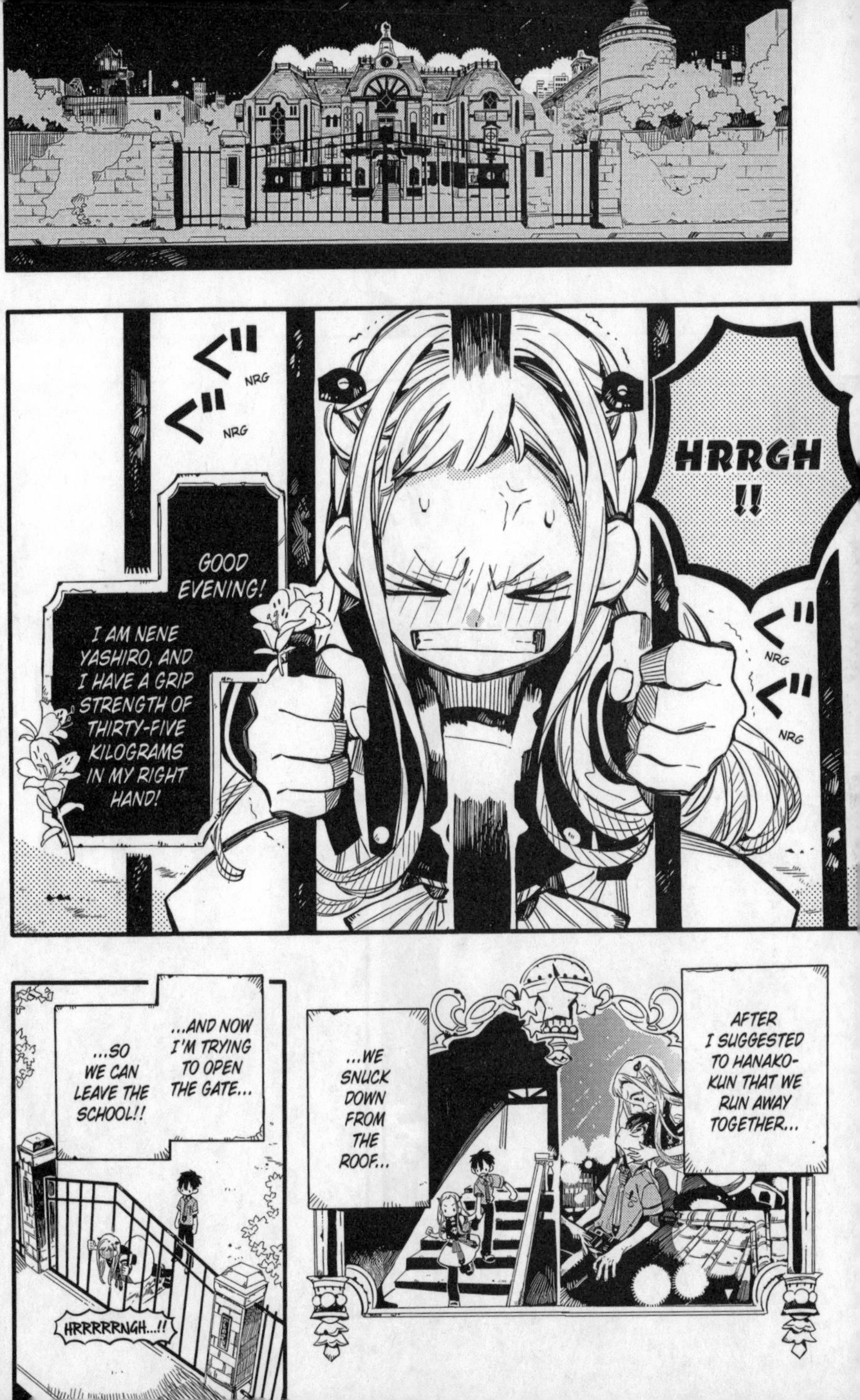
HRRGH!!
NRG
NRG
NRG
NRG
GOOD EVENING!
I AM NENE YASHIRO, AND I HAVE A GRIP STRENGTH OF THIRTY-FIVE KILOGRAMS IN MY RIGHT HAND!
AFTER I SUGGESTED TO HANAKO-KUN THAT WE RUN AWAY TOGETHER...
...WE SNUCK DOWN FROM THE ROOF...
...AND NOW I'M TRYING TO OPEN THE GATE...
...SO WE CAN LEAVE THE SCHOOL!!
HRRRRRNGH...!!

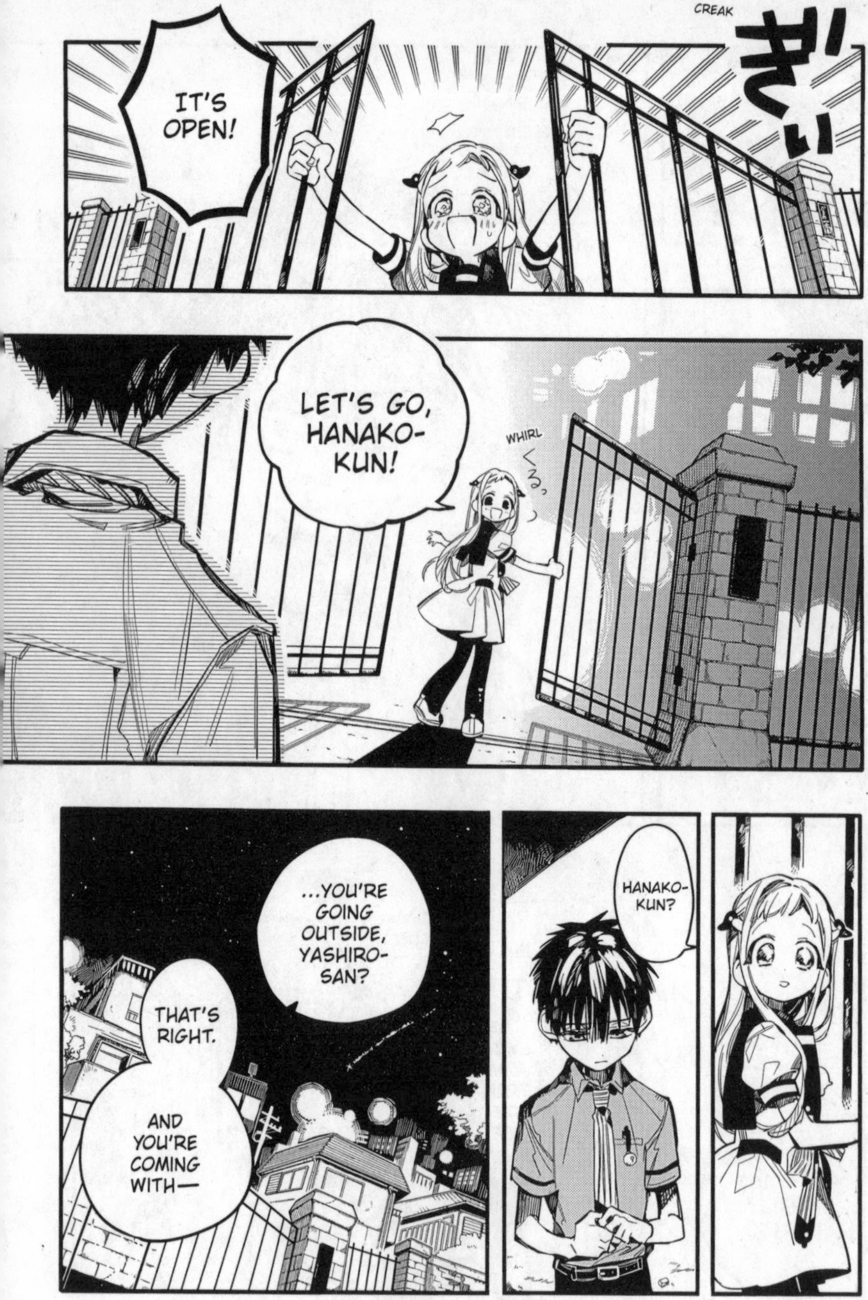
CREAK
ぎぃ
IT'S OPEN!
LET'S GO, HANAKO-KUN!
WHIRL
くるっ
HANAKO-KUN?
...YOU'RE GOING OUTSIDE, YASHIRO-SAN?
THAT'S RIGHT.
AND YOU'RE COMING WITH—

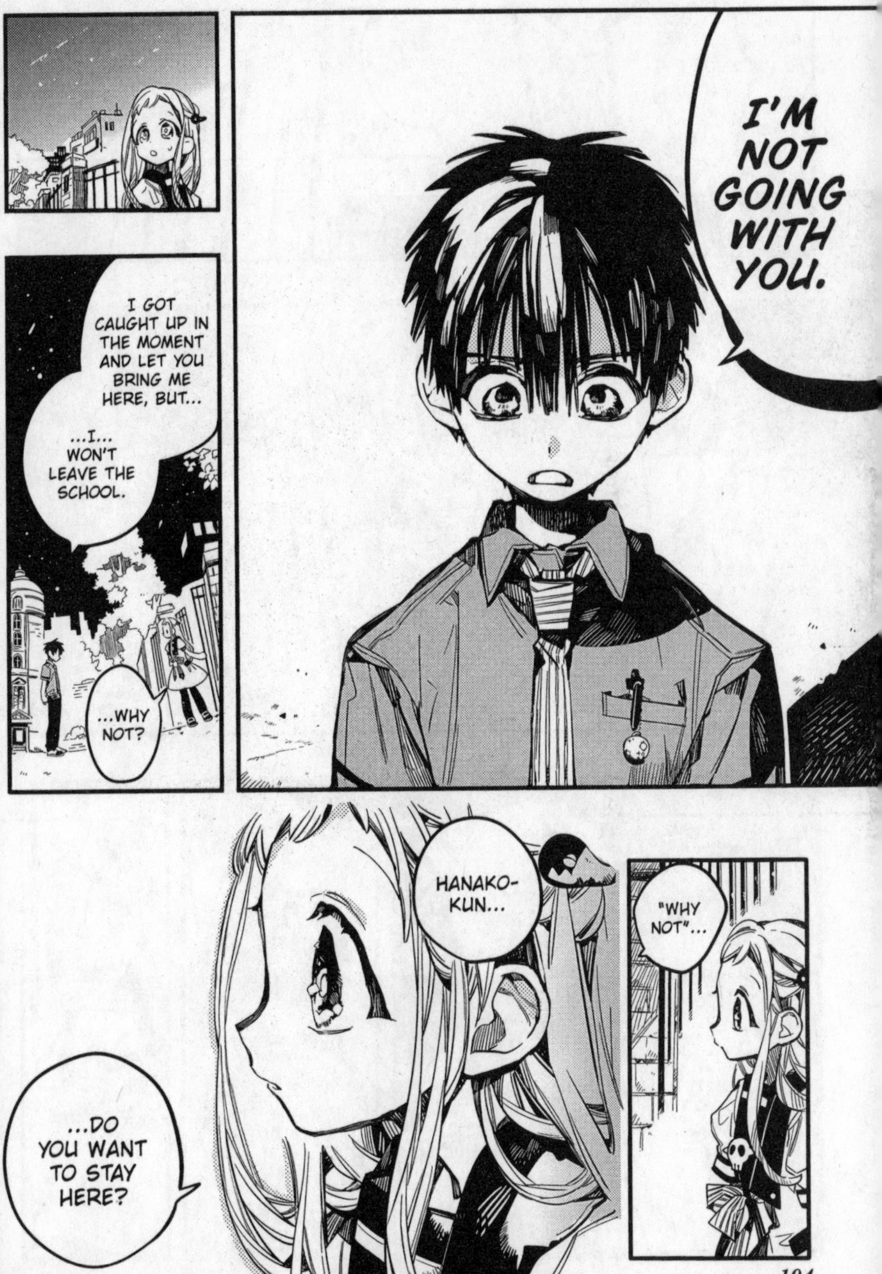
I'M NOT GOING WITH YOU.
I GOT CAUGHT UP IN THE MOMENT AND LET YOU BRING ME HERE, BUT...
...I... WON'T LEAVE THE SCHOOL.
...WHY NOT?
"WHY NOT"...
HANAKO-KUN...
...DO YOU WANT TO STAY HERE?

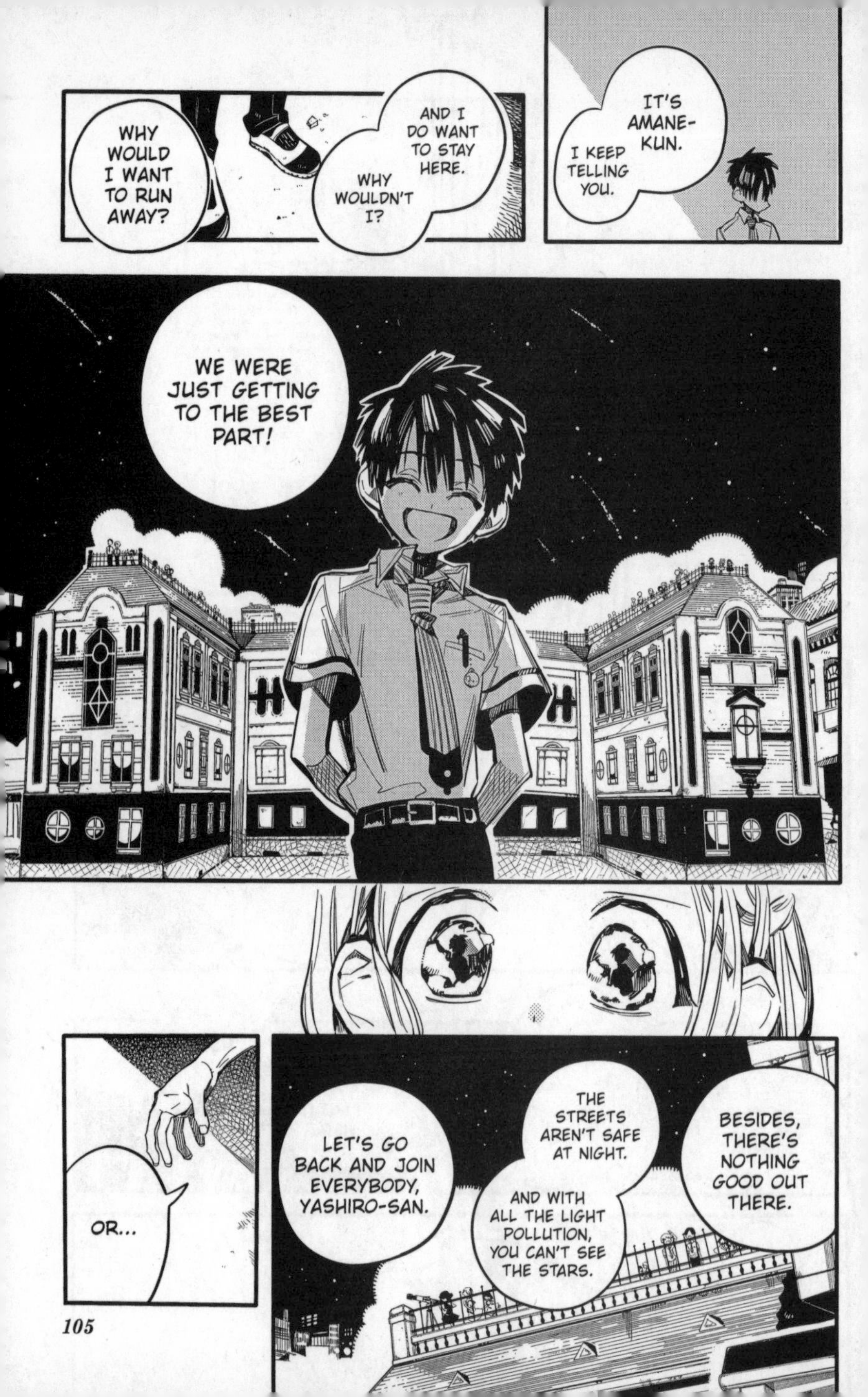

IT'S AMANE-KUN.
I KEEP TELLING YOU.
AND I DO WANT TO STAY HERE.
WHY WOULDN'T I?
WHY WOULD I WANT TO RUN AWAY?
WE WERE JUST GETTING TO THE BEST PART!
BESIDES, THERE'S NOTHING GOOD OUT THERE.
THE STREETS AREN'T SAFE AT NIGHT.
AND WITH ALL THE LIGHT POLLUTION, YOU CAN'T SEE THE STARS.
LET'S GO BACK AND JOIN EVERYBODY, YASHIRO-SAN.
OR...

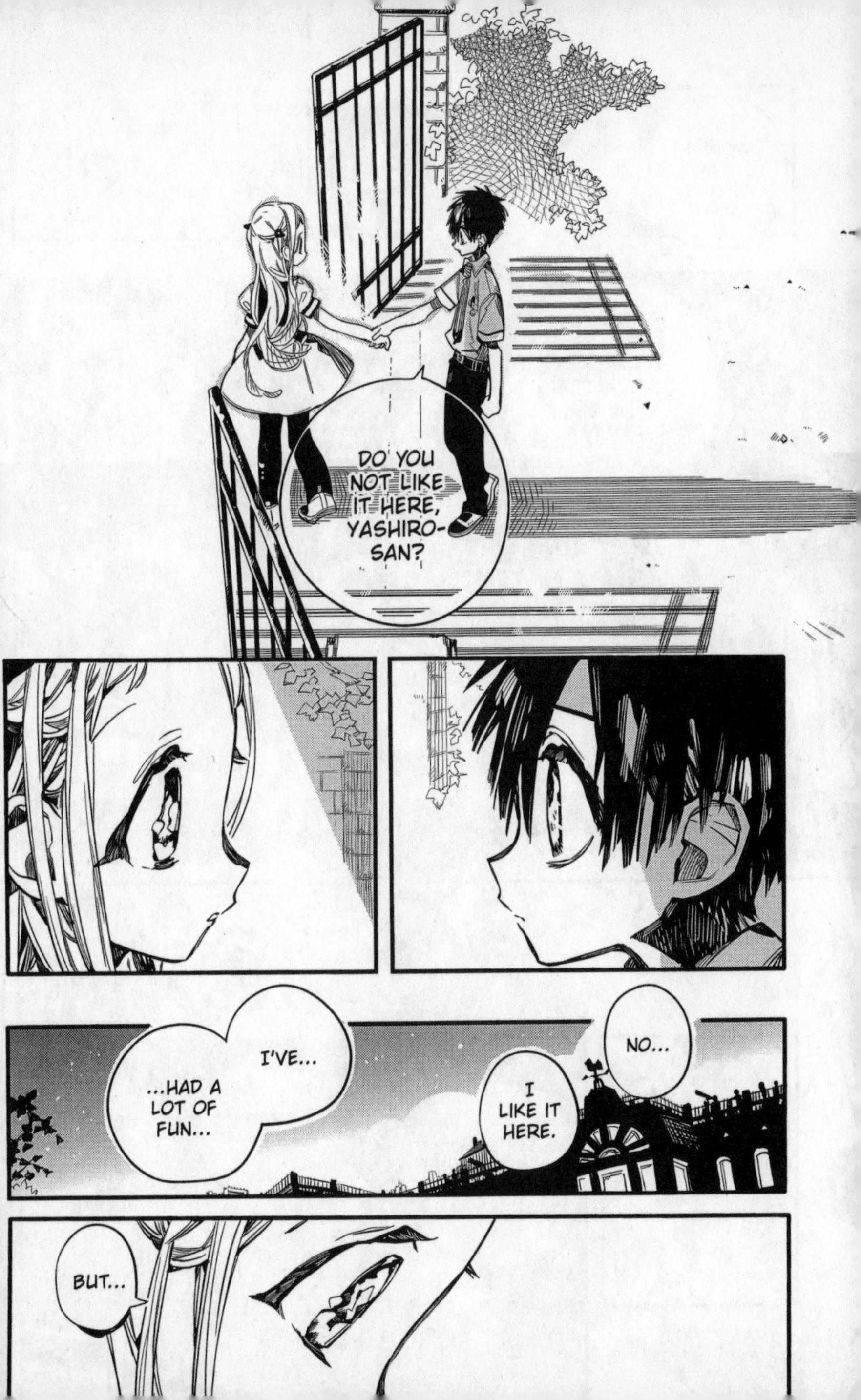
DO YOU NOT LIKE IT HERE, YASHIRO-SAN?
NO...
I LIKE IT HERE.
I'VE...
...HAD A LOT OF FUN...
BUT...

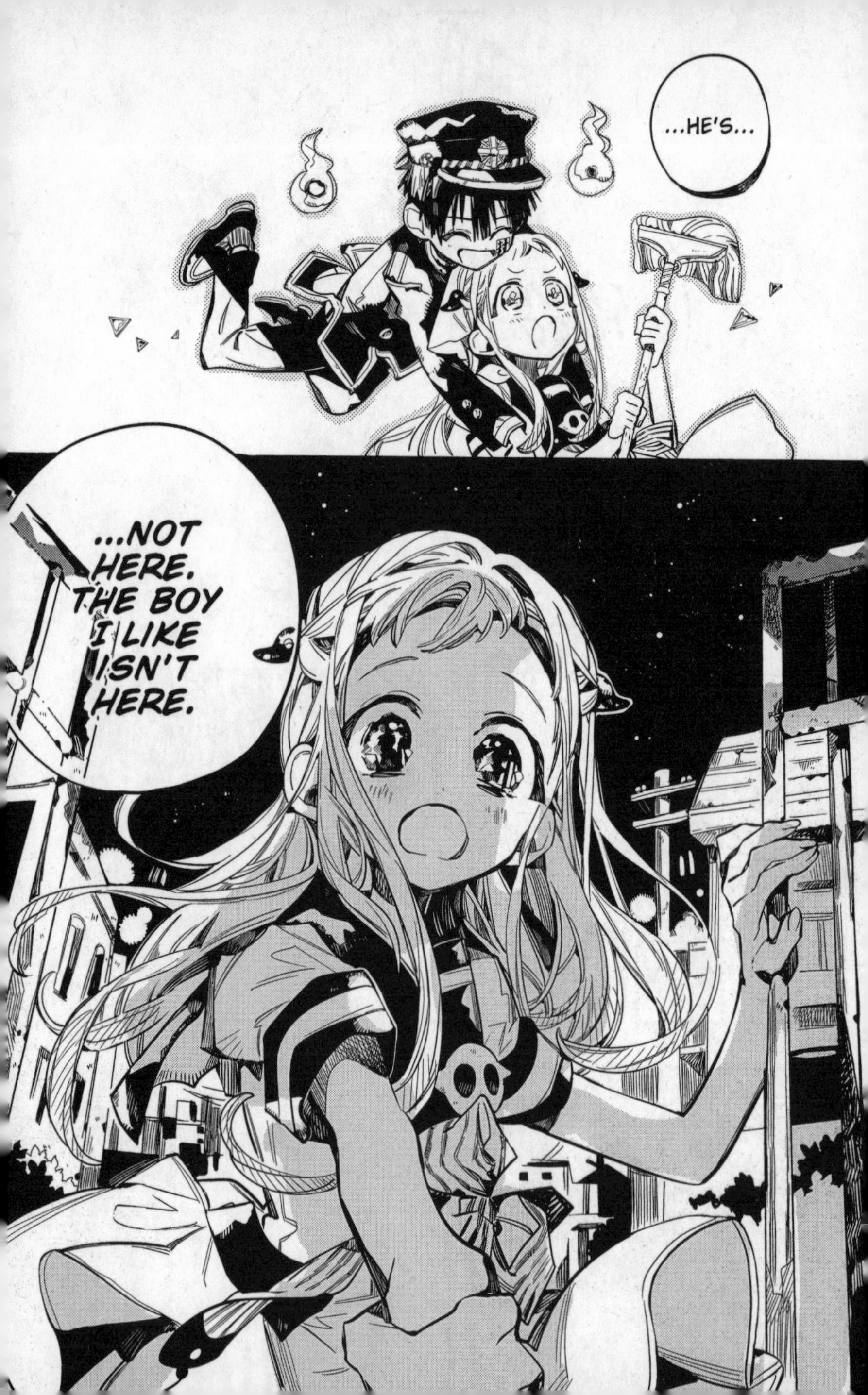
...HE'S...
...NOT HERE. THE BOY I LIKE ISN'T HERE.

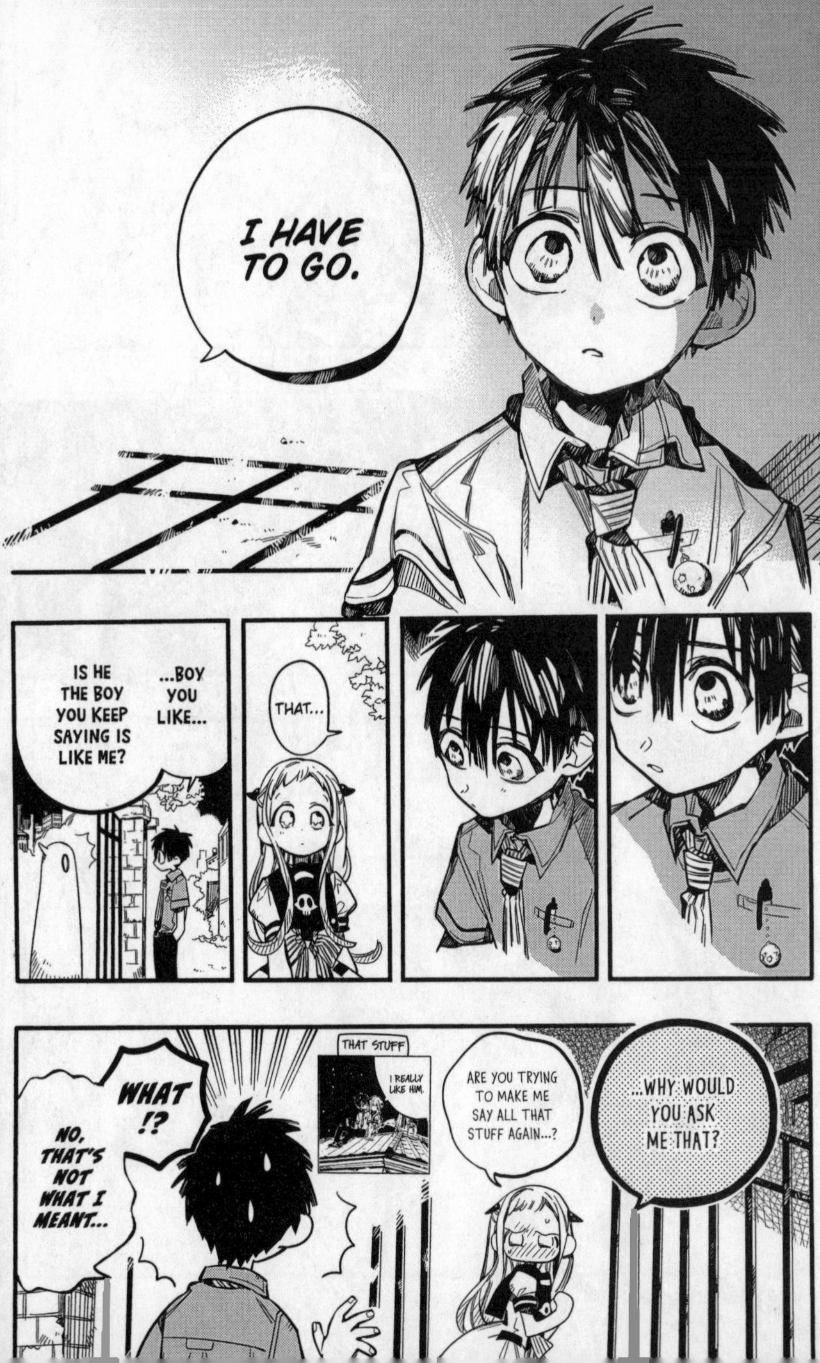
I HAVE TO GO.
THAT...
...BOY YOU LIKE...
IS HE THE BOY YOU KEEP SAYING IS LIKE ME?
...WHY WOULD YOU ASK ME THAT?
ARE YOU TRYING TO MAKE ME SAY ALL THAT STUFF AGAIN...?
THAT STUFF
I REALLY LIKE HIM.
WHAT !?
NO, THAT'S NOT WHAT I MEANT...

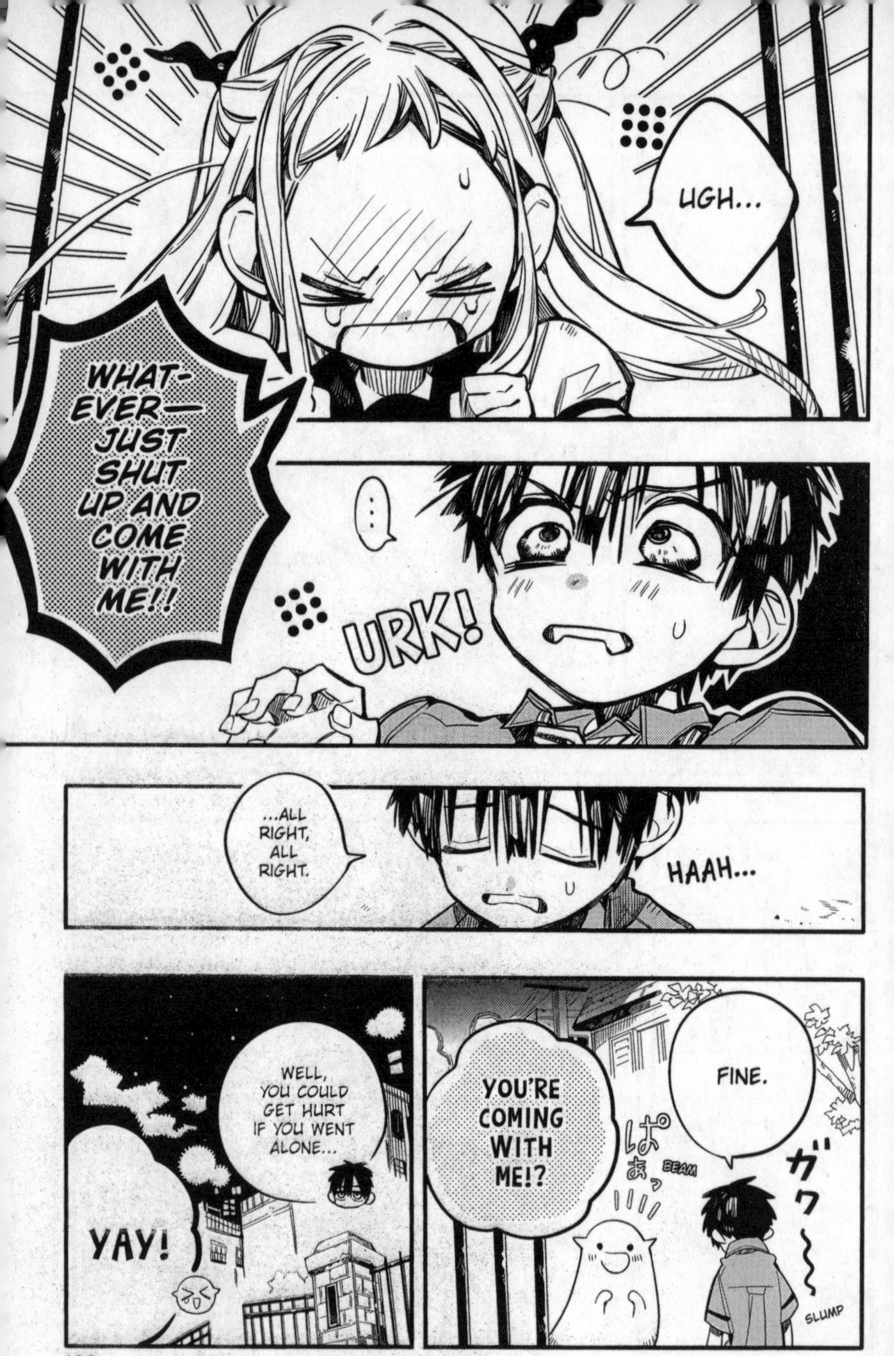
UGH...
WHAT-EVER— JUST SHUT UP AND COME WITH ME!!
...
URK!
HAAH...
...ALL RIGHT, ALL RIGHT.
FINE.
YOU'RE COMING WITH ME!?
ぱあっ
BEAM
ガクー
SLUMP
WELL, YOU COULD GET HURT IF YOU WENT ALONE...
YAY!

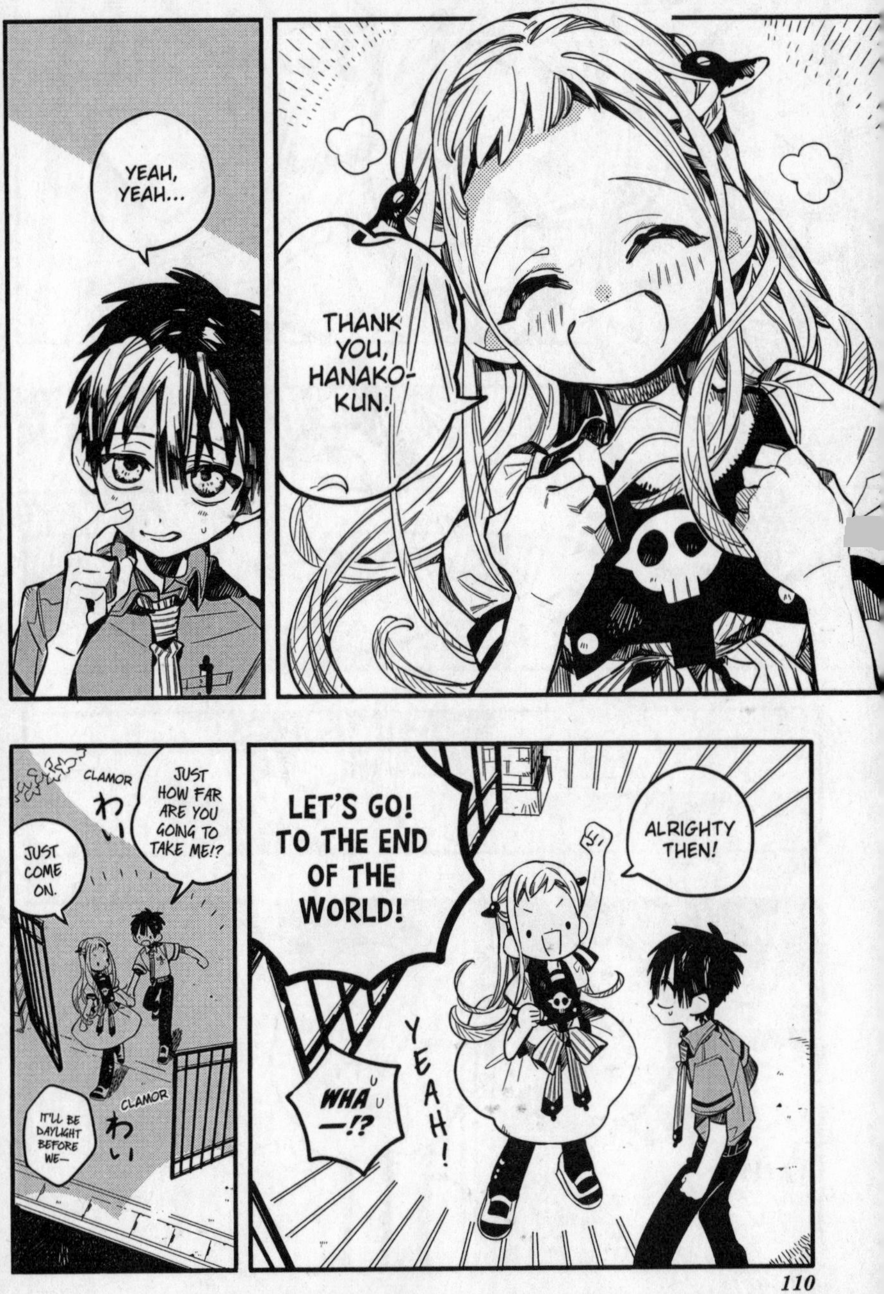
THANK YOU, HANAKO-KUN!
YEAH, YEAH...
ALRIGHTY THEN!
LET'S GO! TO THE END OF THE WORLD!
YEAH!
WHA—!?
CLAMOR
わい
JUST HOW FAR ARE YOU GOING TO TAKE ME!?
JUST COME ON.
CLAMOR
わい
IT'LL BE DAYLIGHT BEFORE WE—

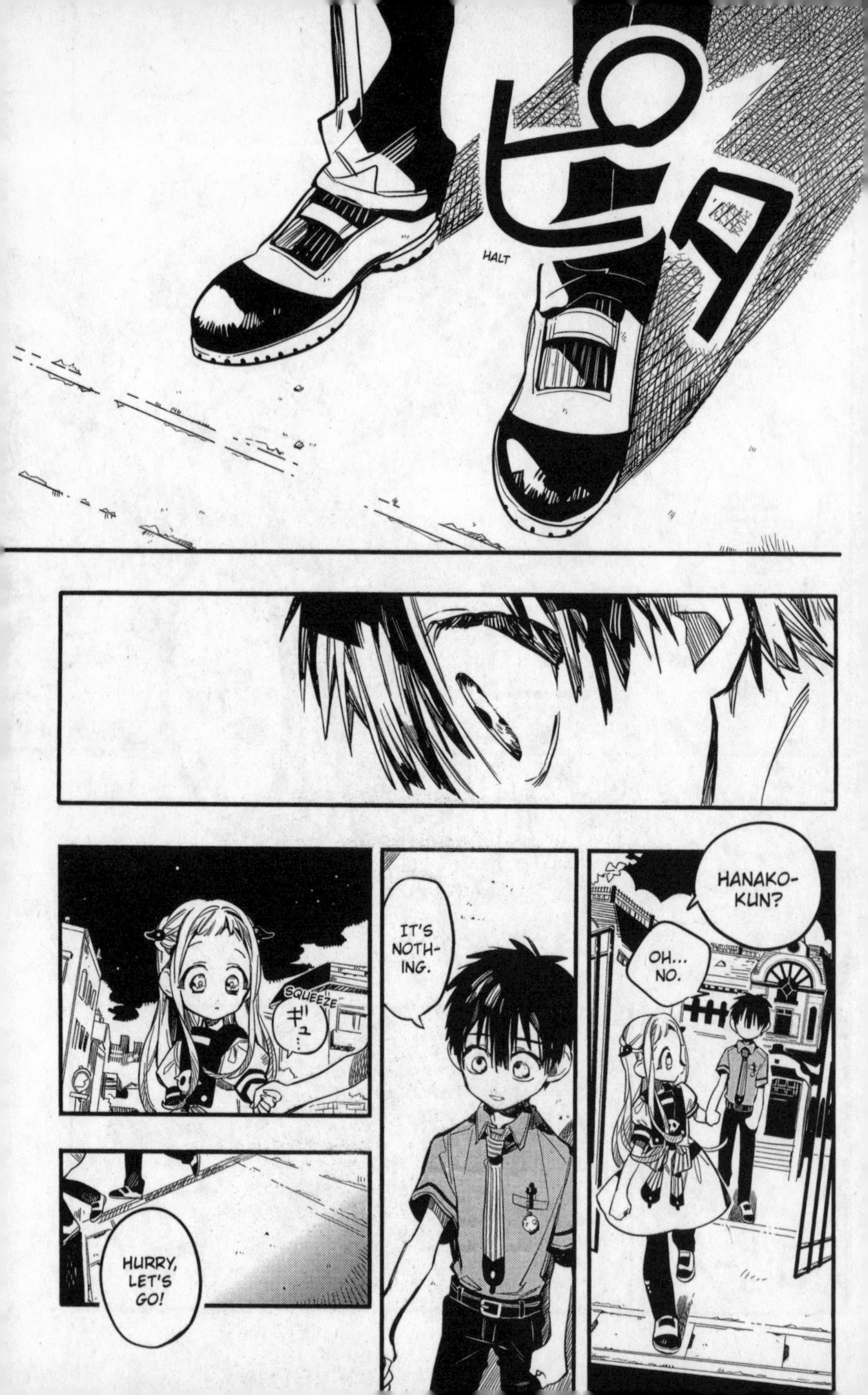
ピタ
HALT
HANAKO-KUN?
OH... NO.
IT'S NOTHING.
SQUEEZE
ギュ…
HURRY, LET'S GO!

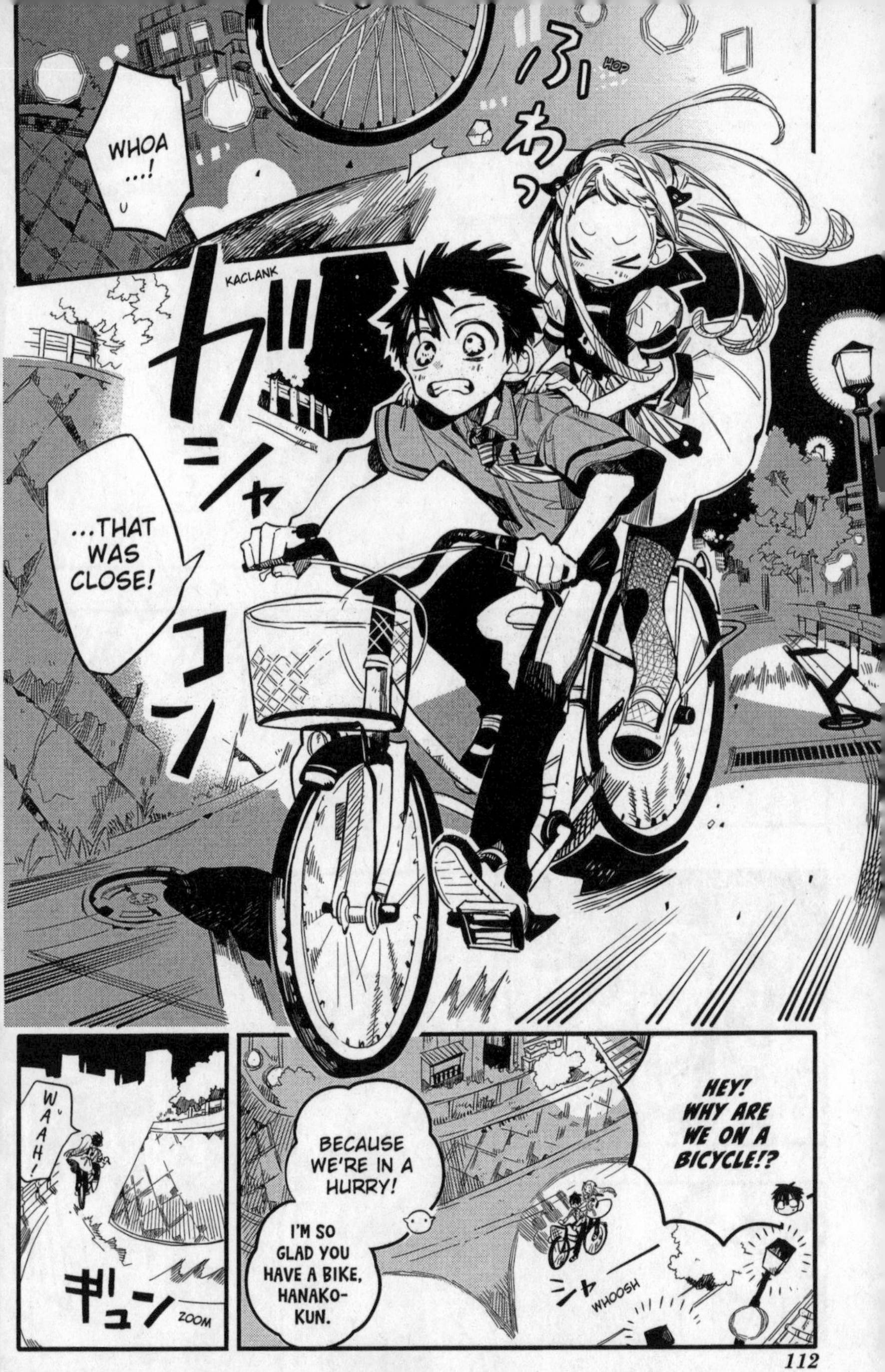
HOP
WHOA ...!
KACLANK
...THAT WAS CLOSE!
HEY! WHY ARE WE ON A BICYCLE!?
BECAUSE WE'RE IN A HURRY!
I'M SO GLAD YOU HAVE A BIKE, HANAKO-KUN.
WHOOSH
WAAH!
ZOOM

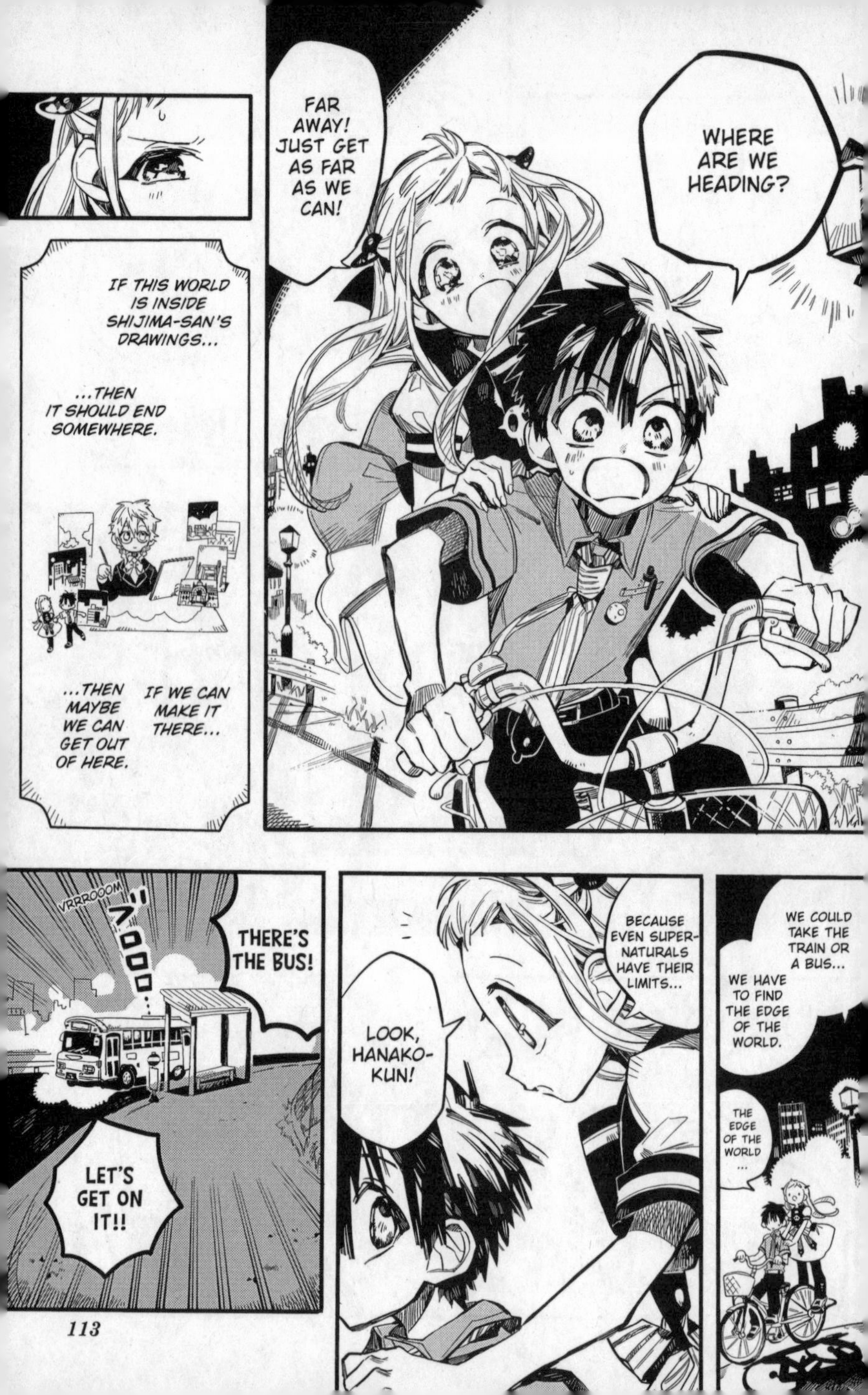
WHERE ARE WE HEADING?
FAR AWAY! JUST GET AS FAR AS WE CAN!
IF THIS WORLD IS INSIDE SHIJIMA-SAN'S DRAWINGS...
...THEN IT SHOULD END SOMEWHERE.
IF WE CAN MAKE IT THERE...
...THEN MAYBE WE CAN GET OUT OF HERE.
WE COULD TAKE THE TRAIN OR A BUS...
WE HAVE TO FIND THE EDGE OF THE WORLD.
THE EDGE OF THE WORLD...
BECAUSE EVEN SUPER-NATURALS HAVE THEIR LIMITS...
LOOK, HANAKO-KUN!
VRRROOOM
ブロロロ…
THERE'S THE BUS!
LET'S GET ON IT!!

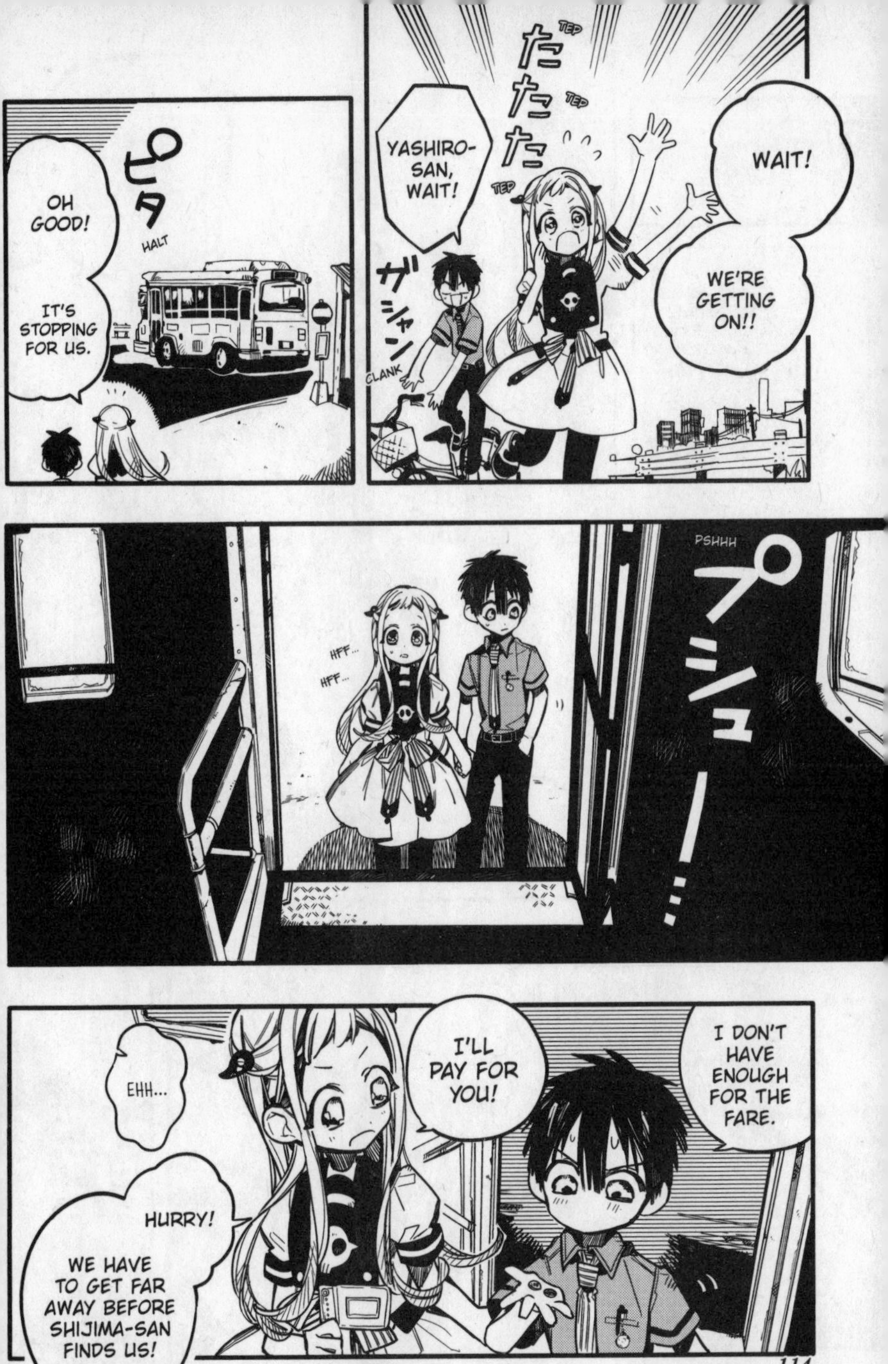
WAIT!
WE'RE GETTING ON!!
たたた
TEP TEP TEP
YASHIRO-SAN, WAIT!
ザシャン
CLANK
ピタ
HALT
OH GOOD!
IT'S STOPPING FOR US.
PSHHH
プシュー…
HFF... HFF...
I DON'T HAVE ENOUGH FOR THE FARE.
I'LL PAY FOR YOU!
EHH...
HURRY!
WE HAVE TO GET FAR AWAY BEFORE SHIJIMA-SAN FINDS US!

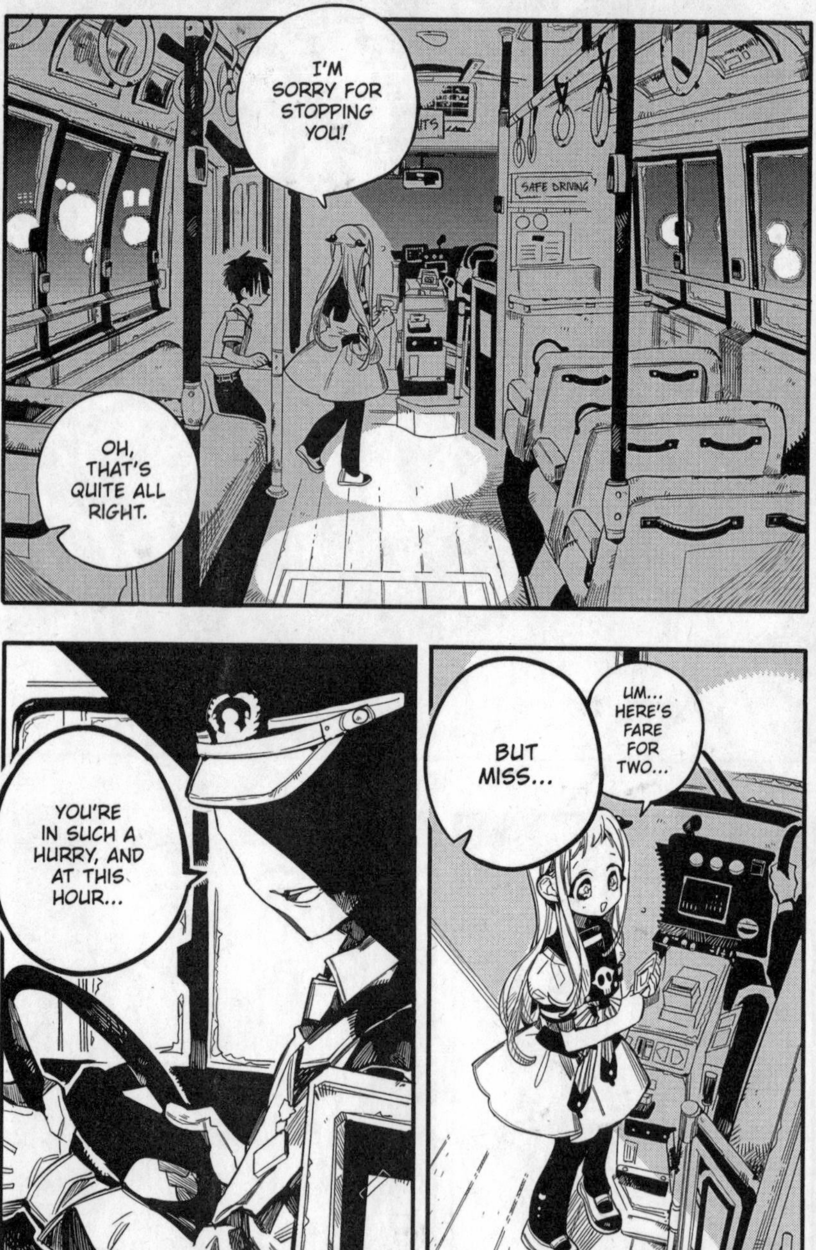
I'M SORRY FOR STOPPING YOU!
SAFE DRIVING
OH, THAT'S QUITE ALL RIGHT.
UM... HERE'S FARE FOR TWO...
BUT MISS...
YOU'RE IN SUCH A HURRY, AND AT THIS HOUR...

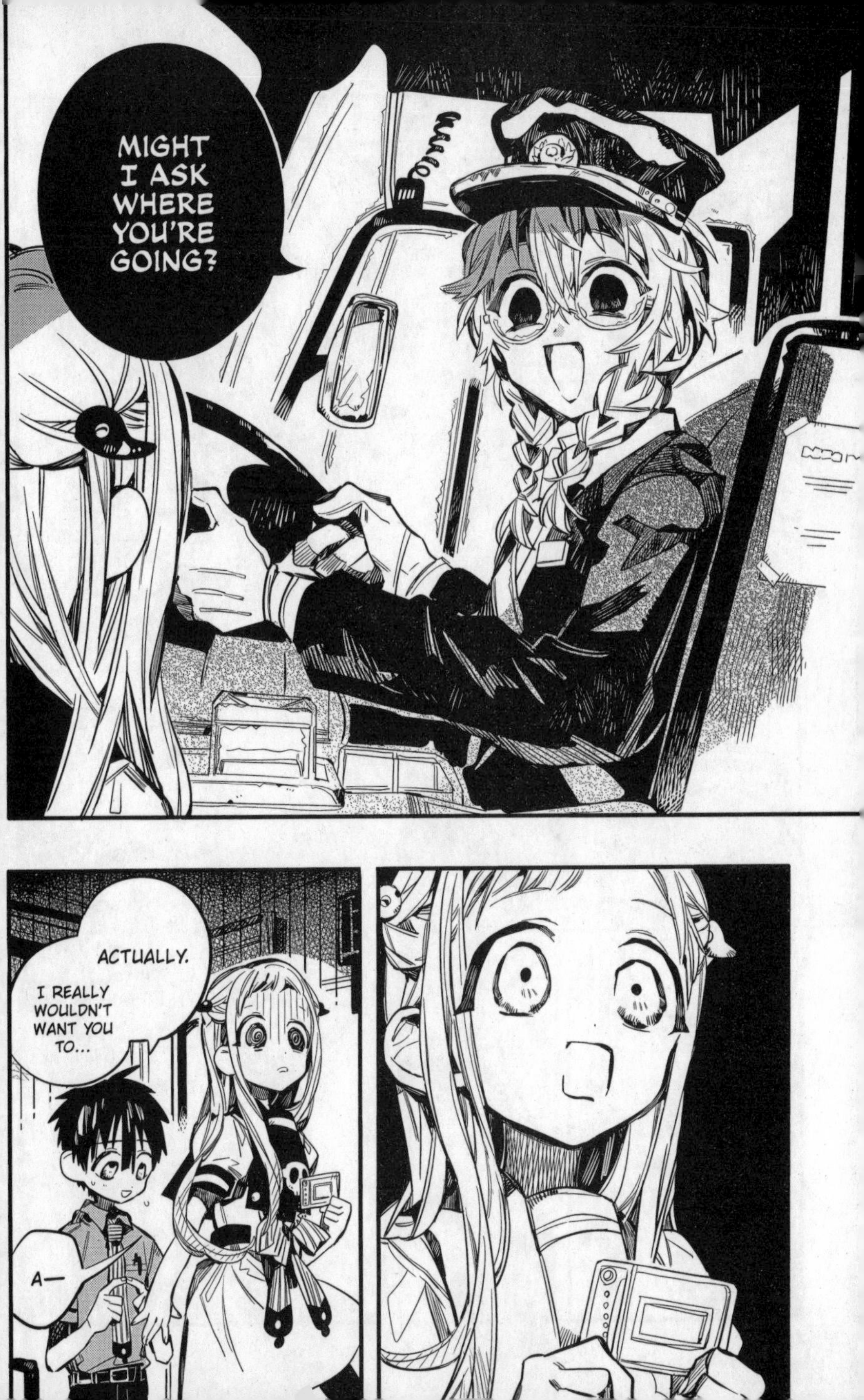
MIGHT I ASK WHERE YOU'RE GOING?
ACTUALLY.
I REALLY WOULDN'T WANT YOU TO...
A—

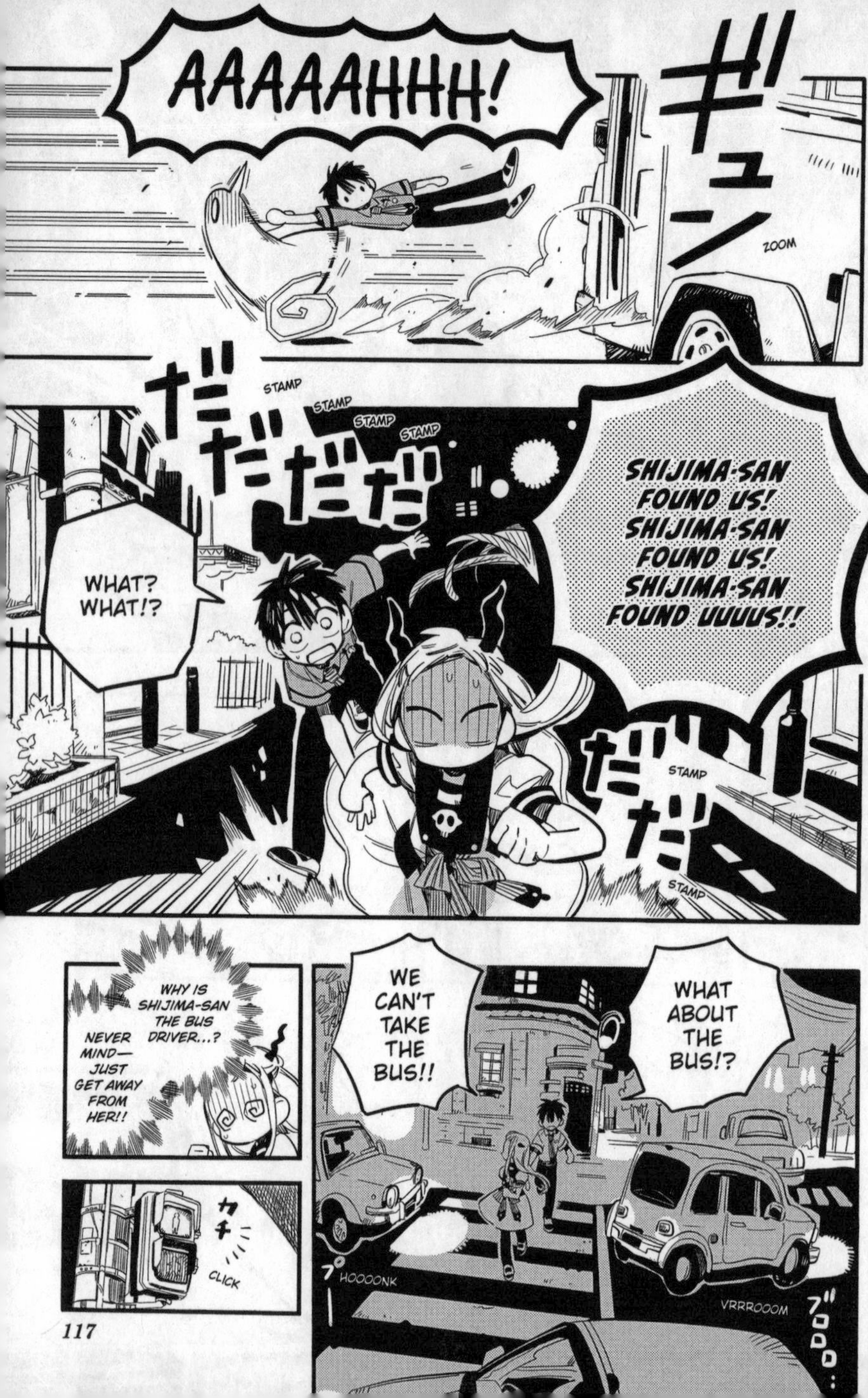
AAAAAHHH!
ギューン
ZOOM
SHIJIMA-SAN FOUND US! SHIJIMA-SAN FOUND US! SHIJIMA-SAN FOUND UUUUS!!
だだ
STAMP
STAMP
だだだ
STAMP
STAMP
STAMP
STAMP
WHAT? WHAT!?
WHAT ABOUT THE BUS!?
WE CAN'T TAKE THE BUS!!
プ
HOOOONK
ブロロロ…
VRRROOOM
WHY IS SHIJIMA-SAN THE BUS DRIVER...?
NEVER MIND— JUST GET AWAY FROM HER!!
カチ
CLICK

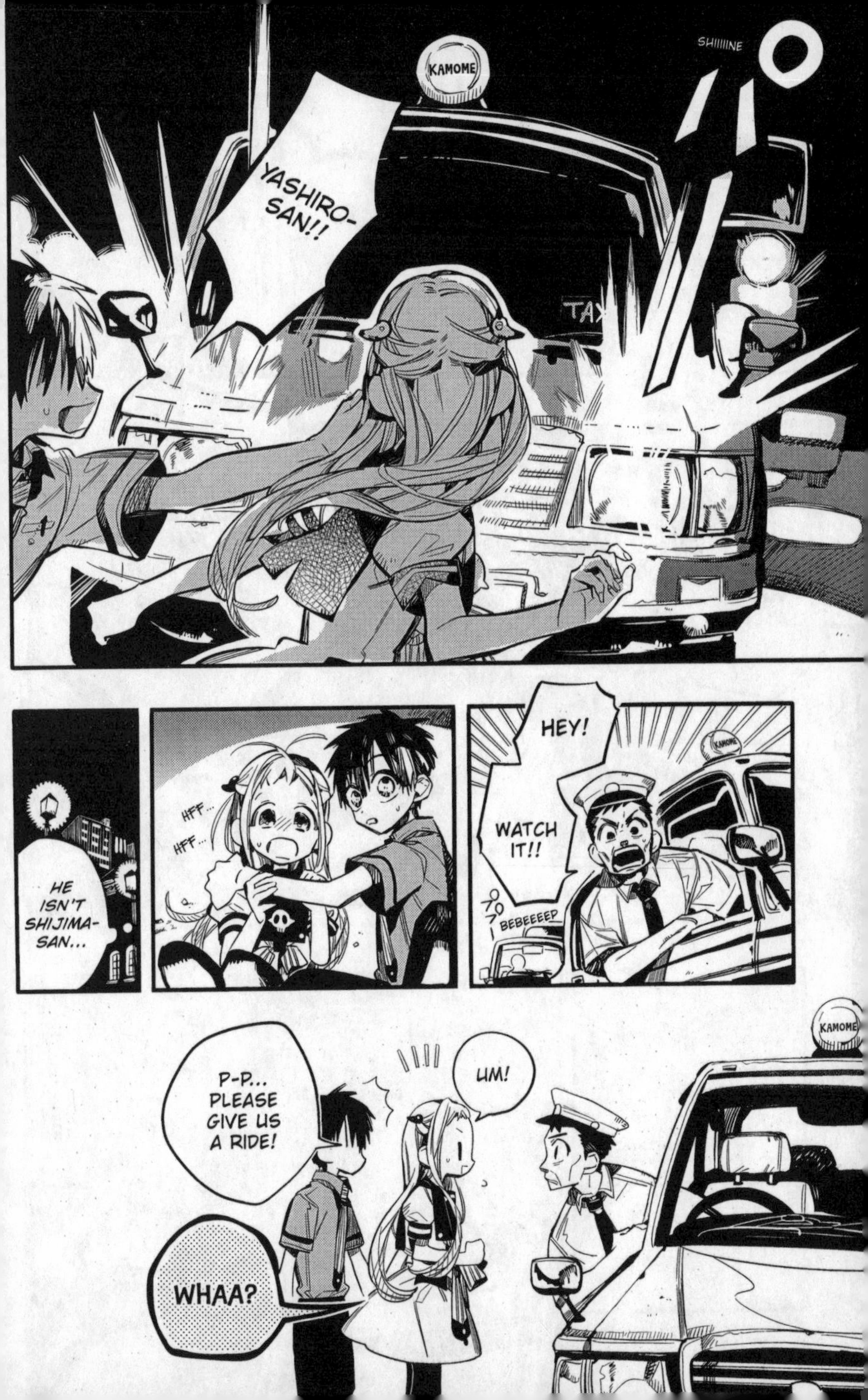
SHIIIINE
KAMOME
YASHIRO-SAN!!
HEY!
KAMOME
WATCH IT!!
BEBEEEEP
HFF...
HFF...
HE ISN'T SHIJIMA-SAN...
KAMOME
UM!
P-P... PLEASE GIVE US A RIDE!
WHAA?

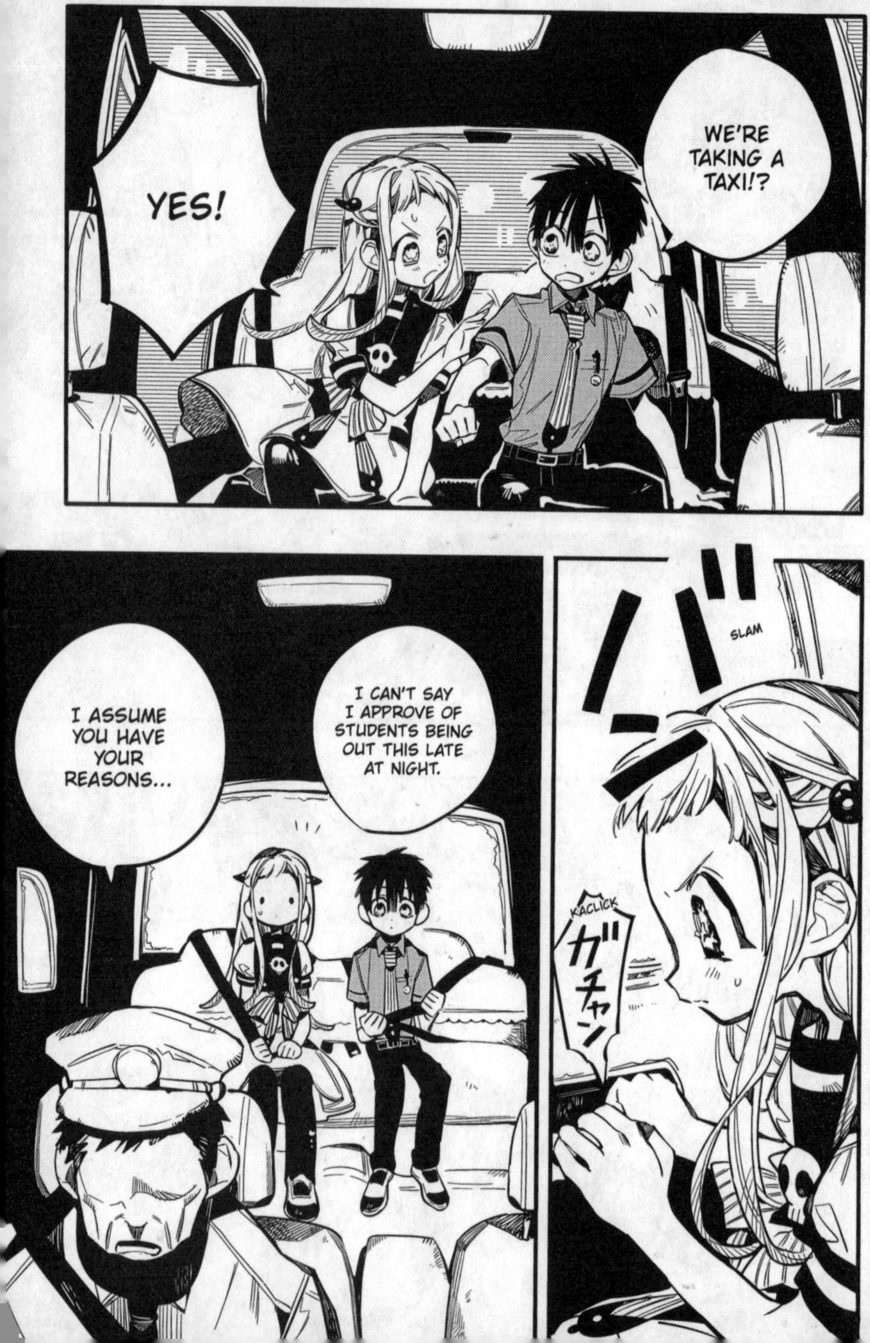
WE'RE TAKING A TAXI!?
YES!
バン
SLAM
ガチャン
KACLICK
I CAN'T SAY I APPROVE OF STUDENTS BEING OUT THIS LATE AT NIGHT.
I ASSUME YOU HAVE YOUR REASONS...

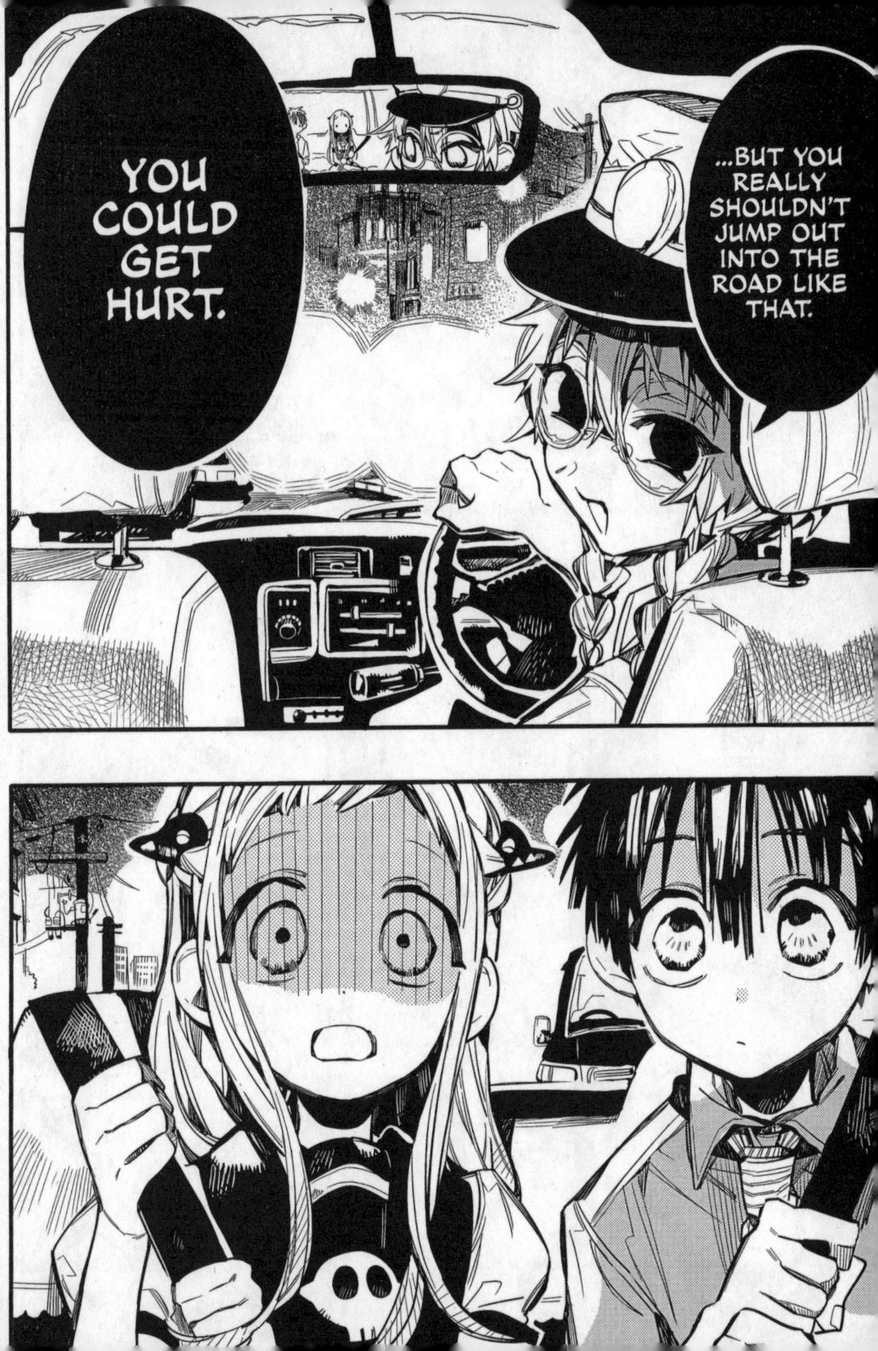
...BUT YOU REALLY SHOULDN'T JUMP OUT INTO THE ROAD LIKE THAT.
YOU COULD GET HURT.

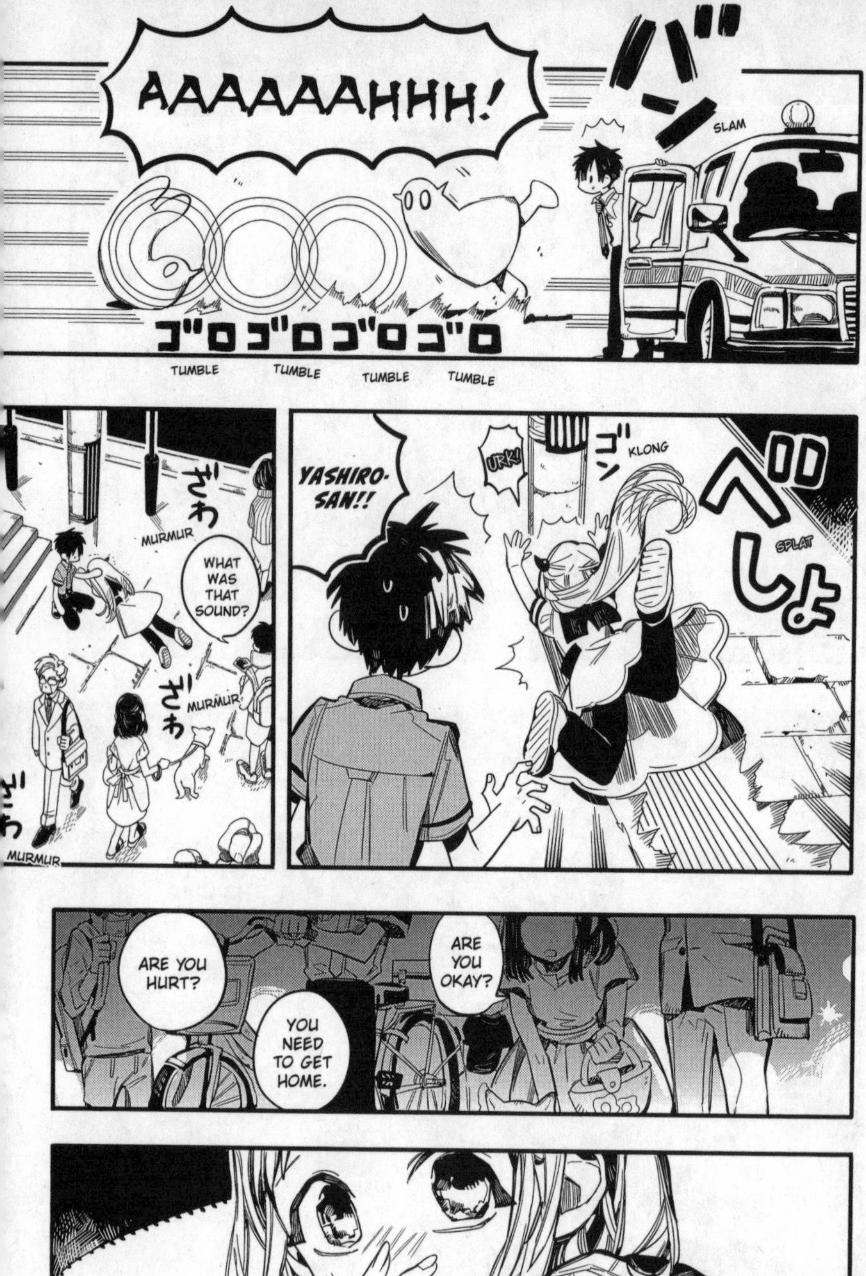

バーン
SLAM
AAAAAAHHH!
ゴロゴロゴロゴロ
TUMBLE
TUMBLE
TUMBLE
TUMBLE
YASHIRO-SAN!!
URK!
ゴン
KLONG
べしょ
SPLAT
ざわ
MURMUR
WHAT WAS THAT SOUND?
ざわ
MURMUR
ざわ
MURMUR
ARE YOU OKAY?
YOU NEED TO GET HOME.
ARE YOU HURT?

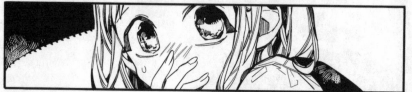

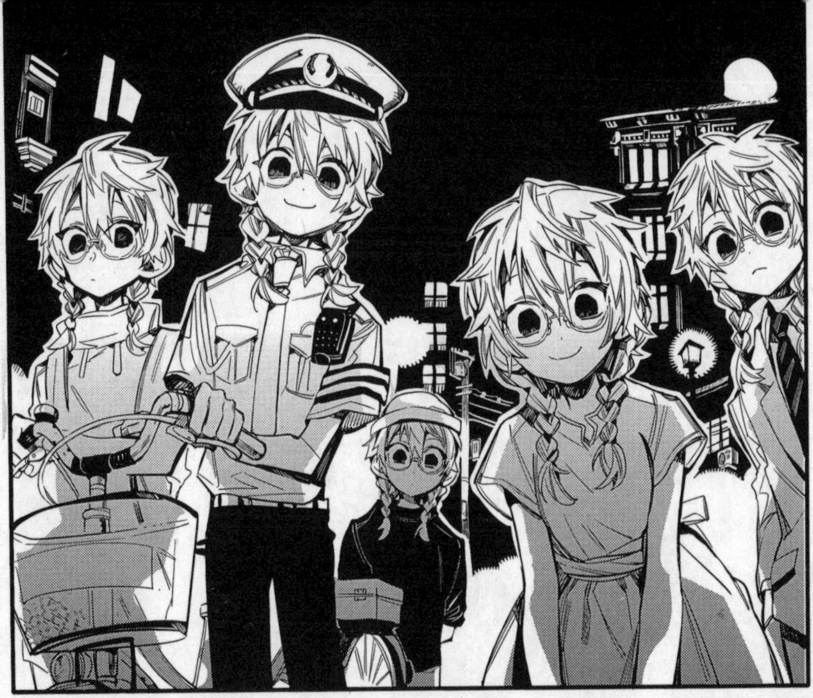

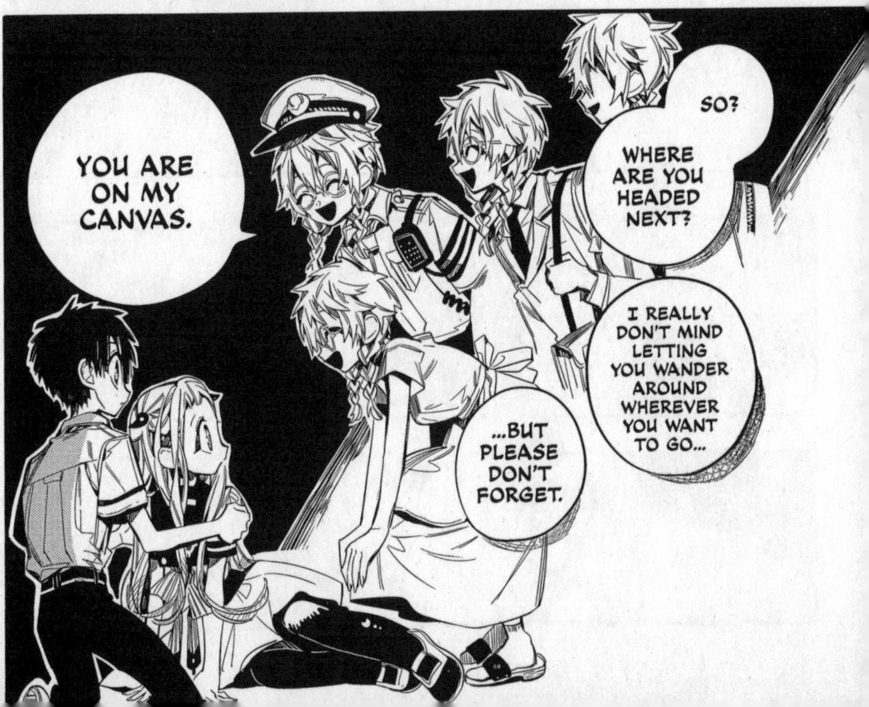
SO?
WHERE ARE YOU HEADED NEXT?
I REALLY DON'T MIND LETTING YOU WANDER AROUND WHEREVER YOU WANT TO GO...
...BUT PLEASE DON'T FORGET.
YOU ARE ON MY CANVAS.

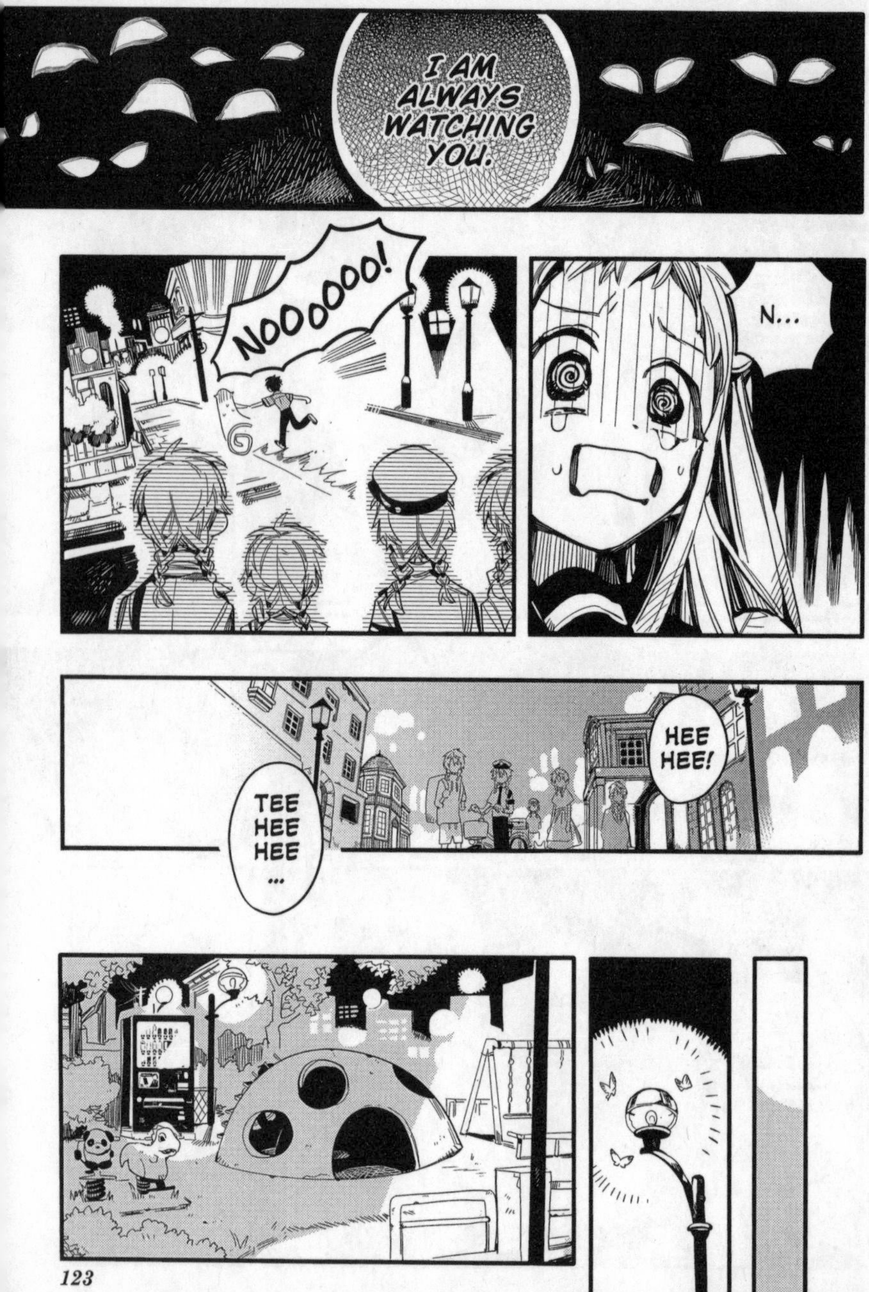
I AM ALWAYS WATCHING YOU.
N...
NOOOOOO!
HEE HEE!
TEE HEE HEE ...

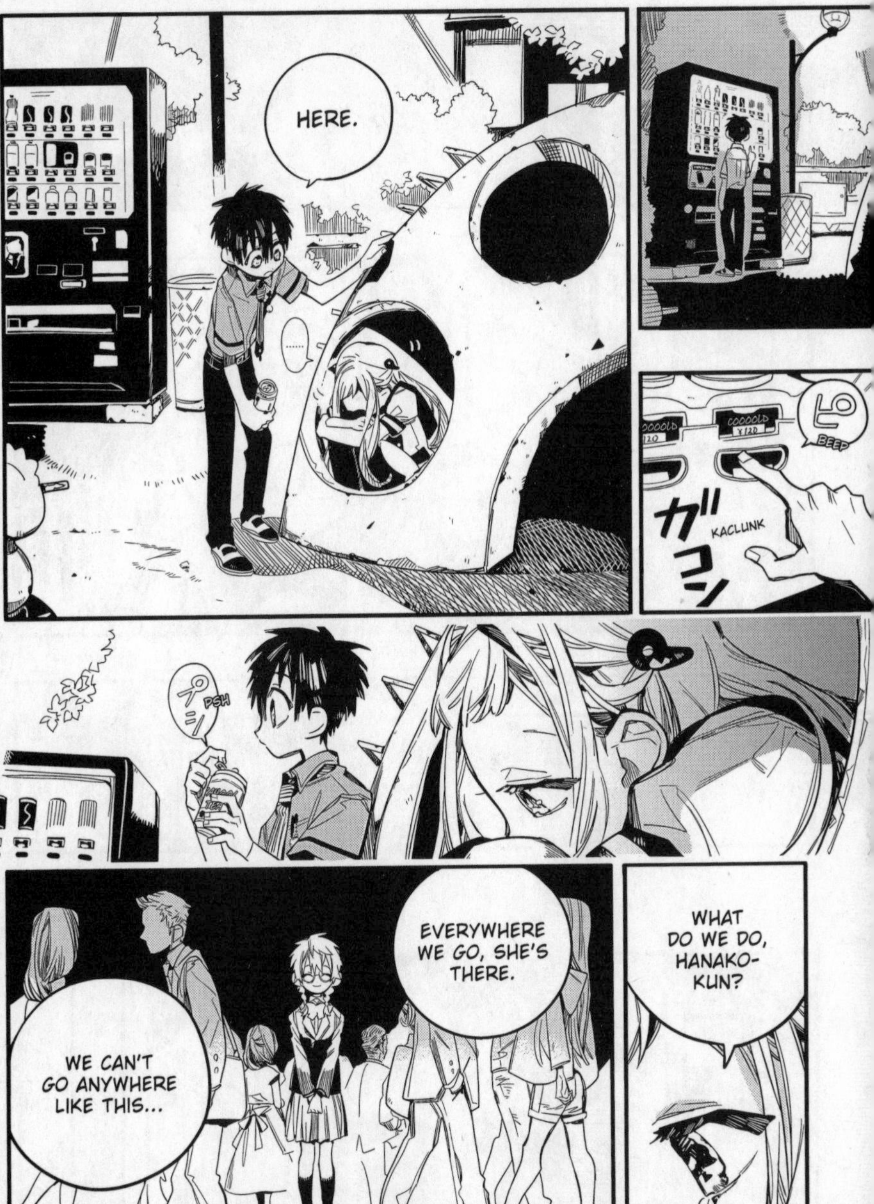
COOOOLD
¥120
BEEP
KACLUNK
HERE.
......
PSH
WHAT DO WE DO, HANAKO-KUN?
EVERYWHERE WE GO, SHE'S THERE.
WE CAN'T GO ANYWHERE LIKE THIS...

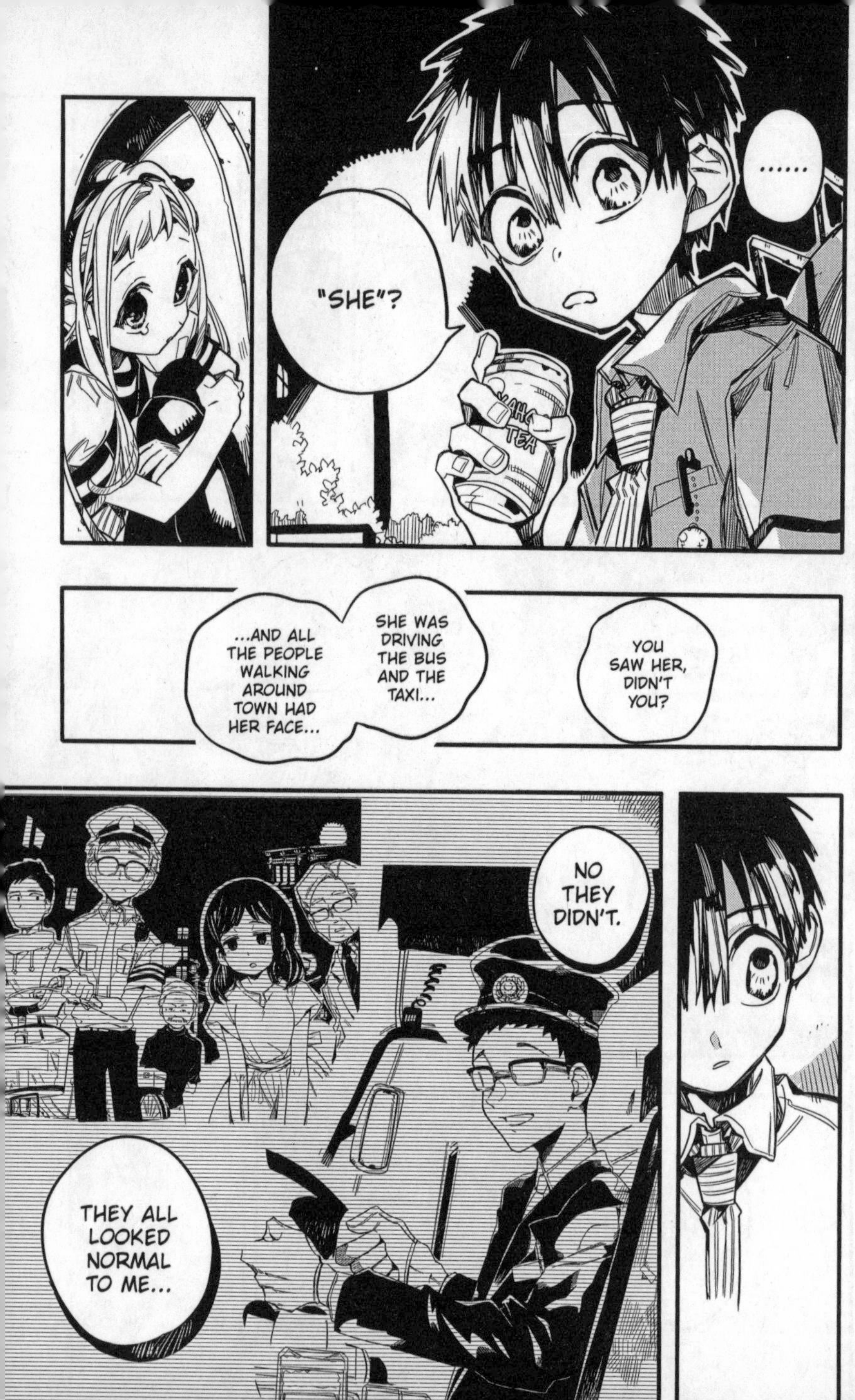
......
"SHE"?
YOU SAW HER, DIDN'T YOU?
SHE WAS DRIVING THE BUS AND THE TAXI...
...AND ALL THE PEOPLE WALKING AROUND TOWN HAD HER FACE...
NO THEY DIDN'T.
THEY ALL LOOKED NORMAL TO ME...

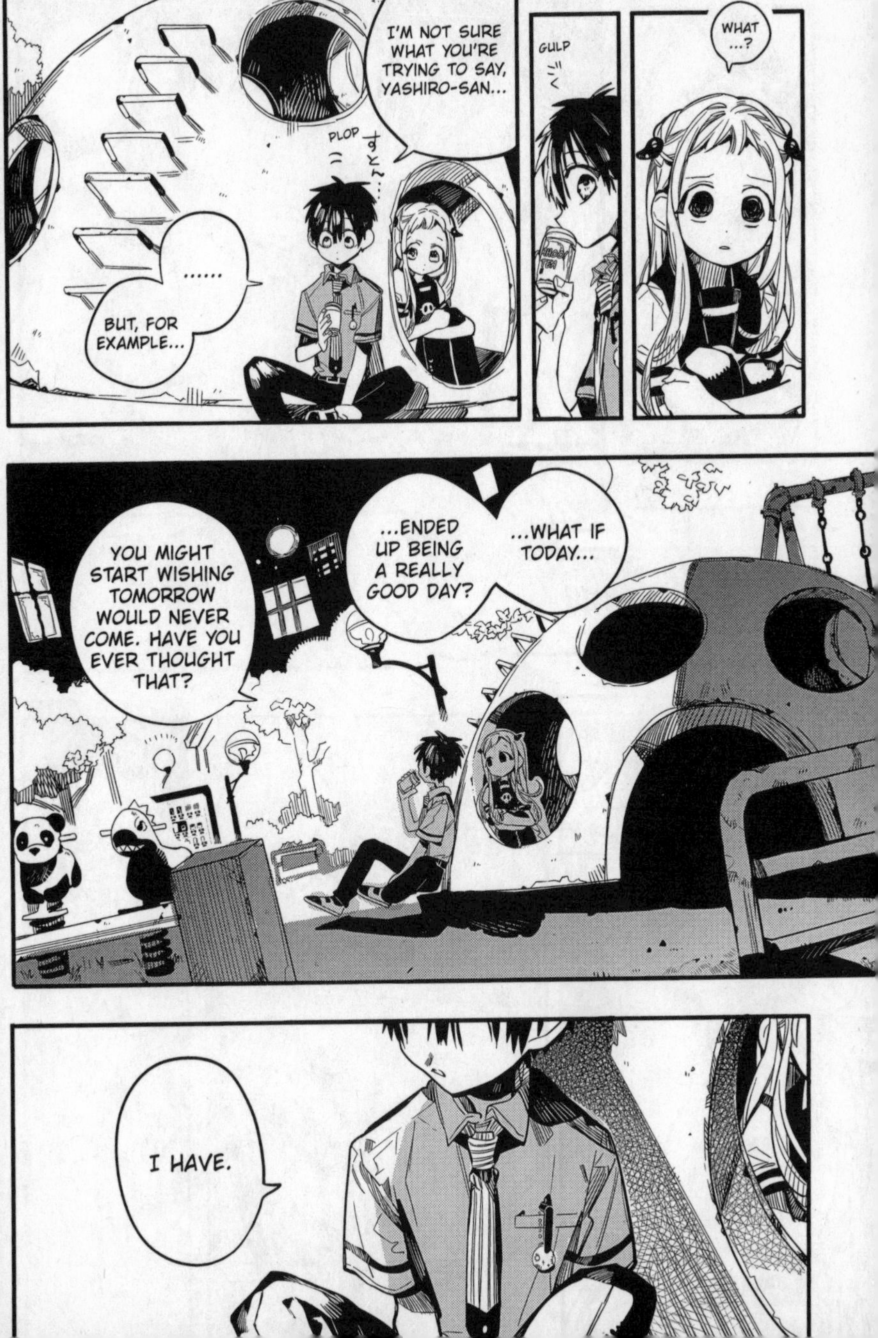
WHAT ...?
GULP
I'M NOT SURE WHAT YOU'RE TRYING TO SAY, YASHIRO-SAN...
PLOP
すとん…
......
BUT, FOR EXAMPLE...
...WHAT IF TODAY...
...ENDED UP BEING A REALLY GOOD DAY?
YOU MIGHT START WISHING TOMORROW WOULD NEVER COME. HAVE YOU EVER THOUGHT THAT?
I HAVE.

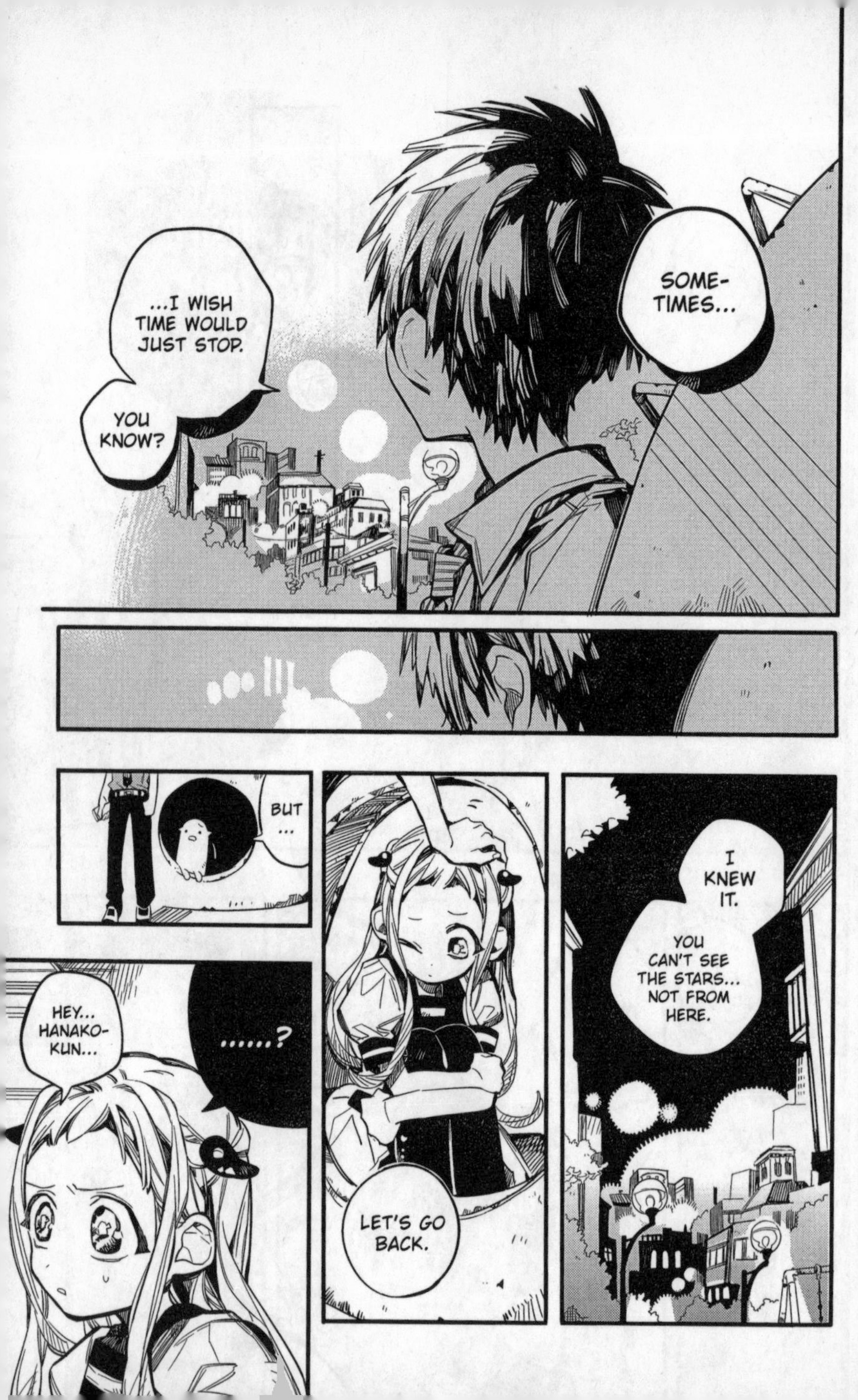
SOME-TIMES...
...I WISH TIME WOULD JUST STOP.
YOU KNOW?
I KNEW IT.
YOU CAN'T SEE THE STARS... NOT FROM HERE.
LET'S GO BACK.
BUT ...
HEY... HANAKO-KUN...
......?

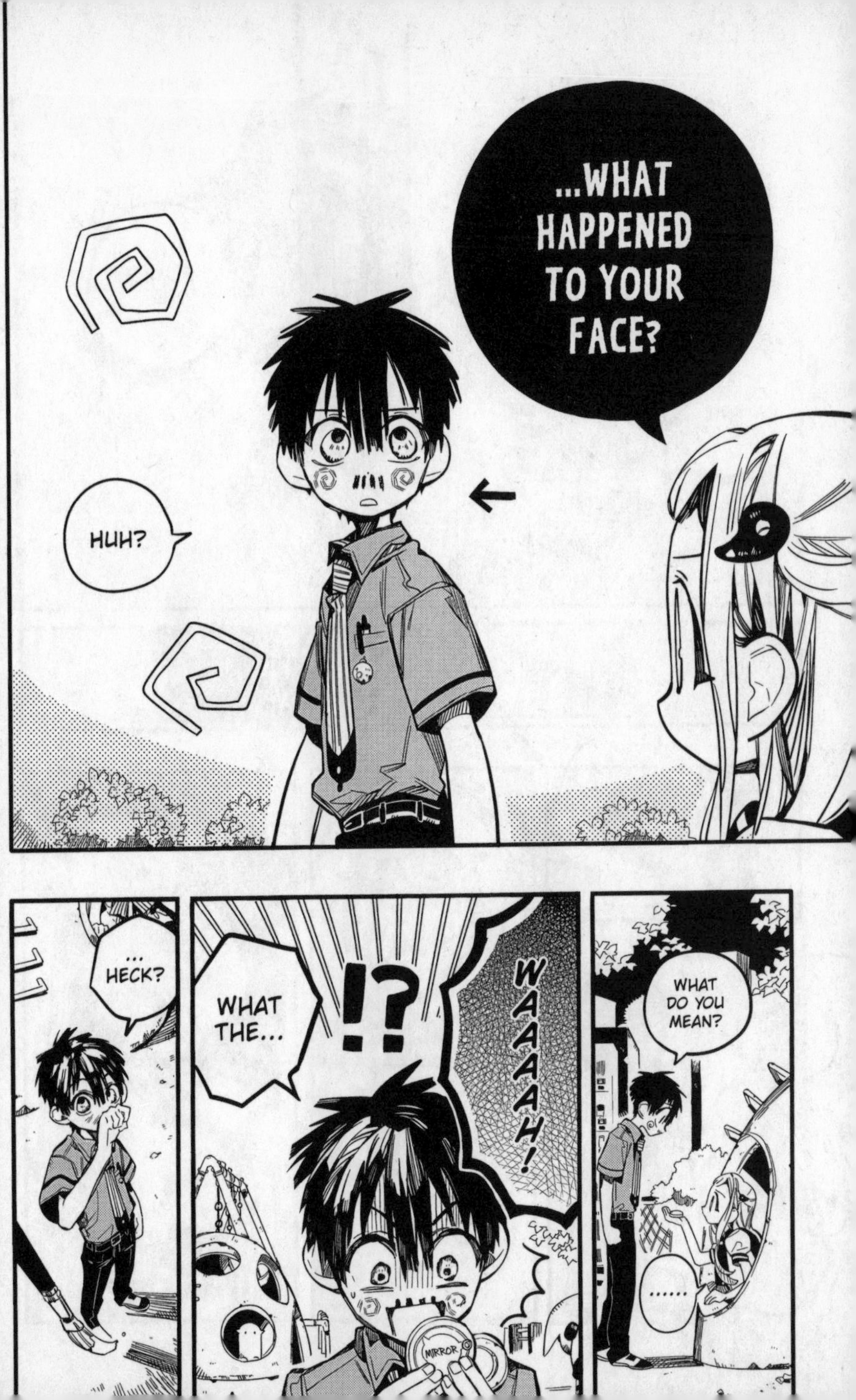
...WHAT HAPPENED TO YOUR FACE?
HUH?
WHAT DO YOU MEAN?
......
WAAAAH!
!?
WHAT THE...
MIRROR
... HECK?

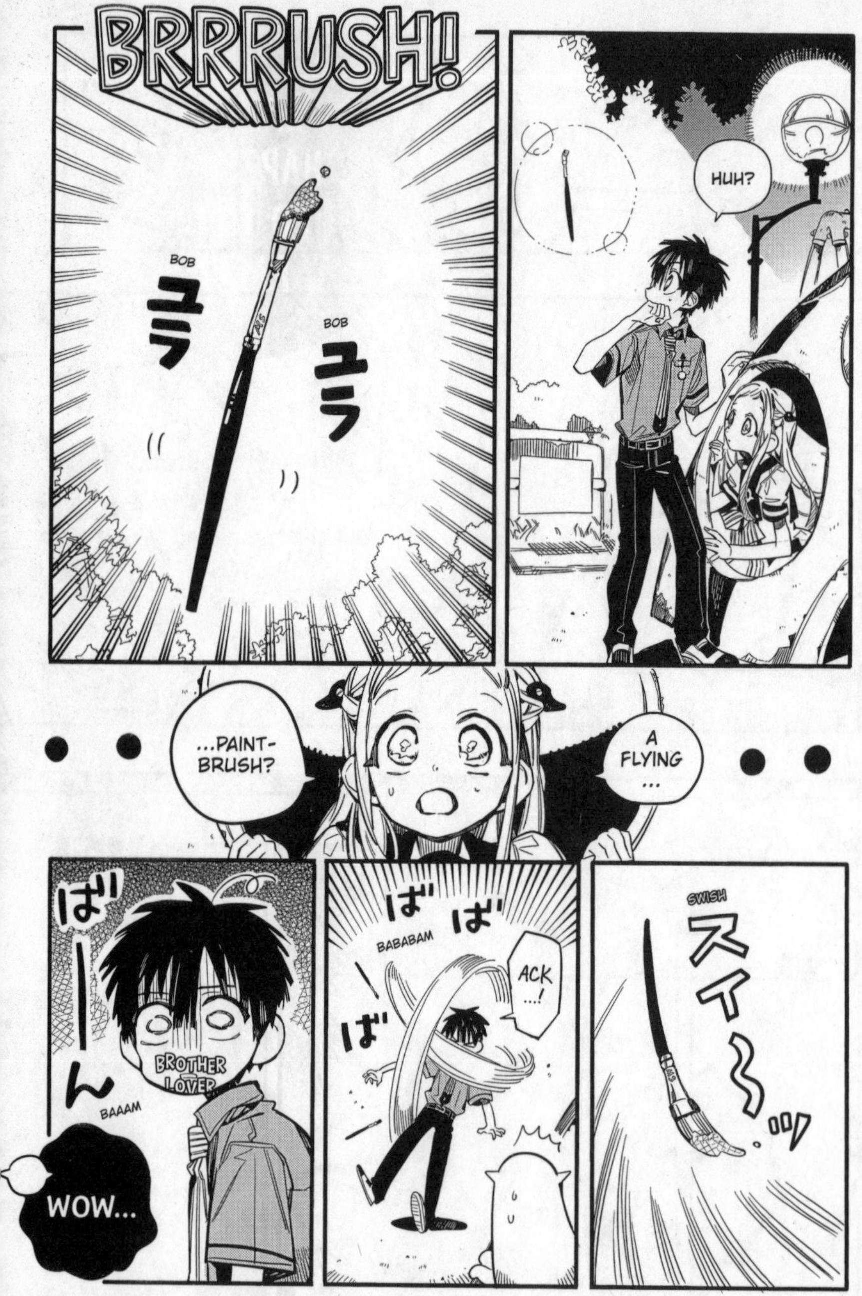
HUH?
BRRRUSH!
BOB
ユラ
BOB
ユラ
A FLYING ...
...PAINT-BRUSH?
SWISH
スィ〜
ばばば
BABABAM
ACK ...!
ばーん
BAAAM
BROTHER LOVER
WOW...

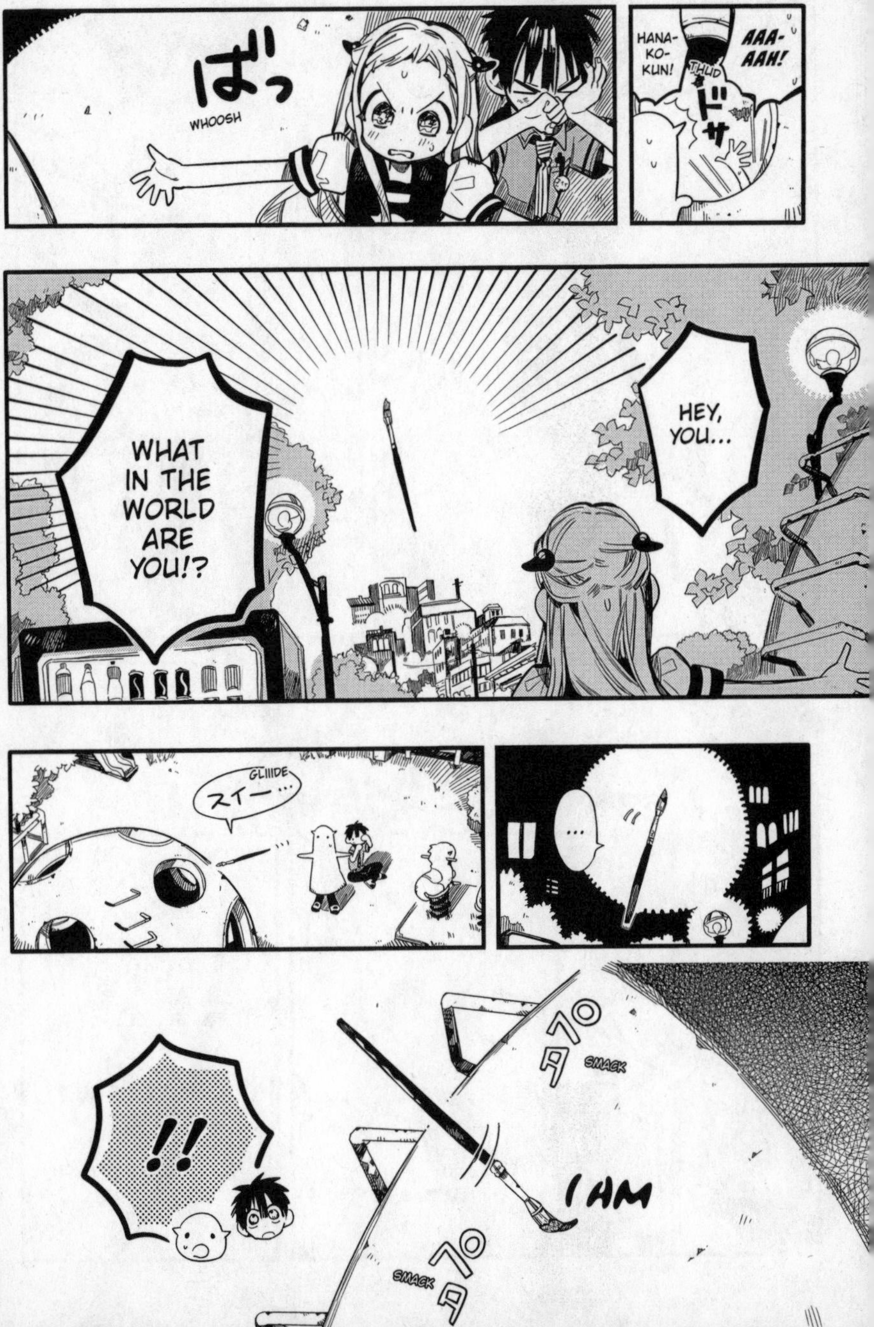

AAA-AAH!
HANA-KO-KUN!
THUD
ドサ
ばっ
WHOOSH
HEY, YOU...
WHAT IN THE WORLD ARE YOU!?
...
スイー…
GLIIIDE
SMACK
I AM
SMACK
!!

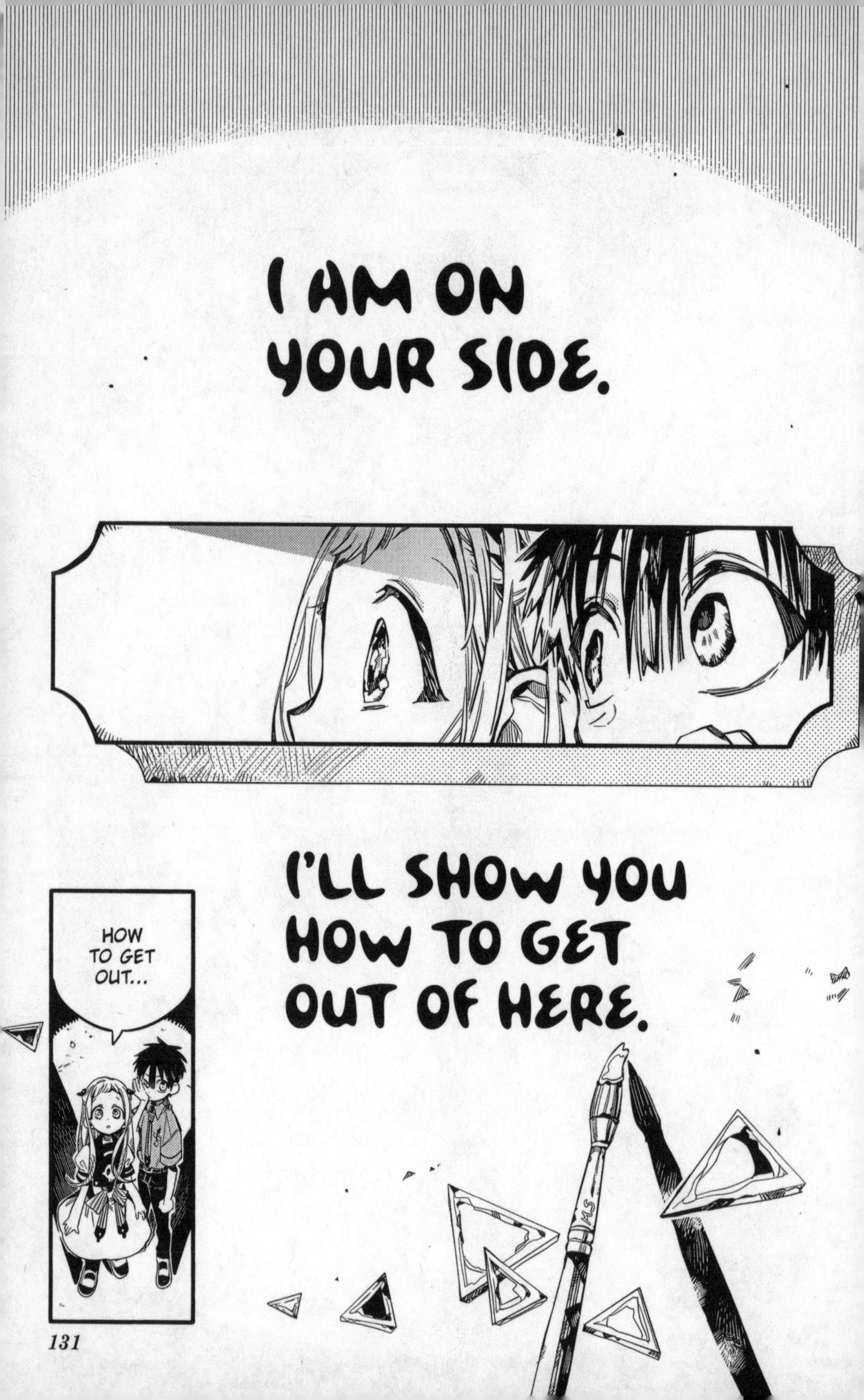
I AM ON YOUR SIDE.
I'LL SHOW YOU HOW TO GET OUT OF HERE.
HOW TO GET OUT...

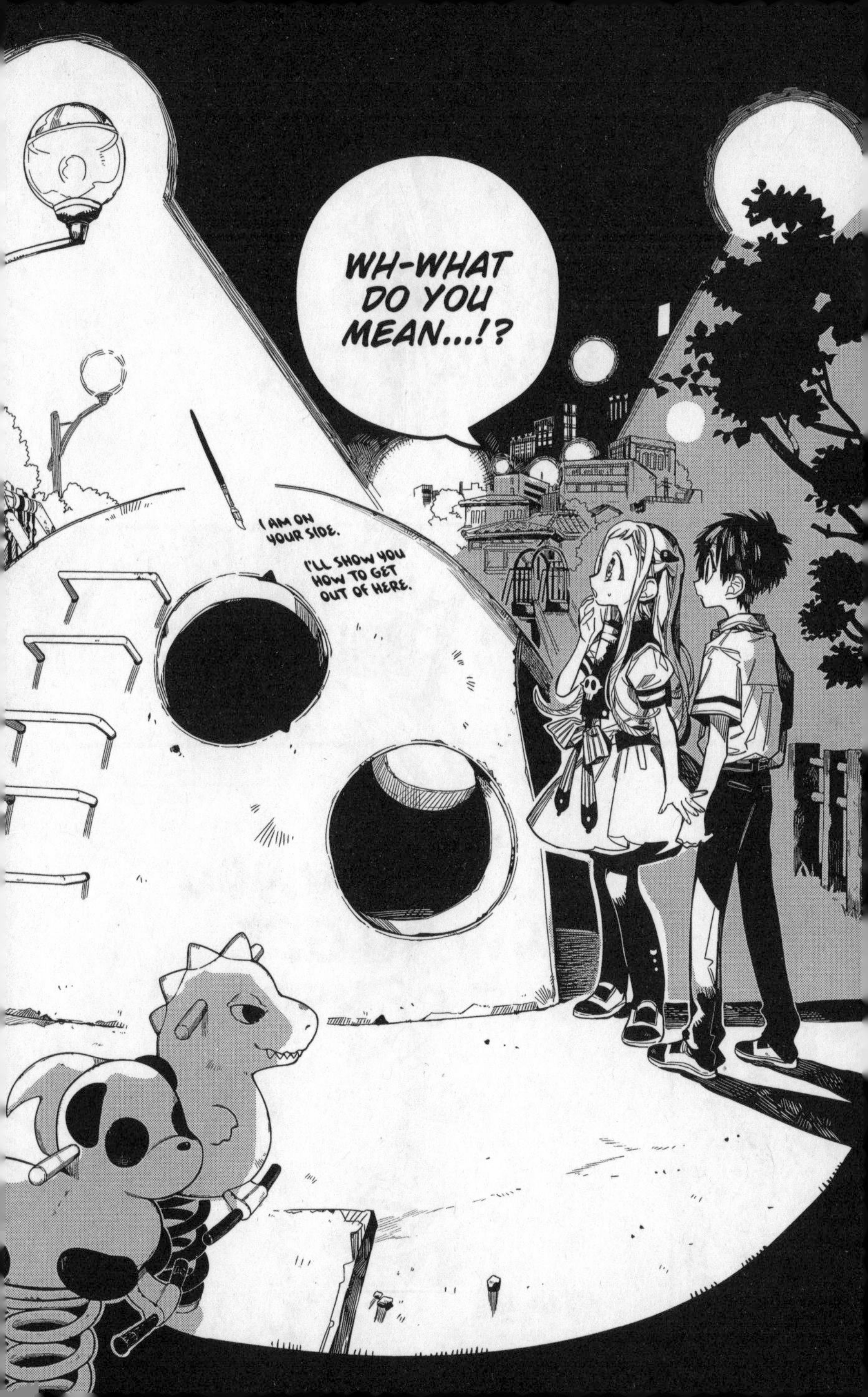
WH-WHAT DO YOU MEAN...!?
I AM ON YOUR SIDE.
I'LL SHOW YOU HOW TO GET OUT OF HERE.

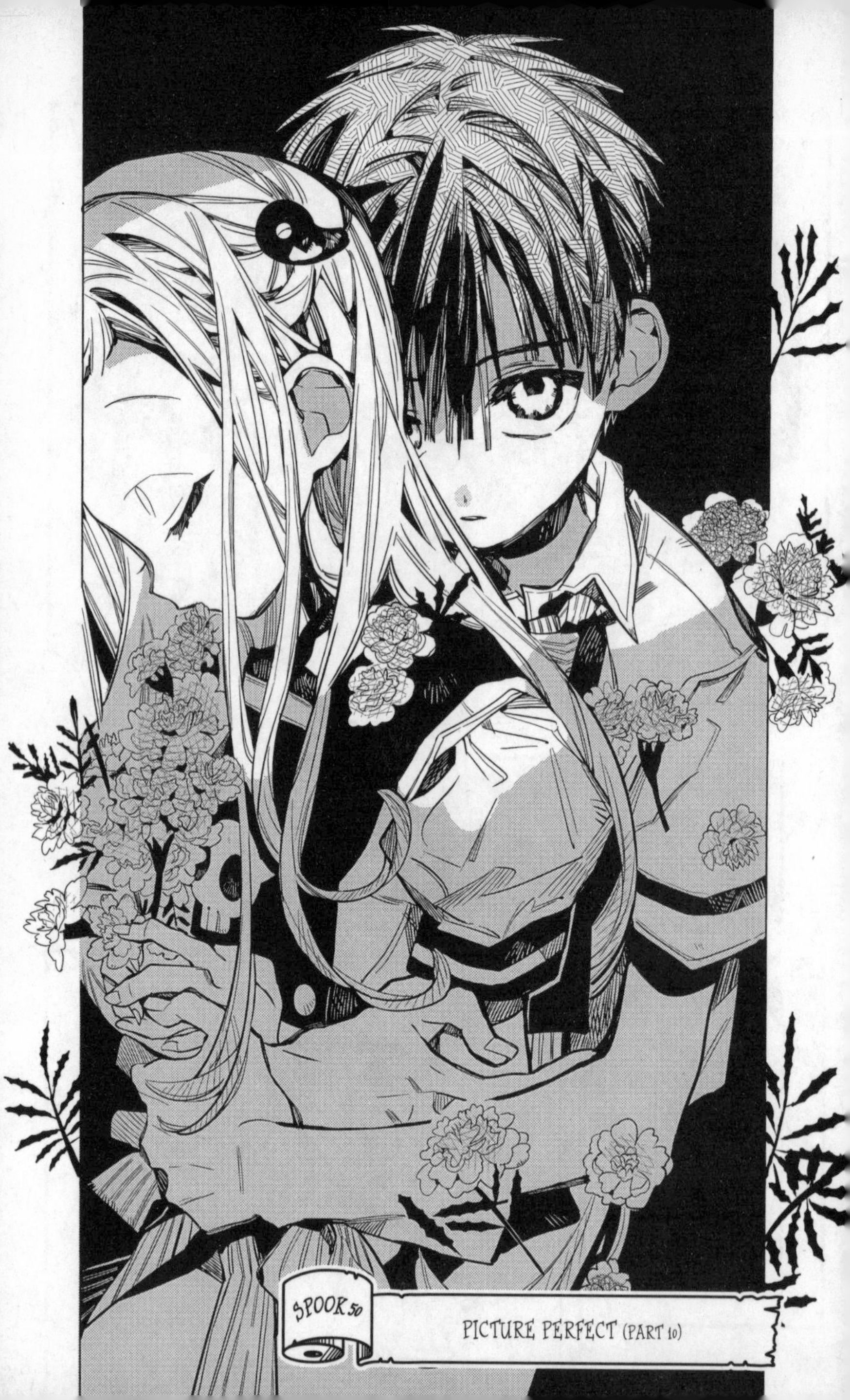
SPOOK 50
PICTURE PERFECT (PART 10)

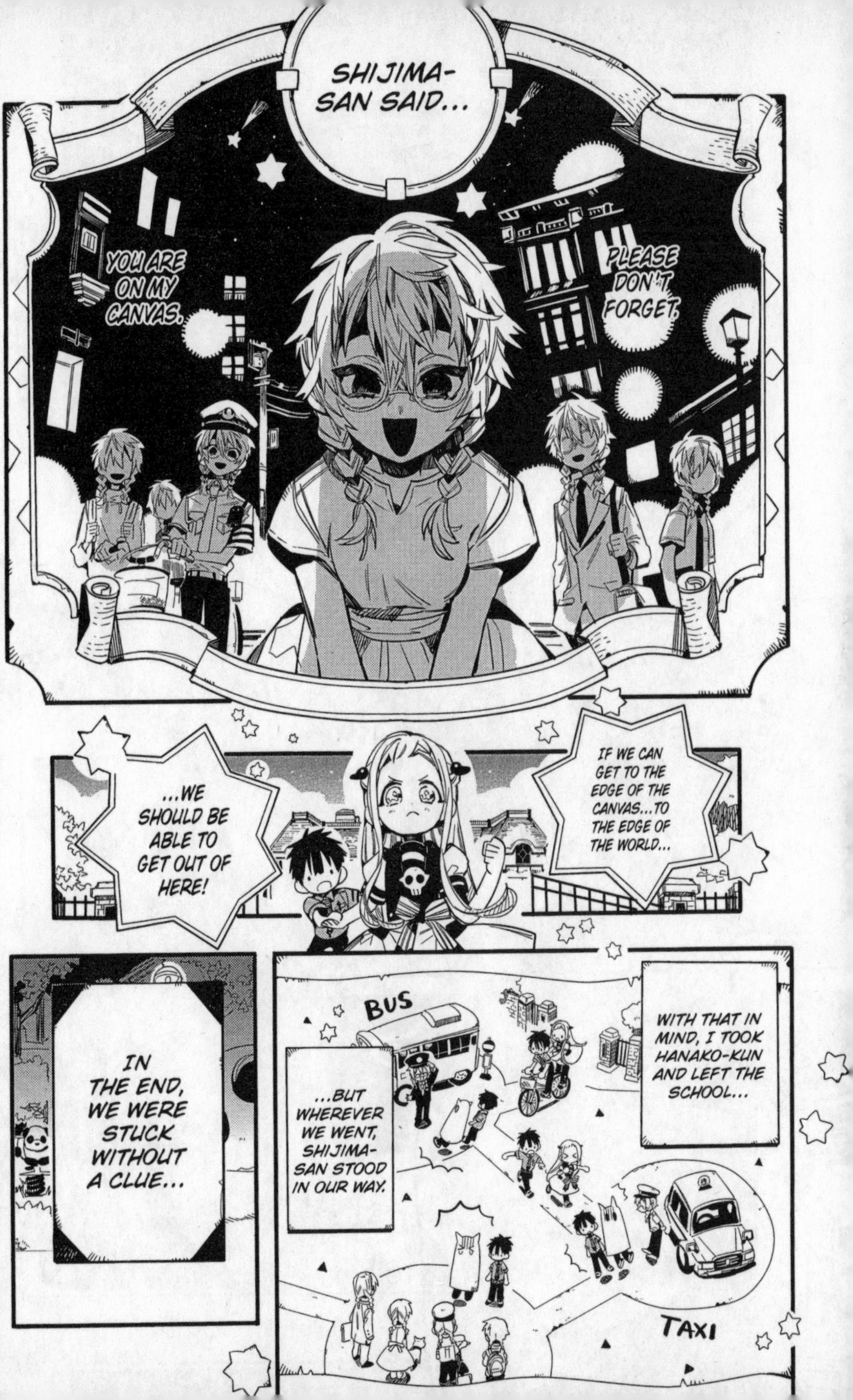
SHIJIMA-SAN SAID...
PLEASE DON'T FORGET.
YOU ARE ON MY CANVAS.
IF WE CAN GET TO THE EDGE OF THE CANVAS...TO THE EDGE OF THE WORLD...
...WE SHOULD BE ABLE TO GET OUT OF HERE!
WITH THAT IN MIND, I TOOK HANAKO-KUN AND LEFT THE SCHOOL...
BUS
...BUT WHEREVER WE WENT, SHIJIMA-SAN STOOD IN OUR WAY.
TAXI
IN THE END, WE WERE STUCK WITHOUT A CLUE...

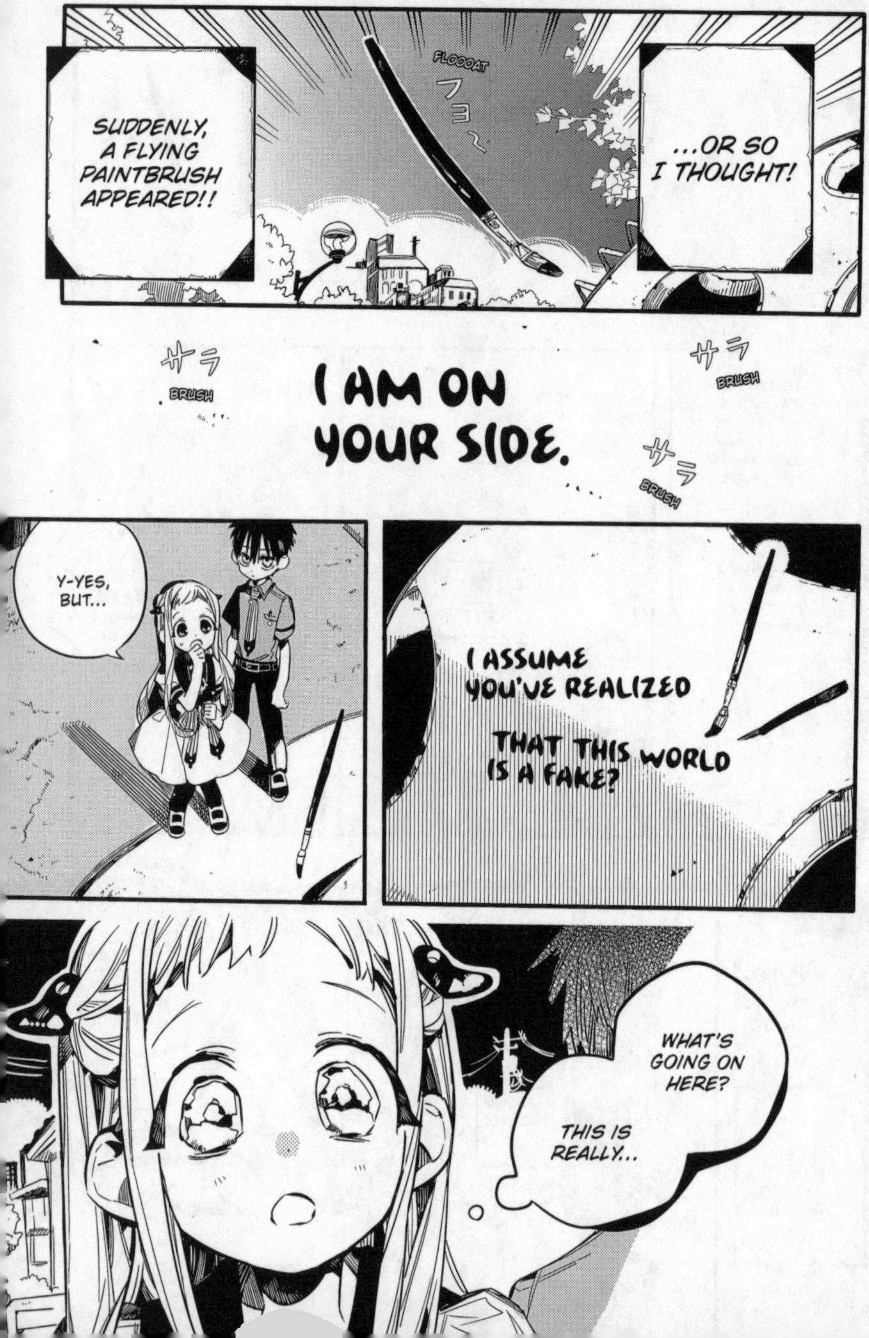
...OR SO I THOUGHT!
FLOOOAT
SUDDENLY, A FLYING PAINTBRUSH APPEARED!!
BRUSH
BRUSH
I AM ON YOUR SIDE.
BRUSH
I ASSUME YOU'VE REALIZED
THAT THIS WORLD IS A FAKE?
Y-YES, BUT...
WHAT'S GOING ON HERE?
THIS IS REALLY...

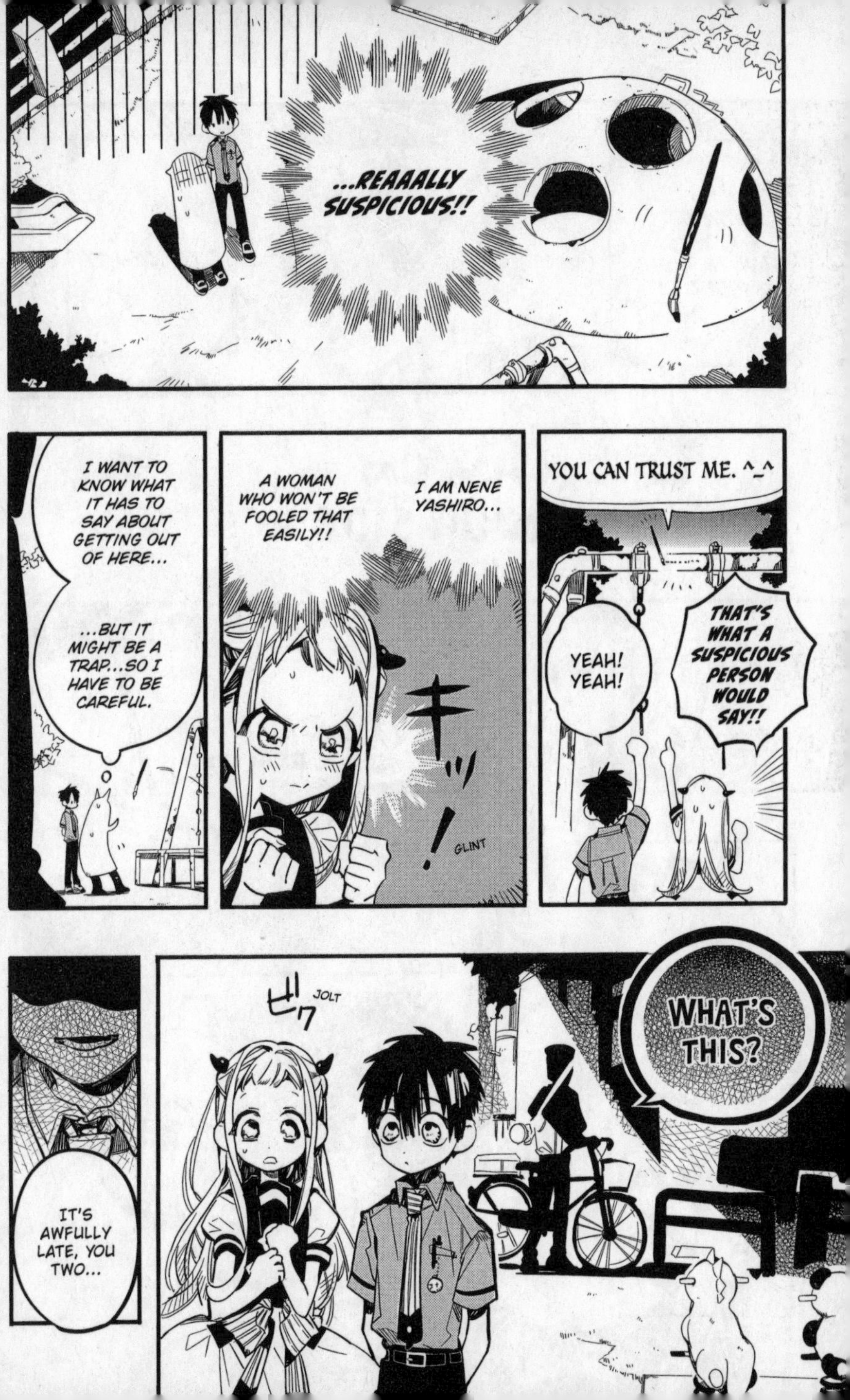
...REAAALLY SUSPICIOUS!!
YOU CAN TRUST ME. ^_^
THAT'S WHAT A SUSPICIOUS PERSON WOULD SAY!!
YEAH! YEAH!
I AM NENE YASHIRO...
A WOMAN WHO WON'T BE FOOLED THAT EASILY!!
キッ!
GLINT
I WANT TO KNOW WHAT IT HAS TO SAY ABOUT GETTING OUT OF HERE...
...BUT IT MIGHT BE A TRAP...SO I HAVE TO BE CAREFUL.
WHAT'S THIS?
ビク
JOLT
IT'S AWFULLY LATE, YOU TWO...

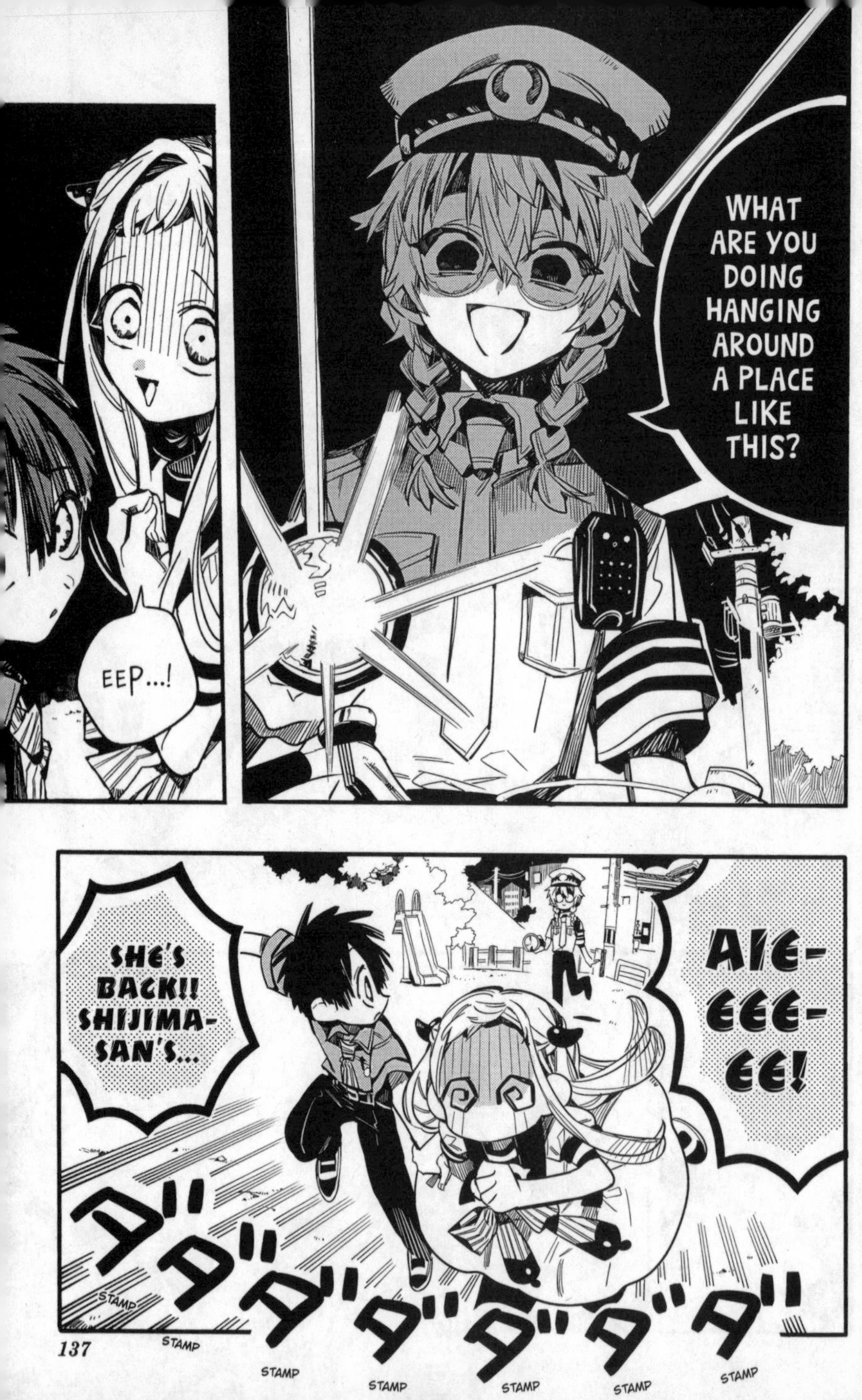
WHAT ARE YOU DOING HANGING AROUND A PLACE LIKE THIS?
EEP...!
AIE-EEE-EE!
SHE'S BACK!! SHIJIMA-SAN'S...
ダダダダダダダ
STAMP
STAMP
STAMP
STAMP
STAMP
STAMP
STAMP

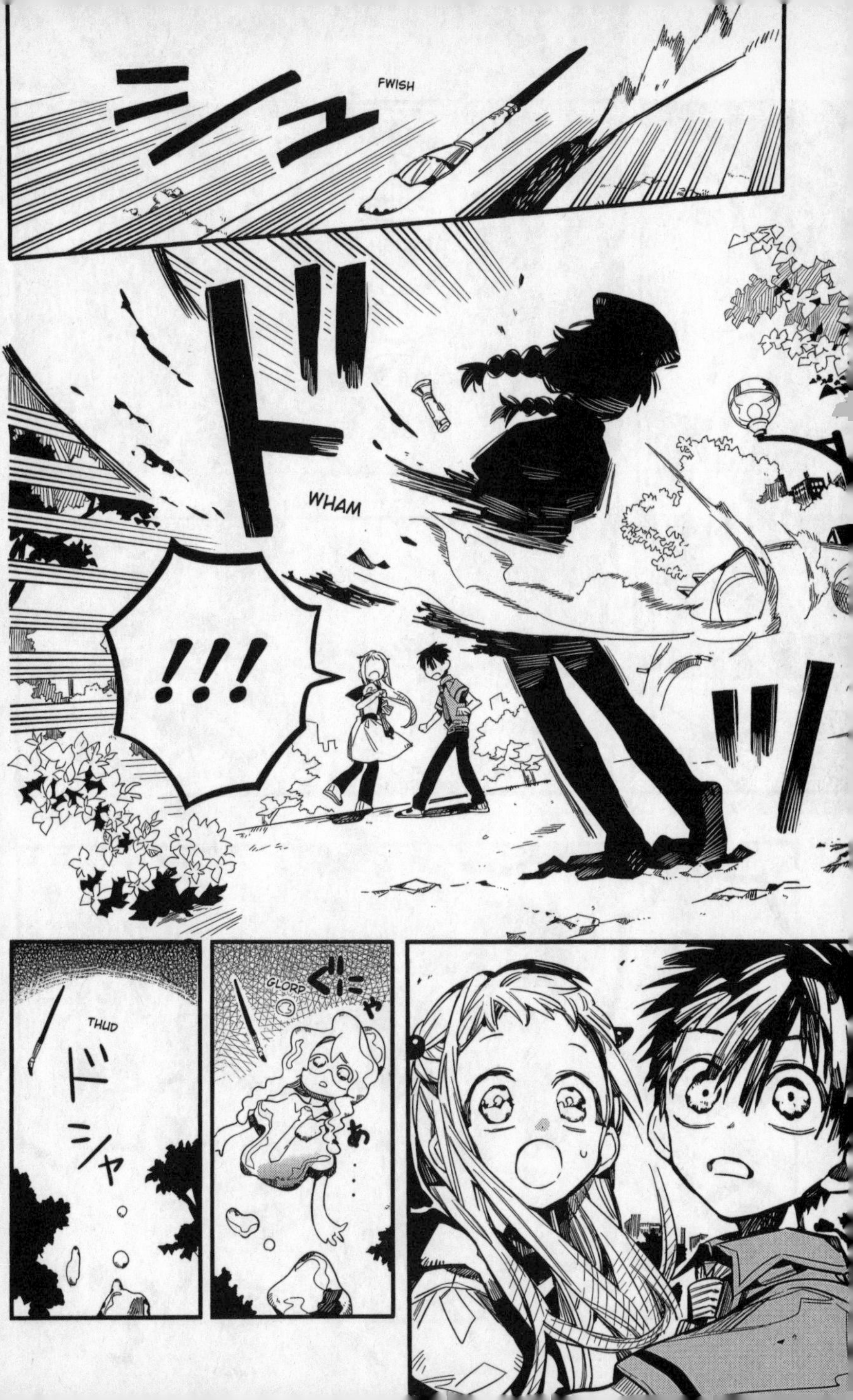
シュ
FWISH
ドッ
WHAM
!!!
ぐにゃ
GLORP
あ…
THUD
ドシャ

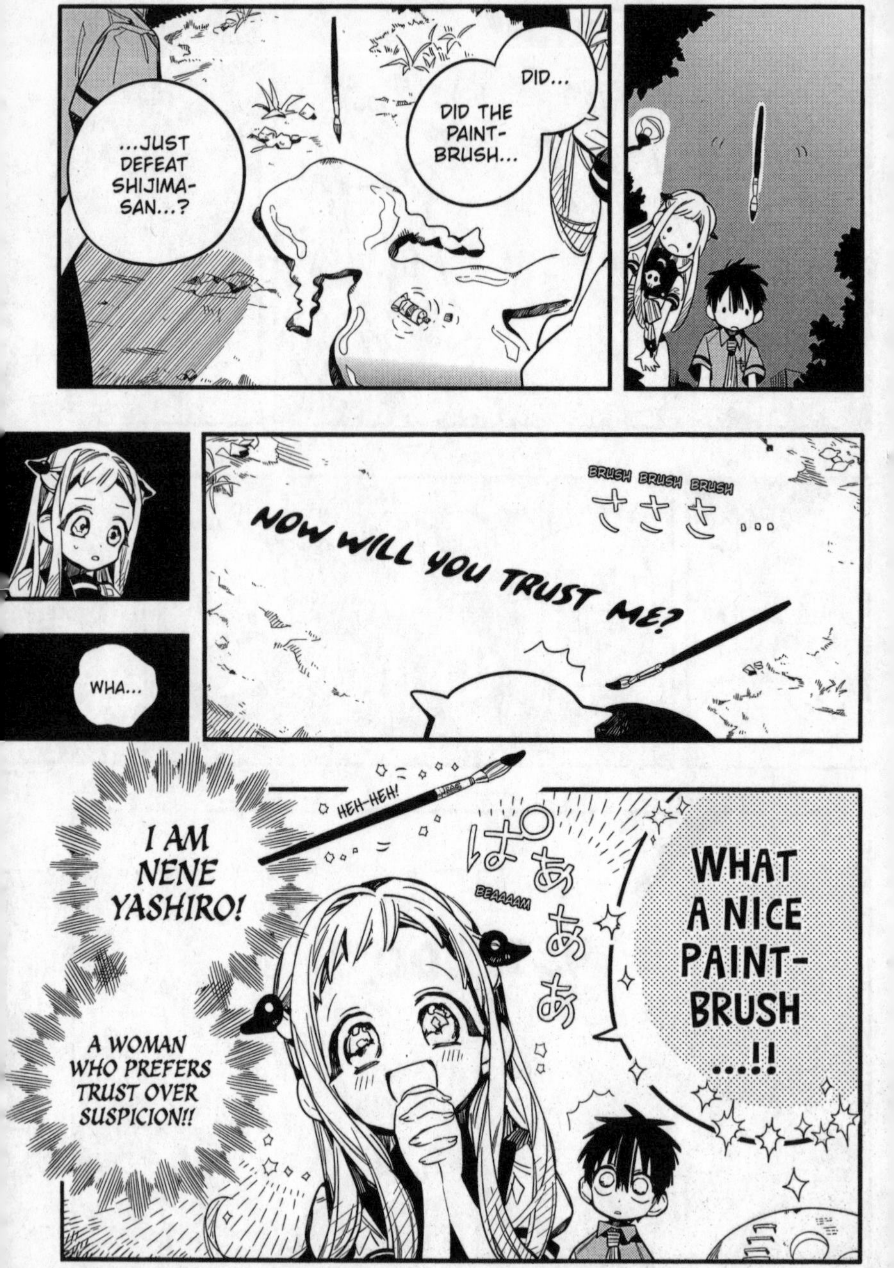
DID...
DID THE PAINT-BRUSH...
...JUST DEFEAT SHIJIMA-SAN...?
BRUSH BRUSH BRUSH
さささ...
NOW WILL YOU TRUST ME?
WHA...
WHAT A NICE PAINT-BRUSH...!!
ぱあああ
BEAAAAAM
HEH-HEH!
I AM NENE YASHIRO!
A WOMAN WHO PREFERS TRUST OVER SUSPICION!!

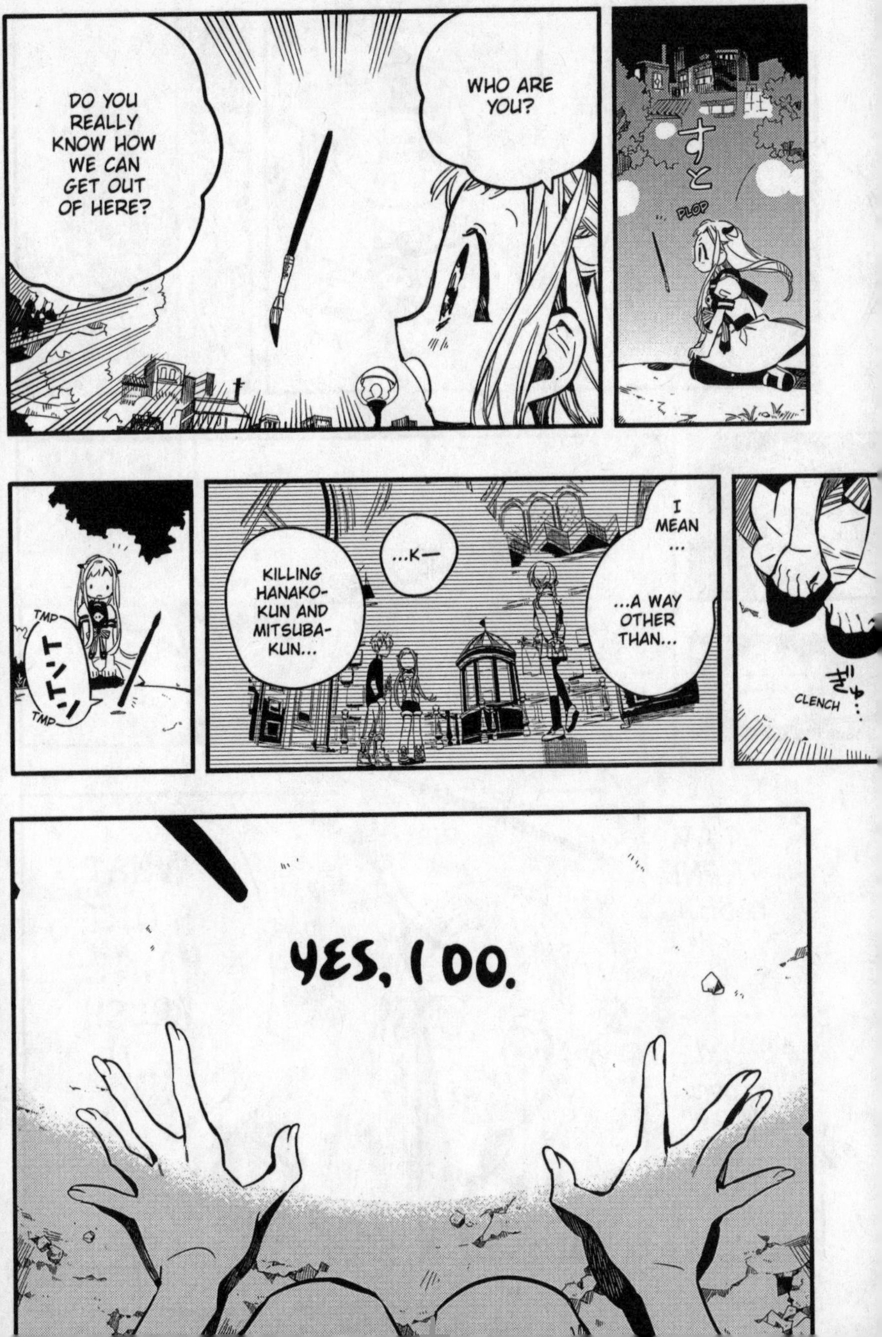
すと
PLOP
WHO ARE YOU?
DO YOU REALLY KNOW HOW WE CAN GET OUT OF HERE?
ぎゅ…
CLENCH
I MEAN ...
...A WAY OTHER THAN...
...K—
KILLING HANAKO-KUN AND MITSUBA-KUN...
TMP
TMP
YES, I DO.

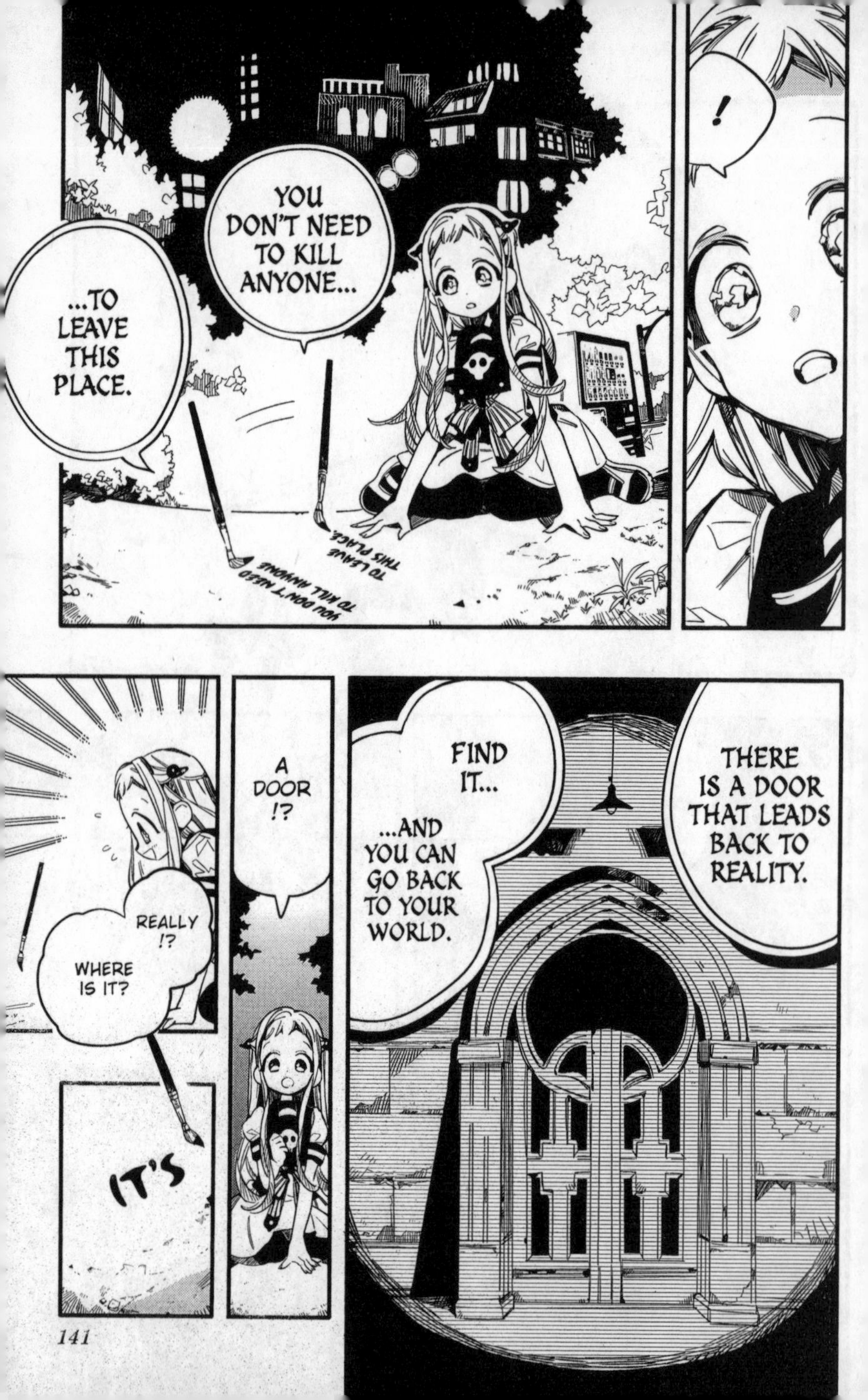
!
YOU DON'T NEED TO KILL ANYONE...
...TO LEAVE THIS PLACE.
YOU DON'T NEED TO KILL ANYONE
TO LEAVE THIS PLACE.
THERE IS A DOOR THAT LEADS BACK TO REALITY.
FIND IT...
...AND YOU CAN GO BACK TO YOUR WORLD.
A DOOR !?
REALLY !?
WHERE IS IT?
IT'S

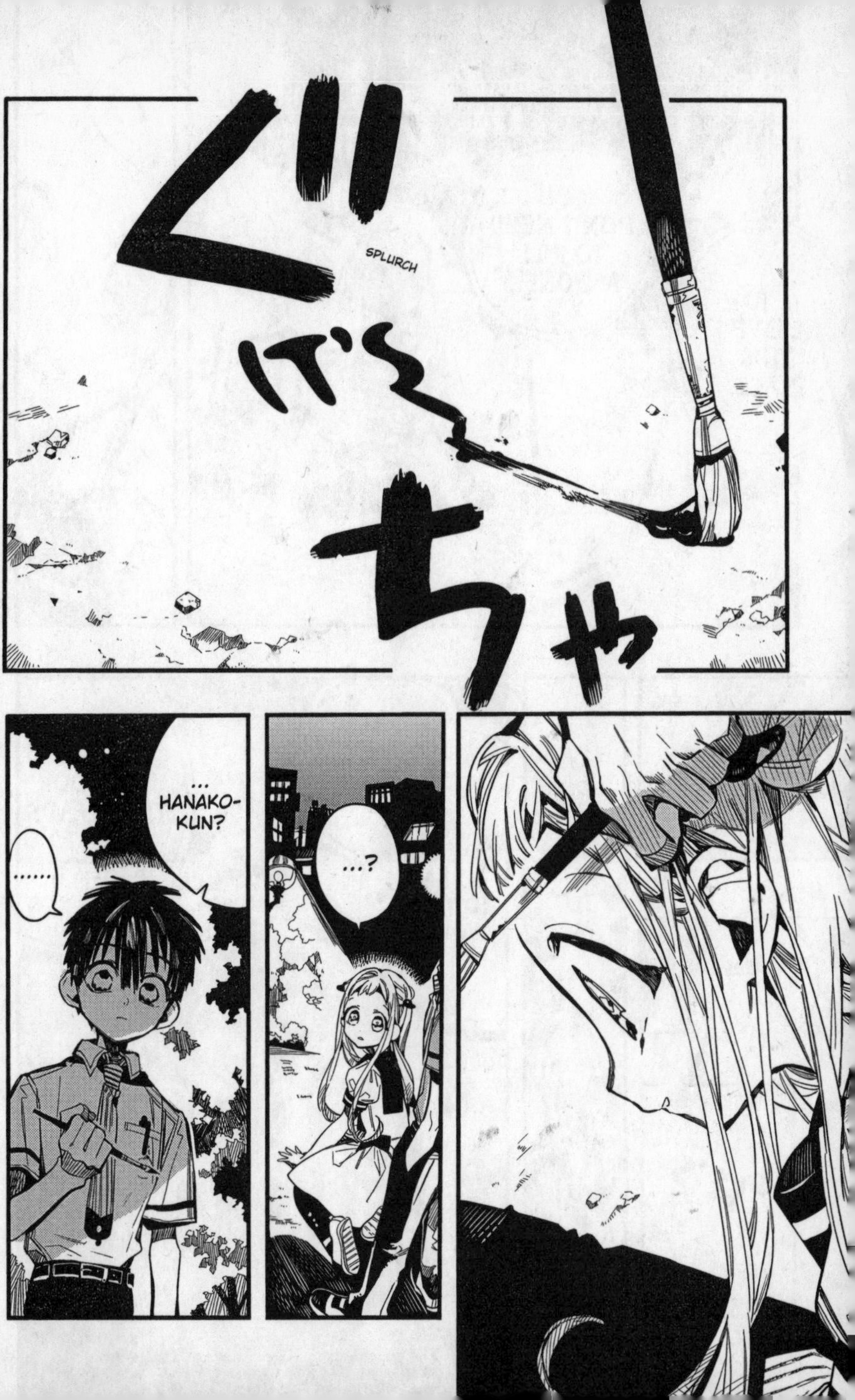
SPLURCH
...?
... HANAKO-KUN?
....

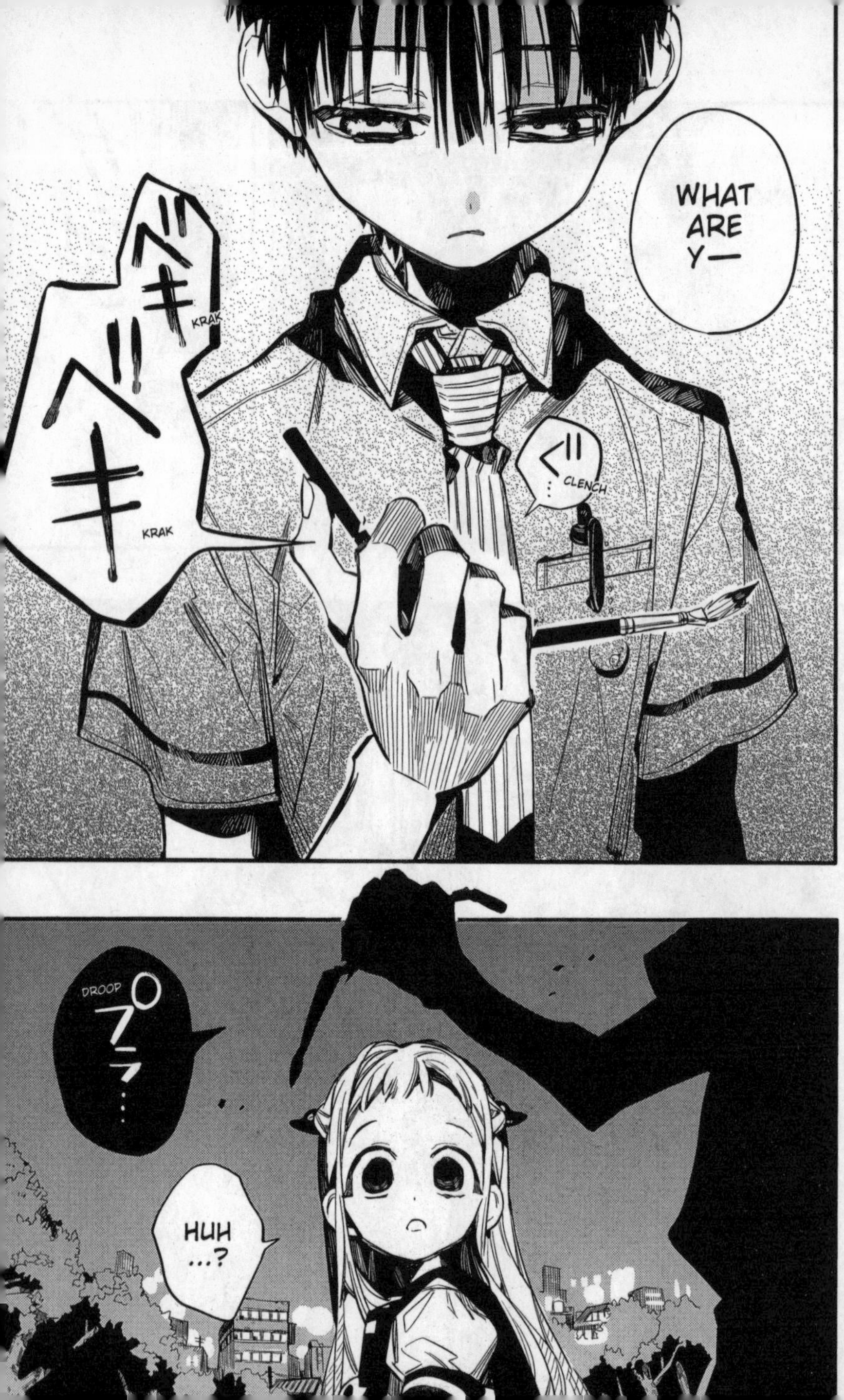
WHAT ARE Y—
CLENCH
KRAK
KRAK
DROOP
HUH ...?

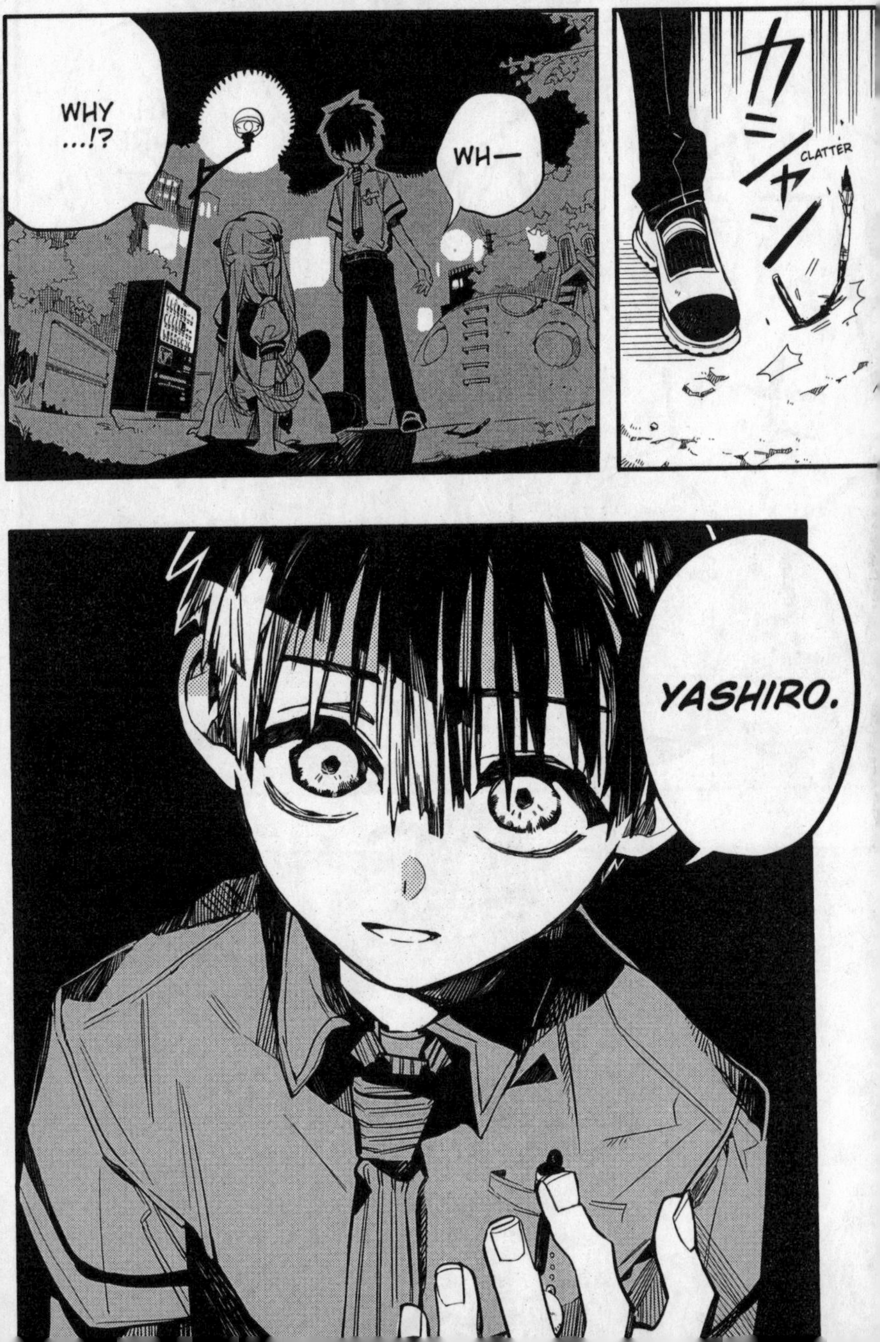
カシャン
CLATTER
WH—
WHY ...!?
YASHIRO.

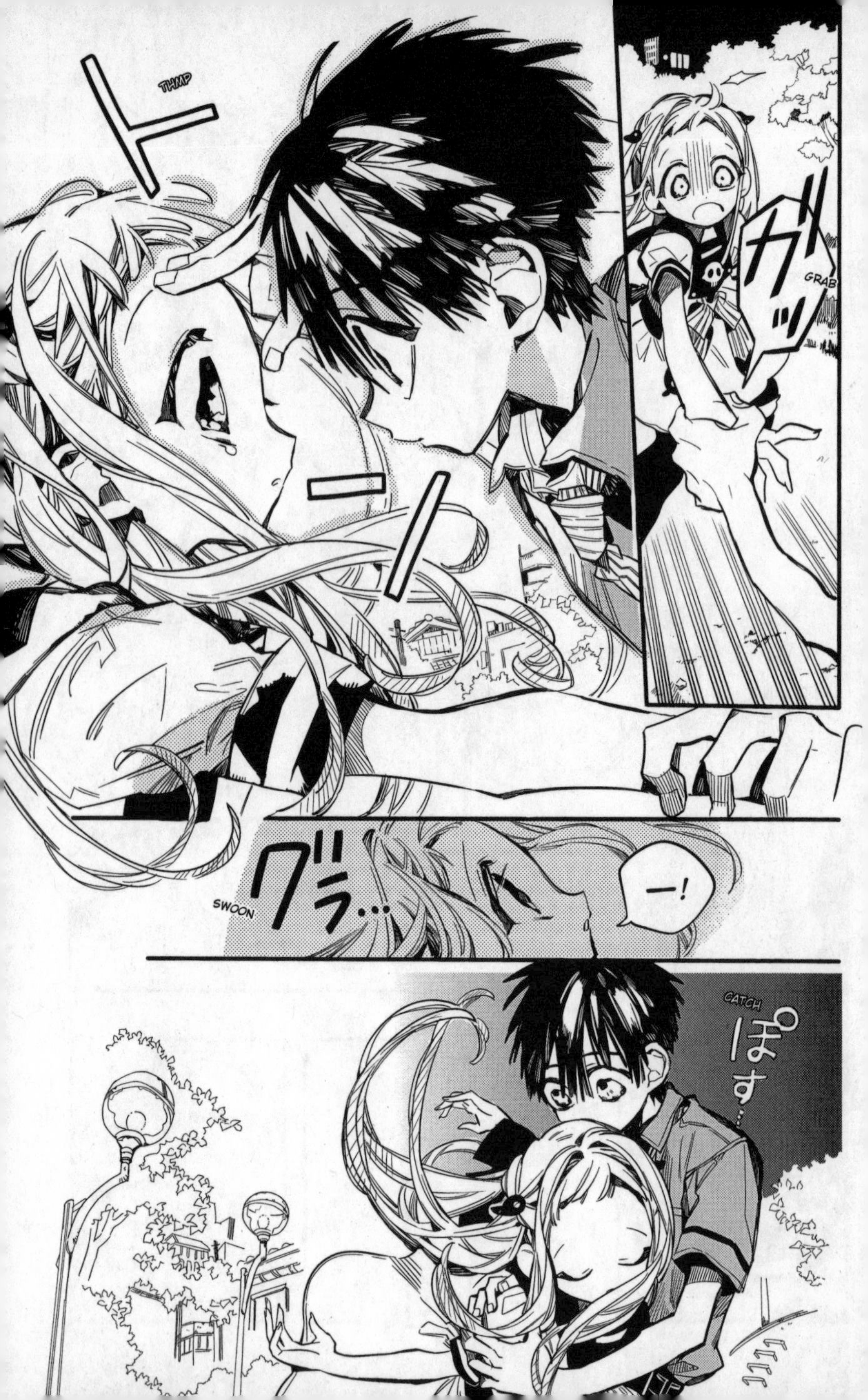
ガッ
GRAB
THMP
—!
グラ…
SWOON
ぽす…
CATCH

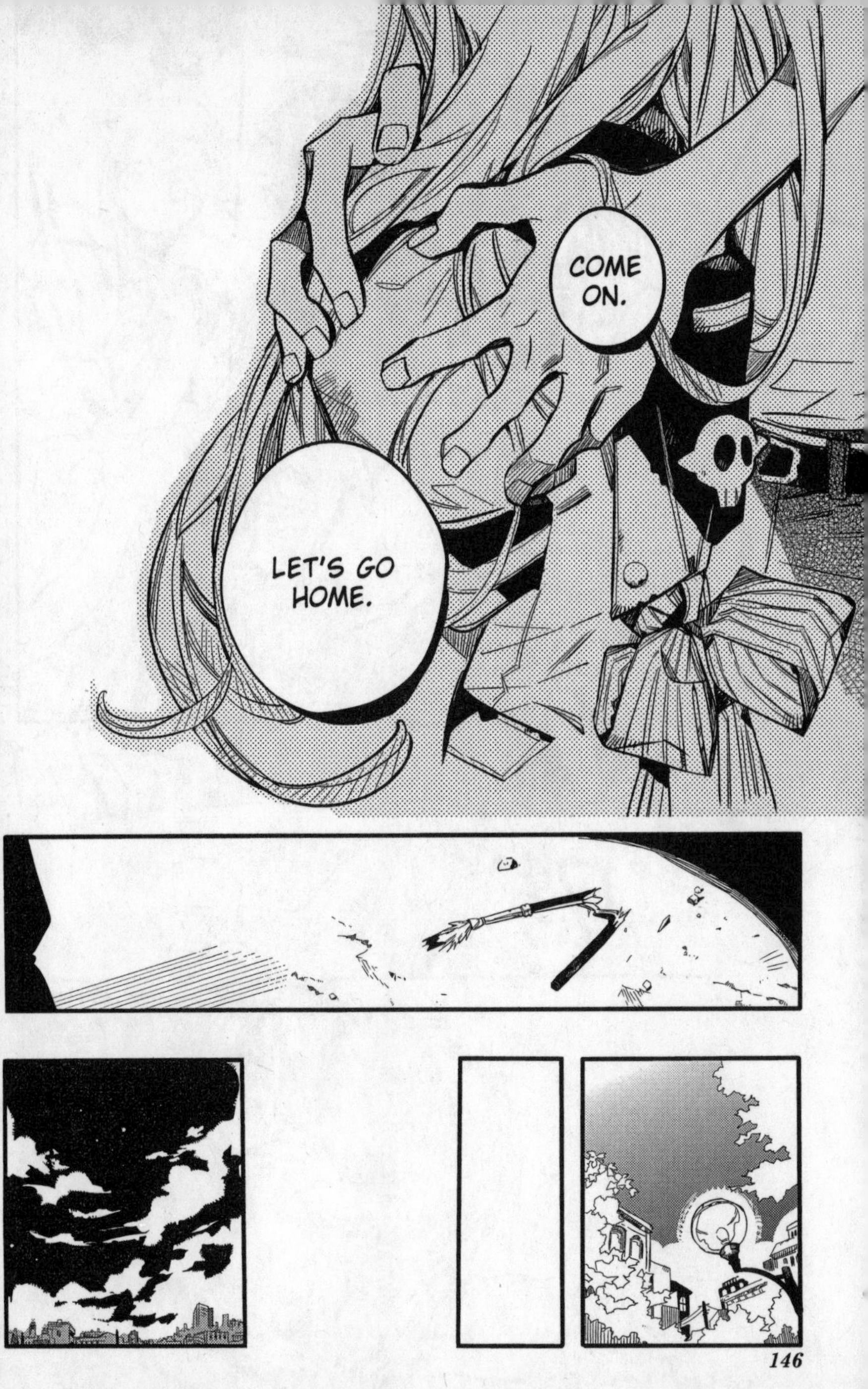
COME ON.
LET'S GO HOME.

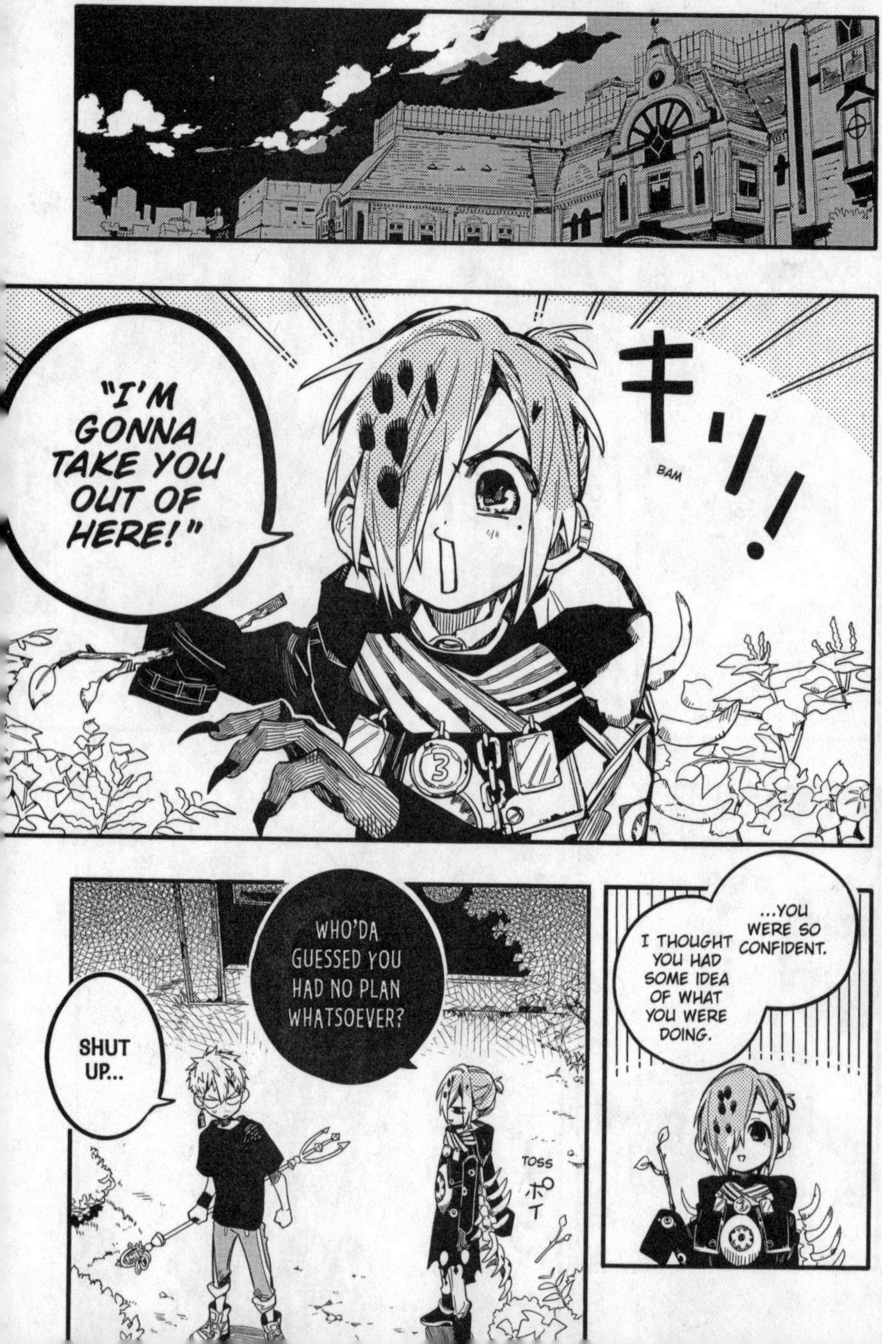
"I'M GONNA TAKE YOU OUT OF HERE!"
キッ!
BAM
...YOU WERE SO CONFIDENT.
I THOUGHT YOU HAD SOME IDEA OF WHAT YOU WERE DOING.
WHO'DA GUESSED YOU HAD NO PLAN WHATSOEVER?
TOSS
ポイ
SHUT UP...

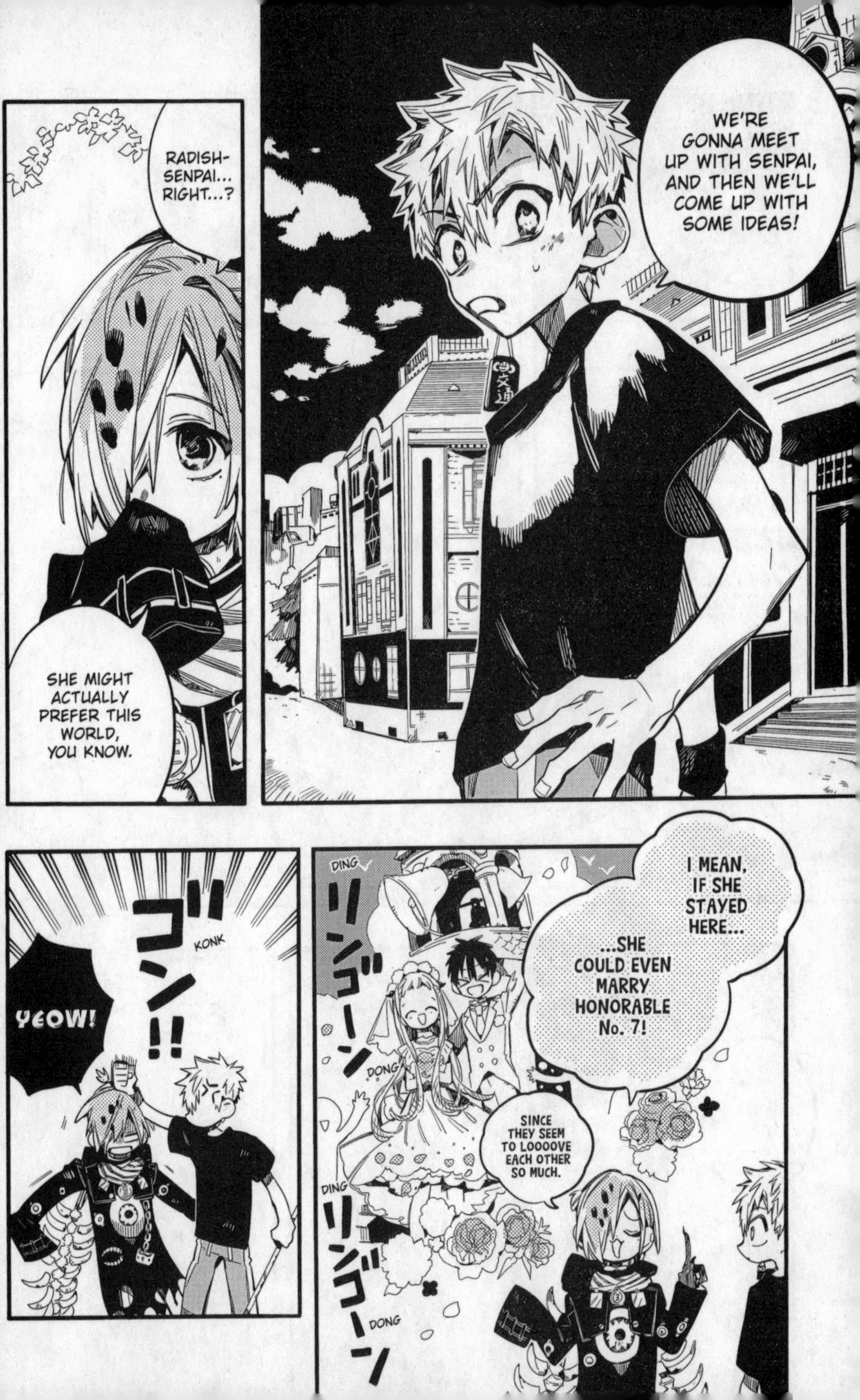
WE'RE GONNA MEET UP WITH SENPAI, AND THEN WE'LL COME UP WITH SOME IDEAS!
RADISH-SENPAI... RIGHT...?
SHE MIGHT ACTUALLY PREFER THIS WORLD, YOU KNOW.
I MEAN, IF SHE STAYED HERE...
...SHE COULD EVEN MARRY HONORABLE No. 7!
リンゴーン
DING
DONG
リンゴーン
DING
DONG
SINCE THEY SEEM TO LOOOOVE EACH OTHER SO MUCH.
ゴン!!
KONK
YEOW!

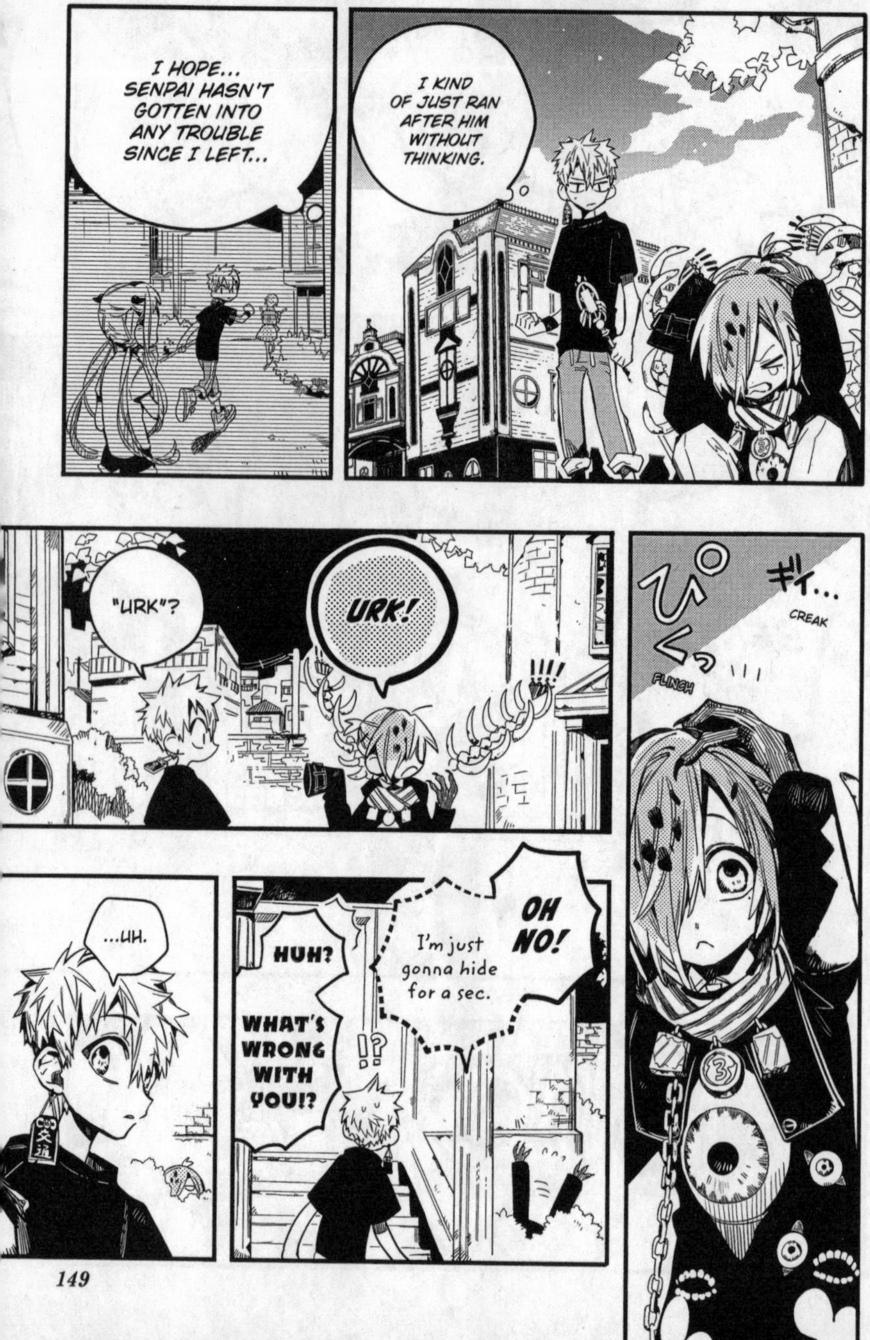
I KIND OF JUST RAN AFTER HIM WITHOUT THINKING.
I HOPE... SENPAI HASN'T GOTTEN INTO ANY TROUBLE SINCE I LEFT...
ギィ…
CREAK
ぴくっ
FLINCH
URK!
!!!!
"URK"?
OH NO!
I'm just gonna hide for a sec.
HUH?
WHAT's WRONG WITH YOU!?
!?
...UH.

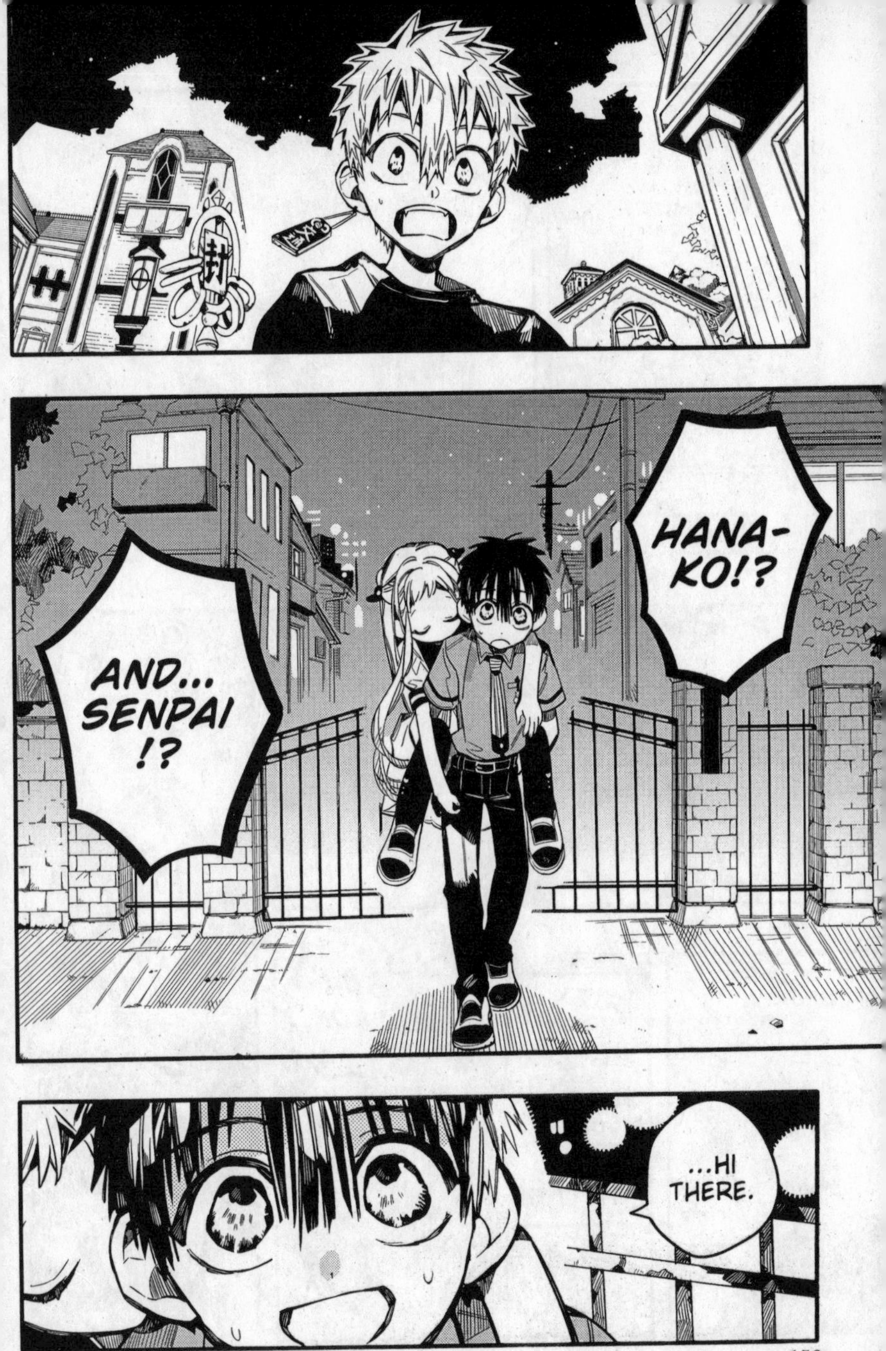
HANA-KO!?
AND... SENPAI !?
...HI THERE.

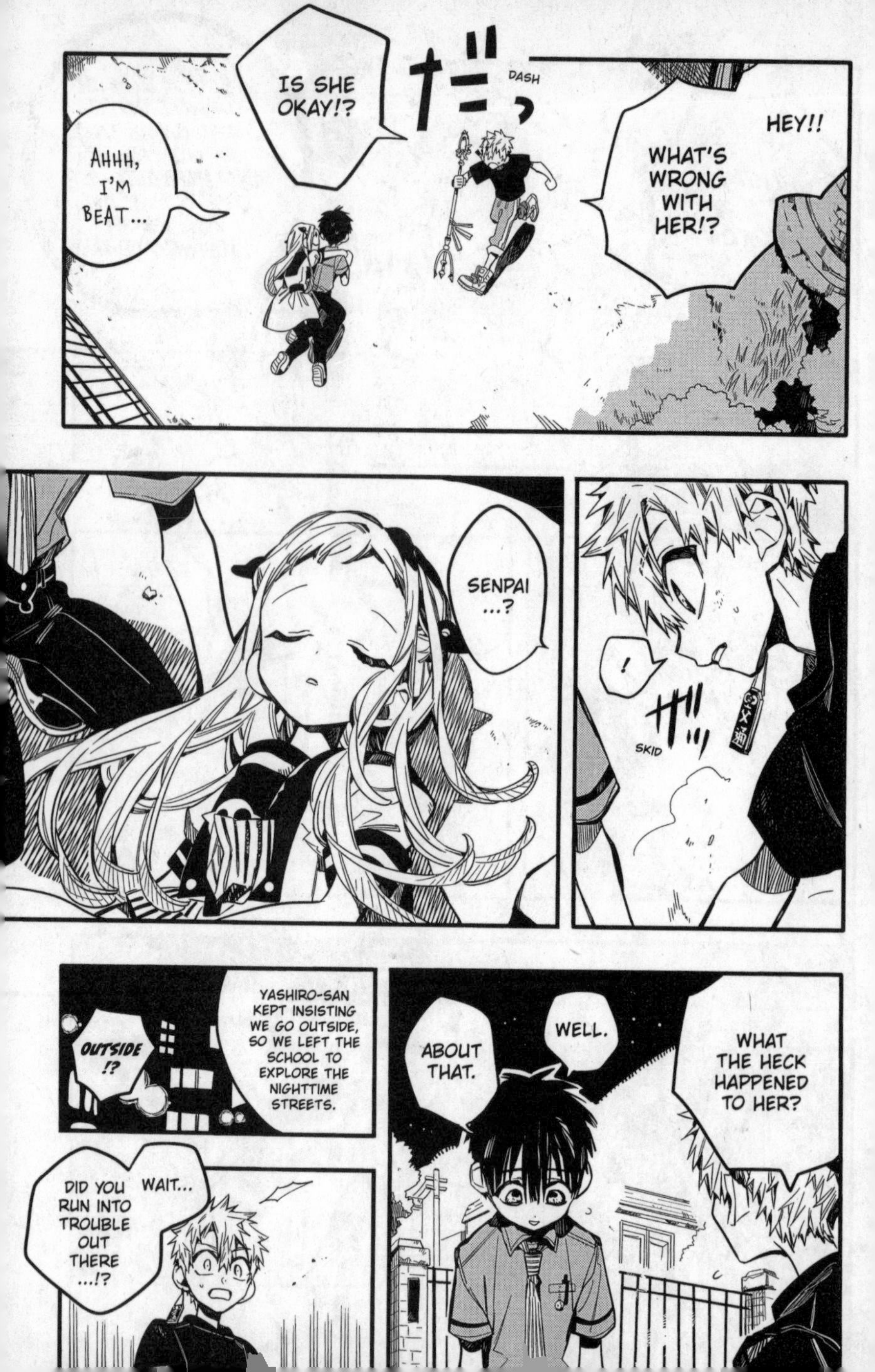
HEY!!
WHAT'S WRONG WITH HER!?
DASH
IS SHE OKAY!?
AHHH, I'M BEAT...
!
SKID
SENPAI ...?
WHAT THE HECK HAPPENED TO HER?
WELL.
ABOUT THAT.
YASHIRO-SAN KEPT INSISTING WE GO OUTSIDE, SO WE LEFT THE SCHOOL TO EXPLORE THE NIGHTTIME STREETS.
OUTSIDE !?
WAIT...
DID YOU RUN INTO TROUBLE OUT THERE ...!?

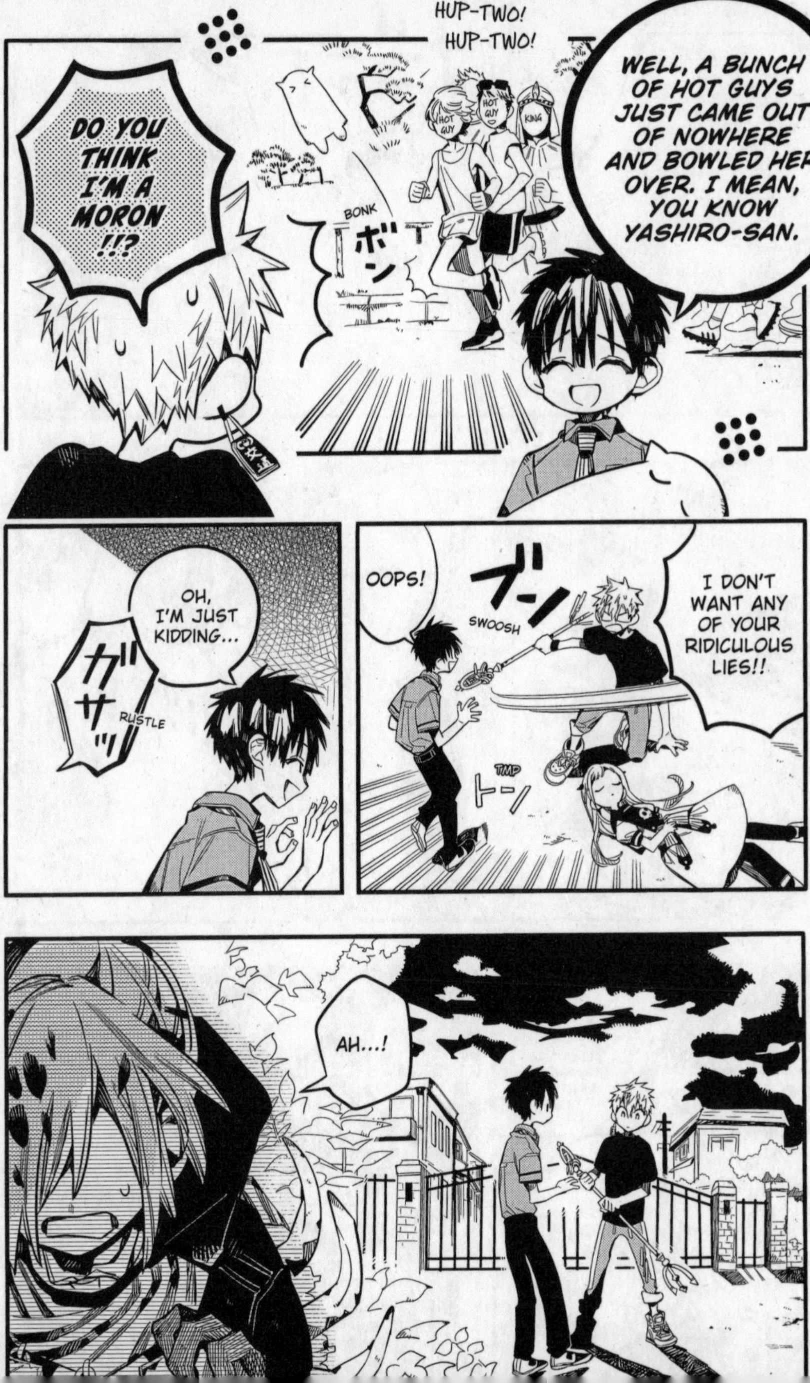
HUP-TWO!
HUP-TWO!
WELL, A BUNCH OF HOT GUYS JUST CAME OUT OF NOWHERE AND BOWLED HER OVER. I MEAN, YOU KNOW YASHIRO-SAN.
KING
HOT GUY
HOT GUY
BONK
ボン
DO YOU THINK I'M A MORON!!?
I DON'T WANT ANY OF YOUR RIDICULOUS LIES!!
ブーン
SWOOSH
OOPS!
TMP
トーン
OH, I'M JUST KIDDING...
ガサッ
RUSTLE
AH...!

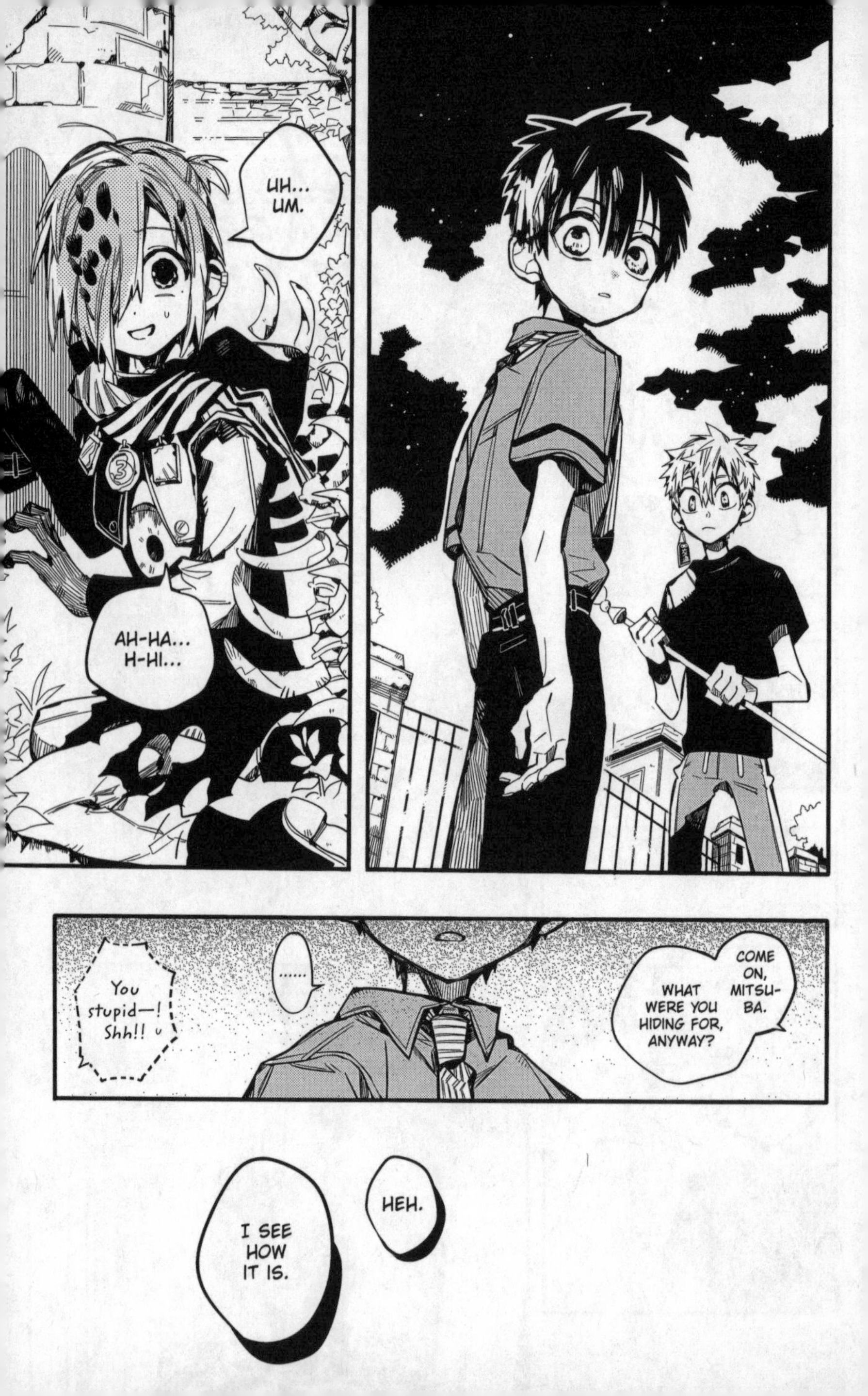
UH... UM.
AH-HA... H-HI...
COME ON, MITSUBA.
WHAT WERE YOU HIDING FOR, ANYWAY?
......
You stupid—! Shh!!
HEH.
I SEE HOW IT IS.

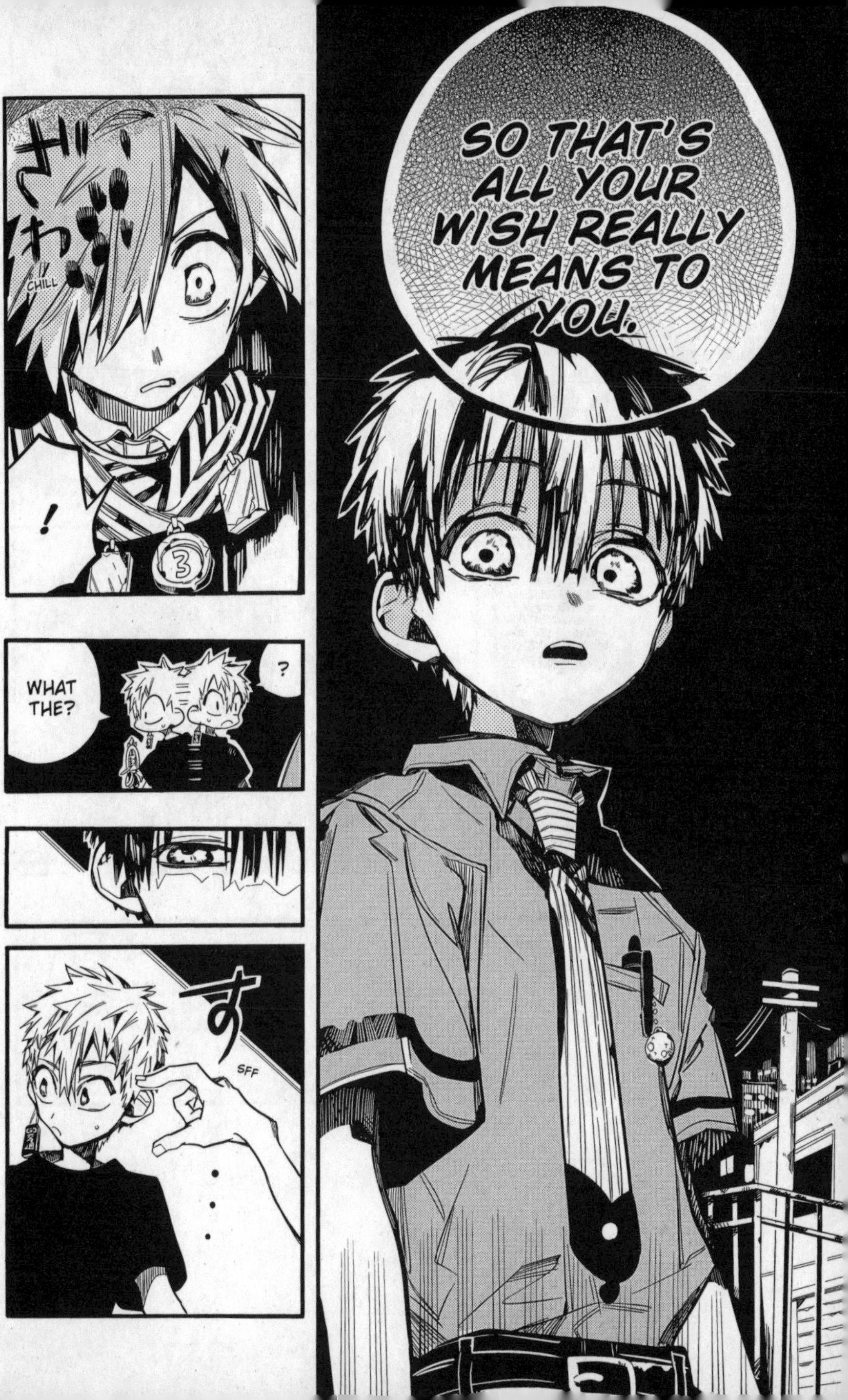
SO THAT'S ALL YOUR WISH REALLY MEANS TO YOU.
ざわ
CHILL
!
?
WHAT THE?
す
SFF
...

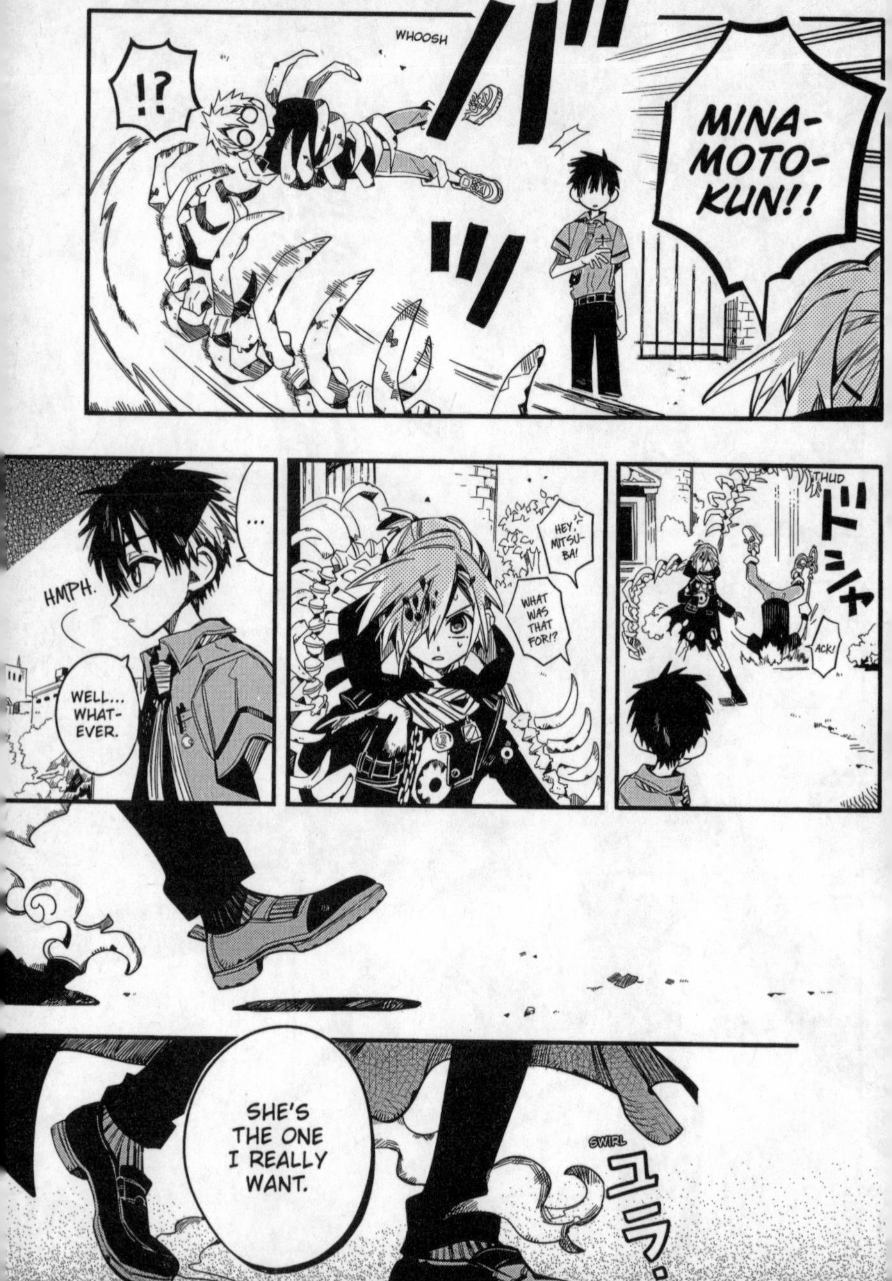
MINA-MOTO-KUN!!
バッ
WHOOSH
!?
THUD
ドシャ
ACK!
HEY, MITSU-BA!
WHAT WAS THAT FOR!?
...
HMPH.
WELL... WHAT-EVER.
SHE'S THE ONE I REALLY WANT.
SWIRL
ユラ

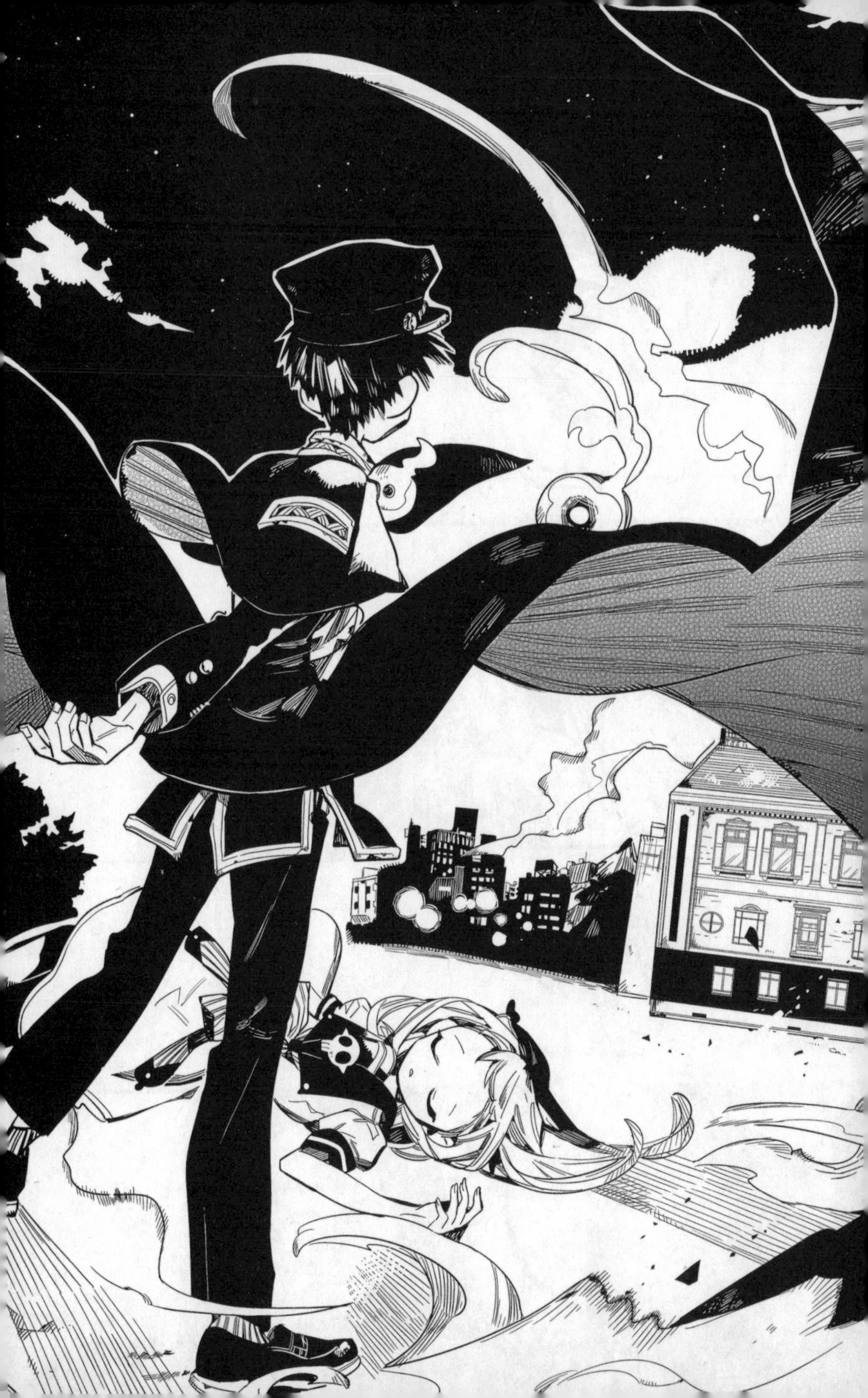

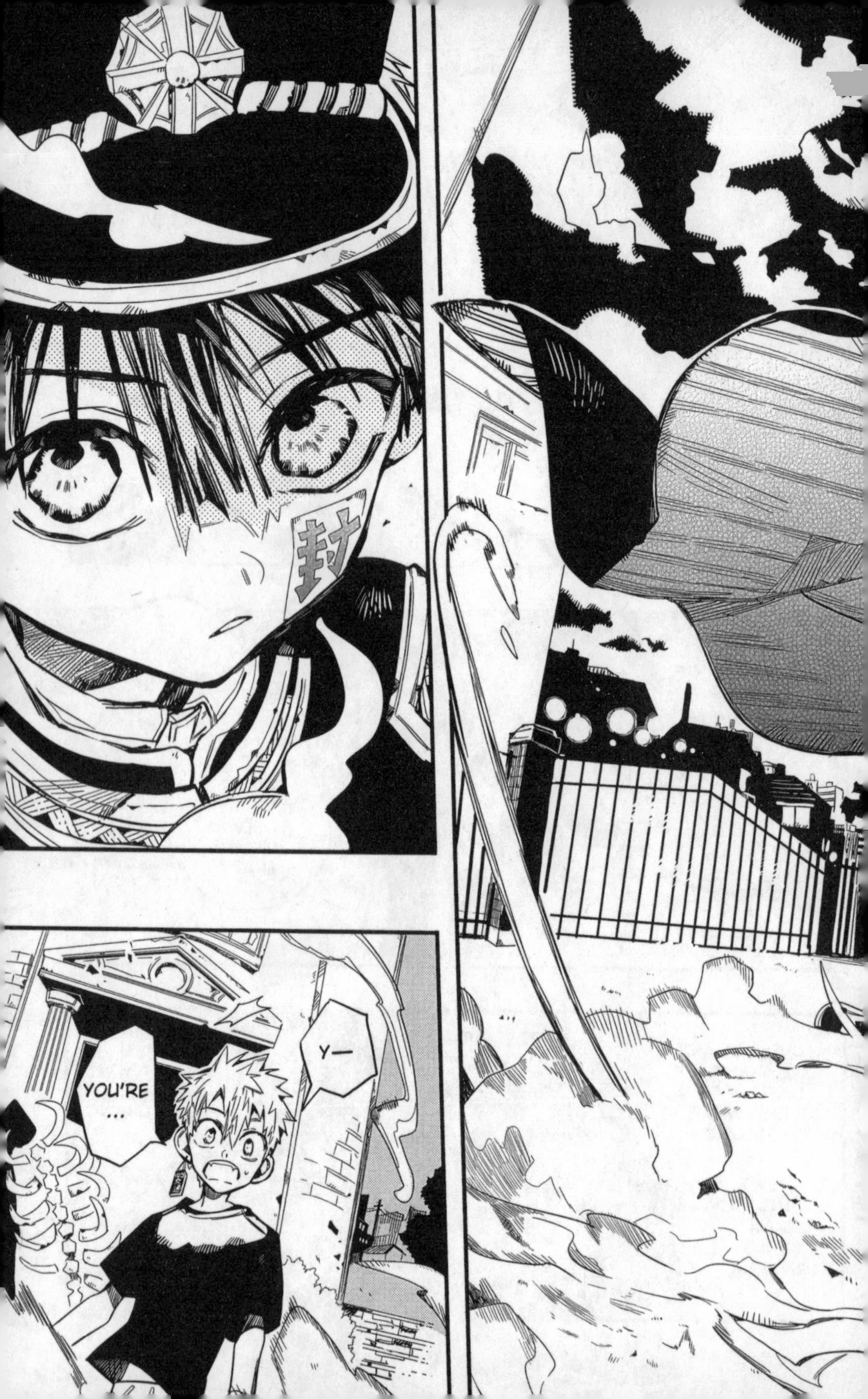
Y—
YOU'RE ...

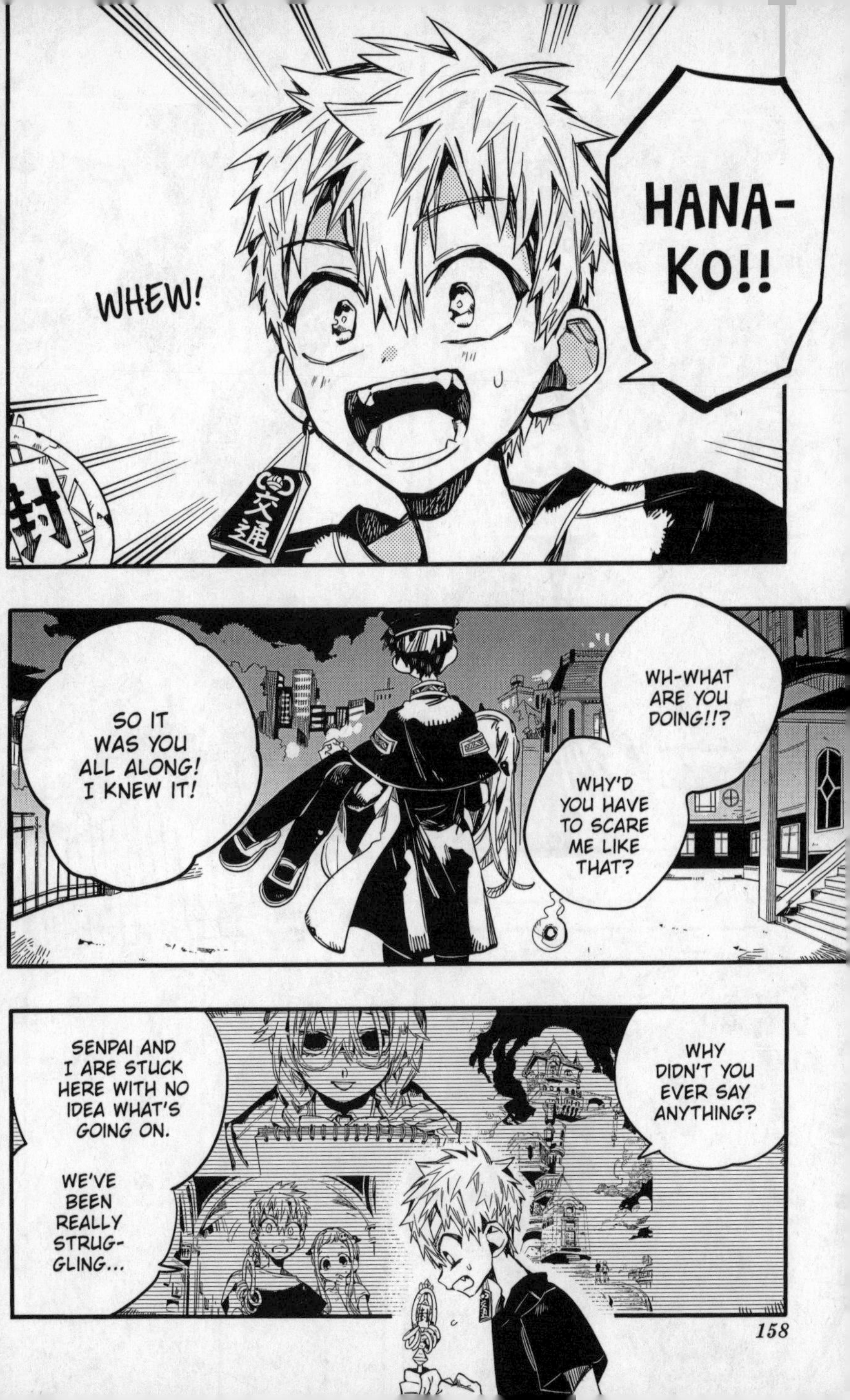
HANA-KO!!
WHEW!
封
交通
WH-WHAT ARE YOU DOING!!?
WHY'D YOU HAVE TO SCARE ME LIKE THAT?
SO IT WAS YOU ALL ALONG! I KNEW IT!
WHY DIDN'T YOU EVER SAY ANYTHING?
SENPAI AND I ARE STUCK HERE WITH NO IDEA WHAT'S GOING ON.
WE'VE BEEN REALLY STRUG-GLING...

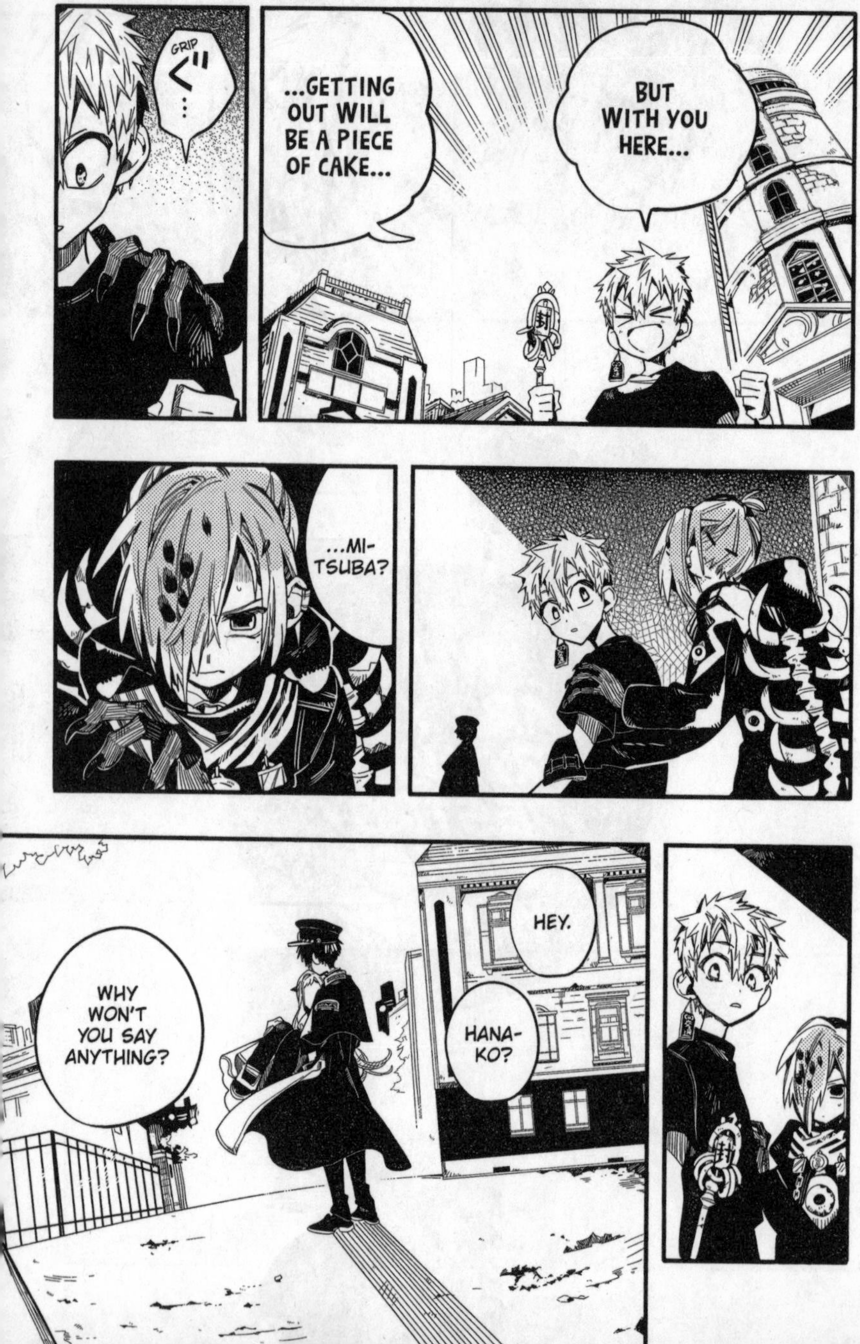

BUT WITH YOU HERE...
...GETTING OUT WILL BE A PIECE OF CAKE...
GRIP
ぐ"...
...MI-TSUBA?
HEY.
HANA-KO?
WHY WON'T YOU SAY ANYTHING?

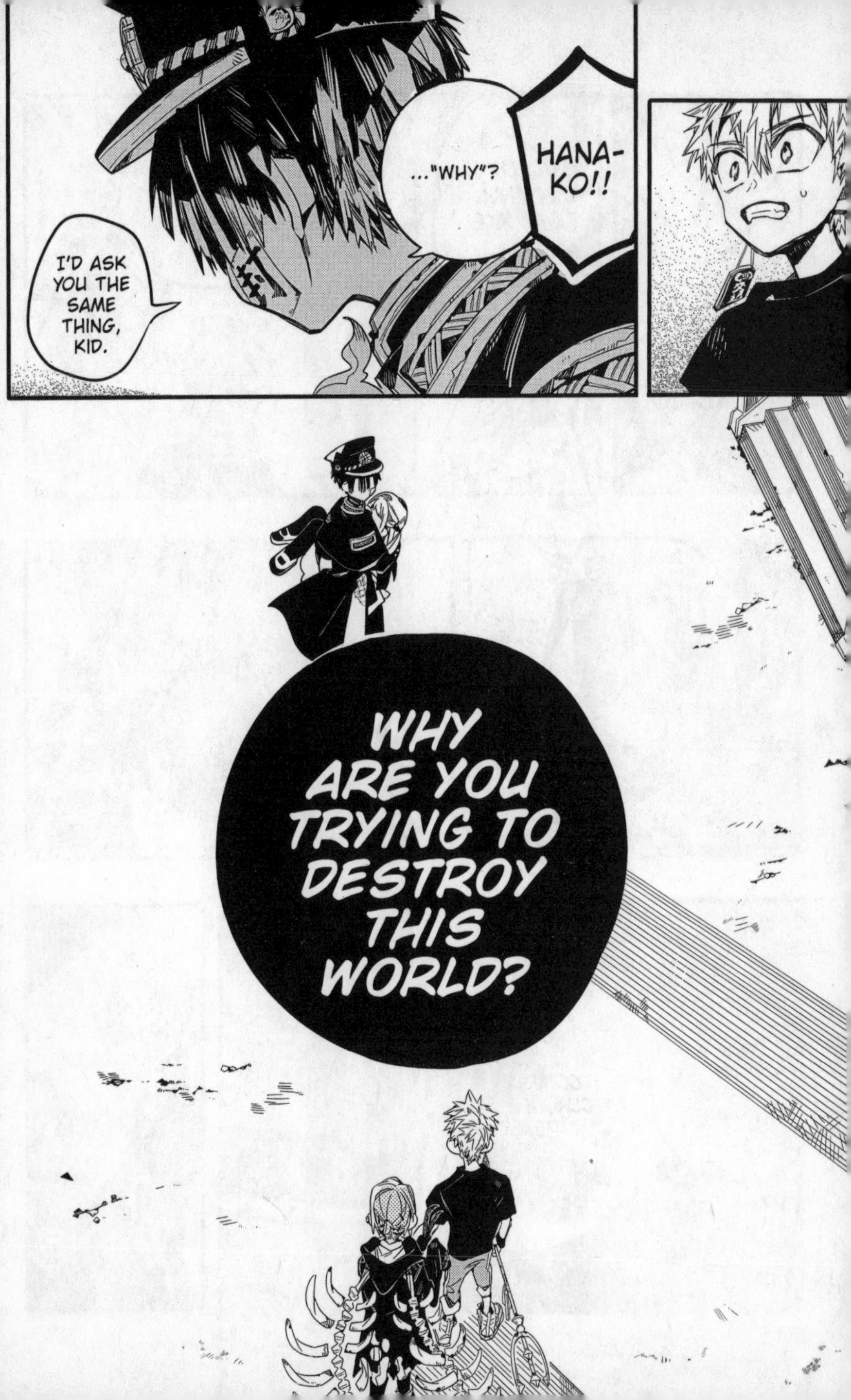
HANA-KO!!
..."WHY"?
I'D ASK YOU THE SAME THING, KID.
WHY ARE YOU TRYING TO DESTROY THIS WORLD?

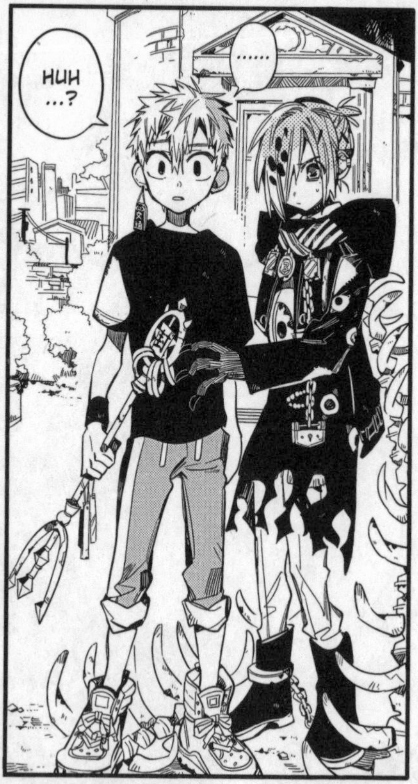
......
HUH ...?
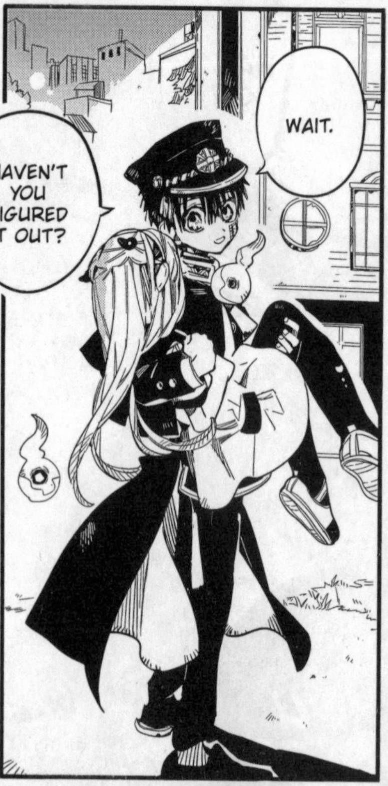
WAIT.
HAVEN'T YOU FIGURED IT OUT?
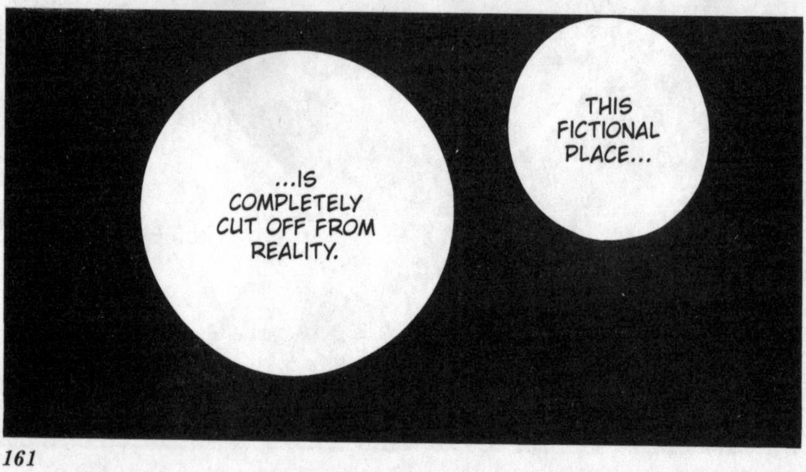
THIS FICTIONAL PLACE...
...IS COMPLETELY CUT OFF FROM REALITY.

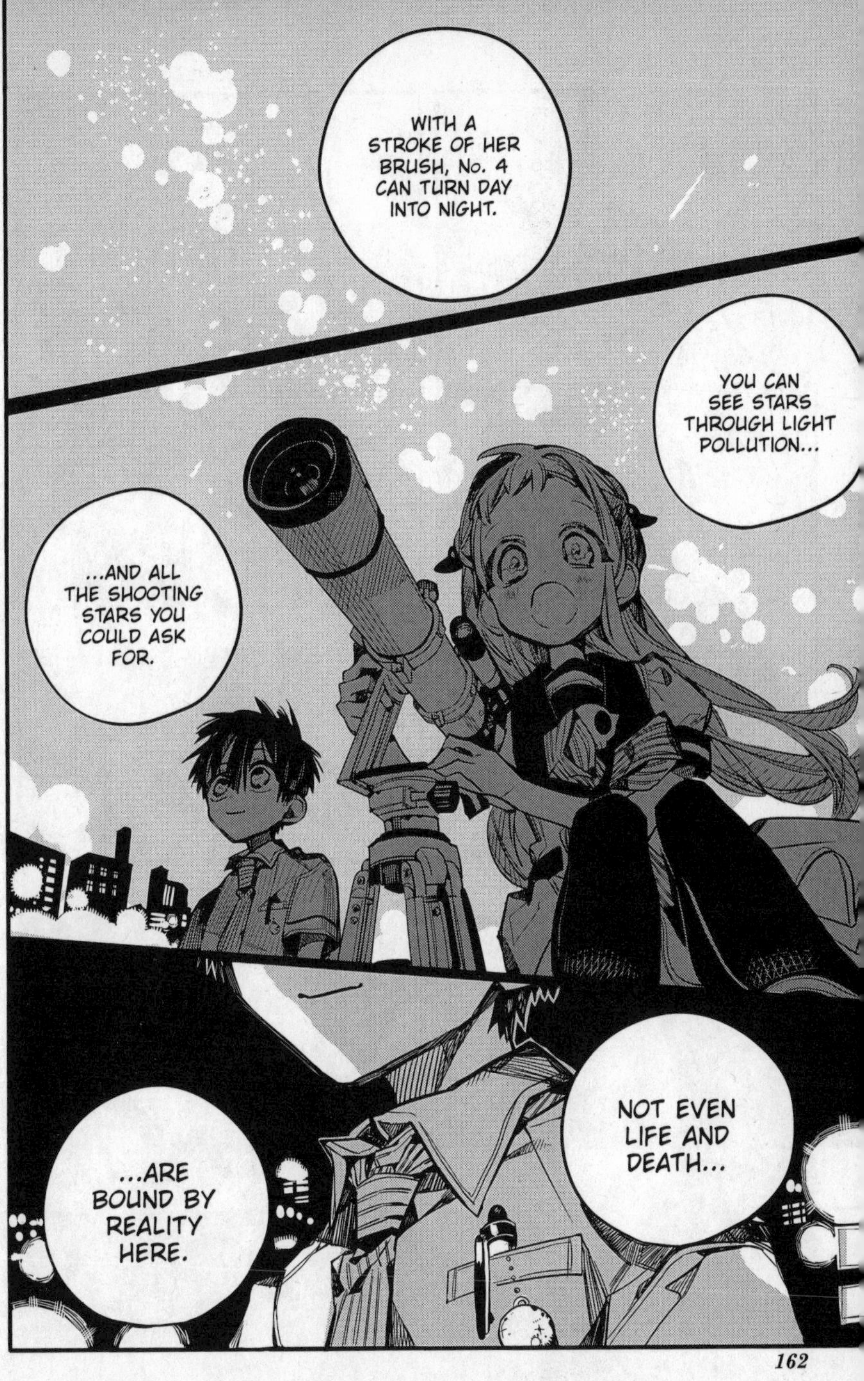
WITH A STROKE OF HER BRUSH, No. 4 CAN TURN DAY INTO NIGHT.
YOU CAN SEE STARS THROUGH LIGHT POLLUTION...
...AND ALL THE SHOOTING STARS YOU COULD ASK FOR.
NOT EVEN LIFE AND DEATH...
...ARE BOUND BY REALITY HERE.

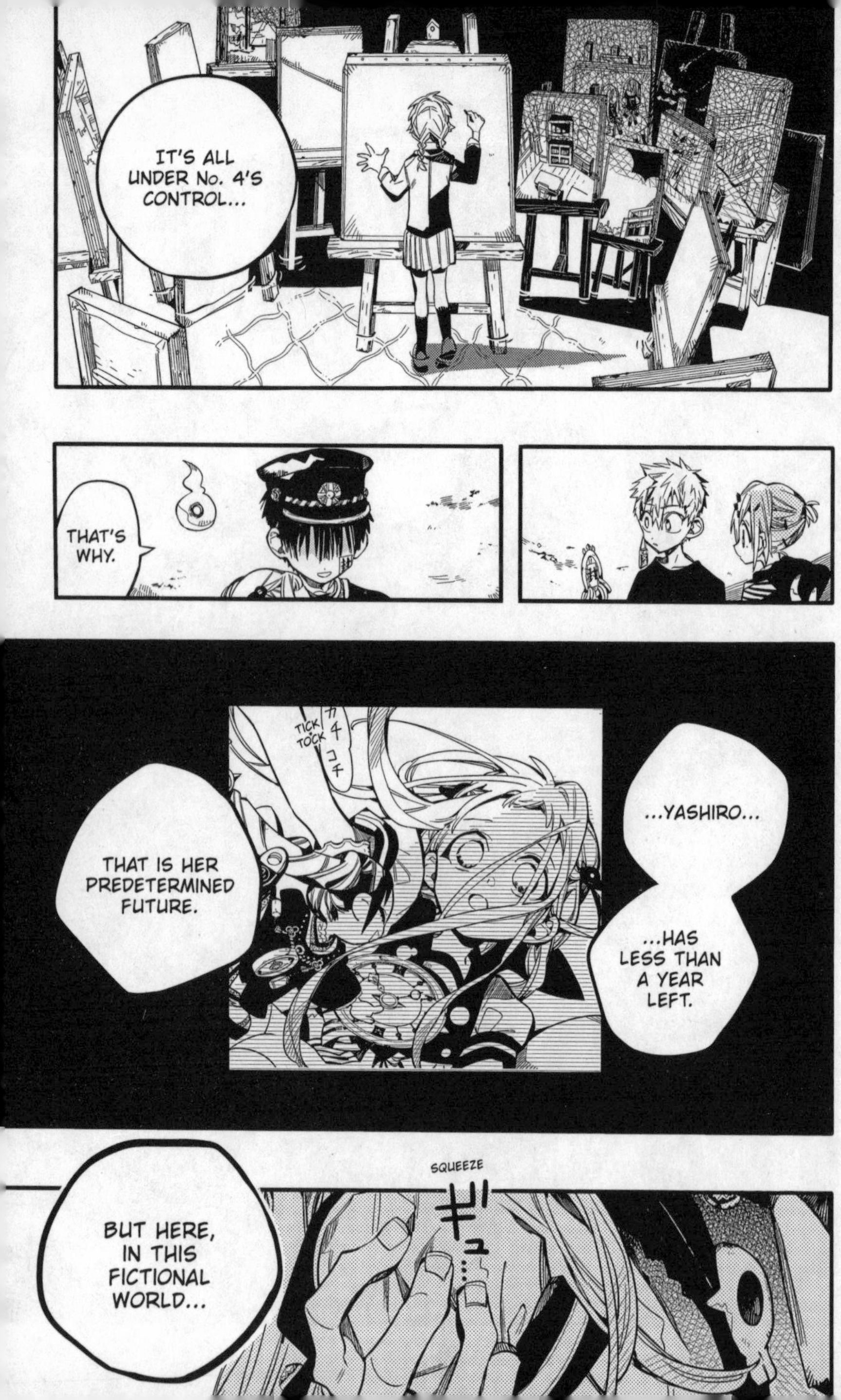
IT'S ALL UNDER No. 4'S CONTROL...
THAT'S WHY.
...YASHIRO...
...HAS LESS THAN A YEAR LEFT.
TICK TOCK
カチコチ
THAT IS HER PREDETERMINED FUTURE.
SQUEEZE
ギュ…
BUT HERE, IN THIS FICTIONAL WORLD...

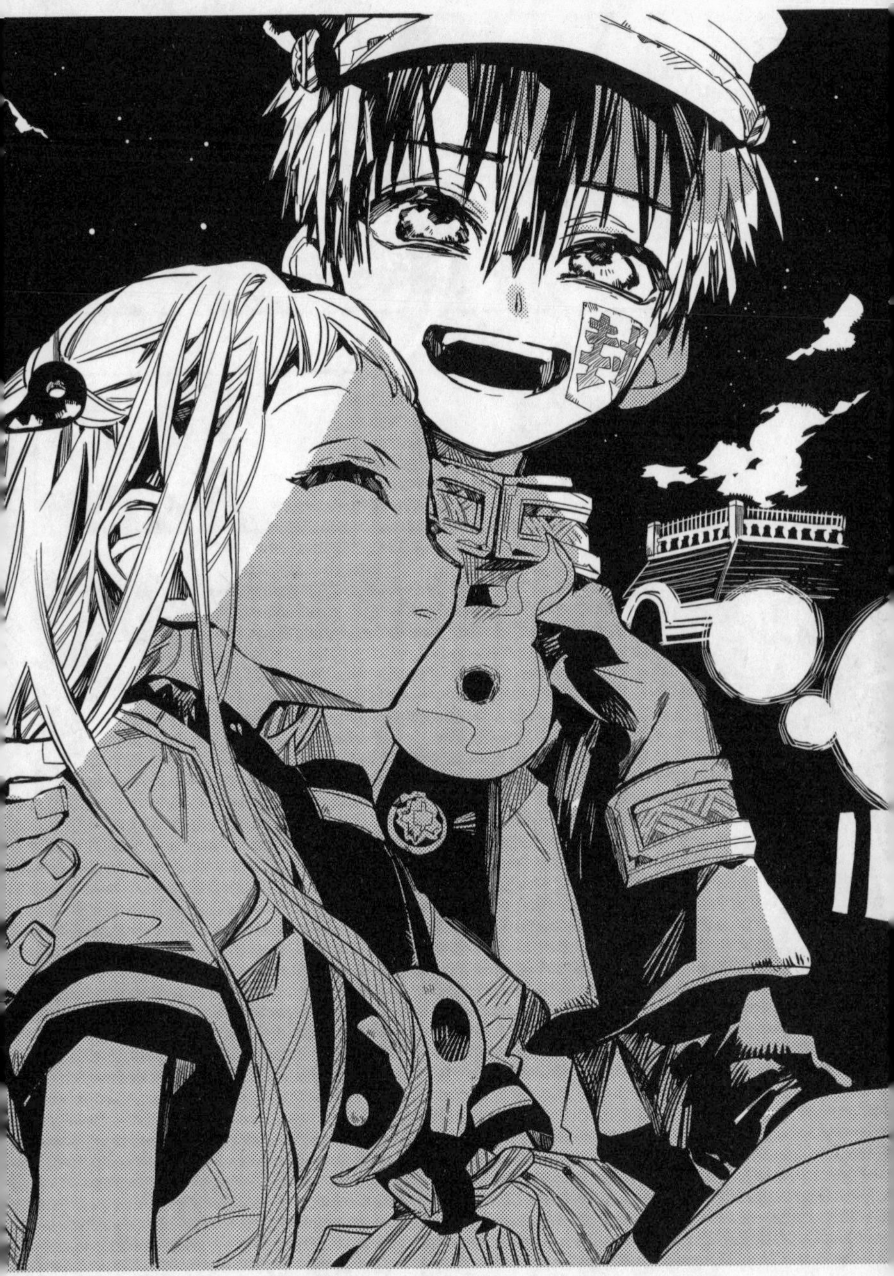
封

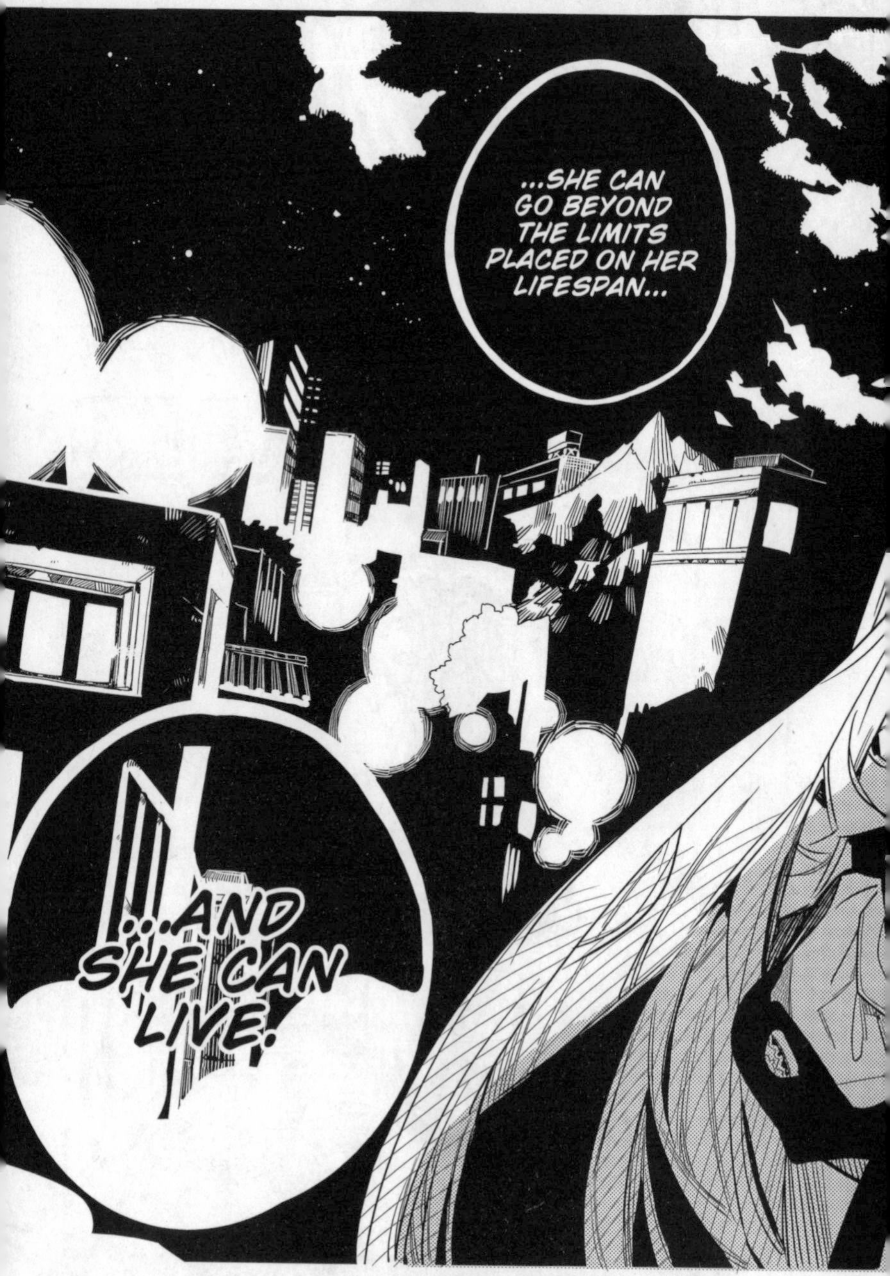
...SHE CAN GO BEYOND THE LIMITS PLACED ON HER LIFESPAN...
...AND SHE CAN LIVE.

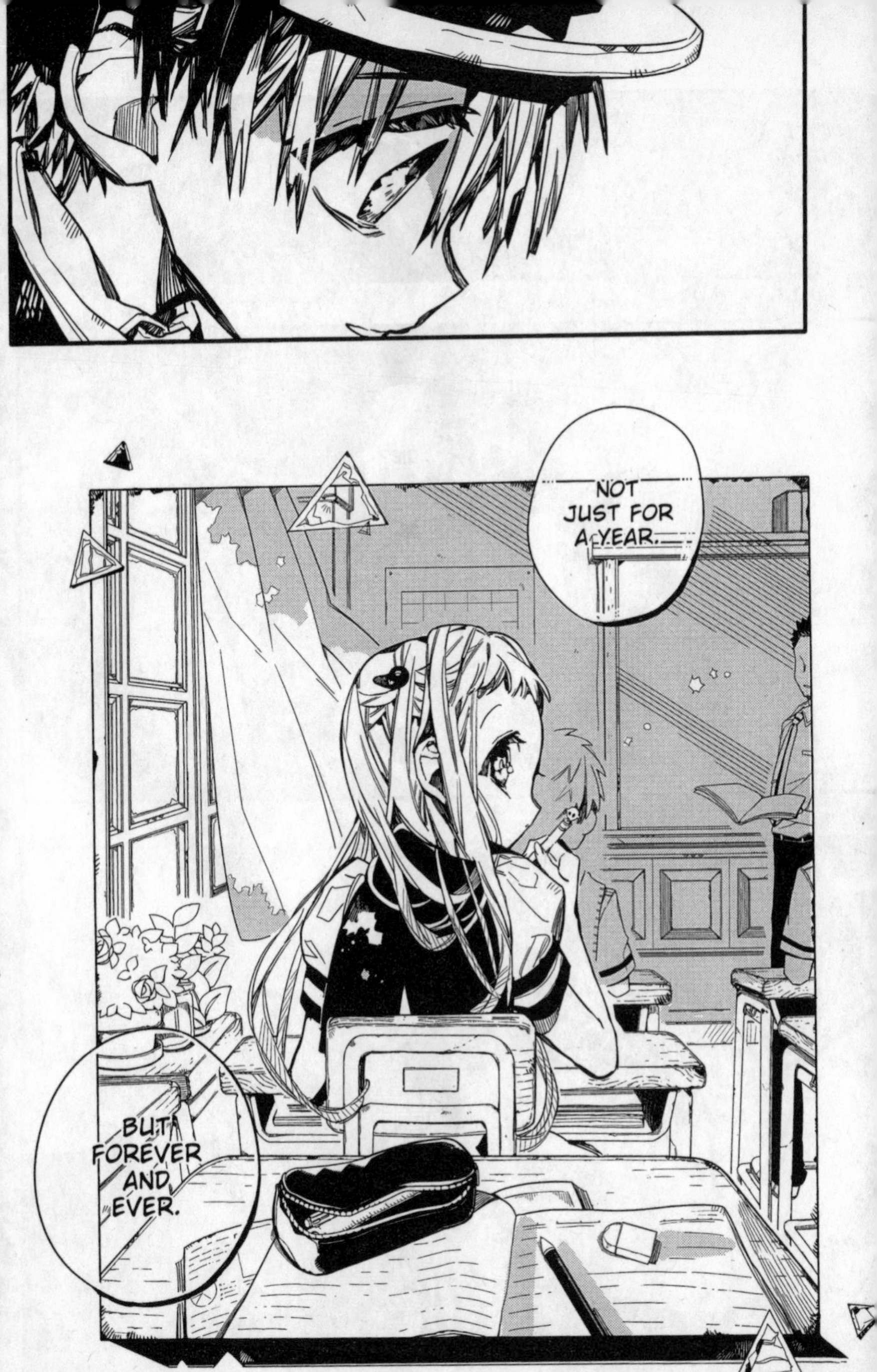
NOT JUST FOR A YEAR...
BUT FOREVER AND EVER.

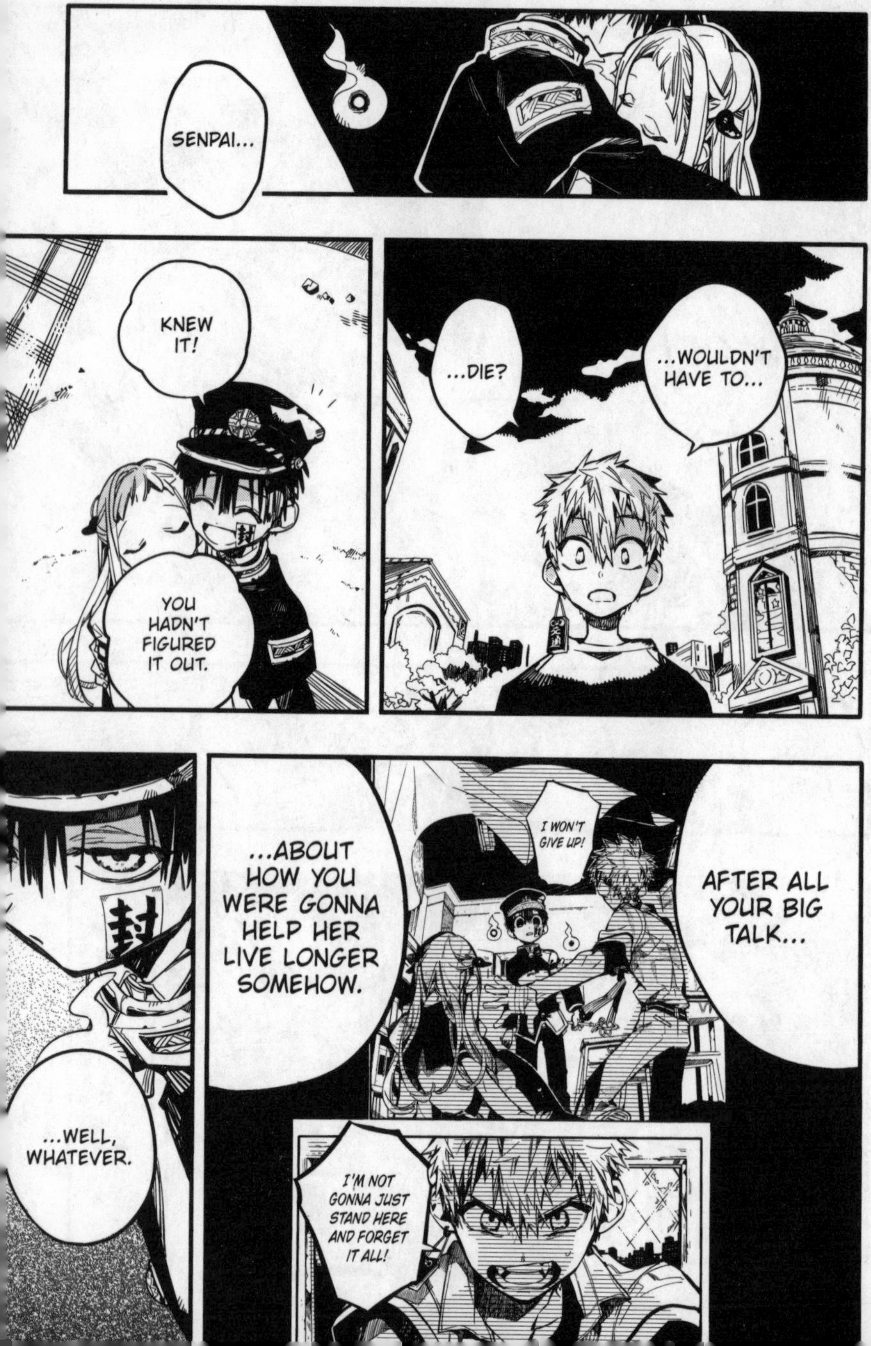
SENPAI...
...WOULDN'T HAVE TO...
...DIE?
KNEW IT!
YOU HADN'T FIGURED IT OUT.
AFTER ALL YOUR BIG TALK...
...ABOUT HOW YOU WERE GONNA HELP HER LIVE LONGER SOMEHOW.
I WON'T GIVE UP!
I'M NOT GONNA JUST STAND HERE AND FORGET IT ALL!
...WELL, WHATEVER.

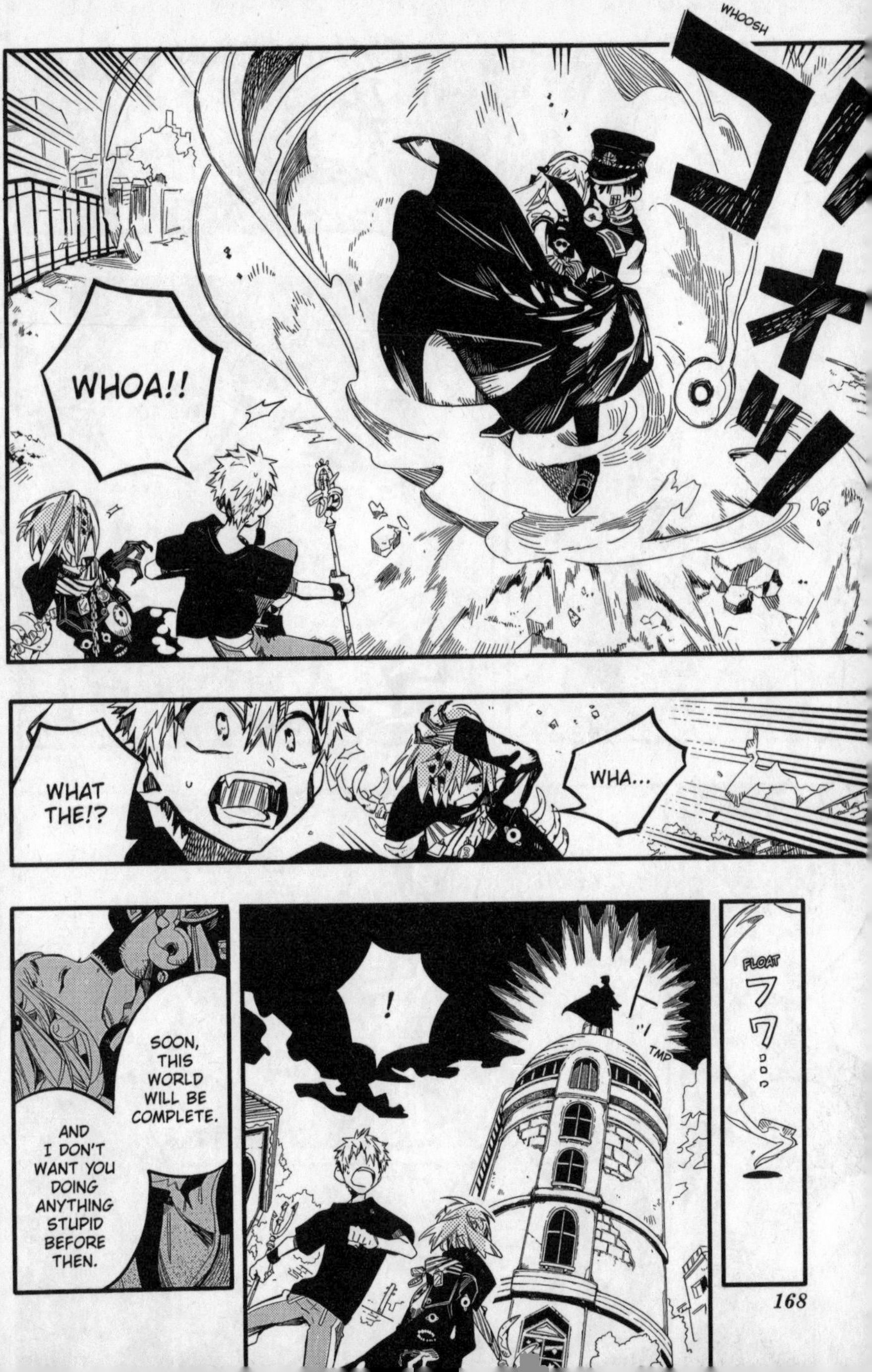
WHOOSH
WHOA!!
WHA...
WHAT THE!?
FLOAT
!
TMP
SOON, THIS WORLD WILL BE COMPLETE.
AND I DON'T WANT YOU DOING ANYTHING STUPID BEFORE THEN.

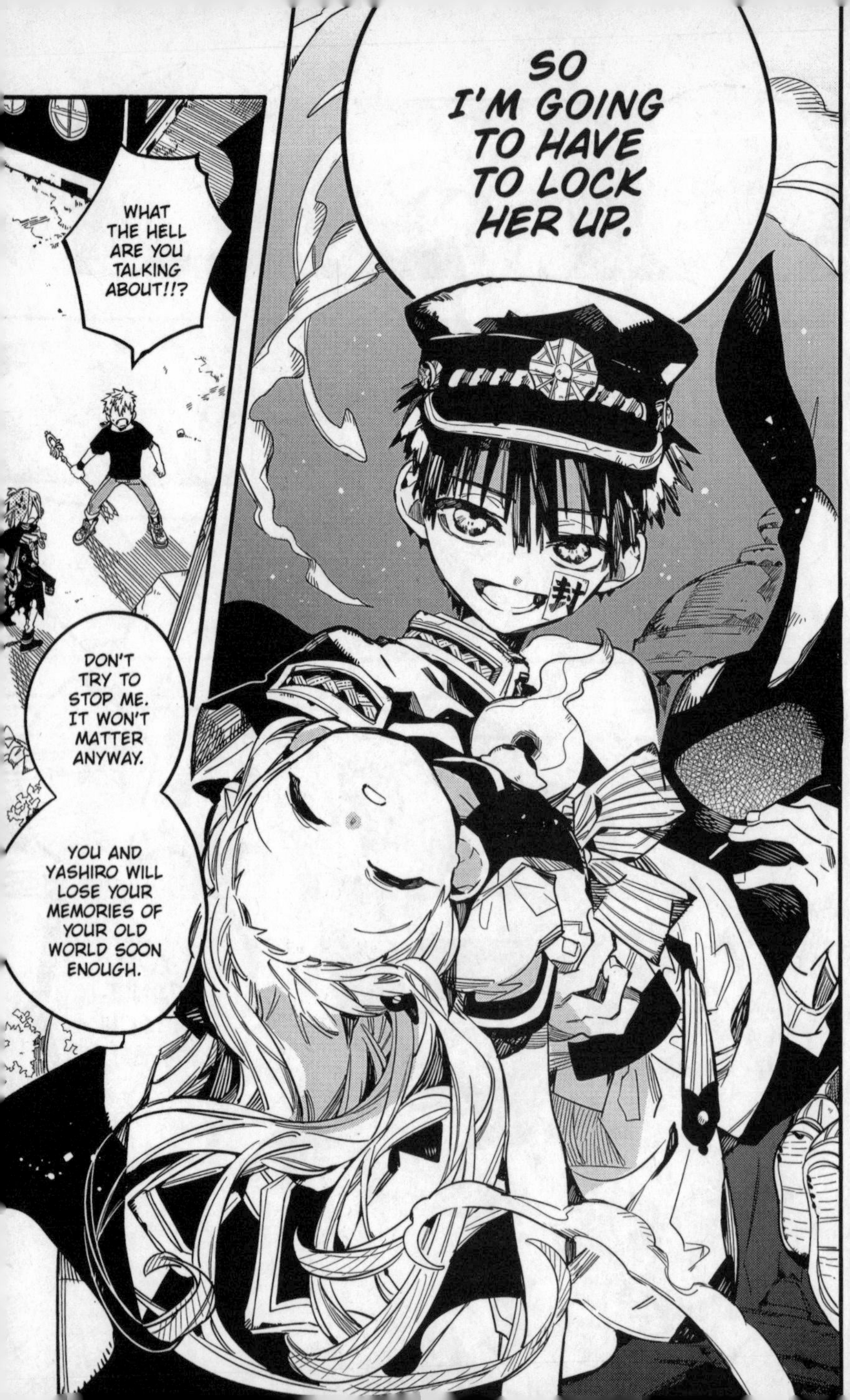
SO I'M GOING TO HAVE TO LOCK HER UP.
WHAT THE HELL ARE YOU TALKING ABOUT!!?
DON'T TRY TO STOP ME. IT WON'T MATTER ANYWAY.
YOU AND YASHIRO WILL LOSE YOUR MEMORIES OF YOUR OLD WORLD SOON ENOUGH.

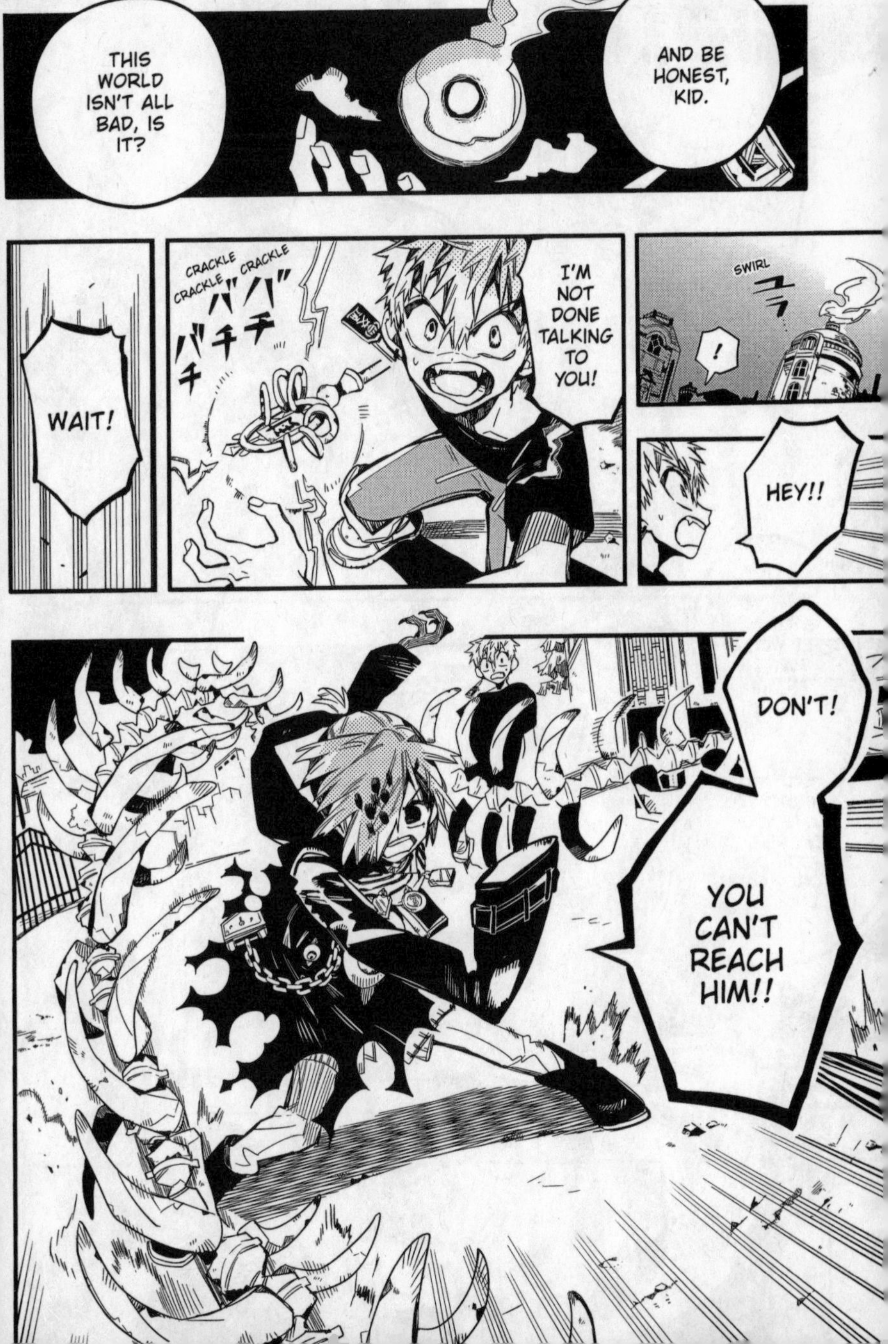
AND BE HONEST, KID.
THIS WORLD ISN'T ALL BAD, IS IT?
SWIRL
!
HEY!!
I'M NOT DONE TALKING TO YOU!
CRACKLE CRACKLE CRACKLE
WAIT!
DON'T!
YOU CAN'T REACH HIM!!

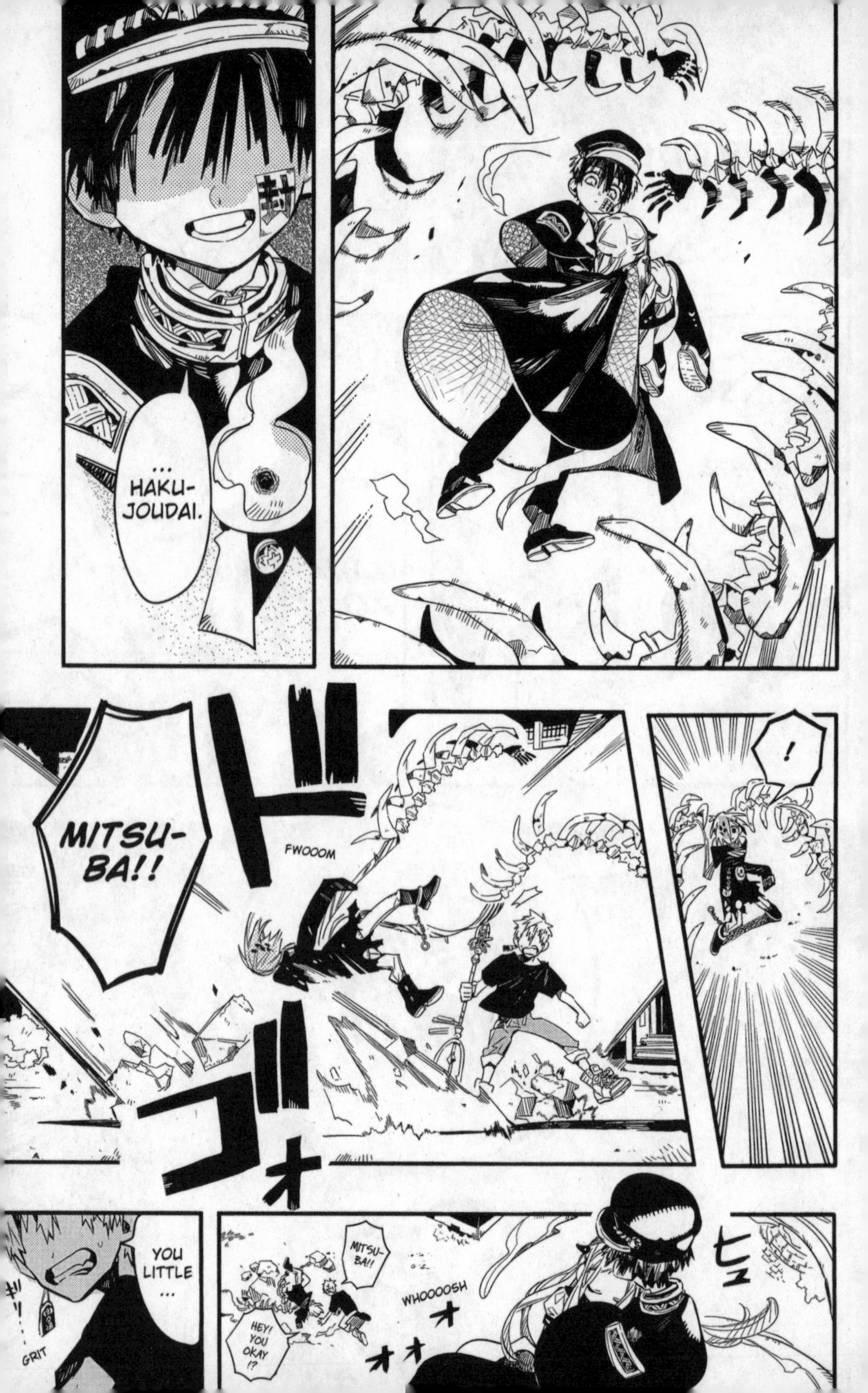
... HAKU-JOUDAI.
!
FWOOOM
MITSU-BA!!
MITSU-BA!!
WHOOOOSH
HEY! YOU OKAY !?
YOU LITTLE ...
GRIT

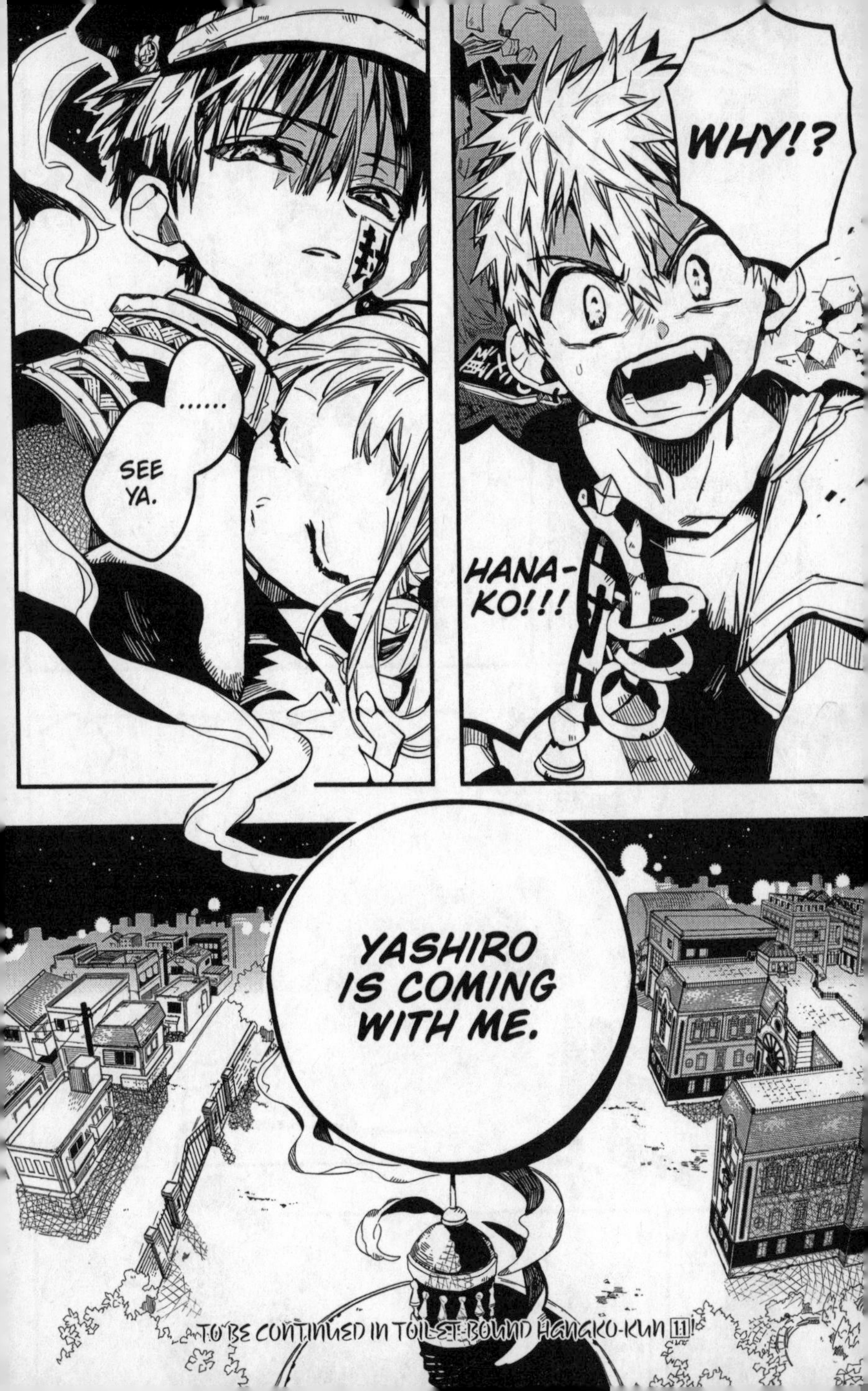
WHY!?
HANA-KO!!!
......
SEE YA.
YASHIRO IS COMING WITH ME.
TO BE CONTINUED IN TOILET-BOUND HANAKO-KUN 11!

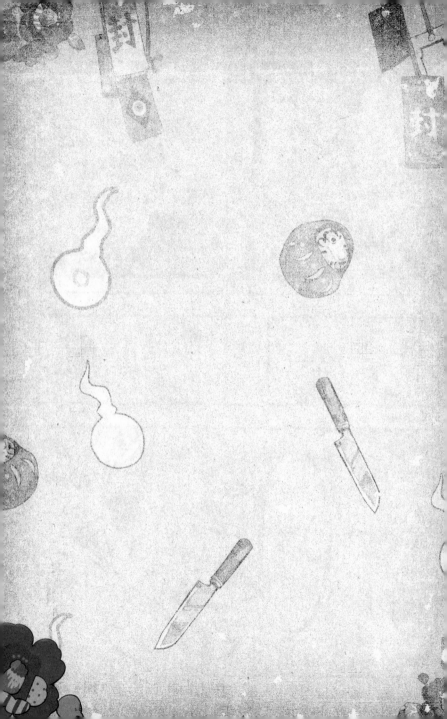

MITSUBA-KUN WANTS TO EXPERIENCE ADOLESCENCE — CUTENESS —

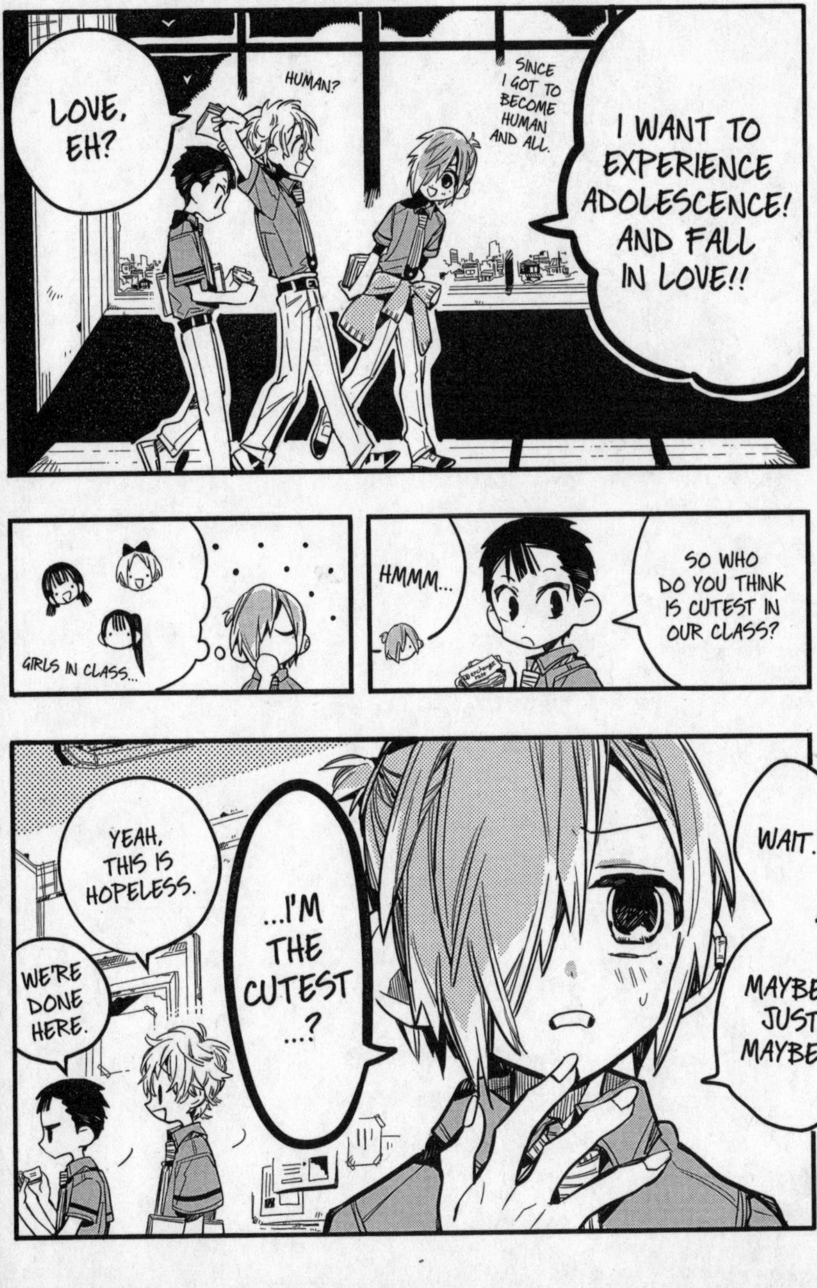
I WANT TO EXPERIENCE ADOLESCENCE! AND FALL IN LOVE!!
SINCE I GOT TO BECOME HUMAN AND ALL.
HUMAN?
LOVE, EH?
SO WHO DO YOU THINK IS CUTEST IN OUR CLASS?
HMMM...
GIRLS IN CLASS...
WAIT...
MAYBE... JUST MAYBE...
...I'M THE CUTEST ...?
YEAH, THIS IS HOPELESS.
WE'RE DONE HERE.

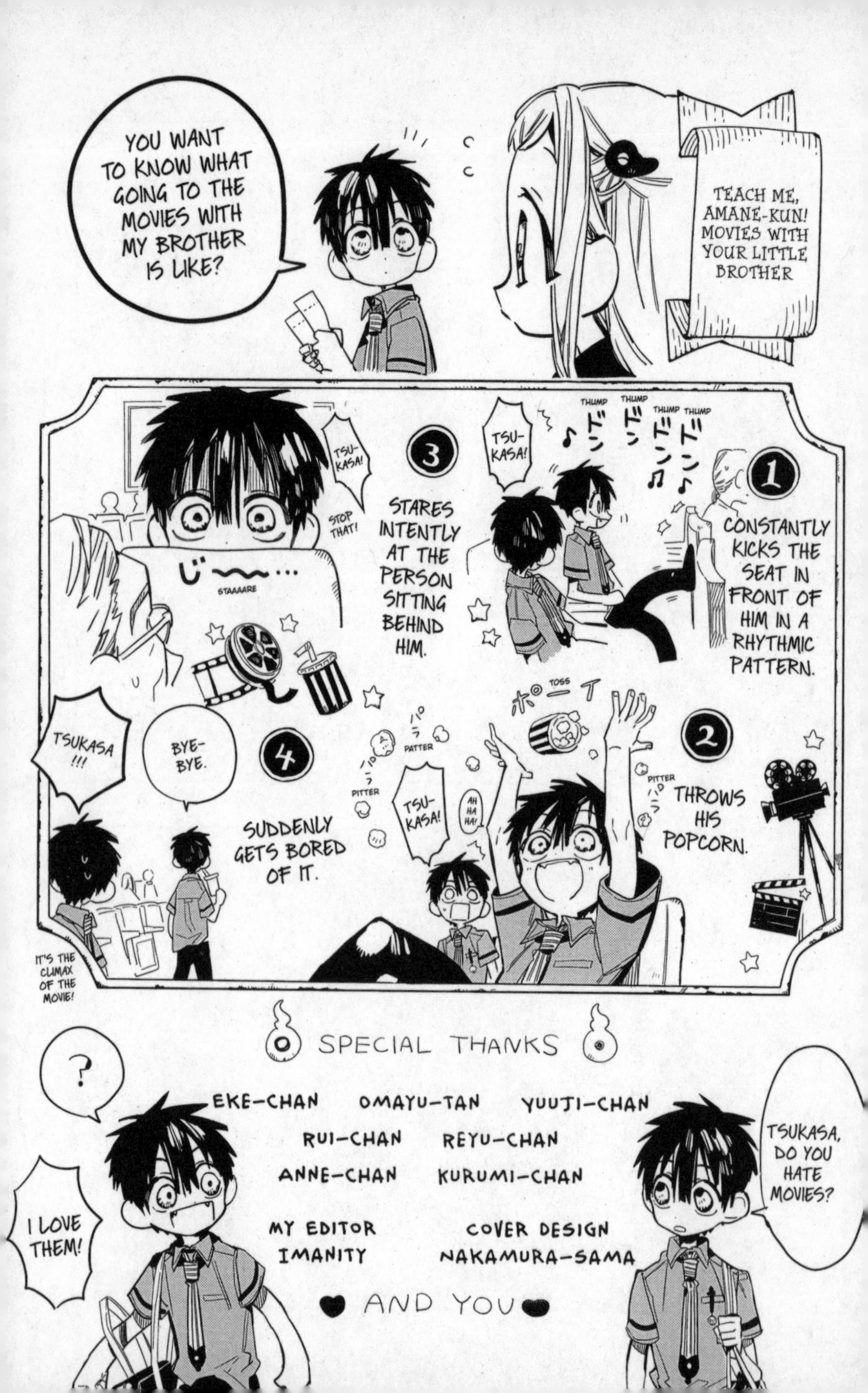
TEACH ME, AMANE-KUN! MOVIES WITH YOUR LITTLE BROTHER
YOU WANT TO KNOW WHAT GOING TO THE MOVIES WITH MY BROTHER IS LIKE?
1
CONSTANTLY KICKS THE SEAT IN FRONT OF HIM IN A RHYTHMIC PATTERN.
ドン ドン ドン ドン
THUMP THUMP THUMP THUMP
TSU-KASA!
2
THROWS HIS POPCORN.
ポーイ
TOSS
パラ
PITTER
AH HA HA!
TSU-KASA!
パラ
PATTER
パラ
PITTER
3
STARES INTENTLY AT THE PERSON SITTING BEHIND HIM.
TSU-KASA!
STOP THAT!
じ〜〜…
STAAAARE
4
SUDDENLY GETS BORED OF IT.
BYE-BYE.
TSUKASA !!!
IT'S THE CLIMAX OF THE MOVIE!
SPECIAL THANKS
EKE-CHAN OMAYU-TAN YUUJI-CHAN
RUI-CHAN REYU-CHAN
ANNE-CHAN KURUMI-CHAN
MY EDITOR IMANITY
COVER DESIGN NAKAMURA-SAMA
AND YOU
TSUKASA, DO YOU HATE MOVIES?
?
I LOVE THEM!

TRANSLATION NOTES

Common Honorifics

no honorific: Indicates familiarity or closeness; if used without permission or reason, addressing someone in this manner would constitute an insult.

-san: The Japanese equivalent of Mr./Mrs./Miss. If a situation calls for politeness, this is the fail-safe honorific.

-sama: Conveys great respect; may also indicate that the social status of the speaker is lower than that of the addressee.

-kun: Used most often when referring to boys, this indicates affection or familiarity. Occasionally used by older men among their peers, but it may also be used by anyone referring to a person of lower standing.

-chan: An affectionate honorific indicating familiarity used mostly in reference to girls; also used in reference to cute persons or animals of either gender.

-senpai: A suffix used to address upperclassmen or more experienced coworkers.

-sensei: A respectful term for teachers, artists, or high-level professionals.

Page 124

The drink selection option reads "Coooold" because most Japanese vending machines are climate controlled, capable of dispensing refreshingly cool soda, piping hot coffee, and everything in between.

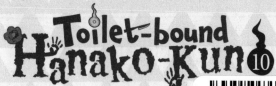

Toilet-bound Hanako-Kun 10

Aidalro

W9-DDZ-434

Translation: Alethea Nibley and Athena Nibley
Lettering: Nicole Dochych

JIBAKU SHONEN HANAKO-KUN Volume 10 ©2019 Aidalro / SQUARE ENIX CO., LTD.
First published in Japan in 2019 by SQUARE ENIX CO., LTD. English translation rights arranged with SQUARE ENIX CO., LTD. and Yen Press, LLC through Tuttle-Mori Agency, Inc.

English translation © 2021 by SQUARE ENIX CO., LTD.

Yen Press
150 West 30th Street, 19th Floor
New York, NY 10001

Visit us at yenpress.com • facebook.com/yenpress • twitter.com/yenpress • yenpress.tumblr.com • instagram.com/yenpress

First Yen Press Print Edition: July 2021
Originally published as an ebook in April 2020 by Yen Press.

Yen Press is an imprint of Yen Press, LLC.
The Yen Press name and logo are trademarks of Yen Press, LLC.

Library of Congress Control Number: 2019953610

ISBN: 978-1-9753-9900-9 (paperback)

10 9 8 7 6 5 4 3 2 1

BVG

Printed in the United States of America

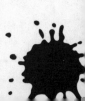